Christmas 2002
Gift from Matt & Katie

CONSUMED IN FREEDOM'S FLAME

More Praise For CONSUMED IN FREEDOM'S FLAME

"Historical fiction is a slippery slope, too often fraught with disconnects between the fictional characters and those real figures of history, too often missing the naturalness of behavior and language; too often erring on either the side of pure history or of fictional device. But, Cincinnati author Cathal Liam has trod deftly in his *Consumed in Freedom's Flame*. This is a book full of romance and adventure woven against the heartrending struggle of the Irish people for independence. In every case, the scenarios created by Liam ring as true as if a cache of long-hidden partisan letters has been unearthed."

Carole L. Philipps, *The Cincinnati Post*

"Unabashed support for the men and women who fought for Irish freedom in the early years of the 20th century is a rarity in these politically correct and revisionists times. Cathal Liam...sets himself against the tide in a story that follows the life of Aran Roe O'Neill, a fictitious rebel who finds himself in the thick of the 1916 Rising and subsequent events."

Ray O'Hanlon, *Irish Echo*

"The conflicts of Ireland are sometimes dubbed simply 'the troubles.' Liam wanted to fill in (their) how's and why's... In *Consumed In Freedom's Flame* (Cathal Liam) follows Aran Roe O'Neill, an Irish rebel, through turbulent times. Only seventeen, (Aran) lies about his age to join the Irish Volunteers. A naïve country boy in the beginning, he is passionate and optimistic about freeing Ireland from British control. (As) Aran's path crosses with many noted rebels, from the idealistic Patrick Henry Pearse to the more pragmatic Michael Collins...Aran's own ideas mature. (The book)...brings history to life..."

Rebecca Lomax, *Cincinnati CityBeat*

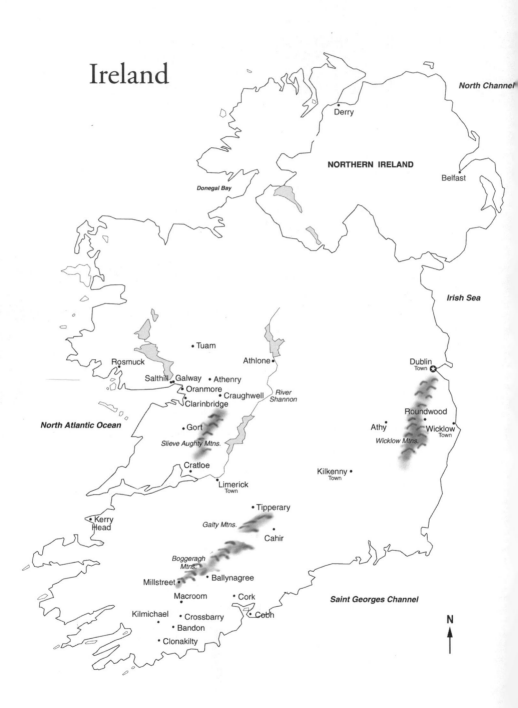

Ireland

North Channel

Derry

NORTHERN IRELAND

Belfast

Donegal Bay

Irish Sea

Tuam

Athlone

Dublin
Town

Rosmuck

Salthill • Galway • Athenry

Roundwood

Oranmore

Craughwell

River
Shannon

Clarinbridge

Athy

Wicklow
Town

North Atlantic Ocean

Gort

Slieve Aughty Mtns.

Wicklow Mtns.

Cratloe

Limerick
Town

Kilkenny
Town

Tipperary

Galty Mtns.

Kerry
Head

Cahir

Boggeragh
Mtns.

Millstreet • Ballynagree

Kilmichael

Macroom • Cork

Saint Georges Channel

Crossbarry • Cobh

Bandon

Clonakilty

N

CONSUMED IN FREEDOM'S FLAME

A Novel of Ireland's Struggle for Freedom
1916–1921

Cathal Liam

St. Padraic Press
Cincinnati, Ohio

Lyrics to "A Forgotten Hero" Copyright © Andy Irvine are used with Mr. Irvine's permission.

Seven lines from "Easter, 1916" and six lines from "The Rose Tree" reprinted with the permission of Scribner, a Division of Simon & Schuster from *The Collected Poems of W.B. Yeats*, Revised Second Edition edited by Richard J. Finneran. Copyright © 1924 by Macmillan Publishing Company, renewed 1952 by Bertha Georgie Yeats.

Please note: With regard to Irish words used in this text, the Irish sineadh fada notation over the appropriate vowel has been purposely omitted. This was done to avoid reader confusion and to simplify the printing process.

Jacket and interior design by Mayapriya Long, Bookwrights Design,
www.bookwrights.com

Set in Adobe Garamond
Printed in the United States of America
First Edition
10 9 8 7 6 5 4 3 2

International Standard Book Number: 0-9704155-0-8
Library of Congress Card Number: 00-107730

Published by
St. Padraic Press
P.O. Box 43351
Cincinnati, Ohio 45243-0351
www.seanchaibooks.com

For my parents, Laura Anne and Russell...
For my wife, Mary Ann...
For Mamo and Pa...
For Patrick Pearse, Michael Collins, Liam Mellowes
and all those many others who have lived and died
so Ireland might be free...

Contents

I'll tell a tale of gallant men
Who in the hills ran cross the glen,
They became a living legend in their day;
Their daring deeds in freedom's fight
Shown like a beacon in the night...
But a song can't bring them back again
Or heal the wound or soothe the pain,
A song can only keep alive the names;
Of gallant women and of men
Their lives consumed in freedom's flame...

The Two Brendans / Irish Brigade

...I write it out in a verse—
MacDonagh and MacBride
And Connolly and Pearse
Now and in time to be,
Wherever green is worn,
Are changed, changed utterly:
A terrible beauty is born.

Easter, 1916 / W. B. Yeats

A Word to the Reader

*T*his story is written from an Irish point of view. It is a strong narrative about the thunder, plunder and injustice Britain visited upon Ireland from the twelfth century onward. Its forceful commentary highlights England's denial and violation of Ireland's dream for independence and self-government. The strength of the commentary reflects the difficulty Ireland has had in breaking the eight-hundred-year-old tether connecting her to England. But, in hoping to retain a reasonable level of historical accuracy, I have tried not to embellish the facts surrounding Ireland's role in its rebellion nor distort Britain's part in the encounter. The principal events happened much as I describe them, though I admit to taking licence with some of the details within those historical occurrences.

This Anglo-Irish turmoil percolated, erupted and subsided many times over the centuries. Then, in 1914, the secret, oath-bound Irish Republican Brotherhood decided it was time once again to try and break the hated link which bound the two nations together. As plans gradually moved toward fruition, a scholar, educator and poet, Patrick Henry Pearse, stepped forward. He helped lead the initial revolt while one of his pupils, the fictitious seventeen-year-old Aran Roe O'Neill, chose to stand and fight by his side.

By telling this story, it is my intention to create a series of informative and exciting events surrounding both historically real and fictionally romanticised characters set against the backdrop of Irish and world events during the early part of the twentieth century. This time is sometimes referred to as Ireland's 'Republican Period' or 'Revoluntary Years.' Furthermore, Aran's adventures are offered as a medium for detailing the chronology of happenings surrounding the 1916 Easter Rising and the 1919-1921 Irish War of Independence.

❧

Aran Roe O'Neill is a fictional character born of my love for Ireland and its storied history. Aran grew up in a unique time: a time when Ireland was making its final and fateful thrust for independence. It was a time of intense dedication on the part of a small group of men and women who felt compelled to employ every available resource to overcome the hurdle of English oppression and forever end its usurping in-

fluence. It was a time of political upheaval, social unrest, economic turmoil and personal sacrifice. It was a time of fear, excitement, violence
and death. It was a time when Irish people turned, not only against
England and the English, but against their own countrymen and women
as well. Sadly enough, the repercussions of these dynamics are still playing themselves out in Ireland today...more than eighty years after the
Easter Rebellion.

In 1916, Aran found himself surrounded by other Irish freedom
fighters and political activists whose names are now legend. Aran was
influenced by many of these people just as real Irishmen and women
were inspired during those early years of the twentieth century. But it
was Aran's spirit and dedication to the cause of independence, kindled
by these soon-to-be-famous historical figures, that form the core of this
story.

Finally, I hope that Aran's adventures challenge you, the reader, to
go beyond these written words and read, visit and/or experience Ireland
in many ways. For it is only through learning and understanding that
the door of yesterday can be truthfully opened and judged which, in
turn, permits a future characterised by veracity, respect and appreciation
of individual differences.

Today, Ireland is crying out to be understood more than ever so that
the tragedies of yesterday will not continually be repeated today and
tomorrow. There is an old Irish expression that says: The east is our
future and the west is our past. In response I might add...though Ireland's
past has often been told in a sea of tears, may her future be awash in
peace and prosperity born on the waves of hope and understanding that
flood both north and south.

A Brief Historical Perspective

> I drink to the death of her manhood,
> Those men who would rather have died
> Than to live in the cold chains of bondage
> To bring back their rights were denied.
>
> *Only Our Rivers Run Free*/Unknown

Shortly before the outbreak of the 1916 Rising, Patrick Henry Pearse and James Connolly collaborated on the writing of a document that was destined to become the cornerstone of today's Irish constitutional government. Contained within this *Proclamation of the Provisional Government of the Irish Republic*, which President Pearse read aloud to the citizens of Dublin from atop the steps of the General Post Office building on Easter Monday, 1916, were the words:

> IRISHMEN AND IRISHWOMEN: In the name of God and of the dead generations from which she receives her old tradition of nationhood, Ireland, through us summons her children to her flag and strikes for her freedom.

and

> ...In every generation the Irish people have asserted their right to national freedom and sovereignty; six times during the past three hundred years they have asserted it in arms...

Yes, six times in the past three hundred years (1601, 1641, 1798, 1803, 1848 and 1867) Ireland rose in revolt but was overwhelmed by her own ineptitude and was outmatched by the forces of the Crown. But in 1916, a group of romantic republican visionaries succeeded in creating the critical-force beginnings that eventually rallied the Irish nation around freedom's cause.

Thus, between the years 1917 and 1921, Ireland experienced a national revival ignited by the men and women of Easter, 1916. Their legacy of self-sacrifice and martyrdom rekindled Ireland's flickering flame of freedom and gradually whetted the nation's thirst for real independence. This momentous swing, initiated by the 1916 armed revolt of the Irish Volunteers and Irish Citizen Army, resulted in Ireland throwing down freedom's challenge to the British Empire. Gradually, this reignited struggle was transformed from a small insurrection in arms against a colonial power to a widespread engagement between two sovereign nations.

The Easter Rising had helped cement the people's commitment to a reenergised ancient dream. This resulted in a heartfelt longing for which all the platitudes of self-rule promised by the British liberals and the Irish constitutional Home-Rulers no longer satisfied.

The leaders of the 1916 Easter Rebellion released a force that finally brought about the birth of a free but blemished nation. Proudly, these revolutionary heroes were prepared to give their lives for a cause they thought was worth fighting and dying for. Sadly, many did.

❧

Since that dramatic spring of 1916, many have argued whether Pearse and the other Rebellion leaders knowingly and willingly engaged in a deliberate conspiracy, a 'blood sacrifice,' intended to draw national attention to their private crusade for Ireland's freedom. Some think that by making such a pledge they were hoping to awaken Ireland and, thus, gain a great measure of sympathy and support for Eireann's long-denied independence.

Of course we will never know the answer to that provocative historical query as the seven executed signatories of the 1916 Easter *Proclamation* left no written confirmation about any personal or collaborative death-wish. But contrary to the speculation of some, especially the noted Irish historian, C. Desmond Greaves,[I-1] I feel certain Pearse and most probably the other members of the Irish Republican Brotherhood's secret Military Council knew what fate held in store for them. They felt their cause was too important to ignore and that a great sacrifice was needed if their plans were to succeed.

A careful study of Patrick Pearse's last years offers an insight into this immolation debate. Forever remembered as a poet, Gaelic scholar and educational innovator, his romantic longing for Irish freedom gradually transformed him from a constitutional nationalist into a revolutionary leader.

Pearse envisioned a new Gaelic Ireland characterised by a shared sense of community, mutual tolerance, economic self-sufficiency and an appreciation of the simple life. In addition his 'new' Irish society would adhere to democratic principles and be insulated from the outside world's troubles.

Through his skilled use of words and his keen insights into history, Pearse drew upon Ireland's symbolic heroes of the yesterday—Tone, Emmet, Davis, Mitchel—to create a forum steeped in high-minded romanticism that supported his pragmatic appetite for war with Britain.

Furthermore, he was greatly influenced by two apparently conflicting ideologies—present-day Catholicism and Ireland's pagan past. Pearse carefully wedded these two differing belief systems and created a justification for his own fatal rush toward self-martyrdom. He willingly entertained sacrificing himself, believing his name and his convictions would live on in the hearts and minds of future Irishmen and women.

Like the pagan Gaelic warrior, Cuchulainn, and the crucified Son of God, his sacrificial memory would continue influencing Ireland down through the ages. If any blood was to be spilled, it would be his own and his comrades. Their symbolic red wine (blood) would wash over the battlefields (Ireland) and nourish its thirsty soil (soul). As a result, Pearse employed the use of Easter, with its powerful theme of redemption, to elevate his actions and justify his probable death. Identifying with Christ, who died on the cross for man's salvation, Patrick Henry Pearse died fighting for Ireland's freedom. Thus, in death, Pearse hoped his spirit and his cause would find eternal life in the hearts and minds of Irish men and women everywhere.

Several years after the Rising, another man, a contemporary of Pearse and Connolly, described this notion of self-sacrifice in one of his writings. William Butler Yeats, famed poet and literary luminary, knew well all of the leaders of the Easter Rebellion. In his famous poem, *The Rose Tree,* he voiced his thoughts about the possibilities that at least Pearse and Connolly had contemplated the eventuality of a blood sacrifice when he wrote:

> ...But where can we draw water,
> Said Pearse to Connolly,
> When all the wells are parched away?
> O plain as plain can be
> There's nothing but our own red blood
> Can make a right Rose Tree.

Pearse's intrigue with self-sacrifice must have percolated within him for several years. In his play, *The Singer,* the hero, McDara, says, "One man can free the people as one Man redeemed the world. I will take no pike...I will go into battle with bare hands. I will stand before the Gaul as Christ hung naked upon a tree."

At the annual Wolfe Tone memorial ceremony at Bodenstown Churchyard in June, 1913 Patrick Pearse spoke of the 'evil thing' (British rule in Ireland) against which Tone, a leader of the failed 1798 Rising, 'testified with his own blood.'

Furthermore, an examination of Pearse's writings after 1914 clearly points to the likelihood of a blood sacrifice which he hoped would awaken the Irish people from their politically induced slumber.

In 1915, at the Dublin funeral of Jeremiah O'Donovan Rossa, a former Fenian freedom-fighter, Pearse, with his comrade Tom Clarke's blessing, boldly stated, "...Life springs from death; and from the graves of patriot men and women springs living nations."[I-2]

Later, Pearse likely spoke for his comrades when he argued, "Bloodshed is a cleansing thing and the nation which regards it as the final horror has lost its manhood."[I-3]

Just like their literary-minded, schoolmaster-friend Pearse, each of the other six Easter Rebellion leaders was also a keen student of Irish history. Each man was aware of the legacies past Rebellions had left to inspire future generations of Irish people. Though the last revolt in 1867 had failed for many reasons, one of its enduring faults was that there were no executions and, thus, no martyrs to inspire the next generation of men and women to reforge freedom's fight.

Certainly, Patrick Pearse and his friends were aware of the powerful impact martyrdom had on the history of the Irish nation. So, there was good reason to believe that yet another dramatic (blood) sacrifice would have a great impact on present and future generations. Surely, they must have been mindful of the old republican conviction that asks, 'Who dares to say forget the past to those of Irish spirit? Who dares to say cease fighting for our place upon this earth? Let remembrance be our watch word and our dead we will not fail for their graves be hallowed milestones on this one-way blood-soaked trail!'

So now, with the outbreak of the First War, the IRB again had an opportunity to fulfill the old Fenian hope that England's difficulty would be Ireland's opportunity. Thus, the 1914 conflict gave the newly rejuvenated Brotherhood a chance to 'have a slap at them' once more. As a result, with world tensions on the increase caused by the growing severity of the war in Europe, Pearse stirred the Irish pot once more with "Ireland will not find Christ's peace until she has taken Christ's sword."[I-4]

Thus, it seems clear that the romantic poet had transformed himself from a thoughtful intellectual into a calculating revolutionary.

Additionally, the words and actions of the Easter Week military leaders seem also to indicate their conscious commitment to the idea of self-sacrifice. These men risked death on numerous occasions throughout the week, leading and encouraging their forces into battle. Contrary to the arguments of others, these actions were consistent with men who had resigned themselves to death. They must have felt they had nothing to lose and refused to direct their followers from the rear. These Provisional government chieftains were not bent on isolating themselves, hoping to preserve their lives for some future execution. Be it now or later, they were willing to lay their lives on the line for Ireland's sake.

In addition, some present-day historians, Michael Foy and Brian Barton, speculate in their book, *The Easter Rising,* that the Rebellion's leadership, trapped in Moore Street on Easter Saturday morning, decided, on the spur of the moment, to surrender themselves and most likely forfeit their lives in return for the safety of their men and Dublin's innocent citizenry. It was, therefore, "...not a strategy carefully thought out in advance, but a gambit hastily concocted as the Rising disintegrated... (It was)...designed not to redeem Ireland but to perform the eminently practical task of saving the lives of their men." On the contrary, this may well have been the enactment of the final phase of a carefully thought out plan.

James Connolly, the labour leader and head of the small Irish Citizen Army, was an avowed revolutionary who wanted to see the end of capitalism and the eradication of British colonial imperialism in his adopted homeland. He knew well of the fatal consequences failed rebel leaders faced at the hands of their military victors and he was not afraid to die for his convictions.

Prophetically, on Easter Monday, just prior to leaving Liberty Hall for the short march to the GPO, Connolly muttered under his breath, "We are going out to be slaughtered!"

When a man standing nearby queried him, "Is there no hope at all, sir?" James Connolly barked back, "None whatever!"

Tom Clarke, the fifty-nine-year-old aging Fenian veteran who had spent a quarter of his life in British prisons, was too frail and too full of British contempt to languish once again behind bars. No, this brave warrior, a survivor of the struggles from the nineteenth century, would much rather have gone down fighting the hatred Sassenach than suffer and die at their hands as an incarcerated man.

Joseph Mary Plunkett already knew he was dying of glandular tuberculosis. In fact, he left what might well have been his death bed to take part in the Rising. Yes, Plunkett knew his end was near and, no doubt, this poetic intellectual had decided to end his days fighting to the death against Ireland's centuries-old foe rather than suffer a painful, gradual death at the mercy of his rapidly progressing disease.

Sean Mac Diarmada was another determined member of this tightly-knit revolutionary band. Tragically, Sean walked with a severe limp, the result of a serious illness (infantile paralysis). But this handicap did not prevent him from travelling throughout Ireland recruiting for his beloved secret Irish brotherhood, the IRB. He was a tough soldier whose final written words to John Daly, a veteran Fenian, indicated he had no regrets about his actions. They simply reflected his desire to join his fellow revolutionaries in death.

> I have been sentenced to a soldier's death—to be shot tomorrow morning. I have nothing to say about this only that I look on it as a part of the day's work. We die that the Irish nation may live. Our blood will rebaptise and reinvigorate the old land. Knowing this it is superfluous to say how happy I feel. I know now what I have always felt—that the Irish nation can never die. Let present-day placehunters condemn our actions as they will, posterity will judge us aright from the effects of our action.[1-5]

Eamonn Ceannt, another of the 'seven tongues of flame' was a patriot and soldier through and through. While awaiting his court-martial verdict, Ceannt wrote to his wife saying, "Trial closed. I expect the death sentence which better men have already suffered."[1-6] Later, on the day before his execution, he penned, "I leave for the guidance of other Irish Revolutionaries who may tread the path which I have trod this advice, never to treat with the enemy, never to surrender at *his* (Ceannt's emphasis) mercy, but to fight to a finish."[1-7] These are not the words or feelings of a man who undertook a revolution lightly. He knew that death might well await him at its end.

Finally, Thomas MacDonagh, teacher, intellectual, poet and an eager *Proclamation* signator, was ready as well to give his life for Ireland. A close friend and colleague of Pearse, MacDonagh revealed his inner thoughts during his court-martial address:

...While Ireland lives, the brains and brawn of her manhood will strive to destroy the last vestige of British
rule in her territory. In this ceaseless struggle there will
be, as there has been, and must be, an alternate ebb
and flow. But let England make no mistake. The generous high-bred youth of Ireland will never fail to answer the call we pass on to them—will never fail to
blaze forth in the *red* (my emphasis) rage of war to win
their country's Freedom...

and

...Take me away, and let my blood bedew the sacred
soil of Ireland. I die in the certainty that once more the
seed will fructify.[1-8]

Yes, it was these seven men, the core of the Easter Rebellion's leadership, who knew what was in store for them if they committed the outra-
geously traitorous act of challenging the military might of the British
Empire and the authority of the Crown. They might have been romantic revolutionaries but they were not unintelligent men. It is inconceiv-
able that during their many hours of plotting and planning they would
not have addressed, in some detail, one of their underlying motives—
that of awakening the Irish people through the spending of their own
'red wine' on Ireland's green battlefield.

In addition to their romantic ideals, these resolute men were well
educated and in full control of their senses. They carefully had outlined
a military maneuver that, if executed to perfection, might very well have
succeeded. Sadly, for Ireland, history records that they did not achieve
their desired outcome.

It also is significant to note that in the days and hours leading up to
the beginning of the fighting on Easter Monday, each of the seven leaders knew full well that their carefully made plans were collapsing around
them like a house of cards. At any number of points along the way, they
could have called off the Rising but refused to do so. In fact, they undertook specific measures to countermand the actions of others who had
tried to stop the revolt from taking place.

It was at this juncture that by pressing on, Pearse and his followers
knew their plans would fail and that, most probably, their very lives
would be forfeited. For example, prior to the Rebellion's onset, the leadership was aware that a large majority of their military followers were

inexperienced and very poorly equipped. They understood full well that their plans for establishing a command post in Dublin would be strictly a pretentious, defensive measure rather than an aggressive, offensive one. This tactic of occupying key buildings throughout the city and waiting for Britain's powerful enemy force to surround and attack them as akin to committing military suicide. Apparently, they rejected fighting a more creative guerrilla war that stood a greater chance of success.

Then, to make matters even worse, the rebel leadership was informed on Holy Saturday, the day before the Rising originally was scheduled to begin, that the German ship carrying its vital supply of rebel weapons had been scuttled near Queenstown (Cobh) Harbour. Additionally, Irish undercover intelligence told the seven that there would be no other material or manpower assistance from Germany or Amerikay.

The leadership also realised that the countermanding orders issued by Dr. Eoin MacNeill, the titular head of the Irish Volunteers, specifying that all military personnel were not to report for manoeuvres as originally planned on Easter Sunday evening, would throw everything into a state of total confusion. The narrow Dublin partisans knew their original strategy of sandwiching His Majesty's forces between their newly occupied city strongholds and incoming Irish provincial forces would not happen.

Lastly, Pearse and the others were mindful that their poorly trained, poorly armed and greatly outnumbered band of brave combatants would not have a ghost of chance against the mightiest empire on the face of the earth. It was akin to leading lambs to the proverbial slaughter yet, proudly with heads held high, Pearse and his comrades led the fateful charge out through the streets of Dublin Town straight up to death's door.

And so it came to pass that Patrick Henry Pearse, his six IRB Military-Council companions along with 318 Irish civilians and republican rebels died for Ireland so that she might be free.[I-9] (British figures state 116 Crown soldiers died in the conflict with a further sixteen policemen killed. The number of wounded include 368 British military, twenty-nine policemen and 2,217 civilians.[I-10] Finally, the first post-Rebellion edition of the *Irish Times,* dated Friday, Saturday and Monday, April 28th, 29th and May 1st, listed 146 large shops and business establishments destroyed.)[I-11]

Specifically, Thomas J. Clarke, Sean Mac Diarmada, Thomas MacDonagh, P. H. Pearse, Eamonn Ceannt, James Connolly and

Joseph Plunkett all died aspiring to and fighting for a united, independent and Gaelic Republic.[I-12]

Today, history notes that only two of those elements have been achieved—independence in 1922 and a Republic in 1949. Sadly, however, a united and Gaelic Ireland is still an unrealised dream. Instead of a united, independent and Gaelic Republic, the leaders of 1921-1922 were forced to settle for less. But as Richard English, noted historian and Irish historical scholar, so aptly notes:

> The separatist Republic as an ideal, and insurrectionary violence as a method, received powerful sanction from the Easter martyrs.

and

> ...Pearse and his colleagues would certainly have taken some pleasure from the fact that their martyrdom was to change the terrain of Irish politics.[I-13]

So, it is this intriguing, tragic and profoundly provocative period of Irish history that forms the backdrop for Aran's adventures as he struggles against the brutal and conflicting forces of British colonial imperialism and Irish republican romanticism.

Acknowledgments

First and foremost I want to thank my parents, Laura Anne and Russell, and my wife, Mary Ann, for their unwavering love and support. Whether life's road is smooth or rough, their caring makes all the difference.

I owe a great debt of gratitude to Marcia Fairbanks, who edited the manuscript. Her incredible attention to detail, her ever-questioning mind and her grasp for the 'feeling' of Aran's adventures is without equal. Marcia's considerable skills add depth and meaning to the story.

I thank Barbara Allen for her calm, confident manner and expert typing skills. Faced with tight deadlines and a seemingly endless parade of minute changes, she accomplished all that was asked and more.

I also thank Mayapriya Long for her wise administrative talents and professional publishing insights. The cover design and interior layout are a tribute to her expertise.

I would particularly like to acknowledge Michael McCarthy of Kilkee, who in 1993 gave me, a stranger, a lift in his car from Limerick to Galway which started me thinking about putting pen to paper; Turlough Breathnach, curator of the Patrick Pearse Museum (St. Enda's School) in Dublin, who has been a constant source of inspiration, help and friendship; Jim Cooney of Macroom, whose thoughtfulness and insights I could always count on; and all of the Wright Clan from Counties Galway, Tipperary and Offaly whose undying kindness can never be repaid.

In addition, I wish to thank those who were interested and generous enough to read and comment on the manuscript. I greatly value their thoughts and suggestions. In particular, I wish to recognise John Casey, Garbriel and Larry Cooley, Kevin Donleavy, T. Ryle Dwyer, Dick and Mary Early, Sam Field, Timothy Foote, Tony Gee, Jenny Kunkel, Robin O'Bryan, Tom Richardson and Father Patrick Twohig. I also thank my colleague, Thomas Armitage, for his invaluable galley notations and for putting up with my bloody-minded blathering; Michael Larkin for his musical survival packets and always Jim 'Lamar' Wendell, an old friend whose great strength and brave determination inspire all those who know and love him.

But, after all is said and done, I accept responsibility for the story's words and ideas. With a contrite heart, I also assume ownership of any glaring errors found in the text knowing full well it is but human to err and divine to forgive.

PART I

The Irish Rebel

1. *Trapped*

O, the night fell black, and the rifles' crack
made 'Perfidious Albion' reel,
'Mid the leaden rail, seven tongues of flame did shine
o'er the lines of steel...

The Foggy Dew / Rev. P. O'Neill

*A*ran Roe O'Neill's chest heaved. His Sam Browne belt felt tight and uncomfortable strapped across the front of his battle-stained, sweat-soiled, green jacket. He reached down, unloosened its buckle and felt the belt's confinement ease. His breathing slowed and his spasmodic gasping stopped. Gradually, Aran's feelings of fear and panic lessened as he struggled to regain some sense of balance and control.

His jacket's polished, brass buttons reflected fiery light against the black sky and partially illuminated his youthfulness. Aran's handsome face, which had seldom known the touch of a razor's edge, was drawn and ashen from a week of accumulated fatigue. It mirrored the excruciating helplessness he felt as he crouched like a trapped animal in the dark, narrow alleyway.

As he huddled in the little Dublin laneway with his back against an old stone wall, Aran Roe's body was tormented by growing feelings of isolation and physical exhaustion. Normally, a two-hundred-yard dash would not have caused him any physical distress but these were not ordinary circumstances. To begin with, he had not had a good night's sleep in over a week...Friday night last to be exact. Secondly, he had not had a proper meal in over two days. The skimpy, hurriedly consumed bowls of food eaten inside the General Post Office were hardly enough to satisfy a growing young man. These two factors combined with the absence of any real, muscle-cleansing exercise threw his normal bodily rhythms off. Finally, to make a bad situation even worse, a British machine gun periodically showered the mouth of his little alley with its deadly rain of fire.

It was those bullets that had prevented him and the others from reaching the top of Moore Street now only a hundred yards away. Those bullets threatened to end his life if he was not careful.

Just an hour ago, Aran and twenty-nine other men had volunteered to follow Michael O'Rahilly on his dangerous dash from the GPO's side door, down Henry Street and up to the top of Moore Street. The distance was less than three hundred yards, but tonight it led straight into the jaws of death.

English troops had built two barricades: one at the top of Moore Street and another atop Moore Lane, about fifty yards to the east. They staunchly defended the British army's northern perimeter around Dublin Town. This particular arc of their encircling ring was demarcated by an east-west boundary known as Great Britain Street.

The O'Rahilly, as Michael liked to be called, wanted to gain entrance to and secure the Williams and Woods Building whose eastern wall abutted the enemy barricade on the corner of Moore and Great Britain Streets.

For the past five days, the Irish Rebel Headquarters was the GPO, but English incendiary shells and bullets had set the great civic structure ablaze and now more than two hundred war- weary Irish soldiers needed to find another place to carry on their fight against the English forces who had poured into the city by the thousands since Wednesday last.

Just as he regained some control of his senses, Aran was reminded of his dilemma by the moaning and gurgling sounds coming from his friend Seamus O'Sullivan's prone body.

During their mad dash up the street, Seamus had been hit by several rounds of machine-gun fire and now lay on the cobbles at the junction of Moore Street and Simpson's Lane. Those unholy sounds only added to Aran's sense of terror and the trapped feelings that welled up inside him again.

Suddenly, there were the distant sounds of English voices and more gunfire off to his right, toward the bottom of the tiny laneway he presently occupied. Aran knew there was not much hope of scrambling to freedom that way.

Seamus's badly wounded body lay in the other direction. If he dared venture out from behind his protective wall, the likelihood that more deadly British bullets would pour down on him was too great a chance to risk. Aran felt hemmed in with no place to go.

Concerned about the state of his friend, Aran inched his way over to his fallen comrade. Seamus lay on his back with his face slightly tilted toward him. Though it was too dark to make out exact details, Aran imagined blood and saliva oozing from Seamus's mouth.

Aran realised he must be badly wounded, or why would Seamus be making those strange gurgling sounds instead of crying out for help?

As he grabbed the downed man's right arm and began pulling him into the safety of the lane, another burst of gunfire made the cobblestones sing and spark just inches away from the two young men. The lead projectiles made high-pitched, pinging sounds as they skipped down the street like flat stones on water.

As he pulled Seamus into the safety of the lane, Aran felt two soft thuds pound into his friend's prone body. Seamus's legs convulsed. His back arched up as his left arm flew into the air. Seamus's left hand, which still held his old Howth rifle, opened wide. Both hand and rifle seemed suspended in midair as if they were performing some sort of ritualistic dance. Slowly, the distance between the rifle and Seamus's outstretched fingers grew wider. Aran, stupefied by his own fatigue and mesmerised by the scene's tragedy, watched the slow-motion ballet. He visualised the rifle becoming a bird in flight as it soared and tumbled away from Seamus's outstretched fingers. Another round of flashing gunfire from the top of Moore Street stunned Aran and, in the eerie light, he fantasised that the 'rifle-bird' was the spirit and soul of his now dead friend. Seamus's immortal being was taking wing and Aran prayed it would find a more peaceful place to dwell.

As the rifle chattered to the street, Seamus's arm fell heavily to his side. A rush of breath told Aran this brave Irishman, who had fought by his side for the better part of the week, was dead.

As he resumed pulling his friend's lifeless body into the safety of the alleyway, the sound of Seamus's metal rifle barrel finally stopped its death rattle. Moments later, more chattering machine-gun fire and bullets ripped through the night and down the gauntlet of death called Moore Street. Their presence quickly changed Aran's mind about retrieving the rifle even though the rebels had precious few of them to spare.

Against his better judgment, Aran cupped a match between his two hands and pushed the little flame toward Seamus's face. His eyes were closed and blood still trickled down from the corner of his mouth. Then he noticed it. The distinctive and unmistakable tracings of a smile were etched on Seamus's lips. His whole face seemed calm and peaceful. There was a sense of satisfaction and, yes, even joy in his final expression.

As he stared down at Seamus, the match burned his fingers and went out. All was black again. Black except for the red glow that gave the night sky a rosy, predawn radiance. The blush from the fires that roared up and down Sackville Street carried their signature of dancing sparks and shooting flames far and wide over Dublin Town for the third consecutive night.

Aran paused for a moment, sat back down and pushed his back up against the alley's stone wall. His now motionless friend lay by his side out of harm's way.

Aran's mind and body seemed numb, lifeless and devoid of all thought and feeling. It was as if he was dead as well. Then, slowly and mournfully, he began moving his lips as he said a prayer for this fallen hero. Another Irishman had died so Ireland might live in peace and freedom without England's cruel, strangling hand depriving Innisfail of its life-breath.

At that moment, from some unknown place deep within his being, Aran's allegiance to Ireland's ancient dream seemed to surge forth. Maybe as much to bolster his own courage as to pay tribute to Seamus, Aran softly repeated the old oath:

> We are willing to fight for the flag we love,
> Be the chances great or small;
> We are willing to die for the flag above,
> Be the chances nothing at all.[1-1]

Aran repeated the oath over and over to himself. With each repetition his depressed spirit regained some of its lost vitality. The ideals of hope and loyalty inherent in that poetic refrain helped bolster his flagging emotions, and he felt a renewed burst of energy course through his body.

He had heard stories of the trenchmen in France singing, chanting and shouting as they plunged forward into battle. He knew that their regimental bagpipes helped bolster the men's spirits as they faced almost certain death. Now, here in this dirty little alleyway in the middle of Dublin, his own inner voice was raised aloud to ward off the fear of death that gripped him.

Moore Street was again quiet. Five...ten...fifteen minutes of endless silence passed. Again, Aran began to feel his body melt with fatigue as he sat in the deathlike stillness of Simpson's Lane. It felt like his motionless being was slowly dissolving into the cobblestones and walls that surrounded him. But after a few more paralysed moments, his mind awoke and began churning once more. Amid the now silent streets, trapped and with nowhere to go, Aran closed his eyes and tried remembering how he had become mired on death's doorstep this Friday night after Easter. Reflectively, Aran Roe O'Neill flipped back through the pages of his life.

❧

Seventeen years ago Aran entered the world as the seventh son of a seventh son. His father, Christopher Shane O'Neill, was a small, successful farmer from a townland near the village of Gort in County Galway.

Aran was raised in a beautiful corner of Ireland surrounded by the shadows and influences of Kilmacduagh, Thoor Ballylee and Coole House. Each landmark made a lasting impression on his malleable being. A being that was blessed with 'special' powers because of his rare birth circumstances.

Kilmacduagh was the ruined, seventh-century monastery of St. Colman. Its beautifully intact leaning round tower had withstood the ferocious early raids of Irish chieftains and Viking warriors. Later, in the sixteenth century, it became the property of Richard, the 2nd Earl of Clanrickard. Adding to the beauty of this holy ground were the ruins of three churches and an abbot's house dating from the eleventh, twelfth and thirteenth centuries.

In Aran's mind, Kilmacduagh represented early Christian Ireland as his ancient land slowly transformed itself from a pagan, Gaelic island to its present twentieth-century, Christianised colony of imperial Great Britain.

Thoor Ballylee was a ruined, fourteenth-century tower house. But lately, rumour had it that William Butler Yeats, playwright, poet and the fifty-one-year-old director of the Abbey Theatre, planned to buy it from Lady Augusta Gregory. It was said he wanted to restore it to its original, simple splendor for his prospective wife and English sweetheart Georgianna Hyde-Lees.

Ballylee was one of those stone-faced, Anglo-Norman fortifications built by the de Burgo clan. They had conquered and ruled most of western Ireland from Limerick to Donegal for more than two hundred years. A Welshman of Anglo-Norman extraction, Richard de Burgo invaded the west of Ireland in the early 1200s and dispossessed the Irish who had lived there for centuries. Eventually, however, the rising power and greed of the Anglo-Irish merchant class dethroned the de Burgos and forced them from their seat of power in Galway Town. But time and assimilation were kind to the de Burgo clan. With their name changed to Burke, they became the Earls of Clanrickard. This renaming and issuing of titles was a strategy instituted by King Henry VIII during the first half of the sixteenth century. His policy of land surrender and regrant helped mollify the Old English who were now more Irish than the native Irish themselves. This clever deception helped Henry solidify his thirst for power as King of both England and Ireland.

It was in these surroundings that Aran's education and understanding of Irish history grew and flourished. Lovingly, his father and grandfather told him of his land's venerable past. From these romantic teachings a special sense of Eireann's antiquity, beauty and misfortune grew within him. Additionally, several of Aran's teachers, his nurturing mother and siblings, and Ireland's other ever-present, centuries-old architectural reminders all added their own influence.

Finally, the old became new at Coole House. The estate home, built in the Georgian style during the mid-1700s, had been in the Gregory family for over one hundred and fifty years. When Sir Gregory died in 1892, his wife, Lady Augusta, and infant son, Robert, continued living there.

It was not the house, however, but its current owner and her guests that made it unique. For it was Lady Gregory and her interest in reviving the Irish language and its ancient culture that created the excitement. It was because of her encouragement of and support for Ireland's Gaelic revivalists, writers, artists, and performers that Coole House became the gathering place for some of the finest and most talented personalities of the day.

It was mainly because of his unusual friendship with Robert Gregory, the son of a wealthy, Anglo-Irish aristocratic family, that Aran, the son of a successful, freedom-loving, bourgeois farmer, was often invited to Coole House. On those special occasions, Aran listened to the inspiring words and heady ideas of Yeats, O'Casey, Shaw, Masefield, Douglas Hyde and on rare occurrences, Patrick Henry Pearse. Like other famous guests, Aran boldly carved his initials into the trunk of a great copper beech that grew in the beautifully walled demesne out beyond the main house. To be in company of such extraordinary people who first thought to etch their initials on the surface of that fine tree was certainly heady wine.

It was in the presence of men such as these that Aran began refining his liberal philosophy and nationalistic outlook on life. From somewhere inside him Aran knew he had a special contribution to make to his family, his country and himself. He believed the hatred and resentment caused by seven-hundred-plus years of foreign occupation and outrageous treatment must end. Deep down in his heart, he wanted to make his contribution to the settling of that old score. Not some fleeting gesture, but a significant accomplishment aimed at ending England's imposed ways.

His maturing convictions, fortified by eleven years of schooling in Gort, were broadened by his own reading, discussing and querying of Irish beliefs and ideas. In addition to his intellectual development, Aran spent many hours working on his family's farm. The hard, backbreaking work of farm life provided a healthy outlet for a growing young man.

Though he was only seventeen years old, Aran possessed the strength, insights and maturity seldom found in one so young. Except for his youthful smile and worldly innocence, he was a man. Standing just over six feet in height and weighing a few pounds less than thirteen stone, Aran Roe was all muscle, bone and determination. He had light-brown, curly hair tinged with both red and blond highlights. His coal-black eyes sparkled and shone like diamonds in a fire's light. They were capable of expressing a range of emotions from fiery anger to warm affection. His facial features seemed as if they had been etched in stone but softened gently by the weathering effects of sun and laughter. He was named after the ancient Ulster warrior, Owen Roe O'Neill, who returned to Ireland from Spain in 1642 to lead Eireann's cause in her ongoing fight against England. Tragically, however, after many victorious engagements, O'Neill was killed in 1649. His death coupled with Cromwell's invasion of Ireland a few months earlier sadly helped cast a dark cloud over Ireland that was to remain for several hundred more years.

❧

Unexpectedly, during the beginning months of 1916, Aran's life took a sudden and dramatic turn. It was late February and spring seemed just around the corner. The early morning brilliance of the bright golden furze bushes illuminated the dark green of the surrounding hills as Aran cycled down the long laneway away from Coole House.

Still filled with surging emotions, he reflected on how last evening had proved to be such a momentous one.

It all began with yesterday afternoon's unexpected appearance of Robert Gregory at the O"Neill farm. Aran was just finishing his after-school chores when his friend arrived. From the excitement written on Robert's face he knew something special was in the wind.

"Aran, you won't believe who's coming for tea this evening!"

Not pausing for a reply, Robert eagerly blurted the answer, "Patrick Pearse, that's who! Will you come up and join us? We'll have him all to ourselves...you, me and Mother, of course."

Without waiting to consult his parents Aran eagerly responded, "I wouldn't miss it for anything and that's the God's truth!"

But now, coasting down a small hill in the road to give his legs a rest, Aran knew his overnight visit at Coole House had been one of those rare and wonderful occasions seldom experienced and never forgotten.

Pearse had driven Thomas MacDonagh, a friend, colleague and the assistant headmaster of Pearse's innovative school in Rathfarnham, a southern suburb of Dublin, to Cloughjordan, County Tipperary. MacDonagh had scheduled a short visit with family and friends near his boyhood home before returning alone back to Dublin. As for Pearse, he planned to stay overnight at Coole House and then drive on to his cottage in Rosmuck near Roundstone on the Connemara Coast the following day. He wanted to check on some repair work being done to his summer retreat after his visit with Lady Gregory and her son.

So, after he had finished his chores last evening, Aran cycled over to the Gregory mansion. He looked forward with great anticipation to meeting this magnetic Irishman and Gaelic League leader once more.

Back in August, 1915, also at Coole House, Aran had first met the noted educator and writer, soon after Pearse had delivered his oration at the grave of Jeremiah O'Donovan Rossa in Glasnevin Cemetery. This eulogistic invitation had been extended to Pearse by Tom Clarke, an old Fenian and Irish revolutionary, while Pearse was residing at his summer cottage in Rosmuck, County Galway.

Later during the spring of 1916, Aran had learned that both Clarke and Pearse were members of a secret, oath-bound society called the Irish Republican Brotherhood. In addition, they were part of its exclusive Supreme Council and its secret, newly-created Military Committee or Council. He also learned that it was this small group of determined men, who in September, 1914 first dedicated themselves to staging an armed revolt against England's rule in Ireland while English resources were committed to fighting a great war in Europe.

Rossa, one of the first Fenians, dating back to the last century, had died in exile in the United States. After a funeral in Amerikay, his body was returned to Ireland for burial in the Fenian Plot at Glasnevin Cemetery in Dublin.

In his written request to Pearse, Clarke had invited him to speak at the gravesite and urged him to make some powerful and provocative statement to the assembled crowd who would be paying their final respects to the dead rebel.

"Yes, whatever ye say, make it strong...make it very strong. Make it as hot as hell!" said Clarke in his directive to Pearse. Old Tom knew that Dublin Castle, the seat of British power in Ireland since the thirteenth century, would be watching and listening carefully to what would be said and done that day. Clarke wanted Pearse to provoke them and publicly challenge their unwanted authority.

Later, as the transcript of his words clearly showed, Pearse did 'make it strong.' It was a brief, powerful oration and one that Ireland would not forget. It proved to be his greatest public speech and its lasting impact reminded many of the words Abraham Lincoln spoke at Gettysburg over America's Civil War dead.

On that August day in 1915, Pearse had spoken of Fenian faith and how Irishmen of today, bound together as they are, must stand in brotherly union for the achievement of Irish freedom.

He closed by stating that the English need be wary and must guard against 'that what is coming.' His final words were

> ...They (the English) think that they have purchased half of us and intimidated the other half. They think that they have foreseen everything, think that they have provided against everything; but the fools, the fools, the fools!—they have left us our Fenian dead, and, while Ireland holds these graves, Ireland unfree shall never be at peace.[1-2]

Two weeks later, Pearse, seated in Lady Gregory's comfortable parlour, had related to Aran and the other assembled guests the background details surrounding the Rossa gravesite story. It was Pearse's first visit to Coole House and his comments raised many queries in Aran's mind. But, being the youngest present, he felt awkward and out of place about asking them.

Aran now recalled his first encounter with Pearse some six month ago as the glow of last night's second meeting still burned within him. This time things were different. He had screwed up his courage to speak, to express himself, and to ask Professor Pearse a query or two.

Now, as the sun's shining light warmed the youthful cyclist's face, Aran felt alive with a new kind of excitement. Many of last night's sentiments expressed by Pearse were ones he too had been harbouring in his heart.

❧

Another burst of gunfire abruptly brought Aran's mind back to the present. The foreign voices to his right and down the lane were closer now and his exposed position along the wall offered no protection from their possible advance.

Slowly he began to inch his way down the dark lane toward them. He hoped to find an open door or alleyway to duck into and hide. Unfortunately, all the doors and windows were locked and barred. If he attempted to break into a building, the noise would give his position away and he would be in mortal danger.

Aran paused to look and listen. Gradually, from out of the shadows, he began to make out what appeared to be English soldiers. Yes, the voices were English. It sounded as if there were only two of them at the far end of the alley.

Standing motionless in the darkness of the laneway, Aran heard the soldiers talking between themselves about building a barricade out of the sacks and wooden barrels they had pulled into the lane from the opposite end of the alley where it turned and ran out into Henry Street to the west of the GPO.

Apparently, they planned to setup a machine gun post and guard this exit from Moore Street and Henry Place. If they chose to fire their weapon, Aran would be cut to pieces. There was no place for him to hide along the narrow confines of Simpson's Lane.

Aran heard the men discussing how the 'bleeden rebel Shinners,' recently run out of the burning GPO, were now hiding in houses between here and the Moore Street barricade.

"We'll give those ungrateful bastards a real taste of British justice," bragged one of the Limeys.

Their conversation caused Aran's heart to pound so hard he feared it would burst. He was trapped. There was no place to hide. Behind him Moore Street was a death trap and now the English intended placing a machine-gun post directly in front of him. With the coming light of dawn, he would be a sitting target.

Aran decided his only chance was to force the issue and use the element of surprise that was still in his favour. He pressed his frame into a six-inch doorway, held his breath and listened to what the British soldiers were doing and saying.

From the racket they were making, Aran guessed he was only thirty or forty yards away from their position. He listened to them roll several barrels over the alleyway's cobblestones.

Apparently they had procured six big kegs for their defensive wall because one of them proudly announced, "Well, this is the sixth and last of these damn barrels. Now, let's stop mucking about and setup the 'spit-fire' and then have ourselves a nice cup of tea and something to eat."

Aran Roe mused to himself that these two soldiers must be as green as grass. Here they all were in the middle of a war with bullets, fire and death all around them and in their casual way these two soldiers sounded like they were organising tea in the middle of a glen.

"If all the British are like them, we'll be marching down Grafton Street waving the tricolour in no time," smirked Aran to himself.

But, quickly he wiped the smile off his face and pushed the sudden feeling of confidence aside. Aran reminded himself to slow down and think the situation through carefully. That was the one thing he had promised himself before this whole affair started. He felt his only chance of coming out of the fight alive was to control his emotions and think things through as deliberately as possible.

Aran nodded his head in mental agreement as he cautioned himself not to go flying off half-cocked and possibly end up a pin cushion for some trigger-happy Redcoat.

Not being exactly sure of what lay up ahead, Aran strained to hear each sound the soldiers made from their end of the alley. It seemed as if his opponents were angry and frustrated by their inability to set up the machine gun in the dark.

Deciding to move a bit closer, he inched his way along the narrow lane toward the enemy's position.

As he closed in on them, Aran could see their ghostly shadows silhouetted behind the wooden-barrel barricade. They seemed to be trying to mount the gun onto one of the barrels behind what appeared to be bags of corn or maybe sand. From their behaviour, Aran guessed the soldiers thought they were completely alone and had nothing to fear from any Irish rebel.

Aran's old single-shot Howth rifle would not be much use in this situation so he slowly bent down and quietly placed the rifle on the ground behind him. Carefully, and for the first time all week, he drew his Mauser pistol known as a 'Peter-the-Painter' from its holster. Then, blessing his decision to take Seamus's 'Painter' from his dead-friend's holster, Aran pulled the other Mauser from his belt. Stepping out into the alleyway he shouted, "God Save Ireland!" and poured a dozen or more rounds into the shapes framed above and behind the makeshift English barricade.

2. Escape

And from the plains of Royal Meath strong men came
      hurrying through,
While Britannia's Huns, with their great big guns, sailed
      in through the Foggy Dew...

The Foggy Dew / Rev. P. O'Neill

𝒫atrick Henry Pearse was seated in a Queen Anne chair next to the huge fireplace in the Gregorys' comfortable parlour. Several big blocks of aged oak and sods of dried turf burned brightly. Their blaze danced and pushed up yellow and orange tongues of flame, warming and illuminating the room. As Aran Roe and Robert Gregory entered the room, Lady Gregory was arranging her finest Willow-patterned tea service on a Victorian table reserved for just such occasions.

Pearse looked up as the two young men made their appearance. Robert was Aran's senior by six years, but did not look it. Both young men possessed airs of confidence and self assurance. They greeted Lady Gregory and shook hands with Professor Pearse.

The evening would be a special one for Aran, as no other guests joined the quartet for tea. They all felt privileged and honoured to have Pearse alone to themselves.

Lady Gregory poured the tea which was accompanied by a large platter of fresh-cut sandwiches, pieces of fruit and slices of sharp-tasting cheese. Initially, the food and tea occupied everyone's attention. Lady Gregory did most of the talking as she questioned Pearse about mutual friends currently residing in Dublin Town.

When Rob asked about St. Enda's, Pearse's bilingual boys' school in the Dublin suburb of Rathfarnham, the professor's eyes lighted up. Regrettably though, most of his replies described how difficult it was to keep the school financially solvent during these lean war years.

This friendly but superficial chatter continued for a time. Then Pearse turned to Aran and asked how his Volunteer training was progressing.

It thrilled Aran that Pearse asked after him and, specifically, about his involvement in the Irish Volunteer Force. He was surprised Pearse even knew of his Volunteer activities.

"Yes, everything is going well after the split, but there continues to be a very serious shortage of arms," commented Aran.

Pearse nodded in reply. Remaining silent for a few moments, then looking at Aran he said, "We owe a big debt of thanks to Erskine and Molly Childers, Mary Spring-Rice and the others. They risked their lives smuggling those Prussian rifles into Howth harbour two years ago. My only regret is that those nine-hundred Mausers rifles and the additional six-hundred landed at Kilcoole a month later were fine for 1870, but not now. Antiquated, single-action, bolt rifles are no match for the new British Lee-Enfields."

The professor was well aware that only a few of those Howth rifles had managed to filter westward. Aran's battalion was not unlike other units throughout Munster and Connacht. Many were forced to use shotguns designed for hunting or to save their money in the hopes of buying black-market British weapons from disgruntled Redcoats. Even more shocking was the fact that a few of the Volunteer farmers in his group were still forced to arm themselves with pikes for weekend manoeuvres. That ancient weapon was reminiscent of Ireland's fight for independence back in 1798.

Pearse, replacing his teacup in its saucer, spoke after a thoughtful pause. "As ye well know, our Volunteer organising is a reaction to the threat of our neighbouring Ulstermen's arming and training."

Clearing his throat, he continued, "I know it only seems like yesterday but it's been over three years since Sir Edward Carson and his myopic Captain Craig openly recruited an Ulster Volunteer Force of 100,000 men. They boldly defied Prime Minister Asquith's and John Redmond's Parliamentary Party attempts to bring Home Rule to our island of Ireland."

The Dublin professor paused and Robert interjected, "Yes, the Irish Parliamentary Party has attempted to politically promote the passage of Home Rule legislation for more than forty years. But not even Parnell's masterful efforts or Gladstone's liberal support ever succeeded."

Robert glanced at his mother seeking a confirming nod.

Receiving one, he went on, "Finally, as ye all know, a Home Rule Bill was eventually approved by England's parliament. It was signed by the King almost eighteen months ago but never implemented. It's still on hold until the war in Europe is resolved and..."

Aran interrupted before Robert finished his sentence, "Ah sure, we all know how the newspapers reported England's great reluctance to enter the war in Europe during that summer of '14. But I wonder so! Was Britain nobly rallying in support of her French and Russian treaty partners or was Mother England glad to be out from under the burden of finally having to resolve the Irish question?"

"No doubt a bit of the both," answered Lady Gregory in reply to Aran's query.

As the housekeeper refilled everyone's teacups, the poised hostess continued, "During the late summer and early fall of 1914, most English, and Irish politicians for that matter, felt the delayed Home Rule legislation would be on hold for only a few months. I clearly remember the optimists boldly stating, 'The war would be over by Christmas!' Unfortunately, German trench warfare proved them all wrong!"

With her voice filled with emotion, Lady Gregory continued, "Sure now, after a year and a half of fighting and with more dead than anyone dares count, that embittered multinational conflict drags on and on with no end in sight so."

"Like lambs being led to the slaughter they are and for what?" retorted Aran. "First, our Northern brethren were willing to pour civil war's blood down upon us all. Now they're gladly spilling it for the King and country they so recently defied."

"Aran's right," answered Pearse nodding his head in agreement with the young Gortman. "To the rest of Ireland's displeasure, the lads in Ulster wanted no part of Home Rule for Ireland. They were not going to give up their favoured economic, political and Protestant positions for 'Rome Rule!'"

Pearse scarcely paused for breath. "The covenant signing, their massive Volunteer recruitment, the ignored Larne gun-running incident, the dirty business over the Curragh 'mutiny,' the Buckingham Palace fiasco just to mention a few were all in defiance of their 'loved' British government. Without question, Carson and his lot were most certainly prepared to go to war with England, Ireland or whomever in order to protect their 'rights.' Such open defiance of Whitehall was nothing more than bloody treason, but the Ulsterites called London's bluff. They won the war of nerves without question."

As Pearse's voice reached a new level of authority, Aran noticed Lady Gregory poised on the edge of her chair dying to slip a word in edgewise.

"Right you are Padraic!"

Ireland's grande dame of the Abbey Theatre rose and gracefully moved to the hearth by the coal-red fire. "Besides all of those political inflammations you so correctly ticked off, at the end of the day Great Britain needed Ulster to fill their trenched, mud-bathed battlefields in France as she fights to free Europe's 'small nations' from oppression."

She stabbed at the fire with a long-handled poker and continued, "Now, in addition to the Ulstermen feeding England's war machine in Western Europe, an eastern offensive in Turkey was initiated last spring. This new strategy required even more British manpower to fill more senseless ditches around Sulva Bay.

"No, Ulster has spoken very clearly. She has definitely won her case for the moment. England will have to wait for the war to end before it can resolve this belligerent Ulster question...her defection from the Empire or Irish civil war looms just beyond the horizon. Only a mad man doesn't see it coming!"

Aran understood only too well what Professor Pearse and Lady Gregory were referring to. Northeastern Ireland's formation of an Ulster Volunteer Force in January, 1913 was indeed provocative. It sparked a reactive countermeasure on Dublin's part.

Though he was only fourteen years old in November, 1913, Aran clearly remembered the Irish Volunteer Force organising in Dublin that winter. Partly in defiance of Ulster's jump-start and publicly as a home defence militia, the IVF was headed by a handful of dedicated Irishmen. Men like Professor Eoin MacNeill, Michael O'Rahilly, Sean Mac Diarmada, Eamonn Ceannt, Bulmer Hobson, Piaras Beaslai and the man seated just before him, Patrick Pearse. Together this group of men and others decided to create their own volunteer force to protect Irish shores from potential foreign invaders while England prepared for possible war in Europe.

The youthful O'Neill recalled his father speaking more than once about the growing fear among those in Irish political power that the British might renegue on their Home Rule promises unless Dublin matched Ulster's northern army with one of its own. Theoretically, this armed contingent of Irish Volunteers could threaten Mother England with their own brand of physical force if the timely implementation of any approved Home Rule bill were for any reason postponed or cancelled. England would not be permitted to rescind their legislatively approved commitment. Aran recalled the many debates of the time as Ireland wondered if the conservatives in Britain might not go back on their parliamentary word. But the

IVF organisers, backed by their armed followers, were confident of their newly strengthened bargaining position.

Unbeknownst to Aran and the vast majority of Irish citizens at the time, the Irish Republican Brotherhood had their designs on using the IVF for their own purposes. It would still be several months before the Gortman learned how veteran Fenian Tom Clarke and IRB organiser Sean Mac Diarmada and others were secretly using the public mustering and training of fellow Irishmen for their own militant purposes. It was their hope that the Volunteers would form the nucleus of an army which could, if necessary, physically wrestle control of Irish affairs away from England while Britannia was preoccupied with their European commitments.

Things finally came to a head when the third Home Rule Bill received its Royal assent in September, 1914 but its implementation was suspended until the war's conclusion. Then, just two days after approval, John Redmond threw a spanner into the works by pledging Ireland's support for Britain's war efforts. He hoped an Irish show of loyalty at this critical juncture would convince England to keep her Home Rule promise. In a bold move of Anglo-Irish solidarity, Ireland's political leader urged Irishmen to enlist in the British army and fight with England 'so small nations might be free.'

The Clarke-Mac Diarmada-IRB militant republican coterie viewed Redmond's actions as Irish treason. The idea of aiding Ireland's longtime foe was out of the question for this small group of Irishmen.

This separatist difference of opinion became a matter of public record as the Volunteer movement split apart. Under Redmond's pro-Anglo-Irish leadership, well over 150,000 men formed a new organisation that called itself the National Volunteer Force. On the other hand, about ten thousand men, loyal only to Ireland but still ignorant of IRB intentions, resisted the break up. They stood fast and continued to call themselves Irish Volunteers. Professor Eoin MacNeill maintained his titular position as chairman and leader of the IVF while in reality he was nothing more than a puppet for the determined republicans.

Lost in thought, Aran had not noticed that both Lady Gregory and Rob had excused themselves from the room. Finally coming to his senses, Aran discovered he was alone with Pearse in the comfortable parlour.

Feeling a bit self-conscious without the others present, Aran stood up and walked over to the dying fire. With agile movements he picked up several large blocks of wood and deftly arranged them on top of half-dozen dry sods of turf.

Moments later Pearse's voice broke the silence, "Aran, tell me how you became involved with the Volunteers here in Gort?"

Turning his back on the newly laid fire and nervously trying to hide his self-consciousness, Aran replied, "Robert and several other of my friends thought it would be a great idea. They wanted me to join them."

Aran was not sure of what to say next. Did he dare risk his secret with the man seated before him? After all, Pearse was one of the officials of the organisation. He did not know how the Professor would react to his confession and he certainly did not want to end his Volunteer involvement. But throughout the evening Aran sensed that a special bond and feeling of trust was growing between himself and the older man. So Aran, with a new found sense of confidence, decided to risk his secret with this important stranger.

Picking up the threads of the conversation again Aran continued, "Mr. Pearse, I must admit that in addition to the urgings of my friends, I had privately been thinking about enlisting but...," Aran paused for just a moment, "...I was afraid that the authorities might discover I was not of age."

Pearse did not say a word. He did not even look surprised.

Aran went on, "The lads all swore an oath not to say anything to anyone and, with my father's consent, I joined up May last.

"I feel rather guilty about telling you all this but my Da actually changed my date of birth and added two years to my age when he signed the enlistment documents. You see, I was only sixteen at the time, not eighteen."

Much to Aran's relief Pearse smiled broadly and nodded approvingly. "Ah son, 'tis not one's age that is the sole determinant of a person's fitness for standing up to what he thinks is right. Age must take the back bench to such qualities as personal conviction, emotional maturity and physical readiness.

"No, Aran, your secret is safe with me too for I can see you are clearly an exceptional young man."

Aran felt blood rushing to his face as embarrassment overtook him. All he was able to utter was a flattered but muted "Thank you, sir."

With a little more prodding from the Dublin professor, Aran briefly described how his Volunteer group trained and drilled on Tuesday and Thursday evenings but, for Aran, the highlight of each week was their Sunday afternoon field exercises in the nearby hills.

Modesty prevented him from telling Pearse that the local commander recognised his natural-born leadership qualities straightaway. This coupled with his many physical attributes, his skill as a crack shot and his tireless determination to learn all he could about military strategy soon saw Aran quickly promoted within his local unit. All of this combined with his other talents, his keen sense of history and his outspoken desire to break the ties now binding Ireland to Great Britain pushed 'Lieutenant' Aran Roe O'Neill into the role of Officer Commanding of Gort's 'C' Company.

Just as Aran was returning to his chair, the two Gregorys rejoined the duo before the fire.

Picking up the threads of their earlier conversation, Aran began telling Pearse how a few of the Howth rifles had finally filtered their way west of the Shannon.

At this point Robert, not one for mincing words, chimed in with, "...and Mr. Pearse, just in case you didn't know, Aran here was assigned one of those Mauser rifles by virtue of his rank and outstanding marksmanship skills."

"Ah, Robert," smiled Aran shyly, "how you do go on."

Patrick Pearse and Lady Gregory both laughed at the two lads as they carried on with each other.

Unbeknownst to the others, however, Pearse's laughter hid one of his more serious concerns. With all the Irish Volunteer's many limitations, he often wondered how any sober-minded individual could place any confidence and trust in such an ill-equipped and ragtag group of men? The Dublin professor was painfully aware that the IVF often raised more eyebrows and chuckles than pride and admiration in the eyes of both Ireland and England.

❧

The sound of the two 'Painters' tore a huge hole in the quiet of the night. The shots seemed to echo and re-echo in the narrowness of Simpson's Lane.

Aran emptied the revolvers into the barricade, threw himself to the ground and quickly rolled several yards back up the lane and into the shallow protection of a doorway.

His heart raced and his breathing came in gasps. His fumbling fingers reloaded both handguns while he tried to calm his frightened nerves.

A long minute passed and the laneway was still quiet. The sky continued to reflect the red glow of Sackville's fires. Aran pulled himself cautiously to his feet and listened for noises from the barrel-end of the passageway. Nothing stirred. He waited several more minutes in hushed silence. Finally, on tiptoe, he crept back toward the enemy's position. Still no sounds from the barricaded soldiers.

Now the outline of the barrier became clearer to him. Yes, there was a machine-gun sitting on top of a barrel. Several other kegs had sacks stacked on top of them, grouped around the gun for protection.

As he moved closer, he could see the barricade was only partially constructed and belts of ammunition were scattered across the cobblestones.

Then Aran noticed one of the sacks was not what he thought it was. It was the body of a man! A soldier lay draped over a barrel with his head slumped down toward the ground. His hands almost touched the cobbles on Aran's side of the barricade. The Irish Rebel's shots had ripped gaping holes in the back of the man's uniform. He had taken the full thrust of Aran's fire in the chest.

Where was the other man? As Aran looked around, he saw a huddled mass sprawled behind the barrel supporting the machine gun.

Tightly gripping both pistols, Aran slowly approached and carefully prodded the form on the ground with the tip of his boot. It was the other soldier. Two bullet holes marked their entrance in the middle of his forehead. He too was dead.

Aran sagged back in horror and fright. These were the first two men he knowingly had killed. Yes, he had fired numerous volleys from the roof of the GPO, but he never knew if his bullets had found their intended targets.

A numbing chill swept over him as he thought to himself, so this is what it feels like to kill another human being. It was so easy to pull the trigger when death was a long way away, but now, when you looked it straight in the face, it seemed different...empty...sad...horrifying...and so very, very final.

Aran tried to steel himself against his fright and confusion. He had to refocus his attention on the matters at hand...self-protection, survival and escape.

He disabled the Lewis machine gun by bending its firing pin with a hard blow from the butt of his revolver. Then he placed the bodies of the two dead soldiers along one wall of the laneway, folded their arms across their chests and covered their faces with their military caps.

He noticed both men carried new, short Lee-Enfield rifles. Aran checked to make sure they both were loaded. He slung a full bandoleer of .303 shells over his back, followed by one of the rifles. With his Mauser back in its holster, Seamus's pistol in his left hand and the other Lee-

Enfield in his right, Aran began making his way down toward the bottom of Simpson's Lane to the point where it made a 90 degree left-hand turn toward Henry Street.

He did not see any human forms through the gap in the buildings straight ahead but as he drew closer to the opening, Aran heard the occasional shout of an English command.

Realising there was not much hope of escape either that way or back from where he came, Aran started turning door handles to see if any were unlocked. Finally, after several attempts, one opened for him.

He felt his way with his boots down a dark, narrow hallway to a door located at the far end. He stopped and listened. Hearing nothing, he slowly turned the knob and eased the door open. Quietly slipping inside, he found himself in a dimly lit room. A skylight allowed a bit of the red-sky glow to illuminate his surroundings. Over in a corner on a low table was a small oil lamp surrounded by three rounded forms.

As the rest of the room seemed empty, he approached the figures and softly but firmly ordered, "Hands up!"

The three shapes sprang to life like startled corncrakes along the River Shannon's marshy flood plain.

"Don't shoot. Don't shoot. We've no guns," came the cry of a woman's voice.

The three forms merged into one as Aran drew closer. It was at that moment that he realised two of the three shapes were children and the other was probably their mother. He relaxed his 'Painter.'

Satisfied that they were alone, Aran demanded to know if there was an exit up to the roof. The woman pointed a bony finger to a ladder on the far wall that led up to the skylight.

After one more quick look around, he pushed Seamus's pistol under his belt. Slowly and carefully, Aran made his way up the ladder and gently nudged open the skylight window. Seeing no one on the roof, he pulled himself up over the window ledge and out onto the flat, tarred surface.

Aran quickly looked around for enemy soldiers. Seeing no one, he investigated possible avenues of escape. With caution, he crawled over to the front of the building and looked down onto Henry Street.

There was a British barricade at the junction of Henry, Jervis and Mary Streets. It commanded a 360 degree view of the intersection, but fortunately there appeared to be no enemy rooftop posts on this side of Sackville Street.

During the past week, the English had stationed snipers on rooftops east of Sackville Street and south of the River Liffey. These enemy riflemen formed a kill-zone stretching from the Amiens Street Rail Station, down to and around the walls of Trinity College and finally, out along the southern bank of the Liffey. It seemed, however, that rooftops north and west of the rebels' former GHQ were unoccupied. Aran guessed the Tommies, confident they had the GPO surrounded and the Irish Republican Army boxed in, felt there was little need for additional aerial coverage.

Weary and lacking battle experience, Aran fought the urge to panic. He took several deep breaths and tried to relax his frayed nerves. He needed to design an escape plan. The bulk of the English army was positioned east and south of him. The sensible move was to head in the opposite direction. So for starters, he carefully began working his way west and north toward Great Britain Street.

Keeping low and warily scrambling from one rooftop to the next, Aran finally descended a fire escape and dropped down into Chapel Place, just south of Great Britain Street.

At the corner, he cautiously surveyed the wide unoccupied avenue. All seemed clear. He took a chance and ran.

After dashing across its broad expanse, Aran worked his way over to King's Inn Street and through a warren of deserted, narrow laneways to Dominick Street Lower.

From there, in the early light of dawn, he finally could see the two British barricades atop Moore Street and Moore Lane. It was the barricade at Moore and Great Britain Streets that he and the others, led by The O'Rahilly, had tried but failed to capture just last night.

Their rebel objective had been to secure the Williams and Woods Soap and Sweet Manufactures Building on the corner. Pearse had chosen it as their new rebel GHQ when the GPO caught fire and forced them to flee.

From a safe distance Aran inspected both British barricades. If by some chance he could disable them, Pearse and the others might be able to flee from their temporary hideouts. If they all could retreat northward, Pearse might be able to establish a new GHQ or join up with Daly's group, which was carrying on the fight in the nearby Four Courts area.

It appeared to Aran the British were using Great Britain Street as their northern perimeter and were focusing all of their military attention southward toward the GPO and the River Liffey.

Forcing open the door of a vacant shop, Aran soon found an access route to the rooftops along the northern row of buildings lining Great

Britain Street. He stealthily made his way to a vantage point directly above and across from the Moore Street barricade.

He had a clear view down Moore Street. There, vaguely outlined in the morning light, were the bodies of a dozen or so dead men. He could also see the spot at the head of the laneway where his friend Seamus had died. Yes, most of the O'Rahilly's brave attack force lay cut to shreds by the bullets from the two Vickers guns located behind the barricade.

Before Aran realised what he was doing, he took aim at a sergeant who strode up and down behind the battlement below. But, just as he began to squeeze the trigger, he stopped.

"Wait, not so fast!" thought Aran to himself as he fought to win control of his trembling emotions.

Regaining command of his senses, he realised his element of surprise would be short-lived once he opened fire down onto the barricade. If he was going to do this right, he first must think things through carefully. After the initial shots from his rifle, the English would turn the tables on him. Aran, the hunter, quickly would become Aran, the hunted.

He paused and tried to formulate a plan of attack and, more importantly, locate an avenue of retreat from this rooftop perch. Trying to shake the cobwebs of exhaustion, hunger and sleeplessness from his nearly numb being, Aran surveyed his position. From this perch, there was a clear view of both British barricades. A two-foot-high crenellated wall extended upward from the top of his building and formed a decorative perimeter around the rooftop. It was a perfect defensive barrier. The gaps between the stone merlons formed narrow loopholes through which he quite safely could fire down onto the enemy's two positions.

His avenue of retreat, however, was less than perfect. Luckily, though, he found a long piece of rope in a storeroom below. Again back on the roof, he tied his find to a chimney stack at the rear of the building. This would allow Aran to lower himself onto the roof of a neighbouring structure. From there he could make his way over to Rutland Square and away from the enemy's likely counter-attack. Aran had attended several Volunteer meetings in the Ancient Order of Hibernian's meeting rooms at #44 Rutland Square. As a result, he was familiar with the building and its layout.

Now Aran O'Neill readied himself for combat behind the battlements along the front of his rooftop perch. If he quickly crawled back and forth between the various openings in the decorative wall, Aran could keep the English guessing as to the number of riflemen that actually were firing down at them.

If he succeeded and if Pearse had posted a lookout to alert the trapped rebels, Aran's gunfire combined with an answering volley from the GPO men would place the British in a deadly crossfire. If all went as Aran hoped, the destruction of the manned barricades would open an avenue of escape for his comrades. They all could flee northward to safety and live to fight another day.

He carefully checked his rifles, pistols and ammunition. Aran felt he could keep the English soldiers busy for ten or fifteen minutes.

Pausing to gather himself, collect his thoughts and say a prayer, Aran Roe, dressed in the costume of a modern-day warrior, thought of some of the other great Irish heroes who had lived and fought before him. He recalled his namesake, Owen Roe O'Neill. He remembered hearing of and reading about such Irishmen as Wolfe Tone, Henry Joy McCracken, Father Murphy, Robert Emmet, William Smith O'Brien and Frances Scott Meagher. Then, there were those groups of poor Irishmen and women who died along the roadside fighting for their starving lives with their teeth and lips stained green from having nothing else to eat but grass. Those Black '47 famine victims died from economic conditions created by England's unresponsive greed, cruelty and selfishness. Yes, the list of Irish heroes and martyrs was almost endless.

Aran did not hate the English per se. What he detested was British authority ruling Ireland, British indifference to the Irish peoples' needs and British loyalty to a throne that viewed Ireland as an underling to be manipulated for English self-interest. If Englishmen or Irishmen died as Ireland fought for its freedom, so be it. If that is what it took to be free of Britain's choking stranglehold, it was worth the price. Better to die here beneath an Irish sky than in some far off place fighting for a colonial cause that was foreign, insensitive, self-serving and destructive of other nations' interests. Like Patrick Pearse, Aran believed it was time for Ireland to stand up and again assert its right to be free. He was ready to sell his life dearly for Eireann's liberty.

The man, Patrick Pearse, and the oft-dreamt word, freedom, were like one in the same in Aran's mind. They seemed inextricably linked. The meaning, the essence, the heart and soul of one was the looking-glass image of the other...indivisible.

❧

Aran's thoughts drifted back once more to that memorable fireside evening at Coole House which he had so pleasurably shared with Pearse, Rob and Lady Gregory. Aran Roe remembered his young friend extolling his rifle prowess and leadership abilities to the schoolmaster.

The Gortman also remembered Pearse gazing longingly into the fire, then turning to look straight at him. For a moment the two were transfixed as if a magnetic field held them fast. Aran felt powerful, prideful feelings and a sense of mutual determination flash between the teacher and himself. The fixation lasted only a moment, but both of them knew they clearly sensed the thoughts and feelings of the other. During that epiphany, they communicated a common sense of purpose and shared spirit of resolve that would forge their lives together in the days ahead.

As the evening had stretched out, talk turned to the Abbey Theatre and the written efforts of new Irish writers and poets.

After some discussion, Aran screwed up his courage again and asked Pearse about some of the things he had said at Rossa's burial. He especially questioned the poet about his comments that warned England to be wary of Ireland.

In response, the Dubliner pulled some papers from the case resting on the floor by his chair. There were some handwritten sheets penned in English. This was a bit unusual for Pearse as Irish was his customary medium of written expression.

When the teacher had finally stopped riffling through the pages, he raised his head and looked at the three eager faces before him. Then in a firm voice he said, "I've just recently rethought some of those very comments and have finally restated my convictions in a poem I'm calling *The Rebel*. I only finished it yesterday."

Without apologising he admitted, "My words might seem crude...even cruel, but they are fresh and heart-felt."

As he read the poem, the turf fire danced in his eyes. His voice was soft, thoughtful but full of passion and desire. He spoke of being born in bondage and of being gifted with vision, prophecy and understanding. He talked of how his heart was heavy with the grief of mothers and how his eyes were filled with the tears of children.

As he continued, he stood up, raised his voice and spoke to his three listeners as if all of Ireland was before him. He said:

> And now I speak, being full of vision;
> I speak to my people, and I speak in my people's
>   name to the masters of my people.
> I say to my people that they are holy, that they
>   are august, despite their chains,
> That they are greater than those that hold them,
>   and stronger and purer,

That they have but need of courage, and to call
    on the name of their God,
God the unforgetting, the dear God that loves
    the peoples
For whom He died naked, suffering shame,
And I say to my people's masters: Beware,
Beware of the thing that is coming, beware of
    the risen people,
Who shall take what you would not give. Did ye
    think to conquer the people,
Or that Law is stronger than life and than men's
    desire to be free?
We will try it out with you, ye that have harried
    and held,
Ye that have bullied and bribed, tyrants,
    hypocrites, liars.[2-1]

The three of them were in awe...speechless. With lumps in their throats both Rob and Aran blinked back tears. Lady Gregory stood up, walked over and held Pearse's hand as she cried softly into her handkerchief. It was one of the most moving moments of Aran's short life.

Pearse put his papers away and they all finished their tea without a word. They were each filled with their own private thoughts and emotions.

❧

The first British soldier to feel the sting of Aran's Lee-Enfield died the moment he was hit. He was sitting with his back to the barricade, smoking a cigarette when the bullet struck him in the chest. He never knew what hit him.

After firing that first shot, Aran ducked down and quickly moved to the far end of the wall. He peered out through another opening and saw half a dozen soldiers looking about with terrified expressions on their faces. They gazed around their position and down at their dead mate. Most remained frozen in place completely bewildered and vulnerable. Two more quick shots from Aran's rifle knocked more soldiers to the roadway. One, shot through the head, sagged lifelessly to the cobbles while a crimson-red flower sprang to life on the front of another man's shirt.

Again, Aran moved as the sergeant yelled for his men to take cover.

The barricade guardians were unsure as to the origin of the attack but they knew they were trapped. Their protective barrier prevented any retreat except forward into the face of the Irish Rebel's rifle fire.

The men by the second barricade at the top of Moore Lane, fifty yards to Aran's left, frantically began dismantling part of their defensive fortification in an attempt to place a few solid objects between themselves and what appeared to be an Irish enemy position behind and to their left. The Moore Lane Limeys were in the process of swinging their Vickers machine-gun around when two of their frightened men toppled backwards as Aran's rifle cracked once more. Both soldiers fell to the ground writhing in pain.

Aran rolled, crawled and peeped down onto the soldiers below him. Several of them had rushed into the buildings opposite his and their rifles were now sticking out through broken windows and open doorways.

"Fire! Fire! Cut the bastards to ribbons!" screamed the sergeant, but no one knew exactly in which direction to shoot.

During the confusion, one of the Englishmen fell as he tried making his escape. The frightened man was in the process of scrambling to his feet when Aran squeezed off another round. The bullet shattered his hip and he now lay paralyzed, limbs askew, on the street below, crying out for help. No one moved except Aran.

Midway along the wall, the Gortman looked down again. This time the soldiers fired in his direction but they focused their attention on his building's ground and first story windows...not up onto its roof.

Glass flew everywhere as Aran noticed other men running down toward his position from Parnell's statue at the junction of Sackville and Great Britain Streets.

Just at that moment, the morning sun rose high enough in the sky to shine down onto the barricades and into Aran's eyes. Its bright, slanting rays blinded him as he looked up Great Britain Street toward 'The Chief.'

Unable to clearly see the second fortification, Aran turned his attention back to the Moore Street defensive structure.

The Gortman was wondering why the trapped GPO forces were not advancing from their hiding places and overrunning the abandoned barricade? Were they not watching what was happening less than one hundred yards away from where they were hiding? Did they not realise this was their golden opportunity to escape?

But Moore Street remained quiet and empty.

As he watched for other rebel activity, Aran heard the laboured sounds of a large motor car off to his left. Slowly coming into view from Rutland

Square was one of those newfangled armoured machines. It was really a lorry encased in metal with a huge Guinness Brewery boiler mounted on the back and a turret on top protecting a Vickers machine-gun. Chugging along, it advanced then stopped halfway between the two barricades. The armoured vehicle screened and protected the men manning the Moore Lane barrier from Aran's fire.

Tut-Tut-Tut-Tut...its heavy machine-gun racked Aran's building. This time gunfire was being directed up at the roof. His position was no longer a secret.

Even though the enemy knew his location, Aran still was free to move back and forth along the wall's one-hundred-foot, protective barrier. The armoured car's oblique angle to Aran's looped openings left him virtually free from exposure unless he stood up or did something equally as foolish.

Unfortunately, the lorry's presence allowed the six surviving men manning the Moore Lane barricade to scramble safely inside its protective metal walls. After a short pause, the lorry crept further down the road toward Aran's hiding spot. It finally came to a stop directly behind the Moore Street barricade just below him.

As the metal monster halted, a soldier waving a white rag tied to a broom cautiously stepped out of an opposite doorway. He paused and then ran over to the wounded man still writhing in pain on the cobblestone street. He dropped the wooden stick, grabbed the man by his jacket collar and pulled his mate safely into the protection of a nearby doorway. The brave Englishman did not know that Aran had no intention of firing down at them during this gallant rescue effort.

A moment later, Aran's attention was diverted by some movement in Moore Street.

Were the rebels making their move now, puzzled Aran to himself?

"Jesus, Mary and Holy St. Joseph!" whispered Aran out loud. "Don't they realise that the lorry's machine-gun will cut them to pieces?"

Aran opened fire and emptied both rifles down onto the plated monster and the store fronts opposite him.

He ducked for cover and rolled to the far right end of his fortification before glancing downward again. When his dizzy head cleared, he saw three people waving white flags coming out of a house about halfway down Moore Street. They headed toward the barricade directly below him.

Were they Irish soldiers? No, it now became clear to Aran who there were. They were civilians moving forward under flags of surrender.

Aran could not understand what kind of an emergency would cause them to run out into the street and place their lives at such risk.

Just then he heard an English voice yell, "Here they come, up the street!"

With that, the turreted machine gun turned 180 degrees and opened fire. Five seconds later, all three individuals lay dead...sprawled, twisted and mangled on the ground. Their simple white flags turned red as blood from three more of the Rebellion's innocent soaked into their surrender symbols now lying in the roadway beside them.

Aran could not believe his eyes.

What the hell was this? Had the English lost control? Was everyone not wearing a British uniform going to be killed? This was not right! The British were supposed to possess a sense of honour and fair play. Was their difficulty in successfully thwarting a guerrilla war in South Africa repeating itself here in Dublin? Aran's mind whirled with a thousand angry thoughts and queries.

On the verge of tears, Aran wondered why Pearse and Connolly did not choose to fight a hit-and-run offensive instead of holing up in city buildings, then waiting for the English to surround them, advance and attack. Ah yes, if only his leaders chose to fight a guerrilla war, things might be very different now.

Aran thought to himself...here I am, one man, successfully tying up fifteen or twenty of the enemy. Five or six have already fired their last shots and I am still hoping a few more will taste death before I make a run for it.

But enough of this wishfulness, thought Aran. Maybe I can manage to hold the enemy off for a few more minutes. Still no sign of Pearse or his men. Now, however, Aran was afraid they would not try anything with that metallic monster guarding the top of the street.

He carefully took aim at the turreted target as it once again turned to face his rooftop fortress.

Staring down at the armoured car, Aran noticed the narrow slit in the turret designed for the gunner to sight through. The little opening offered Aran a real challenge. His first three or four shots sparked off the metal covering but then, as he continued firing, two bullets struck their target.

This time the Vickers machine-gun did not respond to his volley. In fact, instead of firing back, the gun tipped down and remained silent as it pointed its barrel of death at the cobbles below.

Ah, there was some justice after all, thought Aran.

As he looked for his next target, more soldiers poured into the avenue and ran toward the two barricades. They advanced down both sides of Great Britain Street. The Sassenach hugged the walls of the buildings and lingered in doorways as they searched about trying to locate the enemy and its exact position.

Six more times Aran's Lee-Enfield spit fire and deadly projectiles. Three more soldiers fell. This time the English response to his volley was more accurate and sustained.

With hundreds of rounds flying in his direction, Aran decided it was time to retreat.

Taking one of the rifles and its last remaining shells, Aran crawled to the rear of his fortress and down the rope.

He smiled to himself as his escape plan seemed to be working perfectly.

Bending low, Aran ran across several rooftops and clambered over their dividing walls.

Finally, he scrambled down a fire-escape ladder and into an upper-story window of #44 Rutland Square. Once inside the building, he was able to catch his breath. Then, carefully, he moved down the stairs to the front door of the old Georgian building.

He opened the door a crack and looked out. No one in front. All the activity was down at the bottom of the avenue where it joined Great Britain Street. The Gortman ran out the door, flew down the three steps, raced across the street and climbed up over the fence surrounding the Rotunda Hospital.

Safely under the cover of several trees and behind a brick wall, Aran closed his eyes for a moment. He was totally exhausted. His head spun and his legs wobbled. He needed a place to hide, something to eat and a long overdue rest. But where?

On the other side of the square stood #4, another Georgian terraced house and headquarters of his Irish Volunteers. That address offered no sense of security for surely the Crown Forces would search it. But next door, #3 Rutland Square, was the home of Edward Fannin, a doctor with the Royal Medical Corp. It was common knowledge among the Dublin Volunteers that the man was currently stationed in Malta. Aran imagined the house should be empty and would make a safe hideout, at least for a while.

Who would imagine a lowly Irish Rebel having the cheek to hide in a British officer's house? Never mind if the doctor was an Irishman by birth or not. Who would dare trespass on such honourable property?

As he mulled the idea over in his mind, its attractiveness appealed to Aran more and more. His face erupted into a broad grin when, at last, he made up his mind to give it a go.

Slowly, he made his way north around the edge of the hospital complex until he stood directly across the street from #3. Just down the way and to his left was #75A Great Britain Street, Tom Clarke's Tobacco Shop. In addition to its normal retail activities, the little store served as the unofficial headquarters for the IRB and the Easter Rebellion. Aran often had carried messages to and from Clarke's store and Pearse's school in the weeks prior to the Rising.

Fortunately, all military activity seemed to be directed away and behind him, so Aran decided to make a run for it. With his rifle in one hand and Seamus's 'Painter' in the other, he dashed through an open hospital gateway, sprinted across the street and halted on the footpath in front of #3.

He decided that one quick shot, lost in the morning confusion, would attract less enemy attention than an Irish Volunteer trying to hammer down the front door of a house that faced out onto Rutland Square.

He paused on the steps leading up to the door and fired his Mauser pistol. The single round exploded into the ancient lock, shattered it to pieces and blew off its doorknob.

Bracing his body, Aran lowered his shoulder and plowed into the old eighteenth-century wooden door. It held for just an instant. Then, suddenly, the oaken barrier gave way with such an explosiveness that Aran lost his balance. He sprawled wildly forward onto the entryway's floor.

Quickly recovering his senses, he executed a graceful shoulder roll and was back up on his feet in a single athletic motion. With the instincts of a wild animal, Aran, crouching low, surveyed the hallway, turned and slowly opened the parlour's closed door. The room was empty.

Then, suddenly, a uniform appeared at the far end of the hallway. British! The 'Painter' spit fire two...three times. The figure sagged and toppled over.

Carefully sidestepping the body of the dead soldier, Aran cautiously peered into the kitchen. There, at the breakfast table, were two more British troopers. They sat bolt upright in their chairs with their hands in the air. They uttered not a word nor moved a muscle. The two simply stared wide-eyed at the sudden appearance of the Irish Rebel.

For an instant, he wanted to empty his pistol into the lot of them but somehow Aran controlled himself. Instead, he marched them into the parlour, pulled the curtains closed and tied the Limeys up with some rope he had found in the kitchen press. His grandfather, a sailor of some renown in his youth, had taught Aran to tie knots that defied undoing. Not taking any chances, however, the Gortman drenched the knots with water, making sure they would expand tightening the bonds even more. Aran felt confident the enemy would be unable to wriggle out of their restraints anytime soon. Finally, both prisoners were gagged with cloth towelling.

Parting the folds of the parlour's curtains, he looked out on to the street. All seemed peaceful enough. His pistol shots had gone unnoticed amid all the neighbourhood excitement he had recently caused.

With the three enemy soldiers out of action, he quickly searched the rest of the house. Yes, he had the place all to himself.

After shutting and safely securing the front door, Aran returned to the kitchen and devoured the thoughtfully prepared breakfast the English soldiers had organised. It was his first real meal in three days.

He rechecked the ropes securing his captives, then used an upstairs bedroom window to survey the square below. There was a great deal of activity around Parnell's Monument and down Great Britain Street but the hospital obscured most of his field of vision. He guessed the English were still searching for him and his ghostly rebel squad.

Too tired to think or plan his next move, he collapsed onto a bed in total exhaustion. In less than a minute, Aran Roe O'Neill was fast asleep.

3. Surrender

Right proudly high in Dublin Town they flung out
    the flag of war
'Twas better to die 'neath an Irish sky than at Sulva
    or Sud El Bar..

The Foggy Dew / Rev. P. O'Neill

As the hour was late, Robert Gregory suggested Aran Roe stay the night and return home in the morning in time for his daily chores and school. Rob showed his friend to a guest room on the second floor and gave him an alarm clock set for six o'clock.

Still moved by Pearse's words and solemn convictions, Aran nestled comfortably under the warm eiderdown covering. As he stared out through the night-blackened window, the Gortman listened to the wind blowing through the trees outside the old stucco and stone house. The soft bed contrasted with his rock-hard determination and growing desire to play a part in Pearse's plans for the future.

From their brief time together, Aran knew the proud schoolmaster was up to something, something big, and soon, maybe even as early as this spring. Again, he felt some vague, ancient stirring deep inside him crying out for an Ireland free of outside domination and control. He wanted to help Pearse's dream become reality, but how? How could he balance his responsibilities at home and on the farm with his desire to fight for an Ireland free? Even in youth, Aran played an important part in the affairs of the O'Neill household. His parents and elderly grandfather counted on him. His six older brothers were now grown and on their own, but his two younger sisters still lived at home. Many people depended on him so.

In addition to his family, there was also the Irish Volunteers and the company of men who looked to him for leadership. His loyalty to them and their purpose ran deep as well.

As all these thoughts churned through in his head, Aran's mind wondered back in time to ages gone by when kings ruled the land of the ancients. As part of this distant past, he often felt some powerful and magnetic connexion with his Gaelic heritage. Its influence surrounded and guided him in special ways. These feelings were not ones based on power, possession or domination. They were born of responsibility, loyalty and commitment toward a time-worn tradition.

As in old Gaelic society, there was no great exaltation of a higher authority. The land belonged to the people and was held in trust for them by the head of their clan. The leaders and the men of learning were considered equals. There was great allegiance paid to honour, family and a sense of community.

This soulful reminiscing reminded Aran of his recurring dream in which some vague mysterious force always appeared and challenged him to help free Ireland from its chains of bondage. The dream often ended with a reassuring promise of protection from harm and encouraged him to listen to his own innate wisdom and good judgement.

A ghostly specter would say to Aran, "You've the strength and understanding to do the right thing. Listen to your heart and act accordingly." Occasionally, he imagined the spirit saying, "Aran, you have much to offer. Ireland needs men with your strength of dedication and determination."

❧

Aran was dressed and out of Coole House before the alarm clock sounded. He was home milking cows by half six. With his chores completed, Aran washed up, changed his clothes and enjoyed breakfast with his family. He wanted time to think so he chose to walk the three miles to school instead of riding his bicycle.

As he walked, he marveled at the mist rising from the wet hills and green valley. The words of a favourite song danced through his head:

> The stream by the road sings, at my going by,
> The lark overhead wings, a welcoming cry;
> The lake where the trout lies, once more I will see,
> It's there that my heart lies, it's there I must be.
> For these are my mountains, and this is my glen,
> Days of my childhood...[3-1]

The horn of an approaching motor car interrupted his reverie.

As the auto pulled to stop next to him, Aran turned and exclaimed out loud, "Begad, it's you Mr. Pearse!"

"Hop in, Aran. I was hoping to find you this morning. It's time we chatted." Dressed in his usual black garb, Pearse looked in fine form and smiled broadly as Aran climbed into the machine.

Aran Roe O'Neill did not go to school that day. In fact, from that moment onward, his life changed dramatically. In retrospect, it seemed to Aran that he began living his dreams that day.

Pearse and Aran drove directly to Galway Town and met with Sean Mac Diarmada, chief recruiting officer for the Irish Republican Brotherhood and member of its highly secret Military Council.

The three spent several hours talking in the privacy of a home overlooking Galway Bay in the resort village of Salthill just west of Galway. When the discussion ended, Aran felt he had known the two men for years. Though Pearse and Mac Diarmada were almost twice his age, they welcomed the younger man as if he was a long lost brother.

With the O'Neill family's approval, Pearse wanted Aran to begin studying and living at St. Enda's in Rathfarnham as soon as possible. There were men in Dublin who would advance Aran Roe's military education and training while his academic development would be enhanced and nourished at St. Enda's. Pearse recognised Aran's talents, determination and leadership potential. He personally wanted to groom the young man for a role in Ireland's forth-coming push for independence.

❧

Several hours passed before rifle shots woke Aran from a deep sleep. For a few moments, he did not realise where he was. The room and bed were strange and unfamiliar to him. More shots echoed outside his window. Then he remembered where he was...at war with England in Dublin!

Jumping out of bed, he crouched at the window and looked out toward the Parnell Monument.

What in the world was happening? Aran could hardly believe his eyes. Lined up in Sackville Street, facing the statue, were several columns of Irish soldiers totalling 250 to 300 in number. The once proud army now appeared exhausted and defeated. Most of the men looked dejected. Many had their heads bowed while others exhibited signs of all-out fatigue. Some wore bandages and were having difficulty staying on their feet without help.

Aran looked down upon the remains of the bold Irish Republican Army who less than a week ago defiantly took possession of the General

Post Office in the name of the newly declared Irish Republic. He recognised many of the men as fellow comrades who had fought with him in the GPO. Some wore the uniform of brave Connolly's Citizens Army while others wore the mismatched Volunteer outfits of the Dublin Brigade.

Their rifles were piled in the street close to Parnell and the lot of them were under close arrest by about a thousand English soldiers all with fixed bayonets. Occasionally, some of the less disciplined Tommies fired their rifles in the air in celebration of the Irish surrender.

As he looked down Sackville Street, he could see the GPO only three blocks away. There, still hanging proudly from its lofty porch were General Connolly's two Irish flags: The green one with the gold lettering proudly stating, 'Irish Republic,' and the new green, white and orange tricolour...both still flew for all the world to see. However, the flags' tears and bullet holes were so numerous that Aran could even pick them out from his window. The tricolour floated right proudly high over Dublin Town, but the green banner's flag pole was bent almost parallel to the street and seemed in danger of falling.

What in the world had caused this dramatic turn of events? Were Pearse and the other leaders dead or had they simply surrendered? What about the other positions around the city? Would there be any possibility of rescue from forces outside Dublin? Aran did not know what to think as a thousand possibilities reverberated inside his head.

His concern for his fellow soldiers was quickly blotted out by thoughts for his own safety...what should I do and where shall I go? Aran blindly stared at himself in the looking glass hanging on the wall above the room's dressing bureau.

It would only be a matter of time before the British conducted house-to-house searches in an effort to dislodge any isolated rebels.

Should I surrender or run the risk of being shot attempting to escape? Should I walk out the front door with my hands raised or should I fight till the end? Aran's mind was full of confusion and uncertainty.

Suddenly, he remembered the two captured English soldiers tied up in the parlour. They had witnessed him kill their mate. He would be in serious trouble with the authorities if he was captured or surrendered and later identified by either of the two men downstairs.

Aran needed to take stock of the situation immediately. He hurried down the stairs. With a revolver poised for action he looked into the parlour. The two English soldiers were still tied securely to their chairs, but one had tipped his over. The man was now lying on his side in the middle of the room.

Aran guessed he had tried working his way free and had lost his balance in attempting to escape.

In the kitchen, the Irish Rebel filled his stomach with some leftover breakfast bits and pieces.

Taking advantage of the moment, Aran examined and cleaned his two handguns plus the Lee-Enfield rifle using some of the captured Englishmen's equipment. As he occupied himself with his weaponry, the thought of what to do with his two prisoners preyed on his mind. If he made a run for it, he certainly could not take them with him. If he left them tied up, maybe in the cellar, it was possible they would die of dehydration before they were discovered. If they escaped after he departed, the two could testify against him at some future trial. The simplest solution would be to shoot them and forget about it. But his sense of honour, morality and Catholic upbringing ruled out that option.

With time running out, he decided to move the prisoners to the cellar and let them take their chances, just as he was about to do. It was a dangerous game they all played, but that is what war was all about was it not?

Aran explained to his prisoners what he intended to do with them. They nodded in agreement as their gags prevented them from speaking. Before moving them to the basement, he tied hobbles around their legs with more of the kitchen's stout rope. Finally, making sure their hands were secure, he untied them from their chairs and wishing them no future harm, Aran marched them out into the hall.

His captives moved slowly in single file with Aran following a few steps behind them. He held his Mauser ready just in case. Haltingly, the three moved down the hallway toward the kitchen and the cellar stairs.

They were all in the narrow hallway just a few steps from the parlour door when all hell broke loose.

Something hard exploded against the already crippled front door. Before Aran had a chance to react, it flew open and two English soldiers stood framed in the doorway with their rifles at the ready.

Aran dived to one side and sought the protection of the sitting-room doorway. As he fell, he fired his 'Painter' at the invading shapes.

From a prone position under the parlour's archway, Aran saw the lead intruder stagger slightly. Almost instantly the Englishmen began firing wildly.

Aran's two captured soldiers tried to lunge sideways, but it was too late. The confining hallway and their restraints prevented them from seeking safety on the floor.

Luckily for Aran, the soldiers firing from the doorway were at a distinct disadvantage as they peered into the dark hallway. Their eyes were slow to adjust to its dim light after coming in from a sunny spring morning. The British soldiers had reacted to Aran's shots without thinking and were simply firing back in self-defence.

The advantage clearly lay with Aran Roe. He was off to the intruders' side, on the floor, and below their field of fire.

Aran's second volley of shots caught the first man in the stomach, then in the head. The second soldier's field of fire was blocked by his fatally wounded partner. The first man fell forward as he was pushed involuntarily by his mate. The force of Aran's next round of gunfire hurled the second attacker backwards and out onto the building's front steps.

Realising he had only a few seconds before more soldiers from the surrender scene would pour into the house, Aran leaped over the roped, fallen bodies of his captives. He raced through the kitchen, pushed open the rear door, and fled out through the back garden.

As he ran, he cursed himself for not having planned an escape route earlier. Now there was no time for contingencies.

Keeping his fingers mentally crossed and thinking a prayer, he sprinted through a flower garden and pulled himself up onto the top of the garden wall. Straddling the brick fortification, he quickly looked around.

There was no one in the little laneway below, but which way to go? In reality the decision was an easy one. With his feet back on solid ground, he turned and headed away from the troops gathered around the monument at the top of Sackville Street.

Aran ran along Rutland Place to Denmark Street. Stopping briefly at the corner, he peered around...no one about. If I can only make my way over the Royal Canal and into Drumcondra, he thought, I know a family named Richardson living in the Carlingford Road. Young Martin Richardson was his friend and a fellow classmate at St. Enda's. Though Aran had only visited the house once, he remembered its exact location.

Suddenly Aran realised he had made a grave error. In all the excitement back at Fannin's house, he had left his rifle, ammunition and haversack on the kitchen table. His only remaining fire power was the two Mauser pistols...one in its holster strapped to his waist, the other held firmly in his left hand. At the most, the Irish Rebel had only thirty rounds on him. On the plus side, however, his stomach was full and he had slept a few hours. All in all, things were not too bad. Sure, he was still on his feet, there was nary a scratch on his hide and he was free to run.

At that moment, his thoughts flashed back to the Fannin's hallway. He wondered how his two captives were? Had they died at the hands of their own countrymen or had they been lucky? He guessed he would never know the answers to those queries...but those are the vicissitudes of war.

Aran spent the rest of the afternoon moving cautiously from street to street and garden wall to garden wall. The doors that he passed remained locked and silent. As he moved further northward through the city, Aran wondered how he would be received if he knocked up a Dublin family and requested assistance? He realised it would be like throwing dice...he had not a bull's notion who would be behind the door or in what direction their loyalties lay until it was too late.

Then, as if by some miracle, he noticed a small tricolour flag displayed on the inside windowsill of a little house near Croke Park. With new courage in his step Aran knocked on the door. An old woman answered. He quickly explained his predicament and asked her for assistance. Cautiously, she invited him inside. With the door bolted behind them, the woman introduced Aran to her aged husband who was standing in the hallway.

With only Aran's cursory explanation to go on, the elderly man and woman seemed instinctively to understand his plight.

Just as he was about to explain himself more properly to the couple, Aran noticed it. There on the mantle in the parlour was a lighted candle illuminating a faded picture of famed bold Robert Emmet himself. That touching tribute told Aran that indeed he had stumbled upon the right house for sanctuary.

The old man noticed Aran staring at the picture. "Yes...," said the elderly gentleman, "...I too know what it is like to be on the run."

The old woman shooed the two men into a small kitchen at the rear of the house. As she busied herself with the tea kettle, the old man began speaking. He told Aran of his adventures in 1867. How the English soldiers and the Irish Constabulary forced him to flee into the Wicklow Mountains after their little Rebellion had failed.

The old man said their revolt was small compared to what transpired this past week and, as the old rebel talked, his eyes seemed to glow with excitement. He questioned Aran about the fighting in the GPO and what was happening elsewhere in the city.

Unfortunately, the people of Dublin were completely cutoff from the events taking place within their own city. The only newspaper still publishing was the Pro-Unionist *Irish Times*, but it contained little information about the Rebellion. Every word was censored and once again, Britain was writing Irish history to suit its own ends. Yes, the old saw was true: history is written by those that hang heroes.

The other Unionist paper, *The Daily Express,* and the more moderate *Irish Independent* did not publish during the fighting and only turned their presses back on in early May. The one newspaper that would have given a fair and accurate account of the war was the voice of Redmond's Irish Parliamentary Party, *The Freeman's Journal.* Unfortunately, its offices lay among the burned ruins of the Sackville Street fires.

Thus, most battle information was spread by word of mouth: but gossip and rumour totally distorted any shreds of truth or reality. As a result, Dublin's populace was in the dark as to what was happening, why the fighting began and who the real antagonists were.

Aran shared afternoon tea with his hosts and accepted their kind offer to rest in a back bedroom. Before lying down, Aran dashed off a short note to his family in Gort. He was careful about what he said for he feared the British would censor all letters in and out of Dublin. He was, however, able to tell them that he was safe and uninjured. The old man said he would post the letter as soon as it was safe to do so.

Aran's other task before resting was to investigate an avenue of escape from this modest home. In response to his questions, the sympathetic couple put their heads together and drew a rough map of the area. They highlighted the back streets over to the canal and how to navigate around the Archbishop's estate into Drumcondra.

❧

With darkness guarding the streets, Aran was ready to leave. First, however, the three of them knelt and said a few prayers for his safety and Ireland's freedom. In turn, the couple received Aran's thanks for their kindness to him and his hope that they would continue enjoying a long and healthy life together.

Aran Roe stopped just outside the back door, turned and waved goodbye to the republican couple.

The old man smiled at him and said softly, "I stand by your side in your fight. God bless ye, Aran. Keep safe and good hunting. God Save Ireland."

The kitchen lamp was extinguished and the door closed. Aran was on his own again.

Following the couple's map, he kept to the back streets and alleyways. As he approached the Royal Canal, he looked for and found a small container in which to put his pistols and shells. He did not want the water to ruin them as he swam across the narrow body of water. After removing his boots and throwing them safely across the canal, he slid quietly into the waterway. He held the small box above his chest as he floated on his back across to the other side. Once again on land, Aran wished his clothing were as dry as his Mausers and boots were.

There were only a few gas lights in this part of town and most of them were unlit. It looked to Aran as if he was the only person walking the streets on what would normally have been a lovely Saturday evening. With the sound of gunfire still audible, the citizens of Dublin seemed afraid to leave the safety of their homes...and rightfully so. It was as if the entire population had left town.

As he walked, however, he imagined unseen eyes at every window watching him move from tree to garden wall and from shadow into darkness. But slowly and without encountering any military patrols, Aran made his way north and west through the suburbs of Dublin.

It was after midnight when he finally arrived at the Carlingford Road home of his St. Enda's classmates. Martin was a good student, but his eagerness for revolution lagged behind others at the school.

Aran had visited the house once before, about a month ago, after he and his schoolmates had played a hurling match on a pitch next to Croke Park. They competed against a school from Clontarf and, though St. Enda's had lost, Martin's parents celebrated Marty and his three friends' arrival with warm greetings and a fine meal.

Aran had no idea if Martin would be at home. He rather doubted it though. He remembered Marty and most of their other classmates did not board the tram into the city centre on Monday last. He knew some of the other lads were to come to the GPO later in the day but Marty was not one of them. Maybe he had been assigned to another post elsewhere in the city or was slated for guard duty at the school.

Quickly circling the house, Aran noticed a light on in an upper window. Encouraged, he climbed over a low wrought-iron fence and quietly knocked at the back door.

No answer. He knocked again, this time a bit louder.

Finally, a light appeared in the kitchen and a robed figure cracked open the door. It was Martin's mother. She looked frightened and did not recognise the strange military form at her door.

"It's Aran...Aran Roe O'Neill...from St. Enda's...I'm a friend of Marty's...Don't you remember me?"

"Oh, yes...yes of course...Please God, inside with ye."

As he entered the kitchen, she exclaimed, "Look at the state of you! Where in the world have you been? I almost didn't recognise you in that kit. Where's Martin?"

As she spoke, Aran became aware for the first time of the condition of his clothes. He had forgotten what a week without bathing and crawling over, under and around half of Dublin could do to your appearance. Funny thing though...the old couple had not said a word to me about my looks, mused Aran to himself.

But now, here before Martin's mother, he felt self-conscious and mumbled an apology for his unsightly guise.

Then, before he could explain more thoroughly, she spoke, "Never mind...Never mind," as she pushed him into the hallway and up the stairs.

"It's not safe for you to be here," she whispered. "They've been here...searching...twice! Have you seen Martin? They've threatened to burn the house down if they find him here. They keep saying something about harbouring a traitor and that they're watching this house. Aran, where *is* Martin?"

Her words ran together as all her pent-up fears and emotions poured forth at once.

Aran did not say a word as she pushed him up another flight of stairs into the attic. There sitting against a bare wall were Marty's younger sister and elderly grandmother. They did not speak but only stared back and forth at Aran and Mrs. Richardson.

Pausing only for a moment, the woman then hurried across the floor to the far window and looked out.

As she stared intently from behind the drapes, the frantic woman rattled off another volley of words for Aran's benefit, "Two nights ago, my husband, Marty's father, was arrested at work by the police. He's being held as a possible suspect at Arbour Hill Barracks. I was allowed to visit him for five minutes this afternoon."

She was back from the window, sitting stiffly in a chair, and whispering her words as if afraid of being overheard.

"The soldiers are guarding all the main roads and bridges. We can hear gunfire in the distance. It seems like the whole city is on fire. The sky has been red for the last four nights! Where have you been? What are you doing with those guns? What's happened to my Martin?" Her queries just kept coming.

Aran Roe sat down against the top-story wall and began reassuring her that Martin was probably fine...most likely still back at school. No, he had not seen Martin all week. Yes, it looked as if the fighting was over and that the Rebellion had been put down.

This news did not seem to make any difference in her demeanour. She continued to fidget. Suddenly, she jumped up, crossed the room again and looked out the window.

"There...look...I think they're back!" She pointed with a trembling finger.

Quickly, Aran moved to the window. Yes, there was a military lorry parked two houses down the way and a squad of men was lining up on both sides of the street.

Aran was not sure what to do but he successfully fought off the urge to panic. Should I stay here and possibly endanger these frightened, innocent people? He wanted to hide in the house but knew if he was discovered by the authorities Martin's family would definitely be implicated in the Rising. At this point Aran knew the British were in no mood to give any quarter...not even to innocent women or children. But what should he do? Surrender...never! Run like hell...yes!

Flying down the two flights of stairs, he pushed his way out the kitchen door and raced through the back garden. With both Painters in hand, he eased his way past the garden gate, into a small laneway, up over the opposite wall, and out onto Hollybank Road.

If he could only make it to Glasnevin Cemetery, he would be able to hide there for the night.

The Irish Rebel was halfway to the bottom of Hollybank when a military patrol vehicle roared around the corner and headed straight for him. Caught in its head lamps, he dove over and behind a low garden wall.

The machine screeched to a stop. Three men poured out. It was now or never. He must hit them before they had a chance to spread out and close in. Seizing the moment, Aran rose up from behind the wall and emptied both Mausers at the men.

One fell backwards, his head split open. The other two men lunged forward grabbing at their chests while screaming something unintelligible. A fourth man, the driver, put his boot down on the pedal and the vehicle careened off down the road.

Quickly reloading, Aran walked over to the fallen men. Two looked dead and one seemed gravely wounded. There was nothing he could do for them now.

Surely the place would be crawling with English in minutes, so help would be here soon enough. As for me, Aran thought, I had better get the hell out of here and fast!

Running as quickly as safety allowed, Aran zigged through gardens, over fences, in and out of side streets, and across open fields.

It was difficult to run with his pistols in both hands. When he tried to put one of the Mausers into its holster, he dropped it in the darkness.

Aran paused, not knowing what to do...stop and look for the gun or keep going?

It was an easy decision...he kept running.

Finally at Botanic Street, Aran stopped behind a corner house and looked around. All seemed quiet and peaceful.

Quickly, he crossed the road and climbed over Glasnevin's Cemetery wall. He picked his way through the deserted grounds. Would this nightmare ever end? Feeling worn out, beaten and alone, Aran wondered if he should not just dig his own grave here and jump in. It would save the British the time and trouble of digging it for him.

Gathering his wits about him, Aran pushed these defeatist thoughts from his mind and kept on walking, unbuckling his empty holster as he went. Spying a huge Irish yew up ahead, he carefully hid the incriminating evidence among its plentiful boughs.

Finally, thinking he had gone far enough and that there was not a safer place in Dublin to spend the night, he curled up in the folds of a giant oak tree. Aran knew it was going to be a cold night, but at least he was still free.

He pulled his Volunteer jacket tightly around him and tucked his remaining Painter inside the grimy garment, but took care to leave one button opened in case of an emergency. Then, taking several deep breaths, he leaned into the old tree, relaxed his war-weary body and, with great relief, fell asleep.

The next thing he knew the sun was shining and, as he opened his eyes, he was looking straight up the barrel-end of a shotgun. A member of the Royal Irish Constabulary stood over him ordering, "Stand up, put your hands in the air and don't make any sudden moves."

Sleepily, Aran responded to the peeler's demands.

4. *Indecision*

'Twas England bade our Wild Geese go that Small
    Nations might be free,
But their lonely graves are by Sulva's waves or the
    fringe of the Great North Sea...

The Foggy Dew / Rev. P. O'Neill

Aran was cold, stiff and hungry after his short night of restless sleep spent against the rough bark of the oak. Despite his fatigue, he had fallen asleep with difficulty. Now the rays of an early morning sun plus the buzzing of a pesty fly disrupted what little slumber time remained. Delaying his return to fugitive status a bit longer, Aran, with eyes still closed, brushed the insect from his face. The Irish Rebel was pondering where he would go next and what he would do when a booming command frightened him from his reverie.

Ordered to his feet in the quiet of the cemetery, Aran looked years older than he really was. With battle's residue on his clothing, a mop of wildly tangled hair and an offensively pungent odor emanating from his unwashed being, Aran's youthfulness was disguised. In reality, he looked more like an unkempt vagrant than a gallant soldier. The lines of fatigue etched into his face were accompanied by smatterings of grease and dirt. They all helped highlight and magnify his filthy appearance.

"Who are you? Where are ye from? What are you doing here?"

Standing quietly at attention with his hands over his head, Aran desperately tried to think of replies to the bloody peeler's queries.

"Private Peter Casey...Irish Volunteers...Drogheda," replied Aran.

Continuing with his falsified answers he added, "On Wednesday last a couple of my mates and me decided to come down to Dublin. We wanted to see what all the fuss was about. Back home we'd heard there was some kind of a disturbance going on in the city so."

The policeman just looked at Aran shaking his head back and forth in disapproval.

Aran, trying to act frightened and innocent, quivered his lower lip while he spun more lies.

"Yesterday, we saw a group of British Lancers marching toward Ashbourne so me and my mates split up. We hoped to stay out of trouble and meet back near here today. Since I'd no place to sleep, I decided to spend the night here."

Aran tried to focus the onus of attention back onto the policeman by boldly asking, "Am I under arrest here? Sure, I really haven't done anything wrong, have I? Besides, me mother back home will be after worrying about me so."

"Are you under arrest?" cried the RIC man. "You bet your filthy arse you are! It's amadans like you and your lot that's responsible for mucking up Dublin last week. If I'd my way, everyone of you and yis lot will pay dearly for your misbehaving."

As the peeler spoke, he raised his shotgun menacingly. Poking Aran in the ribs, he motioned his captive forward down a rough cobbled path. He pushed Aran toward a small group of buildings one hundred yards up the way.

As Aran Roe walked along in front of the policeman, his mind raced. His Mauser pistol was tucked in the waistband of his trousers. Could he slide it out, turn and get off a shot before the rozzer pulled his trigger? Would the shot bring more RIC, recapture and his likely execution? Or should he just play a waiting game and see what happened? He decided to wait.

The Irish Rebel realised that this RIC man was no professional. Probably his first duty post...guarding a bloody cemetery! The inexperienced copper had not even searched him. What a foolish man!

As the two approached and entered one of the low stone cottages near the cemetery's front gate, Aran smelled the delicious aroma of a breakfast fry. Inside a young woman hovered over the cooker. An older man, maybe her father, sat at the kitchen table watching her prepare the meal.

The policeman motioned Aran toward an empty chair opposite the man. He himself walked over to a small corner desk and picked up the telephone that rested on it. All the while the peeler kept his shotgun trained on Aran.

"This is Constable Nolan from Glasnevin. I caught me one of

your bloody Shinners. He's here in the caretaker's cottage just below the main gate. How soon can you send up somebody to take him off me hands?" The RIC man looked proud as punch.

After a short pause he replied, "Very well, sir. I'll keep him quiet for ye 'til then."

Smiling, Nolan put the phone down and joined the other two at the table. His shotgun rested, ready for action, in his lap.

"They'll be here in thirty minutes or so to collect you," the rozzer announced to everyone present. "Luckily, you're just in time for what may be your last meal," he laughed.

Fear welled up in Aran's throat as he fought to control himself. He tried to consider his options as unemotionally as possible. Should he shoot the copper here on the spot and make a run for it? There was not much time to decide.

The Irish Rebel reasoned that if the troopers or whoever Nolan just called arrived and found his 'Painter,' he would be in serious trouble...maybe even shot on the spot. Waves of uncertainty washed through his mind. Finally, he reached a decision.

Breaking the room's silence, Aran said, "I need the toilet, if you please, sir!" He looked straight and hard at the copper.

Nolan stared back in disgust but rose from his chair, pointed the gun at the door and motioned his prisoner outside.

At the back of the cottage, against the far cemetery wall, was a tiny shed. Nolan opened the door and nodded to Aran.

The cubicle contained a low enclosed wooden bench with two round holes cut neatly into the top of it. Nolan swung the door closed and stationed himself outside.

As Aran settled down to relieve himself through one of the openings, he reached into his jacket and pulled out Seamus's 'Painter.' It had saved his life on more than one occasion during these last two days. But now, in another desperate move to stay alive, he dropped the revolver through the other hole in the bench. Aran had decided to take his chances unarmed.

He stood up, redressed and knocked on the door. Nolan pulled it open, turned his face away from the escaping vapors and marched Aran back to the cottage.

On their return, the young woman offered Aran a basin filled with warmed water and a bar of rough soap.

Nolan shouted, "Sure, there be no need for that!"

But the cailin lashed back, "Up the garden wall with ye. A quick wash before his bite to eat won't hurt a bloody thing. Besides, what's he done to you, Jimmy? Aren't we all Irish anyway?"

Nolan dropped his head. He sat down once again but his shotgun still pointed in Aran's direction.

With the little crisis over, the girl served each of the men generous platefuls of food.

Anticipating the delicious looking meal, Aran thought to himself, "There's nothing as good as an Irish Sunday breakfast, and this one looks like it won't be disappointing!"

The Gortman consumed his share and more. No one, however, passed a comment. They all ate the tasty food in silence.

During the meal, Aran kept his eyes focused on his plate while he wondered what was going to happen next. Finally, looking up, he addressed the constable, "What's going to happen to me now, sir?"

"They'll probably take you over to Marlboro Barracks or maybe Richmond. The British plan on shooting the likes of ye for destroying this beautiful city of ours and thumbing you nose His Majesty's authority. You Shinners have caused a lot of trouble, but this time you sods have gone too far. Sure, your lot just can't be satisfied with how good yis got it, can ye?"

Nolan seemed proud of his little speech. He acted like he enjoyed presiding as judge and jury over his captured grimy outlaw.

After pronouncing his verdict and cleaning up his plate, Nolan rose to his feet and waved his shotgun at the prisoner. Aran was not sure what was going to happen, but once again the young woman interceded on his behalf.

"Jimmy, will ye just get a grip on yourself and sit down? You're acting like you're tuppence short of a pound. This here's only a lad and you're behaving like he's Wolfe Tone himself."

Again Nolan sat down. He tried to wipe the sheepish look off his face as an unsettled peace once more descended upon the four of them.

The calm was short lived, however. Moments later the sound of a motor was heard as it pulled into the circular drive in front of the cottage. Doors opened and English voices filled the morning air. Seconds later, a sergeant with two others in tow trooped into the now crowded kitchen.

"On your feet you bloody devil. Its eejits like you that will pay a dear price for your troublemaking. As far as I'm concerned, I hope you and all your lot are hanging like earrings from trees by week's end."

As the sergeant spoke, one of the soldiers patted Aran down while the other roughly cuffed his hands behind his back.

"I don't think this Paddy saw any action," pleaded Nolan half-heartedly, glancing over at the girl.

"I found him out sleeping there under a tree." Nolan nodded with his head toward the cemetery.

"What's your name? Where're you from?" ordered the sergeant.

"Casey...Private Peter Casey from Drogheda," replied Aran. He tried sounding contrite and looking humble in front of the soldiers, but he had little experience at play acting.

"What're you doing down here?"

"A few of me mates and me decided to come down and see what your noise was about. We heard rumours all week. Guess we should've kept our noses out of it," lied Aran repentantly.

The Irish Rebel saw no point in exacerbating the situation by decrying England's seven-hundred-year-old reign of Irish occupation and boldly stating his desire to put an end to it in any way he could. If he was lucky and played his cards right, he would live to fight another day. If not, he would make his true feelings known before they stretched him with their rope of 'English justice.'

"You bet your grimy Irish arse you should've kept your nose out of it," said one of the soldiers interrupting Aran's thoughts.

With that, the three British soldiers marched Aran out the door and into the waiting machine.

As they drove off toward the city, Aran whined, "Where are yis taking me?"

"Shut-up! You'll see soon enough!" came the curt reply.

"Sounds like the eejit is in a hurry to die, eh Serg?" grunted the driver.

Quiet descended as they drove west around Dublin on the North Circular Road. Since he had little choice, Aran sat back in his seat. The metal handcuffs bit into his wrists.

Having skirted Phoenix Park, the car neared Kingsbridge Station with its Victorian arched roof. Seeing it reminded Aran of Dublin's other main rail complex, the Broadstone, and his arrival there just a few weeks ago.

※

After meeting with Pearse and Mac Diarmada in Salthill, Aran returned to his family's farm just outside the village of Gort.

Calling a family council, he described to his elders the events of the past evening in greater detail than he had at breakfast and of his unexpected meeting today. He told them Professor Pearse wanted him to come to Dublin and attend school at St. Enda's.

After a short discussion, Aran received the blessings of his parents and plans were made for his departure.

The young Gortman's family was well aware of his political passions. In fact, they actively encouraged his nationalistic feelings and wholeheartedly supported his Volunteer training.

Just by lucky chance, Aran's oldest brother and his family were thinking of moving back to the O'Neill farm. Aran's father said he would talk to his eldest son and thought there would be no difficulty finding room for them to live back here at home. His brother's presence would certainly fill the labour gap created by Aran's departure.

The young rebel felt a great sense of relief knowing that things would continue to run smoothly on the farm without him. He knew his older brother would look after everything in his absence.

That afternoon Aran told his two younger sisters he had been offered a unique opportunity to attend a special Irish language school in Dublin. He would move there and live at St. Enda's for the remainder of the school year, maybe even longer. It was too early now to say for sure exactly how long he would stay. Hopefully, they could come and visit him after Easter.

The two girls seemed pleased to share his excitement and good fortune, but were sad he was leaving home. They would miss him very much.

Later that afternoon, Aran excitedly cycled over to Coole House to tell Robert and Lady Gregory his news.

Neither of them seemed surprised by Pearse's offer, by Aran's acceptance, or by his sudden decision to leave for Dublin.

Robert said he would inform their local IVF unit of Aran's reassignment and move to Rathfarnham. He also promised to wish their fellow Volunteers good luck and God's blessings from their OC.

Though their upbringing was different, Aran and Robert were like brothers. Now, with Aran leaving, Robert would be lonely. He would miss Aran's enthusiasm for life and his fidelity to friends and the Volunteer movement. As a result, the Gregory lad soon decided to tread down an old familiar path and honour his dead father's family name. Within the month Robert returned to England and joined the Royal Flying Corps.

Aran's decision to leave home had awakened in Robert his own sense of duty and obligation to his old Anglo-Irish ancestry. Robert's enlistment in the British military followed an old family custom.

Surprisingly, his mother was sympathetic. In Lady Gregory's mind, her son's familial loyalty to his old traditions was as powerful as Aran's allegiance to Eireann's ancient longings for independence.

Sadly, months later, Robert Gregory was accidentally shot down and killed by an Italian Air Force pilot over the wastelands of France. Though still a young man, Robert added esteem and glory to the family name, but he would never know the satisfaction of witnessing his country of birth celebrate its independence. He would not share in the pride of seeing it take its rightful place among the nations of the earth. Finally, in lasting tribute to Robert, William Butler Yeats penned an inspired and touching poem immortalising the young man's spirit forever.

Robert and Aran represented the coming together of many old and powerful forces. First, there were the ancient Gaelic blood lines and traditions that had been diluted by centuries of Viking, Welsh, Norman, English and Irish intermarriage and cultural blending. This intermingling of people and customs created conflicting political behaviours that were intensified by the religious, social and economic confusion of the Protestant Reformation, Cromwell's Puritan invasion, the French Huguenots' emigration and the English planting of Scottish Presbyterians in Ireland.

The resulting mix created many animosities and torn loyalties between individual members of Irish society. In a simplified sense, this resulted, unfortunately, in the establishment of a dualistic world. First, there were the competing forces of a Catholic majority and a Protestant minority. Next, a much larger impoverished lower class was dominated by a smaller, wealthy upper class. Finally, there was the explosive mix of a ruling Anglo-Ascendancy minority who often forced itself upon a subservient Irish majority. These conflicting variables were eventually bound to lead to trouble.

Yes, it was easy to tease out a single issue and hold it up as the measure by which to judge all matters, but in reality, many elements converged causing much confusion and uncertainty. Neither Ireland nor England could be blamed for Robert embarking upon a different path than his friend Aran had taken. Master Gregory was the product of complex multicultural circumstances. His life and death brought honour to the family's name and its proud cultural heritage.

❧

Eventually driven to Richmond Barracks, Aran was only a stone's throw away from the dreaded Kilmainham Gaol over whose main entrance resided, in artistic relief, five bronze snakes. These 'Demons of Crime' were twisted and chained together as a warning to all who happened to pass by or through its sinister gates. But viewed in its totality, Kilmainham's was a grey stone monster of English evil. Its black history was filled with the dead and broken bodies of many an Irish patriot. Recently, it had stopped serving as a civilian criminal centre of incarceration. Today it was being used by the military to house its army prisoners.

With his hands unshackled, Aran's guards marched him into a large gymnasium. On this day it contained several hundred captured Irish soldiers as well as some civilians caught up in that morning's military sweep. Curtly, he was told to get into line with the rest of those 'damned traitors.'

As Aran and the other men stood around the edges of the huge room, detectives, called 'G-men,' from the political division of the infamous Dublin Metropolitan Police Department walked around the room scrutinizing the faces of the Irish prisoners. The G-men were so named because Dublin Town had been divided into six police jurisdictions, A-F. Thus, the letter 'G' was used to designate the next most important area of governance, political investigation. Officially, the abbreviation stood for the Department of Political Investigation and Information of the Dublin Metropolitan Police.

From time to time, one of the G-men would point out a certain individual, and two burly soldiers would yank the unfortunate man out of line. Then, under guard, he was marched out of the room.

From the men being taken away, Aran quickly realised these detectives, mostly of Irish birth, were fingering their own countrymen for the benefit of the British authorities. These earmarked prisoners were the individuals who had helped organise the Rebellion or were known for their anti-British sentiments and subversive political activities.

Soon after his arrival, Tom Clarke was identified and taken away. As he walked out of the room, a voice shouted out, "Remember '16...God Save Ireland!" The guarding soldiers' angry stares and threatening gestures quickly returned silence and order to the gymnasium.

Most of the captive Irish soldiers were exhausted. Many were having difficulty just standing on their own. The expressions on their faces told of their personal sacrifices. Aran knew these men had been victimised, not only by a superior military force, but by their own mates' sparse turnout, by an inadequate supply of arms as well as their own leaders' conflicting orders.

As Aran looked out the corner of his eye, he recognised a familiar face. It was the young captain, Michael Collins. He had been Joe Plunkett's adjutant in the GPO. Additionally, he had been an inspiring leader under the most difficult of circumstances throughout their week's revolt. Collins knew of Aran's friendship with Pearse and of his move from Gort to St. Enda's. In fact, it was Collins who had come up to him and wished him 'good luck' just before Aran and the others followed the O'Rahilly out of the burning GPO on their way to attack the enemy's barricade at the top of Moore Street.

Slowly and carefully, so as not to attract attention, Aran worked his way over until he stood next to Collins.

"What happened to all of ye after I left?" whispered Aran out of the side of his mouth.

"I was just wondering the same about yourself?" replied Collins.

"No talking you bloody sods," barked one of the G-men.

Then, as if to exercise their authority over the prisoners, two of the detectives approached and carefully examined the faces of the men standing by Collins and O'Neill.

"I thought so!" declared one of the G-men. "You, you, you and...you...step out of line this instant."

Aran saw hatred and self-satisfaction shining in a G-man's eyes while the man stood no more than two feet away from him.

With that command, Collins and the three men to his right stepped forward and were told to march.

As they headed off across the floor, one of the G-men shouted out, "You...you at the end of the line—get back there with the rest of these hoors."

So ordered, Michael Collins did an about-face and rejoined the other prisoners.[HN-1]

Back in line again next to Aran, Collins did not utter another word. The Irish Rebel followed his lead.

The longer the ID process lasted, the more the feelings of dread and foreboding spread among the prisoners. The concern on their faces grew more noticeable as more of their comrades were marched off. It was difficult to maintain a feeling of hope and optimism under these most trying of conditions. Aran could almost feel the group's flagging spirits sag when another man was removed to face what only God knew.

This culling process lasted for more than an hour. Finally, those remaining were herded into groups of thirty or so and led into small rooms adjoining the gym. Aran Roe, Michael Collins and several dozen other men were all pushed together into one of those cubicles.

Their detention quarters contained no furniture whatsoever. Its two windows had been boarded up and there was no air circulating around the room. The pungent odor of sweat-caked men and dirty clothing soon filled the communal cell.

To make matters worse, there was only one small pail in the room that was intended to substitute for a chamber pot. Much to everyone's disgust, the British did not have the decency to at least provide cut-up bits of newspaper to substitute for lavatory paper. Thus, with thirty men in the room and nature's occasional call, the little cell and its pail were soon filled with another offensive odor.

No one seemed comfortable sitting on the 'pee-pot' but the alternative was even less appealing. Soon, however, the men discovered it was less embarrassing to relieve yourself facing the corner while turning your back on your comrades. Thankfully, all quickly learned to ignore their fellow prisoners' need to answer nature's call.

As there were no guards in the room, the men freely talked among themselves in hushed tones. After a moment or two, Aran sought out Collins, sat down next to him, and unfolded his story of escape and capture. He described Seamus's death, his flight from Simpson's Lane, and his attack on the British barricades. He concluded his narrative with the Fannin-house adventure and his eventual capture in Glasnevin Cemetery.

There was something though that bothered Aran. It had been on his mind all morning. Should he not have proudly revealed to Constable Nolan and the others his role in the Rebellion and his desire to see the English out of Ireland? He now felt ashamed of lying and appearing innocent when, in fact, he was not. In retrospect, Aran thought he should have stood up and declared his true feelings instead of choosing to lie.

Collins, however, assured him he had done the right thing. "There are plenty of men right now standing up and declaring themselves for Ireland. They'll keep the bloody British blackguards busy for a good while," retorted Collins in his best sarcastic tone.

On a softer and more positive note Mick Collins continued, "This country of ours is going to need many strong and brave men to stand up for her in the days and months to come. No, Aran, you'll have plenty of opportunities to speak up and declare for Ireland. This war with England is a long way from over!"

There was a fierce defiance and look of controlled anger in Michael Collins's eyes and, as Aran glanced around, all the other prisoners were watching the two of them. There was not another sound to be heard in the crowded room. They all stood or sat motionless as each stared intently at the man called 'Mick.'

After what seemed an eternity, the men stirred and again began talking among themselves. Collins smiled at Aran and squeezed his arm.

"Let me bring you up to date on what happened to us after you left." Collins's voice was more relaxed now and his eyes twinkled.

"Yes, yes, I want to know all about it." said Aran.

The Corkman began his story by describing how the rest of the two hundred plus men in the GPO escaped from their fire-filled GHQ. "We hightailed it across Henry Street and up into Moore Place, then tunnelled our way through a row of houses and shops on the eastern side of Moore Street, just opposite your Simpson's Lane retreat. Eventually, we regrouped setting up a temporary rebel GHQ in #16. This was mostly on account of Connolly's painful wounds. To continue hauling him about in that blanket-sling would have been inhuman. For most of us the lion's share of that night was spent discussing what we should do next. Some wanted to continue the fight. Others wished to mount another barricade charge. Still more suggested we try breaking through the enemy's perimeter around Parnell's monument. But of all the alternatives discussed that night, no one ever mentioned the word 'surrender.'"

After pausing a moment to reflect on what he had just said, Collins continued his narrative. "Aran, you remember Saturday morning when the three civilians, each carrying their white flags, were cut down in the street in front of our hiding place...well, that was the coup de grace! The GHQ leadership decided it was time to treat with the enemy.

"Unfortunately, we hadn't posted a lookout, so we had no idea of your efforts to try and create an opening in the barricade for us to push through and escape."

Collins went on. "As you might have guessed, when Pearse asked for terms, the English would have none of it. No negotiating with little old Ireland! It was either give up unconditionally or be wiped out by their 'forces of law and order.'"

Gradually, a sadness crept into the Captain Collins's voice. With their two heads together, he talked and Aran listened. "Who knows how many innocent people would have died or suffered if we'd continued fighting? So nobly Pearse handed over his sword and the bleeding lousers drove him away. The rest of us marched out, under guard, to the top of Sackville Street. We stacked our arms before Parnell's outstretched arm. That's what we were doing when you saw us from the Fannin house.

"We spent the night sleeping rough under heavy guard on the lawn of the Rotunda Hospital. Then this morning they marched us all over to here."

Collins described to Aran the reception the captured Irish Republican Army received as they marched through the Liberties and down Thomas Street.

"Waste from chamber pots, rotten veg and vile oaths were flying at us from every direction. I guess the poor of southside Dublin Town were too far away from the Sackville Street looting to prosper but too close to the action not to have their daily routines disturbed.

"Without their 'separation pay,' without a squalid rat-infested room to go home to, without some menial 'tuppence-ha'penny looking down on tuppence' job to go back to, these underclassed citizens were taking out their vengeance on those they felt were responsible for Dublin's fires, destruction and disruption.

"This display broke the hearts of some Volunteers around me. A few even cried out, 'We did it for yis, you ungrateful thicks.' But no one was listening...and, if they were, they wouldn't have understood. But in my heart of hearts I hoped that some of Dublin's citizenry grasped the importance of what we tried to win...a chance to finally be free of Britain's yoke."

Michael and Aran speculated that their interruption of Dublin's daily life was the most disturbing feature of the Rebellion for many. As the actual fighting was quite localised, the majority of the populace was not placed in a life-threatening posture. But, unfortunately for many Dubliners most of the stores and pubs closed. People were forced to make do with less than they were normally accustomed to having.

Collins thought that some of the outrage displayed toward them, as they marched along to Richmond Barracks, was organised by women afraid of losing their 'separation pay.'

"No one knows what measures the British might impose on the Irish population as a way of evening up the score for our rebellious behaviour toward the Crown," scoffed Collins.

"Sure, you really still can't blame those poor women now can ye? They're just trying to protect their meagre interests and make a show of it in front of the Limeys," interjected Aran.

Collins nodded, "Right so, Aran. I know their lot in life isn't easy. For as you well know, since the war in Europe began, 'Mother England' has provided those wives and mothers with monthly separation payments to compensate for the loss of income brought on by the absence of their husbands and sons who are off fighting for her in Europe."

"Tis a terrible burden they're forced to bear, no doubt. A life without their men makes living doubly difficult...the loneliness, the worry...the lack of a steady income. It's not a pretty picture to paint," agreed Aran.

Collins returned to his description of the morning's march to Richmond, "But Aran, every now and again, someone in the crowd would shout, 'God Save Ireland' or 'Up The Republic' and we'd all stand a wee bit taller and step a little smarter. Once, someone up ahead even broke out singing Kearney's *A Soldier's Song*. We all joined in and were almost through the first verse before the guards put a stop to it.

"Aran," Collins motioned his young friend to slide even closer. With a softer voice he continued, "A group of us are tired of letting the majority of the Irish nationalists take the lead with their constitutional conservatism. Redmond and his kind seem more than willing to trade Irishmen, alive or dead, for more empty English guarantees. You're well aware that to date Irish parliamentary tactics and British legislative promises have not moved us any closer to our long denied freedom. Speaking for myself, your friend President Pearse and my other IRB comrades, we believe force is the only effective way of achieving the ends we seek...Irish independence! The use of violence is the only language His Majesty's government takes seriously. It shows them we mean business."

Aran interrupted by raising his index to his lips.

"Yes?" said the Corkman.

"But don't we owe it to the people to...to...to somehow ask them for their support and blessing in all this. Weren't those Dubliners who were throwing insults and veg at ye along the quays this morning telling you they disapproved of our violence? Weren't they acting in support of more conventional methods for achieving political independence?"

"Maybe they were but I'm betting they'll be some of the first to jump on our bandwagon when they start seeing what we can accomplish. Aran, too rigorously adhering to the democratic process in the early stages of a revolt might allow the majority to make the wrong choice. Sometimes, the minority must take the lead without asking for approval. Once the new direction is clear, I'm guessing most of the nation will gladly follow...but it's our responsibility to first show them the proper way."

The young Irish Rebel nodded affirmatively. "Captain Collins, I want you to know I'm in full agreement with you and your lot. I know Professor Pearse, Mr. Clarke and the others share your feelings. I should know, I've heard them expound on that subject often enough. Yes, a powerful dose of republican violence will undermine England's existing political systems here in Ireland. In the end, we'll have established a new form of government that will fulfill our nation's desire for self-rule."

Aran spoke with such sincerity and conviction that Michael Collins could only smile at the young soldier. The captain held out his right hand and the Gortman shook it warmly.

Returning to his saga, Michael concluded by saying, "Sure, the rest you know. You arrived here shortly after we did so. Oh, one more thing. Rumour has it that General Connolly was taken by ambulance to the Castle's hospital. You can't imagine the pain and suffering that man endured after his wounding on Thursday afternoon. I wonder if he'll make it with that leg of his looking as it did."

Just at that moment, the door to their prison room opened. Two English soldiers entered with several loaves of stale bread and a bucket of water with one dipper.

Someone with a Donegal accent asked if the toilet bucket might be emptied. A guard pointed to a man near the offensive container. He ordered him to collect the bucket and marched him out the door. A few minutes later, the Volunteer returned with it empty. For his efforts he received a huge cheer from his fellow prisoners.

Aran, Michael and the others spent a restless night in their cramped quarters. It was difficult finding a comfortable sleeping position as there was not enough room for every man to stretch out. Most slept in a seated position while leaning against one of the room's walls. During the night many of the men coughed and gagged. Several actually vomited as the air in the room became staler and more putrid.

Yes, lack of physical comforts made life difficult, but the overriding concern of every prisoner was what was going to happen to them next? Everyone tried to steel their nerves against the unknown, but not knowing your fate made time pass slowly and their internment more difficult to endure. Then, to top matters off, the captured men were concerned about their friends and companions who had been marched out of the gymnasium yesterday.

As the long sleepless night wore on, Aran Roe and Michael Collins whispered to one another about their leadership's decision to fight it out from city buildings rather than employing unconventional guerrilla tactics against the overpowering military advantages held by the British authorities.

Collins believed in action as Aran did. But unlike Aran, he did not hold much faith in fancy romantic ideals. Michael preferred avenues of action organised along practical lines headed by realists instead of treading down idyllic paths directed by dreamers. Now, Aran could understand why Collins felt that Pearse's, MacDonagh's and Plunkett's romantic beliefs and self-sacrificing behaviours had compromised the success of the Rebellion.

Michael Collins's last words to Aran before drifting off to sleep were, "Leave dreams to the dreamers!"

❧

Finally, morning arrived. Another bucket of water with some hard biscuits and bits of bully beef were brought in by three soldiers. During their brief stay in the cell, one of the guards mentioned that the rebels were going to be shipped to English prisons in a few hours.

"Enjoy your lovely Irish air for as long as ye can," he quipped, turning to leave.

All the Irishmen began talking excitedly among themselves.

"So we're not going to be lined up and shot after all," whispered Aran to Captain Collins.

"Ah, prison in England...that could be a living hell if we're not lucky," replied the man from County Cork. They both knew of the inhumane treatment many old imprisoned Fenians had received in English jails during the 1880s and 1890s. Stories of what Tom Clarke endured were legend among the rebels' ranks.

Someone in the room suggested trying to organise an escape before they were all loaded onboard ship. Though it seemed pretty impossible considering their present circumstances, Aran's mind started churning.

"Should I risk it and try running if I see an opening?" queried Aran of the Corkman.

"It really depends on the quality of the opportunity, doesn't it?" answered Collins.

"Well, in any event, I'm going to pay special attention to every detail this morning. You never know when a chance will present itself, do ye?" declared the Irish Rebel.

Collins only smiled at Aran's enthusiasm for risking death so casually.

Deciding to keep further thoughts to himself, Aran chose not to say anything to any of the other prisoners about escaping from their captors. If he was going to make a break for it, it would be a decision based on his own assessment of the situation. Besides, Aran figured one man had a better chance of slipping away unnoticed than did a group of desperate prisoners all making a mad dash for it at once. He realised, however, that given the present circumstances any opportunity of escaping without the help of some outside assistance was virtually impossible.

5. *Hiding*

No pipe did hum, no battle drum did sound its
　　loud tattoo,
But the Angelus bell o'er the Liffey's swell rang
　　out through the Foggy Dew...

The Foggy Dew / Rev. P. O'Neill

 Soft warm sunlight filtered through bellowing white clouds blown in on a sweet springtime breeze. This idyllic setting dramatically contrasted with the foul filthy-smelling detention rooms from which Aran Roe O'Neill, Michael Collins and several hundred other prisoners of war now emerged.

Aran and the other Irishmen were so relieved to be outside in the fresh air, they almost shouted for joy. Oh, what a heavenly delight it was to be out in the sunshine once more. This was where Aran belonged and where he loved to be. As if by some special godly sign, Aran noticed a solitary row of flowers blooming beside the foundation of a building that lined the compound's perimeter. They seemed to be cheerfully greeting his release from the awful confinement of the gymnasium prison.

Aran had grown up on a farm. For most of his life he had worked alongside his grandfather, father and brothers. Together they had planted the spring crops and gathered in the autumn harvest. In between times there were cattle to run, horses to care for, sheep to shear and a thousand other chores that necessitated frequent attention. Dry stone walls often needed repairing or rebuilding, outbuildings required renovating and whitewashing, while seasonal fairs and local Saturday markets were always on the list of things to attend. Going to these gatherings to buy or sell family and farm necessities were some of life's pleasures.

After concluding their usual business around town, most of the men spent some time in a favourite pub. They rehashed the highlights of the week, shared other news and, of course, contributed to the local rumour mill. Aran greatly enjoyed these ritualistic social occasions. Besides their entertainment value, they were also instructional. He liked watching and listening to his father visit with their neighbours and friends about everything imaginable. Glassfuls of that magic elixir called porter disappeared as the men discussed, usually at great length and with guarded emotion, how difficult it was to farm in Ireland with England controlling market prices and shipping quotas.

The power of the landlord had finally been broken with the passage in 1898 of the Local Government Act and the 1903 Local Land Act. Most of what remained of the old landlord estates had been divided up. The land, originally Irish, had finally been returned generations later, to the peasants and farmers who had loved and cared for their native soil from which the Stranger had calculatingly padded his wallet with excessive rents and greedy profits.

The land had reverted to the Irish people, though not without a price. England loaned Ireland the money to buy back the land from its landlords. Ireland then resold the land to the locals who, in turn, gradually repaid the Anglo-Irish government. This money was returned to England in the form of annual land annuity payments. It would be years before the Irish finally owned the land titles free and clear. Many adamantly maintained that the British Crown had stolen and wrested millions of pounds from the Irish people since the Act of Union in 1801. Aran realised that the old extortion game was still going on today. It just appeared to be a wee bit more legal and above board than it was in years gone by.

With some luck and much hard work, Aran's father had succeeded and prospered after the 1903 legislation. His original thirty-five acres grew to over one hundred and he was called upon by the local farming community for his sound advice and wise counsel.

Aran closed his eyes and transported himself from the bowels of British military power to the rolling furze and heather-covered fields of Kilmacduagh. In his mind, he found the hollowed-out stone he loved sitting upon and imagined his broad back leaning against a thousand-year-old round tower. He closed his eyes even tighter and imagined looking out upon the ruins of its surrounding ancient churches. Smiling to himself, he thought of a time long ago when Irish kings safeguarded Eireann's ancient land in their dutiful and communal ways.

Reluctantly returning to the pressing realities of the moment, Aran mused to himself, "Ah sure, there's is a bit of the old romantic in me no, but isn't there in everyone?"

Suddenly, the shrill sound of a whistle shook the cobwebs from his head. There were practical matters needing his immediate attention. He needed to be ready for their challenges.

"Fall in, you sons-of-bitches," bellowed a sergeant. "The major has something to say to ye, the scum of the earth!"

For the twenty minutes prior to their being called to attention, the men had aimlessly milled about within a heavily secured section of a grassy assembly area. But now, in rows four abreast, they stood at attention waiting for the British officer to speak.

The two hundred or so prisoners were encircled by five hundred heavy-armed troops. Most of these Limeys looked young and lacked the air of military experience. Aran wondered if they were thankful to be here in Ireland instead of in France where soldiers like themselves were dying by the hundreds of thousands. The ill-planned and misdirected Gallipoli invasion alone had claimed over a quarter of a million Allied lives in less than six months. That senseless Turkish fight had brought down the British government and several of its key military leaders including the Lord of the Admiralty, Winston Leonard Spencer Churchill.

After a brief word with another officer, the major mounted a low platform positioned at one end of the yard. In the bright sunlight his brass buttons, buckles and leather boots shone with military pride. In a strong clear voice he informed the assembled Irish Republican Army prisoners that their involvement in the Rebellion had been a foul and traitorous deed. So, as a result of their foolish actions, they were all headed to prison. With seeming pride, the military man continued to rebuke the defeated men. Finally, he concluded his tirade by stating, "Each of you should consider yourself very lucky. You eejits were simply following orders not giving them." He informed them that as of this morning, the Rebellion's leadership was all in custody. He added, "Those foolhardy lousers will be dealt with in a far more severe manner than any of you bloody wasters!"

The captives glanced around at one another. Their eyes expressed unspoken fears. Nodded heads and shrugged shoulders silently conveyed their alarmed feelings. The grim reality of the British officer's words greatly disturbed the gathered throng. He was talking about their lives and the lives of their friends and commanders.

Aran and the others were informed they would be marched down to the Custom House Quay and loaded aboard a cattle boat bound for Britain. Their imprisonment abroad was to begin immediately! As the major retired from the platform, he could not pass up the opportunity to quip, "A cattle boat suits the likes of ye quite well!"

Minutes later, the prisoners were ordered to form two lines. Under close guard they were marched from Richmond Barracks and out along the Old Kilmainham Road toward the city. Four columns of English soldiers surrounded and escorted the Irishmen. Additionally, several companies of armed men were positioned in front of and behind the prisoners. It was a three-mile walk to the city centre, but with such enemy manpower present Aran realised there would be little opportunity to escape.

During the past several days, the Irish Rebel had been kept busy just staying alive. He had had little opportunity to focus on anything else. But now, as he marched out on this fine May morning, the Gortman thought of his family back home. How would he let them know he was still alive and off to 'jolly old England' to do some 'hard time' for the bully, John Bull, himself?

As they moved east toward town, the parade passed South Dublin Union. Now all was quiet, but until yesterday Commandant Eamonn Ceannt and his second in command, Cathal Brugha, aided by the gallant Volunteers of Dublin's Fourth Battalion, had held the British to a standstill in and around the grounds of that rambling hospital and workhouse complex. The defensive stalemate might have led to an Irish offensive victory had more than twenty percent of Eamonn's men turned up to fight with him on Easter Monday. Ceannt, like the other three Dublin battalion commandants, was victimised by Professor MacNeill's countermanding of Pearse's order to rise on Easter Sunday evening.

Yes, Aran knew that the Rebellion's fate had been sealed prior to any shots ever being fired. All the troubles that had erupted in the week prior to Easter had greatly limited its success potential. A sea of unfortunate confusion and a cacophony of bruised egos were too great a handicap for the Rising's leadership to overcome.

Marching on toward Dublin Bay and England, Aran thought back to the events of that calamitous week. Pearse and the others on the clandestine IRB Military Council had chosen not to inform Dr. Eoin MacNeill, titular head of the IVF, of their intentions for staging a revolt. The IRB thought that once the Volunteers were armed and the Rising actually under way, it would be too late for MacNeill and his conservative friends to interfere. Yes, the need for secrecy in executing their plans was paramount. Ireland's history was so pockmarked with stories of fiendish informers destroying the carefully laid plans of disaffected rebel-patriots that the IRB was unwilling to take any unnecessary chances.

Aran remembered the many converging events that had occurred prior to the Rising's originally scheduled beginning on Easter Sunday.

First, the IRB, from its inception, had been dedicated to the physical overthrow of English rule in Ireland. The Brotherhood's leadership always believed that England's difficulty was Ireland's opportunity to strike for its freedom. So, with the outbreak of the First War, the English difficulty that Ireland longed for was now at hand. But, planning and organising a national revolt was a complex task and the IRB's secret council had had their hands full.

England, however, had problems of its own. The war in Europe, which was to be over in weeks, was now months old and showed no signs of ending soon. The British government was on its proverbial knees begging for American assistance. England felt that with such help, Germany could quickly be defeated. If that were to happen, any military advantage Ireland presently enjoyed over England would dissolve. Once again, Britain would reinforce its 'army of occupation' and be free to refocus her attention on her dissentient island neighbour. As a result, the chance for any successful military engagement would be lost. It was necessary, therefore, to act quickly while war still raged on the Continent.

Secondly, James Connolly and his two-hundred-person Citizen Army was threatening to take on the might of England by themselves. The labour leader was impatient and unwilling to wait any longer. But, rather than have Connolly alert the English that unrest was riper than imagined among the disenfranchised, the IRB invited Connolly and his small but well-drilled Citizen Army to join them. This increased the Volunteer's military strength and removed the possibility of a premature and ineffectual rebel offensive.

Thirdly, Germany had been contacted and had agreed to send a large supply of guns, ammunition and possibly some military advisers to Ireland. With the British Army occupied in France and with the Irish Volunteers properly armed, the balance of power on their little island might shift in favour of the rebels.

Next, Aran recollected the rumour stating how the British government planned a major Sinn Fein and Irish dissonant roundup. England felt a small disharmonious group was stirring up too much trouble. They threatened the Crown's secure position and, besides, they were a public embarrassment. With its leadership deported to English prisons, any possible revolt would have little chance of succeeding.

Another force driving things closer toward a climax was the discordant demands of Ireland's Ulster unionists who sought to remain free of a Home-Ruled, Dublin 'Popish' Parliament. These Northerners wanted to remain within the Union, but if forced to be a part of a united Ireland, were prepared to belligerently establish their own provisional government. They would proudly declare their independence from Britain and if forced to, would boldly fight to defend their 'Ulster' independence. These threats were backed by a solemn Covenant signed by one-third of its population, a military force of 100,000 rifled UVF men and, led by their strident leader, Edward Carson, pledged that 'Uster will fight and Ulster will be right.' Irish civil war or an Ulster rebellion against England seemed like real possibilities.

Besides all of these dynamics, Aran fondly recalled Ireland's antagonistic reaction to the ever-growing Anglicisation of its society. This trend greatly offended many staunch nationalists and their more radical cousins, the republicans. This renewed interest by many Irishmen and women in the revival of Ireland's vanishing Gaelic culture at the expense of Britain's superimposed substitute had been gathering strength since the end of the last century. Additionally, the flames of Irish heritage and self-government were being fanned by a widespread resurgence of European nationalism.

For all of these reasons and more, Easter Sunday had been selected as the date for the Rebellion's beginning. Accordingly, Joseph Mary Plunkett, another member of the IRB's covert war committee, drew up military plans identifying key buildings and geographical locations around Dublin that would serve as centres for rebel occupation and armed resistance.

It was thought that if these key locations could be controlled and held until rebels from the countryside reached the city, the English would be outmaneuvered, out-manned and, hopefully, out of luck. Sandwiched between the Dublin partisans in their city strongholds and with the aid of additional Volunteer forces arriving from the provinces, the IRB felt the trapped British army would be forced to capitulate.

Even if little Ireland could just hold off mighty England for a short while, Eireann's efforts for its own governance would attract worldwide attention.

The Rebellion's leadership felt confident that even if the Central Powers did win the war, Germany would side with Eireann and support her cause for independence. If, on the other hand, the Allies won, Ireland would be in a strong position to petition for its sovereignty from England at the peace conference which would soon follow at war's end. Britain had clearly stated it was fighting the war in Europe so 'small nations might be free,' and was not Ireland a small nation without its freedom? So, no matter who won the worldwide conflict, Ireland felt it would gain the freedom she sought, especially if she rose up and successfully battled her occupying neighbour on Irish soil.

But, during the week before Easter, plans for the Rising fell apart. On Maundy Thursday evening, Professor MacNeill discovered Pearse's plan to use the Volunteers for making war against England.

MacNeill had always viewed the IVF as a defensive force to protect Ireland from unknown enemies and to resist England conscripting Irishmen into its war machine. MacNeill also argued that both the National Volunteers and the Irish Volunteers were formed to assure English compliance with Westminster's 1914 Irish Home Rule legislation now scheduled for implementation after the war's successful Allied conclusion.

MacNeill was furious with Pearse and wanted to call off the manoeuvres scheduled for Sunday. But on Good Friday morning, Pearse and MacDonagh convinced MacNeill it was too late to postpone the Rising. Too many carefully laid plans were even now being played out.

The professor reluctantly agreed not to interfere. On Holy Saturday, however, when news that the German ship bringing arms to the rebels had been intercepted by the British and eventually scuttled, MacNeill acted. He placed a notice in the Irish *Sunday Independent* newspaper cancelling all Volunteer activities scheduled for the following day, Easter Sunday.

At this point, Pearse's and the IRB's leadership plans began collapsing. Without the needed arms, there was little hope of any significant help from rural Ireland. But, deciding there was more to lose by not rising, the IRB decided to proceed with the Rebellion. On Easter Sunday morning, Pearse announced that the call out slated for six o'clock that evening was postponed and would be rescheduled for noon the following day, Easter Monday.

It was now a matter of record. The Rebellion began on Monday but, with all the problems created by the countermanding and reissuing of orders, only one-fifth of the Dublin Brigade took their assigned noontime places. Thus, the Irish military surprise was greatly reduced in both numbers and in its fighting ability.

Aran recalled overhearing English soldiers in the gymnasium talking about the timing of the Rebellion. There were rumours circulating among some units of the British army that something was up with the 'Shinners' for Easter weekend. But when Ireland read of MacNeill's newspaper orders for the IVF to stand down, stay at home and not parade on Sunday the military relaxed. This false sense of security was reinforced again on Monday when a possible early morning attack failed to materialise. As a result, most of the British army and Dublin Castle governmental officials left Dublin Town at mid-morning to attend the traditional Fairyhouse horse races north of the city.[HN-2]

With the Rebellion rescheduled for Monday and ignoring the colossal confusion created by MacNeill's countermanding of Pearse's orders, the IRB made numerous mistakes which only helped the British overcome the initial advantage held by the protagonists. The British munitions dump in Phoenix Park was not destroyed. The rebels failed to occupy a key communications and telephone exchange building in the city centre. Dublin Castle, traditional seat of English command and authority, was virtually unguarded but the misinformed Volunteers failed to seize the opportunity. Next, Trinity College, with its high stone walls strategically located in the heart of the city, was ignored as a key offensive and defensive chess piece. But maybe the biggest mistake of all was establishing the rebel's GHQ in the middle of Dublin Town. The English soon surrounded the GPO raining it with shot and shell. It was finally set on fire and destroyed by a persistent incendiary bomb attack. As a result, the rebels were forced to retreat directly into the waiting arms of the British army. In the final analysis, the redcoats simply encircled the heart of the city and waited for the Irish to run out of their indefensible holes.

❧

The prisoners marched past South Dublin Union. It had only been cleared of rebel activity yesterday. Some of those who had fought there began singing *God Save Ireland*. The rest of the men joined in the salute to their fellow comrades heroic efforts. The English guards protested this behaviour by firing their rifles into the air. The singing eventually stopped but every Irish soldier in the passing parade felt a sense of pride and victory no foreign army could quell.

On they marched toward the Liberties with its world-famous Guinness Brewery buildings dominating the old neighbourhood. Further along, they entered Thomas Street and made a left hand turn down

Footbridge Street. They now trod o'er a piece of sacred and hallowed ground.

It was on this corner, in front of St. Catherine's Church in September, 1803, that the English half-hung and beheaded bold Robert Emmet for his part in that summer's abortive Rising. Prior to his execution, Emmet's famous speech from the courtroom dock has never been forgotten. His hallowed words still ring true in the hearts and minds of Irishmen and women everywhere.

Boldly, the rebel leader declared to his judge and jury, "...when my country takes her place among the nations of the earth, then, and not 'till then, let my epitaph be written."

Reflecting on those words, Aran hoped that the events of the past week would shorten the time to the writing of Robert's epitaph.

With tear-filled eyes and pride in his voice, Aran shouted out, "Remember Emmet" as they rounded the corner. Others took up the cry and its sound echoed and re-echoed off the walls of the surrounding buildings. A thoughtful quiet followed more British rifle reports.

Marching down toward the river, Aran thought of Pearse and his teacher's famous hero. The large wooden block upon which Emmet had given up his head to the British now resided in the hallway just outside the chapel and study hall entrance at St. Enda's. Somehow Pearse had discovered its whereabouts and had it brought to the school for safekeeping. Today, it served as a constant reminder to all of the sacrifice and the dedication required of Ireland in her centuries-old struggle for freedom.

They marched on in orderly fashion across Queen Street Bridge, the oldest River Liffey span still standing. It had been built in the mid-1760s and named for Charlotte, the wife of King George III. Remembering that Amerikay had won its freedom by defeating George III, Aran prayed to God that Ireland might defeat the King's namesake, George V, and win its independence as well.

Methodically, the long column of men turned right onto Arran Quay. Though the spelling was different, it did not matter. He and St. Enda, the patron saint of the Aran Islands, shared this one block of cobblestones to themselves. Aran drew a special sense of pride deep into his lungs. He then looked back across the river to a stone building with its wrought-ironed and stoned wall facing the river.

Just one week ago, inside that edifice called Mendicity Institute, a nineteen-year-old soldier named Sean Heuston and twenty other youths held off a far greater enemy force for some forty-eight hours. Finally, on Wednesday afternoon a British regiment, the Dublin Fusiliers, brought the building and its defenders to their knees. Aran remembered the reports of how enraged the Limeys were when they discovered that such a small band of young soldiers had been able to hold them off for two entire days. Aran bowed his head in prayer to honour all those brave Mendicity warriors.

Moments later, the prisoners, with their guards marching alongside them, passed the Four Courts so courageously defended by Commandant Edward Daly and his First Battalion soldiers. He truly had carried the fight to the British army and only reluctantly surrendered yesterday morning after receiving Pearse's written instructions to do so.

As the rebels passed the main gate, one of the prisoners cried, "Eyes left!" and a lone voice began singing *A Nation Once Again*. Seconds later two hundred voices joined in the singing. This time the rifle shots had no effect. It was not until British bayonets were menacingly pointed in the direction of the singers that order was restored among the marching ranks of Irishmen.

As they neared the city centre, the crowds along the quays grew larger. Angry shouts greeted the prisoners, but here and there friendly greetings and waves erupted. Occasionally, a small packet of food or a parcel of clothing found its way through the armed guards and into a rebel's hands. Some of the British soldiers seemed sympathetic to the sorry plight of the internees. They simply turned their heads and overlooked the sporadic gift giving.

These acts of charity were clear indications by some Dublin citizens of their support for the Rebellion and of the ambivalence some British subjects felt for the Crown's authority in Ireland.

As more onlookers filled the processional street, the guarding soldiers were forced in upon each other and pushed up against their Irish prisoners. All this congestion and growing confusion made uniform marching difficult. The British soldiers were in danger of losing control of the situation and several of their officers shouted at the crowd, "Stand clear of the prisoners! Make way for the marching men! Out of the way...we're the forces of the Crown!"

A major on horseback hollered out to the prisoners, "You there, Shinners, stay in line! Stay in line there! Shut your bloody gobs...no talking!"

Amid all the unexpected tension and sudden confusion, the idea of escape jumped back into Aran's head. He was on his toes and alert to any possible opening through which he might flee.

Then, just as he passed Chapel Street with Grattan's Bridge off to his right, Aran saw Martin Richardson. He wondered how in the world Marty knew where he would be this day.

Martin, whose family lived in Drumcondra and whose frightened mother never stopped asking queries during Aran's brief stay there on Saturday evening, was between his British guards and the low retaining wall separating Ormond Quay from the Liffey. Marty strided with a confident gait as he looked straight ahead. He did not want to alert the British soldiers he was trying to catch one of their prisoner's attention. But, despite Marty's forward stare, Aran saw his lips moving.

The Richardson lad found it difficult to keep pace with his friend with all the people gathered on the footpath and spilling out into the street. With some skillful footwork, however, he managed to stay abreast of Aran.

The Irish Rebel smiled whispering a prayer, "Thank Jesus for all those hurling drills we were forced to endure back at St. Enda's." It was evident to Aran their training had paid off.

Looking to his right, the Gortman strained to decode the words Marty's lips were mouthing. Finally, it came to him what his friend was saying, "Remember the Puddle. Remember the river tunnel. Remember the Puddle Tunnel."

"Begad!" murmured Aran. "What's he thinking? Is Martin alerting me to a possible escape route? Could he be offering an avenue of freedom?"

Just up ahead the small underground River Puddle flowed out into the River Liffey. For the past one hundred years or so, the little tributary had been directed underground as Dublin Town grew up around and over its humble banks. Today, it flowed into the Liffey through a large underground tunnel of stone, brick and pipe fashioned into the larger river's wall.

One Sunday when several of his St. Enda's classmates, including Martin, were on a march with members of the Citizen Army, the River Puddle and its underground channel were discussed as a possible escape route in case of some unforeseen future emergency.

Supposedly, the shallow river's separate tributaries flowed under the streets of south Dublin and emptied out into the Liffey through a giant drainage tunnel just west of the Haypenny Bridge. Independent of the sewer system, the Puddle's water was reportedly quite clean. Dublin children often played down in its tunnels. Everyone at St. Enda's had heard stories about these street urchins and their cunning adventures in, under and around the streets and laneways of Dublin.

Aran remembered a member of Connolly's army carefully pointing out to their little group its underwater opening in the stone wall of the Liffey. Darkened from its source among peat bogs high in the Wicklow Mountains, the Liffey's water was almost black and made the Puddle's opening invisible to the uneducated eye.

With thoughts of escape now racing through Aran's head, Martin and he continued moving toward the Custom House Quay.

As they marched along separated only by a sagging column of British soldiers, Martin suddenly turned and looked directly at Aran. He said, "In ten seconds, we'll block for you!"

Aran nodded his head to show understanding and approval. Simultaneously, both young men began counting silently to themselves.

One, two, three...it was now or probably never. Three maybe four quick steps and Aran would be on top of the river's low stone wall. Once there, he would push off and dive.

Four, five, six...he was a very good swimmer having learned during summer outings at Kinvara and Salthill, both on the shore of Galway Bay. The water there was always cold, but it did not seem to bother him. He swam like a trout in a mountain stream.

Seven, eight...he could swim underwater across the narrow Liffey, surface quickly for air, then head for the underwater tunnel opening. If he found it quickly, he just might make it!

Nine...Aran steeled his body for the run and jump. He would be over the wall in two seconds if he was not tripped and into the water before the guards could draw down on him. From then on, it was in God's hands. He said a short word of prayer asking for His strength and help.

Ten...just at that moment Aran saw Martin and two other boys he did not recognise, run straight across and into the path of the two British soldiers marching alongside him. All five fell into a pile of kicking, pawing, yelling, twisting bodies...arms and legs flew everywhere.

The guards in front of Aran failed to notice what was happening behind them. They were too intent on making forward progress through the crowded street with their rebellious charges. With the front group moving on ahead and the guards next to Aran rolling on the ground, there was an ever widening opening for him to run through...and run he did. In three steps he was at full speed and on top of the wall. Pushing off, he arched his body out over the river, grabbed as much air as his lungs would hold, and readied himself for the plunge into the cold water.

As Aran sailed out over the river, he briefly studied the river surface rising rapidly to meet him.

He was delighted and surprised at what he saw. The river was free of boat traffic so nothing would obstruct his dive or swim and there, along the far wall, was a small boat. Had Marty anchored it at that spot to mark the Puddle entrance? Yes, of course he had. My God, he really had thought this thing through carefully.

In amazement at Martin's detailed planning, Aran's fully clothed body plunged into the river.

The Liffey water was very cold. It almost knocked the breath out of him. He managed to control his surprise and began swimming for his life. His heavy boots pulled him down but he knew he would be grateful for them when he was again back on dry land.

As the seconds crawled by, Aran realised that the first part of the escape plan had succeeded.

He tried to relax and measure the distance he must swim underwater balanced against the air he had swallowed before he had hit the water.

In the darkness of the Liffey, he could not see the opposite wall or the boat tied to it. There was no other choice but to trust his senses and keep swimming.

It seemed forever, but finally Aran was able to make out the wall looming up in the dim light.

He clawed at its rough surface, rolled over with his back against its stony face, and looked up for the outline of the small boat floating on the water somewhere above him.

Finally, he spotted its oblong shape just off to his right.

Quickly, he propelled himself over to the curragh usually found only on the west coast of Ireland, pushed his head above the surface of the river and filled his screaming lungs with air. The long slender boat shielded him from the troopers on the other side. He hurriedly gathered his senses.

No telling what had happened to Marty and his friends. Hopefully, they were able to talk or run themselves out of harm's way. Maybe they would blame his escape on poor British crowd control or their make-believed anger at the Irish rebels for disrupting their daily lives. Well, there was nothing he could do to help them now. He thanked God for their assistance and prayed for His blessings on them all.

Aran resisted the urge to peek around the end of the boat. He was curious to find out what was going on across the river on Ormond

Quay. Instead, he took several deep breaths and with all the air in him he could hold, Aran slid back under the surface of the water and started looking for the tunnel opening. He thought it was off to his left.

Moving carefully, he felt his way along the wall of the Liffey. No opening...damn! Aran's mind was racing. It was then that he realised he had gone the wrong way. He would have to go back up for another breath of air before continuing his search.

It was easier finding his way back to the boat a second time. Cautiously, he surfaced. As he pulled more air into his body, he looked up. Over the edge of the wall and above him on the southern rim of the river he could see a dozen or more heads. They were all intently gazing down at him.

"There he is!" cried one of them. "Look there! Down there!"

Aran saw fingers pointing in his direction. Again, Aran heard the familiar sound of rifle fire. Moments later the water around him began splashing and bubbling as other bullets chipped off the wall immediately above his head.

Thanking the bystanders, who had, so thoughtfully, pointed out his defenceless head to the British gunmen, Aran pushed underwater again. This time he moved off to his right and found the large ten foot gaping hole he was seeking.

"Here I go...please God, help me find a way out of this mess!"

Aran swam along the water-filled channel for several yards. Finally looking up, he began working his way toward the top of the metal pipeline. As he progressed forward, Aran knew if there were any air pockets to be found they would lie along the upper portion of the passageway. Aran Roe needed to find an opening very soon or his chest would explode.

Moments before his air supply expired, the metal tube took a sudden upward turn. Within a few feet his mouth was sucking air...sweet, lovely fresh Irish air. Aran gasped trying to catch his breath. It took awhile but finally he was under control again.

Shaking the water from his ears, Aran held his breath and listened. The only audible noises were the sounds of dripping and gurgling water. He had no idea where he was or what lay up ahead. But his only choice was to follow the tunnel and take his chances. Aran would have to trust his instincts and hope for a bit of good luck.

Slowly, with his senses on full alert, the Irish Rebel paddled and pulled himself along the passageway enjoying the luxury of plenty of fresh air to breathe.

After several minutes, the tunnel divided. Which way should he go...left or right? Thinking that right led toward the Castle, Aran turned left and headed off in that direction.

As he worked his way along, Aran reflected on his escape and rejoiced in the fact that the British authorities had virtually no way of linking him with last week's troubles. They did not know his name or where he was from. There were no pictures of him to publish or pass around for ID purposes. The only people who could pick him out of an identification parade were a handful of guards back at Richmond Barracks, the inept cemetary rozzer and the three men who had driven him away from Glasnevin plus one or two of the soldiers he had rubbed shoulders with on the morning's march toward the quays. Oh yes, there were the ones back at the Fannin house...if any of them were still alive. Ah sure, the only way the enemy could actually link him with the Rebellion was for one of those men to personally identify him. At this point, that chance seemed quite remote. But the more distance he could put between himself and those knowledgeable persons the safer he would be.

But wait a moment...there was one other thing that would give him away...his wet Volunteer uniform. He would have to find different clothes to wear as soon as he was up again on dry land.

On and on he swam. Soon, however, the water level dropped and his feet began touching the tunnel's bottom as metal tubing gave way to stone and brick...top, bottom and sides.

Then suddenly, up ahead through the blackness, he could see several small shafts of light piercing the blackness. Stopping, he again listened carefully. Yes, now he could hear street sounds above him...not many, but there were definitely people and the occasional motor car on the move overhead.

The Gortman knew he was under some Dublin street. The shafts of light were coming through small holes in a hinged metal plate built into the top of the tunnel.

Aran had no idea what waited for him up above. Maybe a British soldier or, if not, some startled citizen. In any case, anyone seeing him crawl out of the tunnel could easily sound the alarm summoning the authorities to investigate.

He had two choices. If he continued further down the tube, he might find a safer exit or, if he waited here until nightfall, he might escape unnoticed through this overhead opening.

He thought for a moment then decided. Rather than risk some

unknown danger further along the tunnel, he would stay put and wait. It would be a long wet one, but it was better than an English prison cell.

Leaning up against the damp brick wall, Aran Roe O'Neill closed his eyes and tried to drift off to sleep.

6. *Fighting*

As down the glen one Easter morn to a city fair rode I,
There armed lines of marching men in squadrons
passed me by...

The Foggy Dew / Rev. P. O'Neill

*T*ime passed ever so slowly. Aran walked up and down the bricked tunnel to keep his blood circulating. His legs were numb from having been in the cold water of the River Puddle. He frequently jumped up and down hoping to ward off the deadly effects of hypothermia. But soon he came to the realisation that if he stayed underground much longer he would die.

Delaying the decision to surface as long as possible, Aran Roe O'Neill walked around in his underground cavern briskly rubbing his hands over his arms, chest and face. In an effort to ignore how cold he was, Aran forced himself to remember the day, six weeks ago, when he arrived at Broadstone Station. Robert Gregory had driven him in Lady Gregory's car from the O'Neill farm to Galway's rail station. They warmly shook hands and said their good-byes. As the train pulled away from the station, Aran, filled with mixed emotions, jumped aboard. For the five-plus-hour ride to Dublin, he was on his own.

Leaving the Broadstone, Aran took a tram to the city centre. From there another streetcar ride past Trinity College, St. Stephen's Green and out through the southern suburbs of Dublin to Rathfarnham. It was his first visit to the big city and he filled himself with its sights and sounds.

After a short walk down tree-lined streets, he arrived at the imposing gates of St. Enda's School. Walking up the long drive, Aran noticed its well cared for gardens, its spacious hurling pitch and its tall rows of stately trees.

As he climbed the granite steps of the large impressive stone-blocked eighteenth-century house, he saw Pearse smiling at him through his ground-floor office window. The schoolmaster waved and motioned him to enter.

Just as Aran placed his hand on the great door's brass handle, it unexpectedly flew open. Standing before him was a smallish man with a big grin. His welcoming voice boomed, "Begad, it must be Aran Roe O'Neill from Gort! I'm Tom MacDonagh. Welcome to St. Enda's."

As the days passed and Aran became accustomed to life at the school, he became friends with both MacDonagh and Eamonn Ceannt. They were on the faculty of St. Enda's and members of the IRB's secret council. In addition, Willie Pearse, Patrick's artistic and somewhat shy brother, lived and taught at the school.

In fact, the entire Pearse family resided in the converted regal residence. His mother, Margaret, and sisters, Margaret and Mary Bridget, were always about. Pearse's English father, James, a stone sculptor, had died some years earlier.

In addition to Ceannt and MacDonagh, Sean Mac Diarmada and Joseph Mary Plunkett were often seen walking the grounds with Pearse, all in thoughtful contemplation and animated conservation.

Aran knew some sort of a revolt was in the works after his Salthill meeting with Pearse and Mac Diarmada, but its exact details remained a closely guarded secret. As these intimate, confidential gatherings became more numerous, the young Gortman surmised that these determined men were now putting the finishing touches on their rebellious plans.

❧

The ensuing weeks at St. Enda's flew by in a great rush of activity. Aran got on well with the other students. He studied Irish, history, mathematics, literature, and spent each afternoon on the green playing fields of the old estate formerly called The Hermitage. It was during this time that he came to know and befriend Martin Richardson, among others.

In addition to his friendships and studies, Aran joined the local Irish Volunteer unit. Many of the other students at the school were members as well. Together, with some residents of Rathfarnham, they formed an eager company of seriously committed young and middle-aged men. Because of his experience with the Volunteers in Gort, Aran was made third-in-command and retained his rank as lieutenant.

The company trained twice a week...mostly in the Wicklow Mountains southeast of Rathfarnham near Enniskerry. Marching, target practice and survival training occupied the majority of Aran's military time in Dublin.

As Easter approached, however, Aran sensed a change in Pearse. His teacher grew even more serious-minded and withdrawn. Everyone knew Pearse had a lot on his mind just keeping the school going but Aran guessed thoughts of Rebellion were consuming his attention.

On Tuesday of Holy Week, Pearse invited Aran into his office. Along with Mac Diarmada, MacDonagh and Ceannt, there was a new face.

As Aran entered the room, Pearse rose and said, "Aran, I'd like you to meet Liam Mellowes, a Dubliner living in County Galway. Maybe you've already heard of him?"

Aran nodded his head in the affirmative.

By way of introduction, Pearse told Aran Roe that Mellowes was the IVF and IRB leader in the west of Ireland. He went on to say that several months earlier, the British had deported Liam to England as a political undesirable and forbade his return home. But, as the rebel was not under close arrest and with the Rising about to begin, Liam disguised himself as a priest. With the welcomed help of his brother Brian, he made way back to Dublin via Glasglow and Belfast.

Much to Aran's surprise, Pearse noted that Mellowes had secretly been residing within St. Enda's maze of rooms for the past several days. The headmaster praised Mellowes for his assistance and added, "Liam's ideas and input have been invaluable. His attention to detail continually proves to be vitally important in these final days."

Pearse's choice of words 'final days' hit home to Aran. They confirmed everything he had been thinking...very soon now Ireland would be at war with England! The thought of it both excited and frightened him beyond belief, but somehow he kept his emotions in check.

The schoolmaster finally concluded his remarks by saying, "Aran, Mr. Mellowes will soon be returning to Galway as final plans are coming together for the distribution of some smuggled German arms scheduled to arrive shortly in Kerry."

Aran glanced around the small office, but none of the others seemed to bat an eye in reaction to Pearse's announcement.

"Liam...," the professor continued, "...as I've told you before, Aran here could be very useful to you in getting things organised in the west of Ireland. He knows the countryside, is a crack shot and can be trusted with your life."

Aran's cheeks flushed. He felt honoured by his teacher's recommendation, but disappointed at the thought of having to leave Pearse and

Dublin Town behind. During the past six weeks, the two of them had developed a close friendship. Aran eagerly drank in the thoughtful, inspiring words of his wise mentor.

Besides, Dublin Town was so rich in history. Aran had only just begun soaking up its intoxicating air. One of the rooms here at St. Enda's had actually been used for a time by Robert Emmet himself! Inside its four walls, Pearse and his young Irish Rebel read and talked of Ireland's history while idly romanticising about living in a land free of foreign domination. On other occasions Pearse recounted details of the 1803 Rebellion as the two of them walked the half mile across grassy fields to Butterfield House...the house Emmet lived in before his execution.

Sometimes, as evening drew nigh, Pearse, Aran and some of the other students would stroll through the school's rambling gardens. Pearse talked and his pupils listened as together they passed along the tree-lined way known as Emmet's Walk. That short path led from St. Enda's to the Priory just across the road from the school. It was in the Priory that John Philpot Curran, Ireland's pre-eminent legal mind of the late-eighteenth and early-nineteenth centuries, lived with his daughter, Sarah, the love of Emmet's life.

It was on those special walks that Aran learned about the men who Pearse so admired...Cuchulainn, Wolfe Tone, O'Donovan Rossa and Napoleon. Aran soon learned to think of them as his heroes too.

Often at the end of their lessons, Pearse would recite some of his own poetry or he would read the words of other poets to them. Once Pearse talked at length about his favourite Ossianic motto: 'Truth on our lips, strength in our hands and purity in our hearts.' It had become St. Enda's motto. The headmaster had the Irish saying sewn onto a banner with each word emblazoned in gold Gaelic letters. The determined teacher displayed the banner inside his school hoping to inspire its young residents. It also served to remind all of Ireland's great legendary hero, Finn MacCool, and of Eireann's fabled, ancient glories of the past.

But of all the men Pearse talked about and thought of so highly, it was Emmet who held centre stage in his mind. Aran imagined that when Pearse spoke of him, Pearse became Emmet. Aran even imagined that Pearse, if given the chance, would have chosen to turn back the clock of time. He guessed his mentor would have proudly fought and died by Emmet's side if given the chance.

On one special occasion, Pearse recited some of Emmet's poignant words from the school's study-hall stage. Aran vividly remembered those prophetic observations:

There are in every generation those who shrink from the ultimate sacrifice, but there are in every generation those who make it with joy and laughter, and these are the salt of the generations, the heroes who stand midway between God and man. Patriotism is in large part a memory of heroic dead men and a striving to accomplish some task left unfinished by them.

Had they not gone before, made their attempts, and suffered the sorrow of their failures, we should long ago have lost the tradition of faith and service, having no memory in the heart or any unaccomplished dream...This the heroes have done for us; for their spirits indwell in the place where they lived, and the hills of Ireland must be rent and her cities levelled with the ground and all her children driven out upon the seas of the world before those voices are silenced that bid us be faithful still and to make no peace with England until Ireland is ours...[6-1]

❧

Aran felt embarrassingly uncomfortable with Pearse's, Mac Diarmada's, MacDonagh's, Ceannt's and Mellowes's eyes all trained on him.

Pearse recognised Aran's uneasiness and said in a soft reassuring voice, "It's your choice, my son. Listen to your own heart and decide for yourself."

It was not a difficult choice for him to make. Pearse had flattered and honoured Aran with his suggestion he become one of Mellowes's assistants. He also realised that he would be close to his family and Robert again. But, regardless of his teacher's laurels and his close family ties, Aran felt his place was here in Dublin under the wise and watchful eye of Patrick Henry Pearse.

"Thank you, sir, for thinking so highly of me. Sure, it would be a great honour to serve under Mr. Mellowes, but, if given the choice, I would prefer to stay here at St. Enda's. If there's to be a fight for our independence, I'd like it to be with ye here in Dublin."

Pearse nodded. The matter was settled. Aran would stay.

With the meeting over, all rose. Liam and Aran shook hands. Mellowes looked into the young man's eyes and said, "Pat thinks the world of you, Aran. Maybe someday, we'll have a chance to work together. Our new Ireland will require talented leaders...brave, dedicated men like yourself."

"Yes, sir. Thank you, sir. As you probably can guess, I've heard your name spoken before in Gort. You're held in the highest esteem by the Volunteer leaders there. I sincerely do look forward to the day when we might work together, but, please, I beg your understanding concerning my wishes to remain here in Dublin."

Mellowes nodded and the two smiled at each other again. Then without another word said, Liam Mellowes turned and left the room.

An hour later, the redisguised rebel leader was on his way down the school's gravel driveway and out into the night. Liam Mellowes's secretive journey back to Galway and the west of Ireland had begun. The Rising was about to commence.

Pearse, with Aran next to him, stood for a long time on St. Enda's front steps. They looked after the vanished shadow of Pearse's friend and colleague. Finally, without saying a word, Pearse turned and reentered his office. The weary professor sat down at his desk and began writing the first draft of the new Irish Republic's *Proclamation.*

❧

With the restricted knowledge that the Rebellion was scheduled for Easter Sunday, Aran readied himself too. He wrote a long letter to his parents and another to Robert, not realising he had moved to England. The Gortman, however, was careful not to divulge any classified information in case the English censored his post. He wanted them all back home to know he was well and that they were in his thoughts and prayers. He told his family of his walks with Pearse and of Emmet's inspiration. He closed his letters with best wishes and God's blessing on them all.

Early on Holy Saturday evening Pearse gathered all the boys together in the back garden of the school. He told them Willie and he were spending the night in Dublin to avoid any possible arrest by a sudden British sweep of Dublin's dissidents. The professor spoke to his students for a full ten minutes then concluded his remarks with a hopeful thought, "Always remember. If you're ever free, it's the son of an Englishman who will have freed you."[6-2]

Afterwards, Pearse took Aran aside. He asked him to gather up his things. He wanted the three of them to go together to Sean T. O'Kelly's house in the city. O'Kelly, a member of the IRB's inner circle, had been chosen to serve as Pearse's adjutant during the revolt.

The next day, Easter Sunday, following morning Mass, Aran peddled one of the O'Kelly's bicycles to Liberty Hall in Beresford Place. There he assisted the three printers, Messrs. Brady, Molloy and O'Brien, with the typesetting and printing of several hundred copies of the *Proclamation Of The Republic*. After the Rising was underway, Pearse planned a public reading of the document from the steps of the GPO, headquarters of the rebel republicans.

❧

With the Rising postponed 'til Monday, Easter evening quietly settled in over the peaceful city. Disappointed about the events resulting in the Rebellion's delay but eagerly awaiting the morning, Aran followed the Pearse brothers back to Rathfarnham. The three had changed their plans, deciding to spend the night with the other residents of St. Enda's. As a family, they would pass the final hours together waiting for the Rising's commencement. (It was the last calm evening Dublin would know for many days to come.)

The following morning dawned clear and warm. Sunshine filed the windows and spilled into the dining room as all the boys and faculty ate their breakfast together as usual.[HN-3]

Afterwards, a small group of the young men, including Aran, gathered together their gear and meagre weapons. After a short walk from their school's gates, they climbed aboard a tram for the city centre. Other students were scheduled to bring in more supplies later in the day. Lastly, a few of the lads had been ordered to stay behind: their assignment was to guard the school, Mrs. Pearse and her two daughters.

❧

The intense cold numbed Aran through to the bone. He knew he could not bear the pain and discomfort much longer. As he was deciding what he should do, the narrow shafts of light streaming down into his pitch-black chamber from the overhead plate suddenly ceased shining. It was as if someone pulled a switch and turned out the lights.

"What in the world!" exclaimed Aran out loud. "What's that all about?"

Puzzled by this turn of events and forced by the cold, wet conditions of his underworld environment, Aran made an abrupt decision. He had to take a chance and leave the safety of the Puddle Tunnel. He needed to find drier, warmer surroundings. He could not wait for nightfall. It was a risk he had to take. His very life now depended on it.

Not wanting to attract any more attention than was absolutely necessary, Aran pulled off his wet IVF jacket and dropped it into the river. It quickly disappeared into the blackness surrounding his feet. Without the jacket, he hoped to look less like a soldier and more like some ordinary citizen. At least, that was what he hoped anybody on the street above would think.

Carefully placing his numb fingers against the bottom of the metal plate blocking his exit from the tunnel, Aran pushed. It did not move. The river's cold had drained the strength from his weary body. Screwing up every ounce of energy he was able to muster, he pushed again...as hard as he could. This time the lid inched open.

Still unable to see what was above, Aran finally pushed the heavy metal cover over to one side. The aperture, a hole large enough for him to scramble up through, seemed to call him back up into the world of light.

Cautiously, he paused. No sunshine streamed down but there was daylight up there. Some sort of wooden structure was positioned directly overhead. Then it dawned on him. A wagon had been parked right over his opening. That was why no one had raised an alarm or cry of inquiry when he slid open the covering...the wagon was obscuring his actions. Aran placed his hands on either side of the gaping hole and thrust his head up above ground just long enough for a quick look around. Yes, directly overhead was an old delivery wagon. That was why the sunlight had stopped shining through the holes in his metal plate. The wagon blocked its luminous rays.

Carefully and slowly, so as not to frighten the horse tied to the cart, Aran scrambled up from the Puddle. Exhausted from the effort, he lay huddled on the cobblestones under the stationary wagon's protection.

After a few seconds, he gathered his reserves and carefully pushed the metal lid back into place. In doing so he covered up any traces of his escape route from the river below.

Fear of discovery momentarily blotted out his coldness. Crouched under the wagon as he was, Aran might attract the unwanted attention of some curious passer-by. So, as gracefully as his deadened limbs allowed, Aran crawled out from under the wagon and onto the footpath. With each wobbly, hobbled step he looked more like an old man with the gout than a gallant young warrior.

Deciding he was in no condition to walk, much less run from any possible enemy pursuer, Aran knew he must quickly find a safe place to hide and thaw out. With few alternatives available to him at the moment, Aran crawled onto the unoccupied, driverless wagon. With clumsy unfeeling fingers, he covered himself as best he could, with the sacks of raw oats and loosely piled hay filling the wagon's bed. The bags stacked around him helped soak up some of his clothing's wetness while the hay provided a fine blanket of warmth and concealment for his chilled body.

Time passed, though Aran did not know exactly how long he had been in the wagon. He was just starting to doze off when he heard voices. He felt someone climb up onto the wooden bench suspended just above his head.

"Well, I'd better be going," said the wagonman's voice. "Those English dandies at Portobello don't like to be kept waiting one minute longer than usual."

"Sure, if ye get a chance, come by tomorrow and we'll have a glass or two. Now that the bloody Rising is over, the houses are open again," invited a second man.

"Aye," came the reply. Moments later, the wagon slowly started moving forward.

Once under way, the driver seemed in a hurry to make his delivery. Seemingly, he paid no attention to the extra weight he was now hauling. Unfortunately for the driver, the warm sun, the heavy load, and the street's uneven cobblestones slowed travel despite the man's constant stream of oaths urging his horse to get a move on.

Well concealed in the wagon, Aran went over in his head his options. He guessed the driver intended to deliver the animal feed straight into the enemy's hands. Portobello Barracks was on the south side of Dublin, just over the Grand Canal in the direction of Rathfarnham.

Aran imagined he was probably in the Dame Street-College Green area of central Dublin. He peeked out through the covering of hay in the hopes of spotting some familiar landmark that would solve the mystery of his exact whereabouts.

Just at that moment the driver turned a corner. From his vantage point in back Aran saw a long row of tall red-bricked Victorian buildings. If he was not mistaken, the wagon was headed up South Great George's Street. Dublin Castle would be just off to his right. He had probably popped up out of the Puddle Tunnel on Crow or maybe Fownes Street. It pleased Aran to know his underground sense of direction had been spot on. From here it was simply a straight shot up George's Street to the barracks a mile or so away.

But, as he was safely hidden in the wagon, Aran decided to stay put for awhile longer. He thought it a good idea to put some distance between himself and the Castle with its Ship Street Barracks located directly behind the longtime seat of British power and authority in Ireland. The added time in the wagon would allow him to warm up a wee bit. He hoped to regain some feeling in his still numbed body in case he was forced to make a run for it. Now, with the wagon bumping and bouncing along, Aran waited and bided his time.

The ride up George's Street reminded him of one of his several trips from Liberty Hall to the GPO Monday last. On one of those occasions he had guided a brace of horses that had pulled a wagon filled with homemade bombs, water jugs, blankets and sacks of flour. The *Proclamation* announcements he helped print were tied in small neat bundles and rested on the wooden bench next to him.

He dearly wanted to save one to show his children, if he lived that long, so the day before he had carefully tucked several of them inside an old coffee tin and wrapped the lot in a potato sack. Then, he found a narrow opening in the wall under the basement stairs at Liberty Hall and secretly squirrelled his parcel away for safekeeping and later recovery. Aran remembered thinking that someday they might be famous documents and valuable souvenirs.

Aran recalled pulling his wagon up to the Prince Street side entrance of the massive GPO and, with the help of several others, quickly unloaded his cargo. Another Volunteer drove the wagon around to the rear of the building while Aran remained at the entrance doorway waiting for his next assignment.

Moments later, Michael O'Rahilly, better known as 'The O'Rahilly,' arrived in his usual grand style. Driving his new opened-topped De Dion Bouton motor car, the Volunteer leader drove right up to the side door where Aran stood. His expensive vehicle was filled to overflowing with rifles and sundry other war material.

Aran knew he was a compatriot of Dr. O'Neill. Pearse had mentioned to him at breakfast that Michael had spent the weekend driving through the Midlands informing IVF units of the Easter Sunday cancellation orders.

Now, however, seeing the high-priced motor and its owner beside the GPO, Aran surmised The O'Rahilly had had a change of heart. He guessed he planned on lending a helping hand with the pending fight. "After all," thought the Gortman, "he is one of our Volunteer leaders. Maybe just maybe, with the O'Rahilly on point, their chances for success looked brighter." In turn, Aran's haunted feelings of fear and uncertainty took a step backwards. Regardless of the odds, however, it was great having Michael O'Rahilly back on their side. He just exuded an air of confidence.

After exchanging greetings, The O'Rahilly smiled at Aran and in a rather sarcastic tone said, "I've helped wind this clock and now I've come to hear it ring!"

On that note, the Irish Rebel followed The O'Rahilly inside. Aran Roe helped the others take-over the building. The rebellious soldiers knocked out the glass from all the ground-floor windows. Next, the Volunteers were ordered to loop them with mail sacks, books, furniture and whatever else they could find that was not nailed down. Anything capable of stopping an enemy bullet was piled up in front of every window and door in the hopes of forming an impenetrable barrier against an enemy attack. There was even talk of someone making a big placard announcing 'The Headquarters of the Provisional Government of the Irish Republic.'

Following this defensive necessity, The O'Rahilly called Aran over and, after a brief exchange, assigned him to sniper duty on the roof. Aran's reputation as a sharpshooter had preceded him.

From Monday afternoon on, the Irish Rebel spent the majority of the week on the exposed, lofty heights of the GPO's roof. Occasionally, he was relieved and tried to nap on the floor below, but constant rifle fire overhead, nearby British artillery shelling, and noisy rebel activity downstairs made sleeping almost impossible.

On Friday, British incendiary bombs rained down on the GPO. Most of the trapped IRA soldiers answered the numerous cries of 'fire' and fought the flames. Captain Michael Collins took charge of the firefighting forces. Aran and he spent several hours working side by side in a vain attempt to extinguish the growing conflagration. Finally, the smoke, heat and fire proved overwhelming. It forced the rebels to flee their headquarters on Friday evening. But rather than tunnelling out and retreating, Aran joined The O'Rahilly's small attack party that had tried unsuccessfully to storm the British barricade at the top of Moore Street. The O'Rahilly, Seamus and well over half of the others died in that brave attempt to escape the Sassenach's strangling net of encirclement.

❀

Suddenly, the wagon Aran was hiding in came to an abrupt halt.

"Where are ye going in that wagon, old man? What's your business on this road? And by the by, what are ye carrying there?" Aran heard every word of the barking, insistent voice.

"Sure, its feed for your horses at Portobello, sir," replied the driver.

Aran could hear the soldier's horse clip-clopping around to the tail-end of the wagon. He could only hope the inspection would be cursory and not a thorough one.

Moments passed. Aran could almost feel the searching eyes of the soldier trying to uncover his hiding place.

Apparently satisfied with what he had seen, the military man gave the driver the all clear, "Permission to proceed, but no deviations...ye hear me?"

"Aye" came the reply as the wagon lurched off up George's Street once more. With Lady Luck again on his side, Aran breathed a sigh of relief under his rather meagre covering.

That unexpected close call made an impression on Aran. He realised how dangerous it was travelling along this main street. There was always the possibility of unexpected discovery, plus, in a short time, they would be arriving at Portobello British army barracks. Aran knew it was time for him to hightail it out of Dublin.

Gently pushing aside the sacks and hay covering, the Irish Rebel lifted his head above the sideboard of the wagon. Quickly, he had a look around. Light road traffic greeted him though there were several people walking along the footpath.

The wagon's bumping and rattling plus the driver's loud swearing at his horse hid any sounds Aran made sliding off the back end of the delivery conveyance.

Rather than running and possibly drawing attention to himself, Aran stood in the roadway, stretched as if he had just awoken from taking a nap in the now receding wagon. Slowly, he walked over to the footpath. Digging his hands into his empty trouser pockets, the rebel gradually increased his pace. As casually as he could while still keeping a sharp lookout for the enemy, Aran glanced at shop windows and the occasional open doorway. After a few steps, Aran decided he should swing his arms to increase circulation and help bring his still chilled body back to life.

After another minute or so, he quickly crossed the main thoroughfare, entered Camden Place and headed east at an increasingly brisk pace.

He glanced around for any signs of uniforms but, thankfully, none were to be seen.

Next, a right turn onto Harcourt Street and, with St. Stephen's Green behind him, he headed for Hatch Street.

Now walking with a renewed air of confidence, Aran crossed Leeson

Street and ducked down a small laneway toward the Grand Canal. His objective was the quiet residential street known as Wilton Place. There were some old Victorian homes along the canal that had carriage houses behind them. He hoped to find one that was unlocked so he could hide and rest until nightfall.

The second stable door opened to his touch. Its windows were grimy and dusty but its interior was unoccupied. The building's murky interior was just partially illuminated by dimly filtered sunlight. He checked for a rear entrance. It was also unlocked and offered him a secondary exit if necessary.

Finding nothing to eat or drink, Aran settled down in a bed of straw used by some former four-legged resident. He promptly fell fast asleep.

As the sun slowly set over the city's suburbs, Aran slept. A long time had passed since his nap at the Fannin's house. His sleep under the oak tree in the cemetery and in the little prison cell off the gymnasium had not relieved his fatigue.

Suddenly, Aran was startled awake by the sound of a motor car in the driveway just outside his temporary lodgings. Instantly, his senses were on full alert. Immediately after its engine was switched off and two doors banged shut, the rebel heard voices...a man's and a woman's. As their feet crunched across the drive's gravel surface, the two seemed in mid-conversation. Aran clearly heard the name of an apparent friend, Arthur Griffith, discussed. From what Aran could understand of their comments, Griffith, Sinn Fein's founder and chairman, had recently been arrested by British military authorities. Apparently, he was on his way to an English prison in Reading.[HN-4]

Inching closer to the carriage-house door, the Gortman guessed from the couple's conversation that they had arrived home just prior to some newly prescribed nine-o'clock curfew imposed by General Sir John Grenfell Maxwell, the new G.O.C. of all British forces on the island. Besides the nine to five overnight restriction, Aran heard the man mention something about martial law which had recently been imposed throughout the country.

The voices grew fainter and stopped all together with the closing of a door.

"Bloody hell!" whispered Aran to himself. He realised if he were now arrested by the authorities, he would be right back where he had started from his morning...in prison!

Refreshed from his nap but starving, Aran made a calculated decision. He would knock on the couple's back door and take his chances. It sounded to him like they were the kind of people who just might help out a stranded, desperate young rebel.

Aran waited until a light came on at the back of the house. Quietly slipping out of the carriage house, he climbed the back stairs, mumbled a short prayer, and knocked on the heavy oaken door.

After a few moments, another light flashed on. Its brilliance shone through the door's etched, frosted-glass window. After a long minute, it swung partially open. An attractive middle-aged woman stood framed against a hallway light. Seeing Aran standing there, her curious expression changed instantly to one of surprised alarm. She pulled back and almost closed the door in his face.

Suddenly remembering his wild-looking appearance, Aran smiled and saluted politely. He realised the state of him was beyond proper description or repair. He must have looked like some creature who had just crawled out of a hole...in fact he just had!

The woman slowly reopened the door as her cautious eyes gave him a careful once-over.

Aran broke the silence. "I beg your pardon, madam, but I've just had a rather unpleasant encounter with the British authorities. I apologise for any alarm I may have caused you, but, believe me, I intend ye no harm. I'm a student here in Dublin and hoped you might have something for me to eat?"

Without pausing, he continued, "Again, I'm so sorry for disturbing you. Please believe me, I'm not accustomed to begging but this is a most unusual situation."

The woman turned and cried out, "Thomas...Thomas come here this instant!"

Moments later, a greying, heavyset man appeared behind the woman. He looked over her shoulder and exclaimed, "What in the world...?"

Slowly and politely, Aran repeated his story to the man.

Thomas whispered something in the woman's ear.

She moved aside. The man took one step toward Aran. After a rather careful visual examination, he asked firmly, "Are you one of Arthur Griffith's men?"

Aran nodded.

"Were you involved in last week's trouble?"

Again, Aran wagged his head yes.

The man turned to the woman. Their eyes exchanged a silent conversation.

Turning back to Aran, Thomas said, "We'd be pleased if you'd come through."

Gratefully, Aran said, "Thank you."

The two stood aside as the Irish Rebel stepped carefully over the doorstep and into the hallway. Aran was mindful not to brush against his hosts for fear of soiling their lovely evening clothes.

"Into the kitchen, if you please," said the woman taking charge.

With a nod of her head, she motioned Aran through into the kitchen and toward a chair at the worktable.

After a quick look around, Aran took the seat. He guessed this family was well-to-do. Nice things were everywhere.

"First things first...what is your name and where do you come from?"

"I'm Aran Roe O'Neill from County Galway, madam."

"Yes, I knew you were from somewhere. But you said you were a student here."

"St. Enda's School in Rathfarnham, madam."

The man and woman looked at each other. After a brief pause she said, "This is my husband, Thomas Coogan. I'm Anna Coogan. As you may have guessed, this is our home.

"Now, young man, something to drink? A tumbler of milk...maybe a large whiskey...a bottle of porter?"

"Actually, I'd like a glass of drinking water...then maybe a whiskey please," answered Aran.

He gulped down the water and politely asked for a refill. After his second glass, the rebel lifted a Jameson to his lips. He savoured the aroma of the Irish whiskey then swallowed a sweet mouthful. The drink burned all the way down, but it seemed to awaken his chilled spirit. Almost instantly, he felt a pleasant tingling sensation behind his eyes and at the back of his head.

After a thoughtful moment's pause, Aran asked, "You mentioned Arthur Griffith. Do you know him well?"

Thomas answered. "Arthur and I grew up together. He was in my form at school. I helped him finance his first newspaper, *The United Irishman.* That was in 1899. Since then, I've quietly backed all of Arthur's interests."

Thomas looked at his wife and continued, "We're both some of his dearest friends. Do you know Arthur?"

"Oh, no!" exclaimed Aran. "But my headmaster, Professor Pearse, knows him."

"Well, I'll be, Anna. I've met Professor Pearse twice. Arthur introduced me to him on both occasions.

"Young man...what did you say your name was...Aran...well Anna, it's just as I thought...Aran here is one of Arthur's Sinn Fein men. Is that right, Aran?"

The wild-looking youth just nodded and smiled as he slowly sipped his whiskey.

Aran, ever cautious among strangers, was impressed with the couple's apparent genuineness. The man just seemed too sincere and forthright to be a fraud.

Thomas continued, "Were you involved in the fighting last week?"

Carefully, Aran looked at both of them. After a momentary pause, he quietly said, "I was in the GPO under the command of President Pearse and General Connolly."

"How did you escape?" asked Anna.

"I was lucky. I left the burning GHQ on Friday night and hid in a nearby theatre. The British never checked. I simply waited two days and walked out unnoticed." Then Aran added, "I hitched a ride in a wagon across Dublin and ended up here. I hid in your stable waiting for night-fall. But, when I overheard you mention the curfew I decided to stay put until morning. Unfortunately, my empty stomach drove me to take a chance. That's when I knocked on your door."

Both the man and the woman studied Aran carefully. With a twinkle in his eye, Thomas said to Anna, "I think there's more to his story than he's telling us. Is that right young man?"

"Let's just leave it as it is. So please, if ye don't mind, may I have something to eat and I'll be on my way," answered Aran, shifting his body in the uncomfortable straight-backed chair.

"We'll have none of it," replied Anna in a firm voice. "First, it's upstairs with you to soak off some of that dirt and grime. Then, into clean clothes before you come back down for a proper meal." The woman seemed most definite about what Aran was and was not to do.

Aran Roe raised a hand in protest but it did no good.

"Now, not a word out of ye, lad," declared Thomas. In a fatherly way he helped Aran to his feet and motioned him through toward the hallway and its stairs.

"As you'll soon learn, Aran, Anna's word is law around here. There's no point in arguing with her."

❧

Thirty minutes later, a new Aran Roe O'Neill walked into the warm kitchen. He was dressed in some of Thomas's clothes that no longer fit his expanding waistline.

Aran had not felt this grand in a long while.

With a fine meal of reheated bacon, cabbage, potatoes and yesterday's apple pie under his belt, Aran knew he would live to fight another day.

His hosts were kind enough not to ask him any more prying questions. Instead, they talked about their married daughter who lived with her family in County Wexford and their son studying medicine in England.

Later, before the couple retired for the night, they asked if there was anything else he wanted?

Reluctantly, Aran said, "Yes."

He explained he did not want to appear cheeky or offensive, but did they have a revolver or rifle in the house that he might have?

Then he quickly added apologetically, "I'm not sure when I'll be able to return it, but I'll do the best I can."

Aran held his breath as he looked back and forth between the kindly couple. It was a daring and bizarre request to be sure.

After a tense moment, Anna turned to her husband, "Thomas, that gun you brought back from Amerikay...do you still have it upstairs?"

"Yes, it's up in the press."

Without another word, Thomas left the kitchen.

When he returned a few minutes later, he carried a revolver and a box of shells.

He handed them to Aran saying, "It's what they call a Colt .45, Six-Shooter in Amerikay."

"It's a real beauty!" marvelled Aran.

"I've never fired it. I bought it on a lark after doing some horseback riding in Ohio," laughed Thomas. "It's yours. May it keep you safe, help bring Arthur back home and amend some of the many wrongs that have befallen Ireland."

"I'll do my best," whispered Aran, but his attention was fixed on the weapon.

He carefully examined every inch of it. Finally, he opened the box of shells and filled each chamber with a bullet. After a loving pat, he clicked on the cut off and tucked the gun under his belt.

Anna stared in surprise at her husband. This was as close to a gunman as she had ever been and it frightened her. If she had it in her heart to do so, she might have sent Aran out of the house that instant.

With the addition of the gun, conversation between the three of them became strained. Finishing her tea, Anna rose from the table. "Aran, let us show you the guest room. It's on the first floor."

The room was very comfortable. Aran checked to see if the window was unlocked. There was a short drop to a low roof just over the back porch. It would make a suitable escape route if he had to leave in a hurry.

With a sincere word of 'thank you,' Aran said good night to his generous hosts and closed the door behind them.

The Irish Rebel was asleep almost instantly with this new Colt revolver tucked under his soft white pillow. The Gortman's hand was but inches away from its carved wooden handle.

❧

After his first good night of sleep in over a week, Aran rose feeling refreshed and rested. He dressed in Thomas's clothes, made himself a cup of tea and was out of the house before the sun's rays broke through the tops of the trees. Thomas and Anna were still asleep so he decided not to wake them. They had all said their goodbyes last night.

Aran walked quickly over the Baggot Street Bridge. Keeping to laneways and side streets, he made his way south toward Donnybrook. He intended borrowing a friend's bicycle and retreating to the safety of the Wicklow Mountains.

He would hide there in some secluded mountain cabin for a day or two while Dublin's intense military activity subsided. With the coast clear, he would finally head west for home. Aran took comfort in knowing that other rebels before him, men like Michael Dwyer in 1798, had sought the safety of the Wicklows in their hour of need.

Just as he began feeling more like his old self, Aran was jolted back to war's reality. As he turned a corner and started down Brendan Road, the sound of gunfire brought him back to the horrors of the last week's nightmare. Immediately he sought cover by diving behind a nearby garden wall.

"Oh, my nice clean clothes," moaned Aran. "Ah well, they wouldn't have stayed that way for very long." He smiled to himself as he grabbed for the revolver tucked into the waistband of his trousers.

Up ahead at the top of the street was a lorryload of English soldiers. They were crouched behind the protection of another garden wall with their backs to Aran.

Aran saw rifle fire coming from the upper story of a Victorian house just down the street from the British position. He guessed the people inside, probably with separatist sympathies similar to his own, were trapped and outnumbered. They obviously had decided to defend their brick-faced home from this rebel-seeking enemy patrol.

From his position Aran could see that the eight English soldiers were safely tucked in behind a chest-high stone wall. They were pouring round after round of rifle fire into the house.

Aran realised the gunfire would soon draw more soldiers to the neighbourhood. He must either join in the fight now, hoping for a quick and successful conclusion, or hightail it out of there before he was caught in an enemy's round-up.

Just as he turned to retreat, one of the soldiers stood up and shouted a volley of oaths at the people inside the besieged house. "Come out here ye bloody Irish hoors...ye Shinner traitors!"

With that, the vocal Limey dashed forward, crossed the street and made it safely to the protection of the embattled building's front wall. To cover the daring move, his mates kept up a steady stream of rifle fire.

Aran watched as the bold Englishman reached into his pack, withdrew a hand bomb and threw it through a first-floor window. The man then hurdled over the low wall and sprinted up to the house itself. With his back against its brick facade, he hammered his rifle butt through a ground-floor window pane and then tossed a second bomb into the house.

The two explosions rocked the building, blew out some of its windows and set the structure on fire.

Aran stopped dead in his tracks and dove back under the protection of his garden wall. He realised that the people inside the house, no doubt rebels like himself, were badly outnumbered and in desperate need of help.

Throwing caution to the wind, the Gortman carefully moved forward through several adjoining front gardens until he was less than thirty yards from the rear of the British troops.

His emotions were on fire. He heard the hateful oaths pour forth from the audacious soldier. Aran felt his own sense of personal rage explode inside him. That man's verbal volley seemed to blot out all sense of reason. He burned with resentment and wanted revenge against the soldiers who occupied his land and were trying to kill his countrymen...Irishmen who simply wanted to free themselves from England's bonds of slavery and oppression.

Carefully, he took aim and, not knowing how Thomas's new revolver would behave, fired six shots into the unsuspecting soldiers.

The results were wonderful and horrible...all compressed together within one moment in time. The Colt made loud reports but kicked very little. The trigger pulled easily and its cylinder rolled smoothly around as the next shell spun up in front of the firing pin. The Colt revolver was a work of mechanical perfection.

One, two, three, now four of the British soldiers threw their arms into the air and fell forward draped over the garden's stone wall.

The other three Redcoats had no idea what had happened but four of their mates were now down and in great pain. That was enough for them. Their hands went up in the air and their weapons fell to the ground.

"Keep your hands high and don't move so much as a muscle!" ordered Aran. He stood up, firmly clutching the empty revolver in his left hand.

The soldier who threw the bombs into the house became confused by the attack on his mates. He ran down the walkway toward the street. The man was in the middle of the footpath when a single rifle shot brought him to his knees.

He screamed and pitched forward while blood rushed from an ugly wound in his chest. Lying stretched across the curb, the man's red flood of life streamed out into the gutter.

A moment later, three men ran from the burning house. One of them shouted to someone still inside to get busy and put out the fires before it was too late. Then, with their rifles at the ready, two of the 'Shinners' rushed over to the surrendered and wounded soldiers. The three erect Englishmen raised their hands even higher in the air. The third newcomer bent over the wounded man in the street but there was little he could do for him.

After quickly reloading his Colt, Aran helped the two strangers tie the prisoners' hands with their own English belts. Pausing a moment, the Gortman glanced at the two escapees and thought they looked as bad as he must have when he knocked on Thomas and Anna's back door last night.

"What unit are ye from?" asked Aran.

"Not here!" came the reply from the older of the three freedom-fighters. "We'll have time to talk later."

Taking the British soldiers' weapons and packs, the four rebels ran between two houses as they headed off on the double away from the battle scene.

Every eye on the block had witnessed the fight. They had peered out from behind lace curtains and over windowsills during the battle. They continued watching as the Sassenach surrendered and the four republicans disappeared down a back laneway.

Moments later, two squads of crack English troopers drove into the street. Their discovery of the bloody battle scene made the authorities fighting mad. Every house on the street felt their rage and paid the price for the dead soldiers shot and killed by a rebel rifle and a cowboy revolver.

7. Running

Ah! back through the glen I rode again, and my heart
    with grief was sore.
For I parted then with valiant men whom I never shall see
    more...
            The Foggy Dew / Rev. P. O'Neill

By Easter Monday afternoon, the excitement of storming the GPO had subsided. For several untried Volunteers, however, the takeover had serious consequences. A number were badly wounded...injured scrambling into the GPO through ground-level windows. Three were killed as inexperienced soldiers carelessly discharged their weapons while fortifying the building.

The dead and severely wounded were taken under the umbrella of a Red Cross flag to nearby Jervis Street Hospital. Minor injuries, however, were cared for in the small emergency medical centre set up inside the General Post Office. But despite a few unforeseen problems, the main floor at the GPO seemed organised and ready for defence by early afternoon.

Just after one o'clock Pearse, Connolly and a few others stepped outside the headquarters' building. Together they watched Thomas Francis Meagher's tricolour and the Countess's green flag, with the words 'Irish Republic' painted in gold letters, hoisted atop the General Post Office. Meagher, inspired by the French national flag, designed the green, white and orange tricolour and presented it to the citizens of Dublin back in 1848. Unfortunately, it had seldom been flown in public until this day. Constance Gore Booth better known by her titled married name, The Countess Markievicz, cut her flag out of a green bedspread and with a mixture of mustard and gold paint hand-enscribed her message of freedom to all the world. Her flag was a homemade effort, but as it flew above the lofty heights of the GPO, it looked quite grand.

With the two flags flying overhead, Pearse, smartly turned out in his Volunteer uniform, stood on the top step of the General Post Office. From there he read aloud *The Proclamation Of The Provisional Government Of The Irish Republic*. A small group of people paused in front of the building to watch in amazement. They listened with only modest interest to the rebels' pronouncements.

After President Pearse finished reading the document, he received a few half-hearted cheers and some polite applause, but most of the people displayed few emotions or little interest. Shaken heads and shrugged shoulders seemed to express the audience's general feeling of indifference. It seemed the idea of real freedom and independence was something people only talked about but never quite believed would ever come to pass. Witnessing Ireland's first few footfalls toward nationhood in decades, the Dubliners seemed stupefied and unresponsive.

In actuality, the crowd appeared more interested in the anticipated arrival of the Dublin Metropolitan Police than in Pearse's strong declaration of independence. As they stood by and observed history in the making, the people expressed more concern about damage being caused to their newly renovated GPO than to the possibility of Ireland finally achieving its own independence.

As Aran listened to Pearse read, he watched the crowd's indifferent reaction. A wave of sadness, disappointment and sense of loss swept over him. He glanced at Pearse from time to time measuring his response. Aran first noticed only a faint smile of satisfaction etched across his schoolmaster's face, but then he saw that Pearse's eyes shone more brightly than ever. Seven hundred and fifty years of slavery to a Crown would take awhile to overcome. Pearse knew this and so did Aran.

With the pronouncement completed, the Irish teacher looked content, but James Connolly was overjoyed. He rushed over to Pearse. The labour leader shook his hand with unrestrained delight and great excitement. The seven members of the IRB's secret Military Council had made their public declaration. They openly intended to break the bonds that tied them to England. Now, the hardest part was yet to come...to make that separation a national and lasting one.

Aran stepped forward into the middle of the street. With the help of several other Volunteers, they passed out copies of Pearse's address to the people in front of the GPO. Then, in an act of pure defiance, Aran placed a copy at the foot of Lord Nelson's one-hundred-seven-year-old column which stood in the middle of Sackville Street just across from the GPO's entrance. He carefully anchored it with a loose cobblestone pried up from the roadway beneath his feet.

With their public declaration made, Pearse and Connolly returned to the safety of the GPO's lobby.

Connolly, chosen as Commandant-General of Dublin's rebel forces, was in charge of all military activities throughout the city. Assisting Connolly was Joseph Mary Plunkett. He had been charged with the responsibility of tracking all Irish and British army movements from his ground-floor 'office.' Plunkett had carefully designed the Rising's military plans that hoped to seal off all British access routes leading to the GPO. When he was not resting from the effects of glandular tuberculosis, the flamboyantly dressed Plunkett poured over city maps and field communiques from the other commandants. He operated from a huge table set up behind the postal counters on which he monitored troop movements and battle reports.

The other two key members of the IRB's Supreme Council, Sean Mac Diarmada and Tom Clarke, plus Patrick Pearse's brother, Willie, were also inside the GPO. With no soldierly responsibilities assigned to them, the trio acted more as onlookers than as leaders or advisers. They possessed no military training and, as a result, played only minor roles in the Rebellion's engagements during the week. None the less, Connolly, showing this sensitive attention to detail, kept them well supplied with updates regarding military activities and battle engagements received from the various outposts positioned around Dublin. This process of keeping his Military Council colleagues constantly informed exemplified Connolly's sense of personal justice and social democracy. He believed in quality and strength of union among the forces under his direction. These same concerns were expressed in several key sections of the *Proclamation* that he had helped to write.

With most of the military activity taking place inside the GPO, Aran's sniper post on the roof was comparatively quiet. As duty stations go though, it was an extremely dangerous one. Irish rebel snipers were the GHQ's first line of defence against a surprise enemy attack. On the other hand, these Irish rooftop rebels became themselves constant targets for enemy sniper fire. But, as long as he kept his head down, Aran had a great observation spot from which to view things. He also liked the idea of being outside in the fresh air under a sunny Irish sky.

Settled in comfortably on their lofty perch and safely tucked in behind their makeshift defensive barricades, Aran and the other snipers eagerly jumped to the ready when they received a warning cry from below. "The Lancers are coming! The Lancers are coming! Be on the ready!"

Their excitement, however, was quickly throttled. Almost immediately The O'Rahilly passed up official orders relayed from Connolly's own lips, "Don't shoot until you're given the command to do so!"

To Aran's knowledge, this was the Rebellion's first battle command. It came directly from Commandant James Connolly, his supreme commander. The twentieth-century fight for Irish freedom was about to begin.

As Aran peered over the roof's railing, now protected by piles of mailbags and several large oak tables, he spied a fine British cavalry unit massed at the top of Sackville Street just in the shadow of Charles Stewart Parnell's statue and monument. The horsemen, under the leadership of Commanding Officer Colonel Hammond, were a crack unit of England's finest. They had been sent from Marlboro Barracks to clean out the rebels who were causing 'problems' in the city centre.

The Irish Rebel watched as the momentous event played out below him. In Aran's remembrance of Irish history, the English army of Occupation had never before charged or attacked an Irish army battalion. But here on Europe's widest thoroughfare, Sackville Street, English and Irish history was unfolding before his very eyes. This famous street designed in the 1700s by Henry Moore, the Earl of Drogheda, and named after his friend, Lyonell Sackville, was soon to record another notable first.

As the elegant and handsomely uniformed troops fanned out across the famous boulevard, they did not appear to be taking their assignment very seriously. In fact, the calvary kept their carbines holstered and only raised their ceremonial lances to defend their Crown's honour against the sodding Irish.

Slowly, they advanced down the street sitting ramrod straight in their saddles astride their sturdy steed. This picture of pride, perfection and military grandeur was shattered moments later when an eager rebel, not waiting for Connolly's command, opened fire.

The Lancers were just passing Lord Nelson's column when more rifle fire broke out from within the GPO. Three Lancers were hit and died before they fell to the ground while a fourth sprawled mortally wounded on Dublin's fine cobblestones. In addition to the human casualties, two of their splendid horses were also shot dead. It was a sight to behold as this highly acclaimed British unit panicked, broke ranks and raced back up the avenue. Aran thought, as he watched the spectacle, how lucky it was for the Lancers that the rebels opened fire when they did. For, if the Irish had waited for their commandant's order, many more British soldiers would have perished...caught in a blaze of deadly rebel fire.

Aran later recalled that this Lancer charge was the only time all week that British forces appeared on Sackville Street. They had learned a hard and embarrassingly disastrous lesson. But, the Dublin civilian population paid a far more terrible price than had the Lancers. English forces surrounded the heart of Dublin and showered a rain of deathly destruction upon many innocent, defenceless citizens and their property.

Inside the GPO, Tom Clarke was beside himself with joy at the results of the ill-fated charge. While being tortuously treated in English prisons for fifteen years, he had dreamed of the day when retribution would be his.

Yes, the Irish Republican Army had struck a real blow against their British rulers . The IRA spoke with bullets for a change...not with easily ignored words. It was the first time this had happened in decades. [HN-5]

Again, in a prideful voice, James Connolly declared that members of his Citizen Army and Irish Volunteers were officially merged into one unified and nationalised body. He said to those gathered around him, "Comrades, from this moment onward, Ireland's fighting force will forevermore bear the title Irish Republican Army. Men, Ireland is our nation...its republican ideals we are here to defend!"

Connolly realised this idea of a united force deployed against Britain was new. It would take some time for the Irish to accept and embrace it. He was aware that during the past seven hundred plus years the Irish people had managed only small disjointed and often isolated attempts at gaining their freedom. For centuries, Ireland lacked a unified, nationalised and organised front orchestrated by a single dynamic leader. Connolly recognised this and proposed a solution which he now called the IRA.

❧

With the Lancers' charge repelled, things quieted down again inside the GPO. But outside the post office it was a different story. With the apparent breakdown of authority, the poorer residents of Dublin went on a looting rampage. They roamed up and down Sackville Street looting shops much to the disappointment of the Rising's proud leadership.

Aran guessed the poor citizens realised that the DMP and English military were not going to interfere so they ran wild. Old shawl-wearing women, called 'shawlees,' and barefooted, homeless children broke into locked stores taking whatever they fancied. Fires broke out as the thieves smashed, ravaged, looted and destroyed everything in their path.

Efforts by Sean Mac Diarmada and a group of priests failed to hold the greedy crowds back. All their efforts to stop the wild looting proved unsuccessful. Unsatisfied desires and years of economic and social suppression bubbled up uncontrollably as Dublin's underclass spilled out onto the streets around the General Post Office.

As the week of IRA occupation continued, British troop levels in Dublin soared from four hundred on Monday afternoon to over sixteen thousand by the following Saturday. Additionally, they brought in artillery pieces of various sizes including two eighteen-inch guns from their military base in Athlone.

Beginning on Wednesday, the British shelled the city centre for three consecutive days. Plunkett said it was the first time a government had bombed a foreign capitol since the French attacked Moscow in 1812.

Connolly, the socialist commandant, had guessed that the English would not resort to artillery as their capitalistic obsession for wealth and power would overrule military necessity. But the British proved him wrong as worldwide embarrassment and fear of losing imperial control outweighed any economic greed. The government justified the bombing and rationalised to its citizens that they could always replace buildings and material goods lost by maintaining control over a usurped land and its bullied people. On the other hand, they would not easily be able to restore Britannia's worldly pride and haughty reputation in the face of a hapless neighbour's possible triumph over the Royal British Empire!

But despite this error in judgment, Connolly felt a moral sense of victory. He expressed these feelings by pounding a fist into his hand exclaiming, "By God, *they* are beaten. The British are beaten!"

Incredulously, however, James Connolly and the rest of Dublin watched in wide-eyed disbelief as up and down Sackville Street fires burned and buildings disappeared into clouds of smoke, dust and flames. Soon all the world would know that the British Empire was beginning to crumble and tumble down. Britain's fear of defeat at the hands of a few hundred Irish rebels exposed her vulnerable underside. The scars of a burning and destroyed Dublin bore grim testimony to what was soon to come. Yes, Easter Wednesday, 1916 was the beginning of the end for Britain's once proud and grand empire.

From the GPO's roof, Aran engaged the enemy in a long-distance war of bullets as English snipers fired on their headquarters and Irish riflemen answered back. Actually, it was a standoff, as few if any casualties were sustained by either side during these exchanges.

Downstairs, in the bowels of the GPO, Pearse kept to himself. His withdrawal increased as the week's events unfolded and, as the possibility of a military victory seemed to slip through his fingers, he spent most of his time thinking, writing and worrying about the loss of life and injury he was causing Dublin and its citizenry.

Aran saw and briefly spoke with him on just three occasions. Aran felt his mentor was searching his soul trying to balance the death and destruction going on around him with the ideals of freedom and independence he had dreamed about for so long. Aran felt Pearse's pain and helplessness but had no salve to bathe his open and aching wounds.

The last time Aran talked with Pearse was on Easter Friday evening as the GPO occupants prepared to flee the burning building. Pearse finished reading a statement of hope and personal praise to his brave, trapped men. After the comments, the soldiers lined up to leave, hopefully for the safety of a new GHQ.

Aran noticed Pearse standing by himself as the evacuation effort was being organised. With his back to the men, a dejected Patrick Henry Pearse stared thoughtfully back at the burning remains of the GPO. Aran walked over to his Commandant-General, the Commanding-in-Chief of the Forces of the Irish Republic and the President of its Provisional government, and shook his hand. They smiled at each other.

Tears welled up in Aran's eyes and he dropped his head in embarrassment as Pearse spoke, "To hold out against England for an hour, imagine! How glorious that would be! But we have done that and more."[7-1]

As Pearse continued his voice grew stronger and more resilient, "You know Emmet's two-hour insurrection is as nothing to this. They will talk of Dublin in the future as one of the splendid cities— as they speak today of Paris. Dublin's name will be glorious forever."[7-2]

Pearse reached out to Aran and he pulled him to his breast. "Aran, we have lit such a flame that from this day forth, it shall never be put out. It will burn from mountain top to mountain top...from stony field to stony field...from Dublin Town to the smallest hamlet in Ireland.

"God bless and protect you, Aran. You are the hope of a new Ireland. We here have passed our torch of hope and freedom to you. Guard it and care for it well. I know it is safe in your strong hands."

Pearse's eyes also filled with tears and he turned away from his devoted pupil.

"It will be safe with me. You have my word," came Aran's soft but firm reply. "God bless you too, sir, and may the Lord protect you with his love, now, forever and always..."

"Aran...Aran Roe O'Neill, it's time we were off!"

It was The O'Rahilly. The barricade-attack squad was ready to leave on its mad rush up Moore Street and its head-on encounter with the British army.

❦

The four rebels ran hard for ten minutes. Over garden walls, down laneways and through side streets. They put as much distance between the Brendan Road shoot out and themselves as possible.

They must have been a strange sight to any onlookers. Rifles slung over their shoulders, haversacks filled to overflowing and pistols in their hands. They gave a warlike look to Dublin's quiet residential neighbourhoods. People stared at them in frightened disbelief as they raced passed rows of neat gardens and peaceful suburban homes.

Finally, the new trio's apparent leader halted their mad dash. Quickly, the four escapees ducked into a carriage house belonging to a large home on Herbert Road. Each of them was breathless and sweating. As they slipped inside the unpretentious building, Aran noticed by some strange quark of fate that they were only a block away from The O'Rahilly's home.

Willie, after catching his breath, walked over to Aran and spoke, "You came along just at the right moment. Those Limeys were giving us a hard time. We owe you our lives and our home. Thanks a million."

"Glad to be of service to yis so," said Aran smilingly.

"Now, to answer your question you posed back there...we are from 'C' Company, 3rd Battalion. We held off the British advance into the city for most of Wednesday at a place called Clanwilliam House next to little Mount Street Bridge. There were seven in our house, but only four of us got out alive. Our leader, George Reynolds, and two others died in the burning building."

Aran nodded understandingly then replied, "Sounds like my escape from the GPO on Friday evening."

The other two men walked over to Aran. They introduced themselves as the brothers, Jim and Tom Walsh.

Without prompting, Tom began describing their ordeal in more detail as his two companions listened. "There were thirteen of us assigned to guard the Northumberland Road and Mount Street Bridge entrance into the city. Sure, our OC, Mick Malone, and his mate, Jimmy Grace, must have died as their position, a house at #25 Northumberland, was blown up after several hours of vicious fighting . We still don't know what happened to the other four of our group positioned in the Parochial Hall just up the way from #25."

While Tom paused to catch his breath, Jim proudly stated, "We really gave it to them so. You should have seen the bridge. It was covered with dead and dying Sherwood Forester soldiers. Most of Northumberland Road, as far down as you could see, was covered with bodies too. I'd guess there were at least two hundred British killed or wounded on Wednesday last. Aran, you should have seen them! The bloody eejits just kept coming at us and we just kept mowing 'em down. At times our rifles were so hot we had to stop firing and let them cool off or we'd have burned our hands."

"How did yis get away?" asked a wide-eyed Aran.

"Dumb luck," answered Willie Ronan. "We made it out the back door and lit out for Merrion Square. The other lad with us decided to go it alone, so the three of us circled around and hid out in Ballsbridge. That's where you found us this morning. We'd planned to stay at my parents' house until that English patrol started searching the block. My guess is one of the pro-British blighters who lives up the way informed on us. Luckily, it was only the three of us in the house plus the caretaker, Joe. I'd anticipated there might be trouble so I sent my parents off to stay with my sister in Bray. We were about to hightail it out the back when you opened fire on them."

Jim interrupted saying, "Willie, you can thank your lucky stars old Joe was there to put out the fires, please God. Your parents would never forgive you if that house burned down."

Willie reached over and ruffled Jim's hair with his hand.

"Jim, what would I do without you two and Joe to save my arse and worry about so?"

The three friends grinned from ear to ear at one another.

"Now that you know our story," said Jim, "What about you and that fancy six-shooter you carry?"

Aran introduced himself as Aran Roe O'Neill from Gort, County Galway. He told them how he had met Pearse, had moved to St. Enda's seven weeks ago and had spent the week sniping at the enemy from the roof of the GPO.

He explained that he was on the run as well and briefly described his capture, his detention at Richmond Barracks and his improbable escape from deportation. Finally, Aran mentioned Thomas and Anna's kindness to him and his planned retreat into the Wicklow Mountains.

"Well, I'll be damned!" exclaimed Willie. "The three of us are after talking about the very same thing. We've discussed running south into the Wicklows too. There's folk in Wicklow Town who'd put us up until things calm down here. Interested in joining us?"

Aran, wanting to keep his options open, replied, "Thanks. I'll sure give it some thought."

The four rebel survivors continued talking among themselves. They all agreed it was a wildly exciting and terribly dangerous time to live in Dublin Town, but they knew their experiences were only a sampling of the many adventures that would be talked about for years to come. Luckily, and by their own personal choice, each seemed to be thriving on the terror, danger and death that now haunted them as Ireland began her long-awaited fight for freedom.

But now, for the moment, they could all relax. Seated on the floor, backs against the side wall, the four rebels shared a small bottle of whiskey from the stores inside Willie's haversack. It was time to plan their next move.

After the short break, Tom scrambled to his feet and, much to Aran's surprise, invited him to follow them into the main house. The outside building, in which the four rebels were hiding, belonged to an uncle of the Walsh brothers. The family's name was Casey and their dislike for the British could be traced back many generations.

After the proper introductions had been made, they all enjoyed some refreshments as they told the Caseys of the Rebellion's latest developments. The Irish newspapers were still refusing to print the truthful details of the conflict that had so engulfed the city.

Members of the Casey family took turns as lookouts while Aran and his new companions washed up and enjoyed a lovely meal. The feast surprised everyone. With all the week's fighting, food was in short supply and dearer than usual. But Mrs. Casey spared nothing serving the war-weary men and her family a meal fit for royalty.

Spicy boiled sausages, roasted potatoes, a mixture of pan-fried cabbage with leeks and freshly baked brown-bread. This was all topped off with homemade scones, butter, jam and cupfuls of hot, strong tea.

After dinner, the rebels poured over a map of County Dublin deciding on their route into the Wicklows. Then, as they waited for nightfall, they took advantage of their hosts' kind offer and rested for several hours. They all knew how exhausting the next few days were likely to be.

❧

It was dark outside when the revolutionaries bid goodbye to the Casey family. But, before they left the house, everyone knelt down in the sitting room. Together they all said the rosary and asked for God's help, protection and safe deliverance from the hands of the enemy.

Back outside in the crisp evening air, the rebels decided to divide themselves into two groups of two. Willie felt they would attract less unwanted attention and one twosome could cover and backup the other duo. Willie and Tom formed one group and Aran and Jim the other.

The men agreed that packing hand bombs and carrying rifles in the open was an invitation to trouble, so leaving the rest of their weaponry behind, each carried two pistols and a generous number of shells. Mrs. Casey organised a small kit bag containing sandwiches and some home-made biscuits. As a final precaution, each man strapped on a British appropriated, scabbarded knife for protection and unforeseen emergencies.

It was half ten at night as they made their way south back through Donneybrook. The second of the twosomes, Aran and Jim, were a hundred and fifty yards behind Willie and Tom. Whenever possible, each pair walked on opposite sides of the roadway.

They had worked out a simple set of signal sounds for 'go' and 'stop.' Military patrols were enforcing the curfew and could appear without warning, so each of them remained alert to every sound and movement around them.

Slowly and carefully, the four proceeded southward. They kept to side streets and paused every hour for a brief five minute rest.

In this manner, they reached Sandyford a little after one in the morning. There were no motor cars or human traffic on the streets that night. Aran realised the Dubliners were certainly taking the English 'stay-indoors' policy seriously.

On the outskirts of Sandyford, they left the road and began blazing a trail through woods, across streams and over open fields. It was slow going in the dark but, at least, the four men were able to walk together, separated now by only a few yards. Their self-imposed 'no talking' rule was strictly adhered to.

By four o'clock they had reached a point just west of Enniskerry. Growing tired, the men decided to rest for two hours. Each took a thirty-minute turn being the lookout.

❧

The sun rose on another beautiful morning. This year, Ireland had been blessed with a mild, dry spring and an early summer. After more map study and discussion, the three Clanwilliam men and Aran headed off toward Roundwood, Ireland's highest village. They would split up there. The three Dubliners wanted to proceed down into Wicklow Town, stay on a friend's boat and fish the Irish Sea with him. After a few months out of circulation, they hoped things would have quieted down at home and they would be able to slip back into life with their families without a problem.

Aran, on the other hand, intended to head west over the mountains, hike across the Midlands, and find safety on his family's farm in the west of Ireland.

At half six on Wednesday morning, they started off again. Further to the south, they met up with a little used byroad around Enniskerry and cut through part of the Powerscourt Estate property. The 'big house' looked impressive in the early morning light. They walked single file and kept a hundred yards between each man. By walking at a strong pace, the rebels hoped to reach Roundwood by mid-morning.

After they had covered more than half the distance, Willie, who was in the lead, rounded a corner and disappeared from Aran and Jim's sight.

Just as Tom, who was second in line, turned the bend in the road, Aran and Jim saw him dive behind a large outcropping of rocks along one side of the narrow road. Following his example, the two of them quickly took cover. Then, with extreme caution, they slowly worked their way up to where Tom was hiding.

Jim spoke to his brother in a whisper, "What the hell's going on?"

"They have Willie!"

"Who has Willie?" questioned Jim.

"The Royal Irish Constabulary that's who!" came Tom's terse reply.

"Those wretched lousers!" muttered Jim.

"How many are there?" asked Aran as he carefully peered around the outcropping. He was hoping to catch a glimpse of something that would give him a clue as to what was going on up ahead.

"Three...maybe four," answered Tom.

"Sure, did you see what happened?" queried Aran nodding his head up the road.

"Well, when I reached the bend here, there was a lorry stopped at the crossroads up the way. Blimey, if there wasn't a bloody copper standing there talking to Willie. I could see Willie pointing this way and that. I guess he was trying to give some bleeding directions to the peelers."

"Then what?" urged Jim impatiently.

"Now, I'm only guessing see, but the RIC man must have become suspicious about what Willie was saying...you know he's really a stranger to these parts. Anyway, the next thing I know sure enough, two of the peelers jump down off the back of the lorry levelling their guns at him. Then, when he threw his hands up in the air, his coat fell open...and there, for all the world to see, were the butts of his two revolvers sticking out as big as life."

Tom took a breath and continued. "They took his guns, frisked him, slapped on the bracelets, and loaded poor Willie into the lorry. With everyone on board, the vehicle made a U-turn in the road and headed south toward Roundwood."

"Just imagine so, after all we went through at Clanwilliam Place and now to have him picked up by some bone idle rozzers...I say, what will we do now?"

"Guess we could cut across country and head for the village. They'll probably hold him there until they figure out what to do next," suggested Aran.

They all agreed it was the thing to do. So with special care, they left the byroad heading off in a southeasterly direction. Once again, the three young men hiked through stands of evergreens, skirted boggy ground, and climbed over stonewalls surrounding fields of spring hay.

After thirty minutes of purposeful walking, they came upon another side road and decided to follow it. As they walked along, an old man driving two milk cows came out of a field up ahead and ambled toward them.

"Dia dhuit," said Aran in Irish.

"Dia's Muire duit and a fine day to yourselves," answered the old man, stopping before the three young strangers.

"Ye boys are not from around here, are yis?"

"No," answered Aran. "We're from Rathfarnham and to tell you the truth, we're a wee bit lost. Could you point us in the right direction for Roundwood?"

"Well, just over that hill ahead and before ye come to Lough Tay, you'll see to a road leading down from the Sally Gap. Turn left and it's about five miles."

Aran cleared his throat. "We were hoping there might be another way...maybe something a little less travelled."

"Afraid of something so...or maybe looking for someone...like a friend of yis?" The old man's eyes sparkled.

"Well, er, maybe," stammered Tom.

"It's a small place around here. News travels fast, especially when there's news worth travelling," teased the farmer.

"You seem to know everything sure. Do you know where he's being kept?" asked Tom.

"Well, the RIC use a small stone cottage as their headquarters in

Roundwood. It's just this side of the village. My guess is they'll hold him until the authorities come up from Wicklow Town to collect him," answered the old man. "If you don't mind me asking, what's he done anyway?"

"Guess he was the wrong person in the wrong place at the wrong time," said Aran, a bit annoyed.

With that he turned and started walking off up the road.

"Hold on there a minute, young man. Don't go flying off half-cocked. If you don't mind me ould legs, I'll walk yis over in that direction and, if we're lucky, just no one might know that we're coming so."

Aran stopped in his tracks and looked back over his shoulder.

"Ah sure, 'tis no trouble for me to show ye the way...and by the by, I'm Frank...Frank Broderick. I've lived most of me life up here among these hills so they're no puzzle to me. In fact I've me a small cottage just up toward the Gap...not too far from here."

The old man stuck out his hand and, in turn, all three gave it a welcoming shake.

The lads introduced themselves by name but stuck to the story of their being on an outing from Rathfarnham.

Frank herded his two cows into a nearby field and secured the gate after them. Thanking Frank again for his kindness, the three rebels and their guide headed off over the hilly ground toward Roundwood.

As they walked along, Frank initiated the conversation. Boldly he speculated, "I'm guessing yis must be on the run from the English. Maybe ye've been in last week's fighting down in Dublin Town?" Then he added, "If I were a few years younger, I'd like to think I'd have been there too..."

The three smiled at each other and nodded to Frank. He answered back with a toothless grin. His eyes were twinkling like stars on a moonless night.

"Best we not be talking now though. Voices can carry on the wind up here and yis rather not want to attract any unnecessary notice, no?"

"Right so," acknowledged Aran.

The four continued on in silence. The three vigilant rebels followed the old man as he led them along little-used cattle paths, across grassy patches, and through sweet-smelling stands of pine trees.

After an hour's hike, they dropped down over a rise. There, visible through some trees right below them was a small but solid stone house standing beside the main road. Tom confirmed that the lorry parked out in front looked like the same vehicle used to transport Willie into captivity. The village itself was another five hundred yards south of the barracks.

Aran saw no iron bars on the windows and, in fact, all the shutters were thrown open. He guessed the local peelers were so excited at finding a possible escapee fleeing the fighting in Dublin that they completely failed to realise he might be travelling with some companions...brothers-in-arms who might try rescuing him.

Frank motioned the three young men to gather around him. "Lads, I know that cottage well. Before the RIC took it over a family called Ryan lived there. Their daughter and I use to meet down by the crossroads for some dancing on warm summer evenings. Ah, but sure, that was well before yis time...more like when your fathers were doing their courting."

Wistfully, the old man stared down at the little stone house before adding, "That was a long time ago...and she sailed off to England with another..."

Another short silence-filled pause was abruptly broken by, "Enough about me, lads. Yis have work to do, no?"

They all nodded their heads in agreement.

"The house there has three rooms with a short central hallway." Suddenly, Frank was all business. "The large room is used for the office while the two smaller ones serve as a kitchen and bedroom for the men."

"Are you sure?" questioned Aran.

"To a tee...I was in there myself only just last week. Came round just to be polite and have a cup of tay with the lads." He seemed a bit annoyed they would question his information.

"Satisfied?"

No one said a word.

Frank continued in hushed tones, "As I was saying, you enter the house through the front door. The office is on the right and the bedroom's on your left. The combination kitchen-dining room is at the back of the house but the door leading to it from the other end of the hallway is boarded shut. The only way into the kitchen is through a connecting bedroom door. There's also a back door from the kitchen that leads directly out onto the porch there below us." As he spoke, Frank used his finger as a pointer.

Aran, looking down onto the stone cottage-cum-barracks, saw the low porch roof and the back door leading from the kitchen.

"Nowadays, there are five or six RIC in residence most of the time. Sure, yis are a bit outnumbered aren't ye?"

"Not enough so as to make any difference!" retorted Aran.

Everyone smiled at his brash overconfidence.

It was now just before eleven on a fine May morning. As the four looked down on the cottage, two uniformed RIC emerged from the front of the barracks and climbed into the lorry. After a moment's pause, they leisurely drove off toward the village.

Obviously, the rebels did not know when the two men would return or if and when they planned on moving Willie. In fact, they really did not know for sure if Willie was in the cottage at all. The chances were, though, he probably was.

Following Aran's lead, the two other rebels moved down the hill a few yards away from Frank. In whispered conversation, they began formulating their battle plan while the old man held his ground trying to catch a word or two of what they were saying. With the two rozzers out of the cottage that left three maybe four inside. No doubt a couple of them were in the office with Willie. Another one or two could very well be preparing dinner in the kitchen. Smoke was coming from the chimney pipe at the back of the barracks.

A quickly drafted plan was agreed upon. While one of the rebels knocked on the front door creating a diversion, the other two would surprise the men in the office and kitchen through the windows along the back of the building.

Their plan left the bedroom uncovered, but it was nearly noon and with all the excitement of Willie's arrest, it was a gamble worth taking. Aran seriously doubted anyone would be asleep in the bedroom under the circumstances.

With Aran assuming the leader's role in Willie's absence, he decided to take responsibility for the rear-office window. Tom agreed to cover the kitchen and Jim opted to pound on the front door. Jim's excuse for knocking up the RIC would be an auto accident in the village. He would tell them his injured wife needed immediate assistance.

A few moments after Jim started pounding on the door shouting for help, Aran and Tom would shatter the glass in barracks' rear windows and order 'hands up' to all inside.

With all the confusion at the back of the house, the rebels thought the RIC policeman, who had answered Jim's pounding at the door, would turn his attention away from the lad and toward the racket behind him. At that point, Jim would arrest the copper directing him back into the office. As Jim covered those present, the Irish Rebel would race around to the front of the building and join Jim. The takeover would be complete when Tom marched his one or two kitchen arrestees up front thus, successfully, wrapping up the compound's capture.

With each man's assignment clear, the three checked their weapons and prepared to head off down the hill.

The old man wished them good luck and God's blessing. He saluted them, turned and headed out of sight back up the slope as the three lads began crawling down the hill toward the cottage. They used long grass, clusters of stone and the occasional furze bush to obscure their approach.

Safely behind the low stone wall that surrounded the barracks, Aran Roc O'Neill and Tom Walsh covered brother Jim as he headed around to the front of the building.

Crouching low, Jim followed the perimeter wall around to the front gate. Slowly, he was to count up to fifty giving Aran and Tom time to spread out, move up to the rear of the house and position themselves under their assigned windows.

"So far everything is going as planned," whispered Aran to Tom as they split up and moved to their spots at the rear of the barracks.

The Gortman counted to himself...forty-eight, forty-nine, fifty, fifty-one, fifty-two...

At that moment, both Aran and Tom heard a loud pounding from the front of the house. Jim sounded desperate as he hammered on the door.

Aran quickly stole a glance into his area of responsibility and swiftly surveyed the office. There were two uniformed RIC in the room with Willie. The Mount Street hero was on the floor with his back up against the wall. His hands were behind him and a rope secured his feet together.

Aran guessed Willie's hands were still cuffed.

One peeler looked up from the writing desk as the other quickly walked across the floor to answer Jim's banging at the door.

Jim really plays his part well thought Aran. Maybe they could use his talents at the Abbey when this is all over. The thought of it made him smile despite the tension.

The RIC man answering the door disappeared from Aran's view as he passed out into the hallway.

Aran slowly counted to three and then nodded to Tom. Both men hammered their revolvers through the window glass yelling, "Get your hands up, NOW!"

The man behind the desk almost jumped out of his chair. His hands shot straight up toward the ceiling.

But Tom was not as lucky. In his nervousness, he had failed to peek into the kitchen before breaking the glass as Aran had done. To his great surprise, when he stuck his weapon through the window, he looked into an empty kitchen.

At that moment, the man who had answered the front door turned to see what the yelling was all about at the rear of the barracks. Jim drew his guns and stepped inside the hallway.

Suddenly, and without warning, everything went wrong. A policeman appeared in the hall's bedroom doorway. He saw Jim's drawn guns and pulled the trigger of the shotgun he was holding. Its buckshot blast hit Jim directly in the chest. The rebel was blown backwards out into the front garden. He was dead before he hit the ground.

At that moment, the RIC man who had answered the door turned and dashed back into the office. He headed straight for the unlocked gun rack on the far wall. Aran fired twice.

The man spun around and sagged to the floor.

In all the confusion, the peeler behind the desk decided to climb over its top hoping to find safety on the other side. O'Neill squeezed off a single shot hitting the man in the lower back. The policeman cried out in pain and, with a heavy thud, slumped over on top of the desk.

Tom, realising something was terribly wrong, shot the lock off the back door. Kicking it open with his boot, he entered the kitchen. As he walked across the floor, heading toward the bedroom, a rozzer rushed into the kitchen with a drawn revolver. Simultaneously, the two fired at one another. Luckily for Tom, the man was a poor shot. The policeman's blast just winged him in the arm. On the other hand, Tom did not miss. The RIC man's chest exploded into a sea of red as two shots ripped into his heart.

While the gunfight in the kitchen was going on, the constable who had shot Jim took a quick look from the hallway into the office. Seeing a strange head peeking around the door frame, Aran fired again but missed. The policeman safely ducked back out of sight only to discover Tom standing behind him with a revolver at his head.

"Drop it, Peeler and get your bloody hands up!" ordered Tom.

As much as he wanted to, Tom could not pull the trigger and shoot the man in cold blood.

Aran raced around to the front door into the office. He cut Willie's legs free. "Where are the keys to your handcuffs?"

"That one over there, the one on the desk, has a ring of keys on him."

Quickly, Aran located the ring attached to the man's belt. With one a mighty yank of his knife, he cut the belt in half freeing the keys.

Moments, later, Willie, free of his restraints, scooped up a shotgun just in case the other two coppers returned unexpectedly.

Pausing a moment to catch his breath, Aran took stock of the situation. Jim was dead, Tom slightly wounded. Both Willie and he were in one piece but both were still shaking with the fear and excitement of it all. As for the RIC...one was badly wounded in the kitchen, another bleeding peeler was still draped across the desk, while a third lay dead on the floor. A fourth man, Jim's killer, lay tied hand and foot on a bed in the other room.

Willie went to the aid of the wounded RIC who lay bleeding on the desk. The other constable in the kitchen was beyond help so only a quick prayer was offered up.

Looking out the front door, Aran saw Tom on his knees beside his dead brother. He blessed himself saying a prayer for the fallen brave rebel. Another name added to Ireland's ledger of honoured dead. Aran wondered how many more would have to pay the ultimate price before the English were driven out and Irish freedom was finally restored. The sacrificial list contained tens of thousands of names. Sure, this struggle was becoming a damnable dirty business indeed! But this was not the time nor the place for such reflections. Time was precious. He could not waste it on the dead no matter his feelings of sorrow or regret.

Aran, wrapping some towelling around Tom's arm, joked, "Ah, 'tis nothing. The bleeding is under control. You'll be grand so in no time."

The Gortman helped Tom carry Jim's body into the house. Once again, a brief prayer was said for the fallen hero of Clanwilliam House.

For a long moment Tom stood head bowed over his brother's body. Looking up, he turned to Aran and Willie and said, "I remember when things were hotting up in Clanwilliam House on Wednesday last. Jim kept saying over and over to me, 'They shall not pass...They shall not pass.' And ye know what? It was a long time before any of those British Foresters ever did."

In a final act of devotion and respect, Tom knelt down and kissed his dead brother on the cheek. Then together, the three of them covered his body with a bed sheet from the other room.

"It's time we decided where we're all going," urged Aran. "Who knows when those other peelers will be back. Besides, surely someone in the village must have heard the shooting."

They hurriedly discussed their options, being careful the surviving RIC could not overhear their conversation or their decisions.

Willie and Tom said they would still head for the coast and Wicklow Town. Away from curious eyes, Tom could heal up safely on the fishing boat. Aran, too, had not changed his mind. He would head west over the mountains and face for home.

After reloading their revolvers, each young man took a rifle or shotgun from the wall case. They also stuffed as much food as possible into the small kit bag Tom carried plus the two haversacks that were hanging on pegs in the kitchen.

As a final act of defiance, they rendered the four remaining police shotguns useless with a sledge hammer found on the back porch.

Pausing a moment to say good-bye to each other, the three young warriors shook hands and parted company. Two heading east, one going west.

It was just after twelve and clouds were beginning to pile up in the sky. It looked like it would be a rainy afternoon in the Wicklow Mountains.

With the weather changing and the barracks's raid behind him, Aran wanted to put as much distance between this stone cottage of death and himself as possible.

He raced back up the slope behind the barracks and there sitting on a stone wall was Frank. He had waited for them to return.

"Bad news?" asked the old farmer.

"Yes," replied Aran. "One of my friends is dead and one wounded but we did free our captured companion."

"...and the policemen?" quietly inquired the old timer.

"Two dead, one wounded and one tied up."

The old man just shook his head. "I fear we're in for some hard times in the days to come so..."

Aran saw tears beginning to slide down Frank's face.

"Better not go down there, sir," warned Aran. "More RIC and, probably, the English will be coming soon."

Frank ignored Aran's advice and started down the hill toward the barracks.

He had walked only a few steps when he stopped, turned and looked back at Aran. "I must go down and see how those men are keeping!"

With that, Frank continued down the hill.

Aran turned away from the old man and the cottage below. He looked up at the darkening sky and headed off in the opposite direction. Tears of pain and sorrow welled up in his eyes too.

8. Murder

O, had they died by Pearses' side, or had fought with
    Cathal Brugha,
Their names we'd keep where the Fenians sleep, 'neath
    the shroud of the Foggy Dew...

The Foggy Dew / Rev. P. O'Neill

The late afternoon turned soft. Aran Roe pulled the collar of Thomas's jacket up around his neck in a vain attempt to keep the gentle spring rain from soaking him through to the skin. Walking over the rough, uneven ground of the Wicklows, Aran wished he had his old broad, black brimmer to shelter him. Like his father, he believed if your head was protected from the weather, the rain and damp were not so bad.

Alone, the young Irish Rebel trod on through the drizzly gathering gloom. As he went, he thought back over the events of the morning. He had been on his feet with only one short break since yesterday evening. More than eighteen hours had passed since he had eaten or rested properly. Hunger and fatigue were now his only companions and, though he felt tired and off colour, Aran knew it was vitally important for him to keep moving west through the mountains and away from Roundwood.

Ignoring the mighty weariness slowly enveloping him, the Gortman doggedly maintained his measured stride and steady forward progress. He was proud of his recent accomplishments but wise enough not to take any foolish chances at this late date. Despite his fatigue, his senses were on full alert. He actively refused to let the intoxicating power of the Rebellion's residue go to his head...especially after all he had been through to come this far.

Outwardly, the cut of him would have turned many a head. An odd collection of borrowed, dirt-stained clothing girded his six-foot frame, cloaking his muscular physique. Aran's once shiny black boots now were covered with mud. His hands were filthy while his thick, curly-brown, unkempt hair looked oily and matted from the day's damp.

Inwardly, Aran was not his usual self either. As the day wore on, his energy reserves neared the point of exhaustion. He was tired, hungry and felt out of sorts. Despite all this, however, his coal black eyes still sparkled, fired by some deep well of inner strength. His unusually taut facial expression now seldom revealed the youthful playfulness born of happier and more innocent times.

On he trudge with slowing pace as night began to close in around him. Calling upon his dwindling stores, the young man skirted north around the beautiful valley of Glendalough, famous for its Saints both Kevin and Lawrence O'Toole. With heightened concentration, he pressed on through open fields and along winding trails compacted by generations of meandering sheep. All around him low hanging clouds clung to the mountaintops while a rising mist issued forth from the glen below. Occasionally, a wintry-like rain shower peppered down on him from an increasingly foreboding sky. A bad situation was rapidly becoming worse.

The fear, however, from what he fled was overpowering. He did not have to remind himself how important it was to keep moving westward. So, staying above the sparse tree line, the Irish Rebel made his way across country over marginal pasture land. His path was often criss-crossed with clumps of heather, patches of grass sprinkled with stands of yellow furze all accented by frequent outcroppings of rocky granite. There were few houses or people living in this part of the Wicklow Mountains. This grassy boggy land was used almost exclusively for cattle and sheep grazing by local farmers.

In this remote part of the Irish countryside there was only a solitary road heading west through the mountains. From Aran's vantage point just below the ridge line, the retreating soldier had an excellent view of its winding path. If they were still on his trail, the fleeing Irishman knew the British military or Royal Irish Constabulary would have a difficult time surprising him up here.

To the Gortman, raised on the west coast of Ireland, those two groups were the embodiment of economic oppression and political domination. The British for so long had one hand in Ireland's pocket and the other around its throat. Aran had been reminded of this fact over and over while growing up in a household strongly governed by its nationalistic sentiments. Aided by a sound formal education and accelerated by his early maturity, Aran was outraged and incensed at the Saxon Stranger's seven-hundred-year-plus dominance of his homeland. He knew of

Eireann's long suffering and, with a deepening sense of loathing and disgust for British politics, this youth had vowed to do something about standing up for Irish independence. That and self-preservation were the main reasons for his now rigorous march through the Wicklows in less than desirable circumstances.

Though on his own this dirty evening, Aran Roe was well armed and, hopefully, prepared for most eventualities. He had one revolver tucked in his belt under his jacket, another concealed in the haversack slung over his right shoulder and a single-barreled shotgun bobbed up and down in the crook of his left arm.

Prior to fleeing the barracks in Roundwood, Aran had selected a shotgun instead of a rifle for protection. He thought its presence would attract less attention in the countryside than a military-like rifle. Besides, it would support his carefully concocted cover story of being on an Easter holiday hunting excursion from his Dublin suburban school.

On he trudged. In an effort to ward off the hellish effects of numbing fatigue, Aran recalled the myriad stories that had circulated throughout Dublin Town after the IRA's unconditional surrender. These rumours vowed that the ringleaders would be dealt with in 'a most severe manner.' As President and Commanding-in-Chief of the newly declared Irish Republic, Pearses's life might be forfeited. But, what about the others? Would the British execute them all?

For the past several months, Aran had listened to his beloved Pearse speculate about his death in battle or, if the Rebellion should fail, his execution by the aggrieved English. Neither eventuality seemed to trouble this romantic intellectual. No, Pearse was not afraid to die for his country. This thoughtful educator firmly believed that the Irish people must be awakened from their slumber and given a new sense of hope, thus sparking a renewed desire for freedom from its present colonial overlords.

Pearse maintained that every Irish generation had the responsibility to rise up and demand its independence. Once he even told Aran that he believed bloodshed was a cleansing and sanctifying thing and that any nation who regarded it as its final horror had lost its manhood.

The schoolteacher believed that those who died fighting for Ireland's cause gave their lives so this ancient land could be reborn. Aran remembered Pearse's hero, Robert Emmet. He had died a brutal death at the hands of the Sassenach after his aborted 1803 Rebellion. Pearse said Emmet died for Ireland so Eireann might once again be free.

No, Pearse was not afraid of death. His Ireland was a cause worth living, fighting and dying for. Those close to him knew and understood that his Irish passions ran deep.

Aran thought of the people with whom he had brushed shoulders during the past week and of his St. Enda's classmates. What was going to happen to the school now? Would the British destroy it for its symbolic representation of Pearse's defiance of their power and authority? What of Pearse's mother? His two sisters? Would the Stranger arrest them or worse? What of Pearse's brother Willie? He never really played an active role in the planning or fighting. He was just Patrick's friend and brotherly sounding board.

Aran recalled the night he had spent as a prisoner in Richmond Barracks. His brief exchanges with Michael Collins had a powerful impact on him. Collins shared the same fierce drive for freedom from England that both Pearse and he felt. The Corkman, however, expressed his feelings more directly and with less poetic idealism than did Aran's beloved teacher. Hopefully, the three of them would survive all this and continue, somehow, fighting for their native land's independence.

Aran realised that Easter 1916 had been Pearse's turn...his generation's opportunity to strike for freedom. They had all fought well...even to the bitter end. But now it might be up to himself and others to carry on the age-old struggle.

❧

Now, with heavy black rain clouds overhead, darkness quickly closed in around Aran Roe O'Neill. If only he had a home cooked meal and a warm bed waiting for him just over the next rise, but that was too much to wish for up here in the mountains. Then, Aran smiled to himself. Wasn't he the seventh son of a seventh son? His father and grandfather had often told him of a special aura that encompassed him. It was there for his protection and safekeeping. They had often talked in hushed tones about this unique force and unusual dividend that was part of his birthright. Suddenly shivering with cold, Aran quickly reflected back over the events of the last ten days. He wondered if there might not be some truth in their superstitious beliefs after all.

As the immediacy of night bore down upon him, the young rebel's thoughts turned to a more practical issue when he spied a small shed up ahead. With no prospects of anything better to serve as shelter, he headed up a steep slope covered with lush green grass dotted with little patches of yellow buttercups.

To his delight the shed was empty and even some clean, dry straw was piled in one corner. He carefully spread it on the floor opposite the door thinking to himself that if anyone should happen to barge in on him tonight, they would have a rude awakening looking down the barrel of his loaded shotgun.

Not daring to light a small fire for fear of attracting unwanted company, Aran sat down and leaned back against the shed's wall. The tiny structure was bathed in silent darkness. Slowly, he ate the last remaining bits of food left in his haversack. It was neither filling nor tasty and did not satisfy his peckishness.

After finishing his solitary meal, Aran curled up on his bed of straw. He was slowly drying off, but his still damp clothes clung to his skin, making falling asleep difficult.

Before succumbing to his fatigue the Gortman recollected some of the stories Major John McBride had told him of living rough when he had fought with the Boer guerrillas in the Transvaal during the 1899-1902 Boer War. It was a new kind of war that used hit-and-run tactics instead of conventional military assaults. McBride had helped organise an Irish Brigade to fight the British back in those days. He had sided with the Dutch farmers in their quest for independence. Later, in 1910, that land was annexed and became part of the new Union of South Africa. But before its political amalgamation, the English had staked their claim to the newly discovered South African gold fields and diamond mines. Again, British imperial greed would stop at nothing short of total victory as their ever-expanding colonial lust cried out for more.

In addition to both sides refining the art of guerrilla warfare at the turn of the century, British Major General Horatio Herbert Kitchener, born 1850 in Ballylongford, County Kerry, Ireland, introduced the world to another new first...the concentration camp. In his now infamous 're-location camps,' thousands of Boer women, children and old men died of disease, malnutrition and abuse. Always willing to overlook their own faults for their own greater good, the appreciative English venerated Kitchener for bringing the war to a successful British conclusion.

Today, this fabled warrior was serving as Great Britain's Secretary of State for War. His latest brainchild saw men from the same family as well as those from neighbouring villages and towns all assigned to the same battalions fighting in France. These Kitchener 'buddy units' were intended to raise the men's morale and sharpen their fighting spirit. It may have accomplished those ends, but as the war dragged on, those special units of British soldiers were forced to charge from their trenches across the muddy killing-fields of France. Britain's battle-weary frustrations were urged on by their foolhardy desire to bring the war to a rapid end. Their misguided battlefield tactics resulted in tragedy not victory.

Those fields of war, clogged with tangled barriers of razor-sharp barbed wire, swept with murderous machine gun fire and obscured by clouds of poisonous gas, witnessed the systematic decimation of British families and the masculine depopulation of entire English towns. Great Britain lost most of a generation of young men in one tragic and needless stroke of thoughtless planning and senseless annihilation.[HN-6]

❧

When at last he drifted off, Aran slept fitfully. A storm raged throughout the Wicklow Mountains that night. Finally, just as dawn arrived, a tremendous flash of lightning illuminated the darkness, startling him awake. Its following clap of explosive thunder frightened him so that he sat bolt upright clutching his shotgun.

It took Aran several seconds to regain control of his panicked emotions. Cautiously, he pulled himself up onto his feet, opened the shelter's door and peered out. The rain had stopped and the storm had vanished. Morning's faint glow etched itself into the eastern sky as Aran's eyes searched the waning darkness for any signs of movement.

Finally, with his heart still pounding but satisfied he was alone, he returned to his straw pallet. The brilliant flash of lightning and its accompanying crack of thunder had marked the end of the night's storm.

❧

Two days were to pass before Aran learned that at dawn, on the third of May, the day of the RIC barracks' raid and the night of the big storm, Patrick Henry Pearse, the first President of the Irish Republic, was executed by a British firing squad in Stonebreaker's Yard, Kilmainham Gaol, Dublin.

Over time, Aran pieced together the events surrounding his teacher's death. After Pearse's surrender to General Lowe and his son on Saturday afternoon, the 29th, the English drove Pearse to Parkgate, British Military Headquarters, to meet with Ireland's new British Commander-in-Chief, General Sir John Grenfell Maxwell. There was little to discuss, however, as Pearse had unconditionally surrendered.

Besides a personal fascination for meeting his defeated foe face to face, Maxwell, an ardent believer in the Empire, wanted Pearse to dictate the Order to Surrender instructions to his four Dublin battalion commanders. Aran found it interesting that Connolly's Second-In-Command and Chief of Staff, Michael Mallin, refused to obey Pearse's surrender orders until Connolly, his Commandant, had added his personal instructions and signature to those of Pearse's.

By Sunday evening, all rebel positions had been reoccupied by the British authorities and all the freedom-fighters, except those lucky enough to escape, were under military arrest.

Later on that Saturday evening, Patrick Pearse was driven to Arbour Hill Barracks and placed in solitary confinement. He remained so imprisoned until Tuesday morning, May 2nd, when he was transferred to Richmond Barracks for court-martial and sentencing. Additionally, Tom Clarke and Tom MacDonagh were tried, convicted and sentenced that same day.

The English Field-General Courts-Martial were directed by British General Charles Blackadder and three other associates. These four men were British through and through.

Like so many of their judicial predecessors, they possessed no interest or knowledge about the centuries of Anglo-Irish conflicts including its social-religious persecutions or its political-economic intrigues. Their understanding of the relationship between the two island neighbours was nil. Unfortunately, this historical void prevented the magistrates from forming an opinion founded on a factual, realistic and fair-minded point of view. Their bias, strictly speaking, was British, British, British. The court's foundation was an imperial one born of colonial domination, suppression and submission to the British Crown, the British parliament and the British army.

In addition to its one-sidedness, proper legal proceedings were not followed. Though courteous to the Irish revolutionary leaders, they denied the prisoners their right of counsel. Additionally, they were refused their right to cross-examine witnesses for the prosecution while some were not permitted to call witnesses in their behalf. The court did allow the rebel leaders one concession. In front of the assembled judges and prior to sentencing, the prisoners were permitted to make a statement in defence of their actions and to offer justification for their 'offensive and illegal actions.' In the true spirit of Robert Emmet, some took the opportunity to utter inspired and thoughtful declarations while others offered simple statements in defence of their beliefs, motives and character.

As a fitting and final touch, no court stenographer was permitted to be present, so the trial dialogue was recorded in longhand. This greatly slowed the proceedings. Later, this omission prevented an accurate review of the trial's sequence of events and its sworn testimonies.

In reality, all the courts-martial trials were nothing more than kangaroo courts orchestrated and controlled by General Maxwell and his lieutenants. Thought the British did try to give the hearings the appearance of proper legal deportment, they were simply and carefully covering their own tracks as they prepared to carry out the most heinous of deeds.

When their trials were ended and their death sentences pronounced, Pearse, Clarke and MacDonagh were driven from Richmond Barracks to Kilmainham Gaol. There they spent their final few hours of life united in spirit but separated by the cold stone walls of that 1796 prison.

On that same May 2nd evening, several miles from Kilmainham's bleakness, General Blackadder, surrounded by the elegance of Georgian architecture, French wine and soft candlelight, was the guest of honour at an elegant party. During dinner the conversation turned to the Rebellion and how the first day of courts-martial trials had gone. The General was said to have given some innocuous reply. When pressed further about his personal opinion of Patrick Henry Pearse, Blackadder was reported to have said, "Today, I had the most distasteful duty of sentencing to death one of the finest men I've ever had the pleasure of meeting."

One of the dinner party invitees, who secretly sympathised with the rebels' attempts at freedom, wondered if the General truly meant what he had said about Pearse or was just trying to soothe his own guilty conscience.

❧

Patrick Henry Pearse, the uprising's figurehead, chose to pass most of his last remaining hours doing what he loved...writing. Besides recording the carefully chosen words he had spoken at his court-martial, in defence of his Easter Week actions, he wrote a short poem entitled *The Wayfarer* plus individual letters to his mother, sister Margaret and brother Willie.

Then, just before midnight, Pearse requested to see a priest. Father Aloysius, a Capuchin, came and gave Ireland's first president Holy Communion. It was to this man that he entrusted his last precious written thoughts.

Patrick's mother was finally given permission to visit her son. She had planned to arrive early in the morning of May 3rd. Unfortunately, the British solder sent to collect Mrs. Pearse at St. Enda's was unable to complete his assignment. Continual sporadic rebel sniper-fire made

Dublin street travel too dangerous. To further compound English ineptitude, the authorities agreed, too late, to allow Willie a final visit with his brother. As he was being taken to Kilmainham, Willie and his guards heard the shots ring out that sent his brother, Pat, to his death.

Tom Clarke, the first to sign the *Proclamation* out of deference to his age, his loyal devotion to the cause of Irish freedom and his dedicated IRB leadership, was the first to die at dawn in that small cobblestoned courtyard on the third day of May, 1916.

MacDonagh was shot next, and, then, it was Pearse's turn. As the clock neared half three in the morning, the condemned military leader heard the soldiers marching along the prison's dank corridors. They were coming to escort him to his death. But, before leaving his place of confinement, the British captain in charge permitted Pearse a final favour. Dropping to his knees one last time, the brave teacher asked God's blessing saying, "Lord, it's over! It's finished. I gladly give myself up to you and to Eireann. Please forgive me for any unjustness I've done while thirsting for righteousness."

Rising to his feet, Pearse turned to leave his solitary cell. Its opening, however, was so low that he had to stoop down to exit. As he lowered his head to leave, Pearse reminded the guards that his act of bending down was not to be interpreted as yielding to English authority or bowing to British justice.

As he walked along the dim hallway, lit only by gas-lamps, Pearse passed the cells where his two imprisoned comrades and fellow freedom fighters had dwelled. He recalled the names of other great Irish revolutionaries who too had been incarcerated in Kilmainham Gaol. Dubliner James Nappier Tandy, the United Irishmen leader, who rose and fought the British in 1798 had been here. John O'Leary, O'Donovan Rossa and John Devoy, all Fenians and part of the IRB's early history begun in 1858, had walked these halls. Charles Stewart Parnell, the Irish parliamentarian and political revolutionary, had resided rather comfortably in his 'grand' cell. That was back in 1881-82 while the 'Uncrowned King of Ireland' and British Prime Minister William Gladstone bargained about rents and land control. Yes, Parnell had slept behind these same stone walls as well. But unlike Pearse and his followers, all of these earlier heroes had walked out of Kilmainham. They had lived to fight another day for Irish freedom and English justice.

Not surprisingly, Pearse thought of his great hero, Robert Emmet. It was from this prison on the twentieth of September, 1803, that the English took Emmet to his brutal execution in Thomas Street. It was said by those who were there that day that Emmet smiled as he faced death.

Now, it was his turn. He too would smile. Yes, and he also hoped that in the days and years to come the name of Patrick Henry Pearse would live in remembered glory in the hearts and minds of Irishmen and women everywhere.

At the end of the corridor, Pearse turned right and walked down the stairs. Stopped on the flagstone landing, one of his guards securely tied Pearse's hands behind his back. A blindfold was placed over his eyes and a small white patch of cloth was pinned to his jacket just over his heart.

As Pearse quietly waited with his guards in the courtyard doorway, another volley of shots echoed through the ancient prison. Thomas MacDonagh fell dead on the cobbles.

Finally, the soldiers directed the condemned president forward into the fresh early morning air heavy with the sweetness of the previous night's rain yet bitter with the bouquet of Irish blood and British gunpowder.

As Pearse walked out, he felt his way along the uneven surface of the prison yard with the soles of his boots. Reaching the far end of the cobblestoned yard, the procession stopped. His guards faced Pearse about.

Behind him and to the right of this proud revolutionary were high walls. To his left was the massive stone prison building itself. In front knelt six uniformed British soldiers. Six more stood directly behind them forming a second row of executioners...all with rifles...all ready to speed him on his way.

❧

Early on Friday morning, the twelfth of May, Dublin Brigade Commandant James Connolly was brought to the same Kilmainham slaughter house. He was delivered by ambulance and strapped into a chair by some of the same soldiers who had faced Patrick Pearse ten days earlier. Unlike Ireland's president, however, this bold Irishman, radical socialist and confirmed rebel was unable to stand on his own. His infected left leg would not support his poisoned, dying body.

Connolly was twice wounded on Easter Thursday. On that fateful afternoon, Connolly had planned to supervise the building of a barricade on a side street near the GPO. As he left the GHQ with his men, he was grazed in the arm by a stray enemy bullet. This incident, unnoticed by his men, necessitated his immediate return to the GPO. Connolly, with the wound dressed and with his jacket sleeve hiding his bandages, came back to supervise the barricade construction. Thirty minutes later, as he returned to the GPO, Connolly was hit several times in the left ankle by sniper bullets. While bleeding and in great pain, Connolly managed to crawl back into the safety of the General Post Office.

After the GPO leadership's surrender on Saturday afternoon, the British, fearing Connolly might die of his wounds before they could execute him, rushed him to Dublin Castle's small hospital for medical treatment.

In spite of the best medical care available, Connolly's condition worsened. So, thirteen days later and in violation of all known rules of military protocol regarding the treatment of wounded officers, General Maxwell's men rushed the socialist and union leader from his hospital bed to his death in Stonebreaker's Yard.

Ever the courageous soldier and brave Irishman, James Connolly urged his murderers on by crying out, "Yes, Sir, I'll pray for all brave men who do their duty according to their lights. [8-1] Then he shouted, "Fire and don't make a mess of it!" Thus, James Connolly added his own blood to the growing stain that was slowly blotting out England's colonial honour and reputation as a democratic, humane and responsible world power.

❧

Standing tall before his firing squad, President Pearse smiled as he thought Emmet might have smiled on his execution day. A great calm passed over him as he realised how few men have the opportunity to live out their dreams and how even fewer have the chance to die as they wish. He was dying for Ireland so his ancient land might again live and be free. Satisfied that his work on earth was finished and, with nothing more to be said or done, Pearse knew his wheel of life had run down.

"READY?...FIRE!"...and at that moment, Patrick Henry Pearse, Aran's beloved mentor and Ireland's first president, slipped into the arms of God and immortality...his earthly life ended.

❧

The rainstorm's dramatic departure had frightened Aran. Lying on his bed of straw, the Irish Rebel felt a strange and terrible sense of despair well up within him. The sensation flooded his entire being. It intensified and quite overwhelmed him. Sprawled paralysed and helpless, he listened to the ringing sounds of silence.

Unable to understand his sudden anguish, Aran closed his eyes, wishing for the comfort of his family and home. With his body curled into a protective ball, the Irish Rebel gratefully fell into a deep dreamless sleep.

❧

When he awoke two hours later, the sun shone down on him through the shed's dirt-streaked window. The unexplained terror inside him had disappeared. He felt like himself again.

Suddenly, realising the hour's lateness and that he must be off, Aran gathered up his belongings, headed out the door and, again, set off for home. 'Twas a grand morning and he had a long road to travel.

With a fine day before him, the sun's warmth on his face and a following breeze, Aran confidently resumed his westward trek. He was unaware, however, that once again the torch of Irish freedom had been passed to yet another generation...for each new beginning starts with an end.

9. Westward

But the bravest fell, and the requiem bell rang
    mournfully and clear
For those who died that Eastertide in the springtime
    of the year...

The Foggy Dew / Rev. P. O'Neill

The warm morning sun dried the last bit of dampness from his clothes as Aran walked down the western slopes of the Wicklow Mountains. While he hiked along well-worn cattle trails, over yellow furze-covered hills and along shady boreens, Aran longed for something to eat. The thought of food triggered memories of yesterday, of the storm and of the frightening flash of lightning that had awakened him so abruptly early this morning. He remembered the terrible feeling in the pit of his stomach. Did it signify something in particular or was it just an intestinal upset? He was not sure what it was. Maybe that feeling he experienced was nothing serious at all...a simple little ache fed by an overactive imagination. But a haunting suspicion deep inside him told Aran something terrible had happened...something that would change his life forever.

Traces of his old dream moved through his mind, reminding him of Ireland's need for brave and loyal patriots. Men and women who would give their labour, love and wisdom to see the best of yesterday's old Gaelic world restored and merged with the best of today's new Irish world. It had been Patrick Pearse's dream as well as MacDonagh's, Ceannt's, Plunkett's and many of the others who had led the Rebellion.

Both the schoolmaster and his student wanted to see Ireland returned to the days when Eireann was joined spiritually and socially by a common set of laws and way of life.

As they were fleeing the burning GPO, Pearse had reminded Aran that Ireland needed young people like himself to help her wake up from the state of passive acceptance that had resulted from years of English oppressive domination. Pearse knew Eireann had the strength and resources to throw off the yoke that bound her, but the people must first unite and work together before the British demons could be cast aside. Aran thought he had the will and, hopefully, the skill to aid Ireland in her struggle to assert itself. Over the past months, Pearse and others had started Ireland back down that road toward national independence. Now, it was up to him and others to carry on the work with or without his teacher's leadership.

Lost in thought, Aran Roe found himself on the outskirts of Athy, a small village in County Kildare. Fearing an armed stranger would attract unwanted attention, Aran stashed his shotgun, haversack and Colt .45 in the ruins of an old abandoned building which was well hidden from the road by a grove of trees and an unkempt hedgerow covered with wildly blooming fuchsia.

As he walked through the town square, Aran noticed it was almost eleven o'clock by the old market house clock.

The ringing bells of a church several blocks away called little groups of villagers and lone individuals to its sunlit and candle lighted nave. The churchgoers headed across the arched River Barrow bridge, past White's Castle, over hard packed earthen streets and through Athy's cobbled laneways. They climbed the hand-cut Wicklow granite steps in hushed silence, disappearing inside the old building in prayerful reverence.

He had not been to Mass since Easter Sunday though he had been blessed, had said the rosary on several occasions and had received Holy Communion last week inside the confines of the GPO.

Aran, secure in the knowledge that the authorities did not know his identify or political convictions, felt quite safe. If questioned, he had decided to state that he had been staying with friends in Rathfarnham while he looked for work in Dublin. But his efforts to find employment had been interrupted by the Rebellion. Out of money and concerned for his own safety, he decided to head for home and the security of the family farm in County Galway.

Just in case the authorities queried him further, Aran recited aloud the second half of his alibi. "Ah sure, 'tis such a fine spring, sir. With all the grand weather, I decided to take in some of the countryside on my return journey home. I've never before ventured very far from Gort and, as I'm now seventeen, I thought it was about time I did some travelling and seeing of this fine world of ours. "Unfortunately, sir, things just didn't work out as I'd planned them so I'm going back home to my family."

Convinced his cover story was plausible, Aran entered the village church and knelt down in a pew near the back.

Carefully, he looked around to see if his presence had created a stir. Satisfied he had not drawn attention to himself and, as nothing seemed out of place or unusual to him, he closed his eyes in prayer.

During the Mass, the priest briefly spoke of last week's 'troubles' in Dublin. He talked of the needless and wasteful loss of life and of the wanton destruction of private and civic property. The clergyman pointed the finger of blame at dissatisfied and selfish 'Shinners' who had caused the rioting and fighting. He thanked God that Irishmen in the surrounding countryside had refused to join in the fight with the ungrateful Dubliners.

The priest summarised last week's 'troubles' with, "What can't be cured must be endured."

He concluded his sermon with sincere and heartfelt prayers for the Irishmen fighting for freedom from oppression and tyranny in Europe.

Aran wondered how the priest could accept the deplorable conditions that existed in Ireland today while condemning similar circumstances that prevailed in other parts of Europe currently being brutalised by the ravages of war? How could he criticise Irishmen who had risen up and struck a blow for their own much deserved freedom? Had not England been a despicable and outrageous overlord for centuries? How the priest could condemn Germany for the same behaviour he accepted from England made no sense to Aran.

Yes, with rare exception, the Irish Catholic bishops had taken the safe and conservative course regarding Anglo-Irish politics. They had consistently opposed any violent or physical force measures designed to throw off the bonds binding England with Ireland.

This practice of mixing politics with religion was an old one. The clergy, especially among its upper echelon, were, in effect, a counter-revolutionary force against the old-time Fenians, against many of the original Land League organisers and now, this papal representative voiced his opinion against the things Pearse and Aran had fought to reverse.

So often the Church's dictates sprung from the concepts of self-protectionism and social conservatism. In fact, Aran remembered that Desmond Ryan, one of Pearse's former students and more recently his personal secretary, had often questioned, "Why were the Bishops always the second line of the British Army of Occupation?"[9-1]

Aran puzzled about the priest's disapproval of Irishmen and women fighting for Irish freedom on Irish soil while he approved of Irishmen fighting for Belgium's freedom on French soil.

Aran had long ago learned that Irish church politics were forever confusing and nothing in the past weeks had happened to change his opinion.

The priest's comments reminded Aran of stories his father and grandfather had told him about Parnell and his Irish Parliamentary Party colleagues during the 1880s. The Catholic clergy was jealous of Parnell's Protestant power as he and others fought the English for Irish land reform and Home Rule. Parnell and his party employed the non-violent tactic of abstaining from voting on key parliamentary issues. The British political party in power at the time, the Whigs, held only the slimmest of majorities over the opposing party, the Tories. Thus, when the Irish party voted as a block, they held and controlled the balance of power in Westminster. By effectively influencing and leading the Irish Parliamentary Party's vote, Parnell became a powerful person. Both British parties constantly played up to him, tried to impress him and courted his voting leadership within the Irish delegation.

Holding such a commanding position with the ability to influence others, the Catholic bishops feared Parnell. They were delighted to see him fall from power and grace when a love affair with a married woman become public knowledge. Though the woman had legally divorced her husband and had married Parnell, the ecclesiastical authorities and many priests blackened his name and publicly destroyed his reputation. Tragically, a forty-five-year-old Parnell died soon after his private life became exposed to public Catholic ridicule.

Aran recalled another time forty years before Parnell when Daniel O'Connell's successors, the largely Protestant-led Young Islanders, received little or no support from the Catholic Church in their efforts to rise up against the might of Great Britain. They had unsuccessfully tried striking a blow for Irish freedom during the turbulent years of the 1840s.

❧

With the Mass over, Aran decided to wait for the small crowd to disperse to their homes or work places. While he knelt waiting, he noticed an attractive young woman guiding three small children up the aisle.

He watched her as she walked past. The woman was about his age or maybe a couple of years older. She wore an embroidered, probably handwoven, full-length skirt and her freshly ironed white blouse was partly hidden by a handmade Irish jumper.

But it was not her clothes that caught Aran's attention. It was the bright, flashing green eyes set in her radiantly tanned face that captured his fancy. Her long, reddish-brown hair fell out from under the white scarf covering her head. The colleen's nose was straight and slightly up-turned. Her figure, though slight, was feminine and appealing. He had never been so drawn to a woman at first glance as he was to this passing stranger.

The way she walked and carried herself told Aran she possessed both strength and fitness gained from some type of physical activity...probably farming. But what struck Aran most of all was the shining glow that illuminated her face when a beam of sunlight fell upon the young woman as she walked past him.

Aran was not sure if it was the sun or his fixed stare, maybe both, but just at that moment, her face turned toward him. Their eyes met. A sudden rush of warmth and excitement surged through him. Her gaze was powerful, intense and, at the same time, gently inviting. It all proved too overpowering for Aran. He closed his eyes and turned away.

A moment later, he reopened them. Hoping to catch another glimpse of this vision of beauty, Aran looked toward the aisle but she had vanished.

Had the woman really walked past him or was that visual encounter a figment of his romantic, adolescent imagination? He was not sure what to believe, but if she was just a dream, why was his body trembling and tingling so?

No other woman, real or imagined, had ever had such an immediate and powerful effect on him. Yes, he remembered sharing the company of young women at crossroad dances, fairs and other social outings, but he had never been attracted or drawn to them as he was to this mysterious vision. Aran had always been more taken with family and farm responsibilities, school and reading interests. More recently, the Irish Volunteer and IRB activities dominated his waking hours. He had never given women or romance a very valued place in his life. Aran always thought there would be plenty of time for such things later.

Back out in the May sunshine, Aran surveyed the village streets. Everything seemed peacefully quiet but, disappointingly, there was no sign of the young woman or the three small children.

Looking on the bright side of things, however, he had not seen a military patrol or the RIC since he had left Roundwood yesterday. Maybe the old man Frank had something to do about that?

As he stood and looked around at the quiet village, Aran wished he had a few 'bob' in his pocket for dinner and some supplies to take along with him on his journey. But without so much as two pennies to rub together he retraced his footsteps back to the ruined building where he had hidden his things.

After a moment of thoughtful contemplation, he decided to circle north around Athy, stay off the main road and cross the River Barrow at an ancient ford he had read about that once was used by his ancestors. He would then head northwest toward Marysborough. If he was lucky and could earn a few shillings along the way, he might shorten his cross-country trip by catching the Dublin train to Galway.

❧

Wet from the waist down after he waded across the river, Aran kept to the byroads and, as he walked along, the Irish Rebel wondered about how the men he had fought with in Dublin were getting on. He fondly remembered Frank, the old man back in Roundwood. He understood the man's torment. Frank loved Ireland but he also cared for his Irish friends who had chosen to support British rule by serving in the RIC. Aran was a realist too. He knew everyone had to earn their crust, but taking the King's shilling...no, not for him...never!

As he continued along the quiet back road, Aran thought of Pearse, Tom Clarke and the wounded James Connolly. What was going to happen to them now that the fighting was over and the Rebellion crushed? Would England tighten its already firm grip on Ireland? How would he keep Patrick Pearse's spirit and quest for a free republic alive in the west of Ireland? Maybe he should try to locate Pearse's friend, Liam Mellowes. Aran wondered if he could count on help from the Irish Volunteers or had they been disbanded and outlawed by Maxwell's newly enforced British law? Everything seemed so uncertain and directionless.

As he imagined the consequences of Ireland's victory in its struggle for independence, Aran dismissed the petty significance of labels or names. It really did not matter to him what the new Ireland would be called...Republic, Dominion, United Free State, Democratic Union...as long as she had her freedom from England's Army of Occupation and was able to determine her own political, economic and social future. He thought of Emmet and again wondered when Ireland would be able to take its rightful place among the free nations of the world?

As he rounded a sharp turn in the road, Aran was surprised to see a stationary horse and butt. The small wagon was filled with children and piled even higher with farm supplies and provisions...all probably just were purchased in Athy. And there, lo and behold, not one hundred feet from his startled step, was the young woman he had seen in the church.

Her white scarf, off her head now, was tied about her neck. The jumper was knotted around her waist and she stood with arms akimbo looking at the horse. Posed there by the little wagon, she exuded an air of frustrated confidence and self-assurance. Her silhouette, again framed by the sun's rays, stirred and quickly intrigued him once more.

As Aran approached, his feet disturbed the chippings on the un-paved surface of the little road. She turned in surprise.

A smile lit her face. "Well, sure I was wondering if I'd ever see that face of yours again?" Pausing, she then continued, "You're not from around these parts, are you?"

"No, I'm just passing through on my way to Marysborough so," replied Aran.

As he spoke, he quickly glanced over her shoulder and decided to change the subject. "Something wrong with the wagon or your horse?" asked Aran. He nodded his head in the rig's direction.

"Yes, as a matter of fact. My horse has picked up a stone. I just can't seem to get it out. Unfortunately for us, I don't have my knife with me this morning."

He could hear the exasperation rising in her soft voice.

During the brief conversation with the young woman, Aran noticed that the curious horse was eyeing him suspiciously. Additionally, the three children in the wagon were peering intently over its sides at him as if waiting for something to happen.

"Here, let me have a look," said Aran. He took the horse's reins from the woman's grasp while carefully handing her his shotgun. She took it with a knowing hand.

Aran stepped up to the beast and gently patted the nervous animal. While he rubbed its forehead and neck, he spoke softly into the horse's ear. With this special attention, the powerful animal calmed down and now stood quietly with the stranger holding its bridle.

With movements learned through many years of practice, Aran lifted the horse's leg and placed the tender hoof between his knees. He slipped his hunting knife out of its sheath, applied careful pressure under the offending stone, popping it loose.

Releasing the leg, Aran again patted and stroked the huge animal. It turned and nuzzled his shoulder as if to say thank you.

"There, that should see ye safely on your way. I don't think your horse should have any more trouble, but you might just keep an eye on that hoof for a day or two," declared Aran. He took back his shotgun, recradling it in the crook of his arm.

"Well, thanks be to God you came along when you did," said the smiling woman as she turned toward the children.

They smiled too and nodded expressions of gratitude in Aran's direction.

Then the youngest one, a girl of about six, said in a loud, hopeful voice, "Why don't you come home with us and have some dinner?"

Before Aran could politely refuse, the other two children chimed in, "Yes, yes, come home with us. Can he Brigid...can he?"

Aran grinned, but replied, "I better be on my way."

He turned and started walking on ahead of the horse and butt.

Before he had taken more than three steps, she spoke, "...then it's all settled. I hope you like lamb and roasted potatoes?"

His empty stomach and racing heart stopped him in his tracks. "That sounds wonderful...if it isn't too much bother?"

"No, it won't be, but we wouldn't tell you if it was," came her honest reply highlighted by her twinkling green eyes.

She continued, "Mind you, you'll have to walk. The wagon is too full for another body. But, just so you don't get lost, I'll ride back and pick you up after I drop off the children and supplies."

Her soft musical voice rang with confidence and a sense of humour. He guessed she was used to giving orders from her manner and tone of voice.

"Just keep walking along this little bit of road for about two miles. Turn right at the first laneway immediately after passing over a little stone bridge. Follow that boreen for about a mile...it's the first house you come to. You can't miss it, but I'll have caught back up to you before then."

With that, she was up on the wagon seat and trotting off down the road at a steady clip.

Aran did not know what to think. Becoming tangled up with this family was the last thing he wanted. He did not feel relaxed around strangers. Not knowing their political sentiments made him feel uncomfortable when talk turned to important issues.

He thought he had better keep to himself and continue putting Dublin's ruined Rebellion further behind him.

Though the choice was a difficult one to make, Aran took careful note of the stone bridge and boreen when he passed by them thirty-some minutes later.

When all the 'troubles' were over and things had settled down, he would return and properly introduce himself to that lovely woman who had momentarily cast a spell on him.

❧

Aran had walked a short distance past the little bridge when he heard the sounds of horses coming up from behind. Deciding to avoid any possible danger, he jumped a low stone wall and ducked down behind it. From his position, Aran had a limited view of the road through the gaps in the loosely stacked stones.

As the horses drew nearer, Aran cocked the hammer of his shotgun and waited.

A moment later, a vision of beauty galloped past him. It was Brigid. She rode a well-groomed black mare that was followed by a riderless chestnut-brown stallion several hands taller than her own horse.

Aran wanted to stand up and wave, but something inside him told him to stay down and remain hidden behind the wall. Obeying this inner voice, Aran permitted the young woman to ride past undisturbed and out of sight down the road.

After several more minutes of hiding, Aran decided he was being too careful. He did not know if it was his stomach or his heart or both taking command. Nimbly he climbed back over the stone wall and started walking down the road in the direction the colleen had ridden.

In a few minutes, Brigid rode back into view trotting toward him. She waved and he returned her salute as she closed the distance between them.

"Changed your mind, did you so?" laughed Brigid. "Any man who decides to miss one of my meals has either just eaten or is running away from something.

"You've said you're a stranger and from the looks of ye you've been living rough. I'd guess you've been through some hard times. I heard your stomach growling back there when you were minding my horse. I'm guessing you must be on the run from something or someone."

She spoke honestly and with a frankness Aran was not accustomed to hearing from a stranger, much less a female one.

"Yes, I did change my mind about eating with you and your family. I didn't want to be a bother to anyone," lied Aran.

"Do you know how to ride a horse?" interjected Brigid not wanting to discuss the matter any further.

Aran nodded yes. A big smile crossed his face.

"I thought so. Here, Connor should suit you just fine. Oh, by the way, my name is Brigid...Brigid Eileen O'Mahony."

She tossed the big stallion's reigns in Aran's direction and nudged her horse in the side with her riding boots.

As Aran pulled himself up onto the broad-backed, saddled stallion, he responded, "I'm Aran Roe O'Neill from Gort, County Galway. I'm on my way home after not finding work in Dublin."

But his last few words were lost to the wind as he urged his mount onward in a vain attempt to catch the youthful woman on her fast-flying steed.

A left turn just before the bridge and up a long gentle incline to a tree-lined ridge. Then, down a curving lane, past several fields of ripe corn, over a small stream and along a low stone wall and ditch. Finally, she turned right into a tidy farmyard dominated by a thatched cottage on one side and well-kept byre on the other. Behind the barn was a stable. Some farming equipment was stored under an open-sided shed off to one side.

Two sheep dogs announced the riders arrival and an old woman surrounded by the three children came out to greet them as they tied their horses to a wooden railing next to the house.

Brigid introduced Aran to the others and for a few moments all five stood looking at him without saying a word.

"He's the man who fixed Old Sean's hoof, Gran," announced the little one, breaking the brief but awkward silence.

"Where are you from?" "What were ye doing walking down our road?" "What's that gun for?" "What are you about?" The children's questions exploded like water over rocky falls.

Coming to Aran's aid Brigid commanded, "Hush now, all ye! Aran's from County Galway. He's heading home after not finding work in Dublin."

Aran stood in amazed silence. He was surprised she had heard much less understood what he had said as the race for the cottage had swallowed his words.

But, as he stood in the front garden displaying an unaccustomed boyish awkwardness, she disappeared inside the cottage herding the children along in front of her.

He was still looking around the farmyard when Brigid reappeared, interrupting his thoughts. "Are you coming in or do you want to be served where you're standing?"

"I'll be pleased to join ye inside if I was ever formally invited?" returned a teasing Aran.

"Dinner will be ready in a few minutes. Let me show you where to wash up," retorted Brigid returning his grin.

As she led Aran through the cottage and out the back door, she chattered away to him over her shoulder.

The three children were all waiting for them on the back porch...lined up as if they were expecting to meet someone important. "This is Annie, the little one with all the questions. She's rising seven. Next to her is Rory. He's eleven. Last, but not least, is eight-year-old Mary. In the kitchen...that was Gran, our grandmother. She's putting the finishing touches on what should be a brilliant meal. Now, Rory and his sisters will show you where we clean up for dinner."

With that, the vision of loveliness disappeared back inside the cottage.

Rory filled a metal basin with warm water from the kitchen cooker and gave Aran a new piece of soap along with a clean soft fluffy towel.

With the children curiously watching from a discreet distance, the Irish Rebel began washing his hands and face.

As he did so, Aran reflected on his quick tour through the one-room cottage. He had noticed the kitchen and dining area were confined to one part of the big room. The flagged sitting room occupied the other half of the home. There were big fireplaces at both ends of the comfortable dwelling and he guessed everyone slept up above in the loft just under the thatched roof.

Outside, along the back wall of the cottage, was a wooden porch covered by a low roof that had been added after the cottage's initial construction. The addition looked quite new, while the original stone building was years old. On the porch was a long narrow wooden form that held other basins for washing, some freshly folded clothes and an assorted collection of empty glass bottles and jars.

Four comfortable sugan chairs were grouped around a small table at the other end of the porch. Garden flowers bloomed in well cared for beds bordering the new addition.

After his refreshing and much needed wash up, as modest as it was, the Gortman walked back into the kitchen.

"Ah sure, this place smells just like home," exclaimed Aran to Gran who was busy serving up the dinner. Being in this comfortable cottage with its home cooking and friendly smiles reminded him of just how homesick he really was.

Brigid called everyone to the table and Aran could hardly wait to taste the delicious-looking, steaming hot food.

Rory thanked God for their bountiful meal and welcomed the newcomer again.

As they sat around the table enjoying Brigid's and Gran's culinary creations, Aran learned Brigid and her grandmother were the heads of the family. The three children, Rory, Mary and Annie, were motherless from Annie's birth. Brigid had an older brother, Andrew, who lived with an aunt in Kilkenny and the oldest sibling, a sister named Hannah, had been away in Amerikay for almost five years. She worked as a housekeeper for a wealthy Irish-American family living on the east coast.

Brigid's father, an officer in an Irish regiment of the British army, had been killed in France during the early part of the First War. He had left the land to Andrew but his son showed no interest in managing a farm. He wanted to be a banker and businessman. Greatly relieved of its burden, Andy was glad Brigid took an interest in the family land and its growing prosperity.

Brigid declined to state her age in response to Aran's leading question, "Farming is hard work for such a young woman...how do you manage?"

With a look of proud determination and resolve, she stated, "I manage quite well, thank you!" Softening her tone, Brigid continued, "Besides the wonderful help of those around this table, excluding yourself of course, Peter Ryan, his family and I are very well able to make a go of it on our own."

Aran soon learned that the Ryan's, a tenant family, provided strong backs and wise council to a grateful Brigid. They lived just up the lane on twenty acres given to them in Captain O'Mahony's will.

The farm itself, excluding the Ryans' land, was an impressive seventy-eight acres in size. They grazed fifteen milk cows plus almost one hundred head of sheep. In addition to the livestock, the O'Mahonys grew barley, wheat and hay. Gran and the children kept a large vegetable and flower garden behind the cottage and the four of them took turns caring for the hens, geese and Queenie, the family pet goat.

Brigid's father had purchased the farm after the Wyndham Land Reform Act of 1903, thus maintaining a six-hundred-year-old family tradition. Members of the O'Mahony clan had worked this land for centuries with the exception of a hundred and fifty-odd years between 1651 and 1803.

In 1649, Oliver Cromwell, England's Lord General and later its Lord

Protector, led his New Model Army into Ireland to rob, murder and terrorise the Catholic population. He ran the O'Mahonys and others like them off their native soil that had first been taken from them in the 1500s during the Tudor reign. But the English planters of the sixteenth century needed farm labour so the former landowners were allowed to stay on their old land working as surfs for their new 'masters.' But then, with the Puritans in power, the Irish peasants had to flee their prosperous land. They were forced to find shelter on the rocky, mountainous land west of the River Shannon. Cromwell had promised this usurped Irish land to his soldiers and supporters in payment and reward for their barbarous and murderous transgressions committed in the name of religious vengeance and Protestant purification.

When the table conversation turned to Aran, Brigid was quick to divert the talk away from him and on to other topics. Aran sensed her awareness and appreciated her protectiveness. He did not want to go into detail about his recent adventures though he did speak freely about his life at home on the family farm.

After the fine meal was finished and the dishes washed, Aran and Brigid sat quietly alone on the back porch. A storm was brewing and swift-moving, boiling black clouds were piling up in the sky. The wind had shifted and the smell of rain was in the air. The hawthorn, chestnut and sycamore trees surrounding the cottage moaned and their green leaves waved wildly, exposing their whitish undersides to the sky above.

Aran was about to ask if he could wait and resume his journey after the storm passed, but it was Brigid who broke the silence. "Aran, I know there is a lot you haven't said, but all in good time. Right now, I need some extra help here on the farm. If you wouldn't mind staying over a few days, I've a crop of early hay to cut and my sheep need shearing. Peter and I could use another experienced hand. You can sleep over there in the byre, have your meals with us and I'll pay you a shilling a day if you'll stay and work with us. Interested so?"

Aran sat in thoughtful contemplation as his insides churned. But, before the rational side of him could formulate an intelligent "no", he replied, "Yes, I'll stay a couple of days to help out...but no longer."

Later, as he rethought his decision to remain, it made good sense to him.

He reasoned that on this secluded farm he would be out of the authority's sight, allowing more time to elapse since the Roundwood episode. Hopefully, the RIC would lose interest in trying to find him, if in fact they were on his trail at all. There were only three more people who could identify him...Frank and the two surviving RIC policemen. Yes, staying was not such a bad idea after all, besides there was Brigid...

But at that moment, sitting on the porch with her and watching the storm blow up, he was not so sure he had made the right decision.

She smiled at him and said, "We both know our meeting was more than mere chance, but let's not analyse things just yet. We'll know and understand more in the weeks and months to come."

Aran felt uncomfortable. He was not used to having serious conversations with unknown women. Most of his life had been spent being with and working around men or members of his family. Talking with such a beautiful and intelligent woman was a new experience. He thought caution and prudence were the wisest avenues of approach, at least for the moment. He would keep his guard up and his mouth shut for a little while longer.

Before the rain arrived, Brigid took Aran to the byre and pointed out a truckle bed in one corner. She covered its mattress with clean sheets and a feather-filled eiderdown. After some searching, they found and cleaned up an old brass oil lamp. Again, shining like its old self, Brigid put it on the small table next to the bed.

When she had finished straightening everything up, she turned to Aran saying, "There now, you should be quite comfortable out here. Sure, is there anything else you're after needing so?"

"No, you're grand Brigid...everything is perfect. I'm long overdue a good night's sleep in a proper bed. I'm sure I won't have any difficulty falling asleep here." Aran smiled down at the attractive woman standing next to him.

With the formalities decided as to where he would sleep and with a rough idea of the farm work required of him for the next several days, Aran excused himself. He went out to the stable and helped Rory rub down, feed and water the horses. It was time he started repaying the O'Mahonys for the generous hospitality they had shown to him.

❧

The storm finally arrived and, as the rain continued to fall without much hope of its letting up, Aran spent several hours cleaning out the stable, spreading fresh straw and sharpening the two scythes hanging on their wall pegs.

Finally, the steady rain stopped. Only a light mist was falling as Aran finished up his chores. Looking up from his work, the Gortman was surprised by Brigid who had a clean shirt, trousers, socks and underclothing that had been her father's. With the prospects of clean clothes to wear, Aran asked about the possibilities of a bath.

Thinking of his privacy, Brigid dragged out to the byre a big zinc bath tub that was stored under the back porch. Aran filled it with water pumped from the well while Rory kindly brought out several buckets of steaming hot water heated on the big black range in the kitchen. Its addition took the chill off his bath and made soaking in the tub a delight.

As he lingered in the soft warm water, Aran let the soap work its cleansing power as it penetrated his every pore. It had been three days since his bath at Thomas and Anna's house in Dublin and he had walked many dirty miles of dusty Irish roads since then.

Upon emerging from his soak, Aran Roe felt clean and new again. His skin glowed and he felt like a changed man. The afternoon farm work and now the bath were a refreshing release from the terror and physical stress of war and life on the run.

With a meal, a bath, a clean change of clothes and his renewed feeling of vitality, the days Aran had spent in the GPO and his subsequent escape from the British authorities seemed a lifetime ago. If it was not for his continued concern and apprehension about Pearse's and the other's well-being, he did not have a care in the world.

Aran joined the family for evening tea. Afterwards, all six of them gathered around a turf fire in the sitting room. Brigid, Gran and he enjoyed more cups of tea while the children sang school songs and recited little verses from memory.

Gran told stories her grandmother used to tell about the Penal Years when the Irish were forced to worship outdoors around Mass rocks and children were taught by travelling teachers who instructed their charges under the shadows of hedgerows.

Aran spoke of his friendship with Robert and Lady Gregory. He talked about the times he had spent beside the ancient round tower of Kilmacduagh. He noticed, however, that everyone was careful to keep politics out of the conversation. It was an understandable caution given the current level of unrest in the countryside around Dublin. Aran was still a stranger and they were as careful as he to avoid bringing up any controversial issues.

As the fire grew low and the hour late, Aran stood up, excused himself and said, "Good night." He again thanked everyone for the grand meal, the lovely evening and their kindness to him.

Brigid walked him to the back door and offered him a small red-globed oil lamp to guide him safely out to the byre.

Later, as he stood looking out the doorway of his humble lodgings, he saw her standing on the back porch looking up at the now clear night sky. Aran knew Brigid was no ordinary woman. An eerie feeling crept over him that destiny had somehow brought them together. Yes, it seemed the special spirit surrounding him from birth appeared to be looking after him once again. Was this woman destined to play a significant role in his future...maybe even share the rest of his life with him?

As he tucked himself into bed, Aran thought about her sainted name-sake, Brighid, who helped bring the gift of Christianity to Ireland fourteen hundred years ago. Once again the Irish Rebel wondered if this modern-day Brigid was somehow going to aid him in his efforts to free Ireland?

He closed his eyes and remembered how that sixth-century Brigid had woven crosses made of reeds to illustrate and explain the concept of the Trinity to pagans. Now, was this lovely saint-like, twentieth-century Brigid going to help him raise Ireland's cross of freedom so all the world might honour and respect Eireann's right to be a free, democratic and independent nation?

His last conscious thoughts were of Emmet and Pearse...Hopefully, the day was not too far off when Robert Emmet's epitaph could finally be written...and that Patrick Henry Pearse would be alive to celebrate that monumental occasion.

Deep and dreamless sleep finally interrupted his fantasies as a faint smile illuminated Aran Roe O'Neill's peaceful face.

10. *Home*

While the world did gaze, with deep amaze, at those
fearless men but few,
Who bore the fight that Freedom's light might shine
through the Foggy Dew...

The Foggy Dew / Rev. P. O'Neill

The next day was filled with backbreaking work. The reaping hook, pitchfork and scythe flashed under a bright blue sky dotted with billowy white clouds. Rory and the dogs rounded up the sheep while Aran and Peter clipped and sheared a winter's growth of wool from the backs and bellies of the bleating animals.

From early morning till past sunset, they worked together...Aran, Brigid, young Rory and the four Ryan's. The O'Mahonys' neighbour, a man called Sonny, arrived with his two sons just after midday. They willingly pitched in to help with the afternoon toiling.

Gran and the two girls made contributions as well. With their buckets of tea strong enough to trot a mouse across the top of it, sandwiches and lovely apple cake, it was truly a collective effort.

Later that evening, after Brigid had returned to the cottage to help Gran with the family's tea, Sonny stopped by once again on his way back home from Athy to tell Brigid that he and his two sons would return in the morning to lend a hand. He had just left when Aran walked through the back door after having a quick wash up.

From the kitchen porch Aran heard Sonny say, "...isn't it a terrible thing...and they were such fine Irishmen too."

His comments were followed by the sound of the front door closing. The Gortman guessed Brigid's neighbour was heading home for the night.

As Aran strolled through the kitchen and into the sitting room, he noticed Brigid seated on the couch before the fire, pouring over a newspaper. Sonny must have dropped it off for them to read.

Tired from his day's labour, Aran slowly walked over to the fire and tossed another wooden block onto its dancing flames. He knew Gran was out on the porch and he had seen the children in the back garden feeding Queenie.

Turning to look at Brigid's dirt-stained face, still unwashed from the day's work, Aran Roe was surprised to see tears running down her cheeks. Their wetness stained the newspaper spread out across her lap. Her hands shook while her lips formed a tight line of stern determination.

"What is it, Brigid?" inquired Aran, sitting down beside her.

But before she could answer, Aran noticed the newspaper's bold headlines, "FOUR MORE SHINNERS EXECUTED." It was *The Irish Times* dated yesterday. Without saying a word, she handed the newspaper to Aran then buried her face in a handkerchief.

Aran quickly read the paper's accompany story. "Early this morning four more leaders of the Sinn Fein Rebellion met their just desserts at the hands of General Sir John Maxwell's firing squad. The four executed men were Joseph Mary Plunkett, age twenty-eight, Director of Military Operations for the Irish Volunteer Force; Edward Daly, age twenty-four, First Battalion Commandant of troops that had been stationed in and around the Four Courts complex; Michael O'Hanrahan, age thirty-nine, Quartermaster-General of the Irish Volunteer Force and Vice-Commandant of the forces which had occupied Jacob's Biscuit Factory; and William Pearse, age thirty-four, art teacher at Scoil Eanna in Rathfarnham. William's brother, Patrick Henry Pearse, the school's headmaster and Rebellion leader, was executed yesterday."

The article went on to detail how on Wednesday, May 3rd the first of the Rising's leaders were shot...Thomas Clarke, Thomas MacDonagh and the self-declared President of the Irish Republic's Provisional Government, Patrick Pearse.

Aran was dumbstruck! Tears wells up in his eyes. A huge lump filled his throat. He dropped the newspaper on the floor and stood up. Walking over to the fireplace, the young rebel stared into the tongues of flame licking at the blocks of wood and glowing sods of turf. Brigid rose and followed him across the room. Her strong hands reached out in a vain attempt to comfort his trembling shoulders.

Aran's mind was a whirl. The guards at Richmond were right. How many more would die before it was over? Beside the military leaders, he found it difficult to believe poor Willie was dead too. That was murder!

He had nothing to do with the Rebellion. He had just tagged along behind his older brother, Patrick. His execution was revenge...pure and simple revenge.

Before the paper had fallen from his hands, Aran also noticed a short clip stating that Joe Plunkett and his fiancée, Grace Gifford, had been married in Kilmainham's candlelit chapel just prior to his execution. English soldiers had acted as the couple's witnesses, while after the ceremony, other guards were posted inside his cell. The authorities allowed the newly married couple ten minutes of supervised togetherness before Plunkett was taken out and shot.

❧

As the days passed, Ireland learned that another eight men died as a result of Maxwell's orders. Major John MacBride, who had played a very minor role in the Rising was shot, no doubt, because of his anti-British and pro-Boer activities. Some fifteen years earlier, he had been a leader of the militant Irish Brigade in South Africa's Boer War. Eamonn Ceannt, one of Aran's favourite teachers at St. Enda's, was executed for his fighting leadership as Dublin's 4th Battalion Commandant positioned at South Dublin Union. Young Sean Heuston and his youthful colleague, Con Colbert, who together were responsible for all the student military training at St. Enda's died before yet another English firing squad. Michael Mallin, Chief of Staff for Connolly's Citizen Army, also met his fate in Kilmainham's Stonebreaker's Yard. Even charismatic Sean Mac Diarmada, Chief Recruiting Officer for the Irish Republican Brotherhood, crippled from a childhood illness, received no mercy. After Sean's early morning execution on May 12th, James Connolly himself was carried into Stonebreaker's Yard, tied to a chair, and filled with British bullets. It was a typically British response to the difficult Irish question...might over right because might equals right! Finally, Thomas Kent, a confirmed Nationalist and loyal member of the Volunteer Executive in County Cork, was captured by Crown forces after a shoot-out. Eventually, he too was executed on May 9th in Cork City.

In ten days, fifteen leaders and heroes of an occupied Irish nation were coldly murdered, forever earning General Maxwell the Irish nickname 'Bloody' Maxwell. Fearing the rebels' graves might become martyrs' shrines to Ireland's lost freedom and British injustice, Maxwell buried his fourteen Dublin bodies in a mass grave filled with quicklime at Arbour Hill Military Cemetery. The General knew the lime would make quick work of their mortal remains, leaving nothing for future Fenians or 'Shinners' to venerate and worship. He was determined not to reward the Rebellion's violence despite the age-old injustices Britain had allowed to fester in Ireland.

Maxwell, however, failed to calculate the power and strength of the dead men's spirits. Within days of the Rebellion's end, the country's anti-nationalistic feelings toward the Rising's leaders dramatically changed. Maxwell's murder of Pearse and his followers plus the imprisonment of more than two thousand Irish citizens turned the tide against the English occupation in favour of Irish independence.

Pearse's gamble was paying off after all. Though his carefully planned Rebellion had failed in a military sense, it had touched the hearts and souls of the Irish people. Soon they would unleash a newly ignited nationalistic spirit that would not subside until Innisfail had rid itself of England's domination.

Pearse was right again when he had said, "To die for Ireland is to live." Though dead in the physical sense, the leaders of the Easter Rebellion continued to live in the hearts, the minds and the spirits of millions of Irishmen and women around the world.

Within days of the executions, an Irish newspaper featured a chronology of the Stranger's rule in Ireland. It demanded Britain's immediate renouncement of the 1800 Act of Union that had legally bound the two nations together for more than a century. In calling for Eireann's long overdue independence, the article included a statement uttered in 1903 by Eamon de Valera, one of three Rebellion battalion commandants to escape a British firing squad. Back then de Valera was still a student at University College Blackrock in County Dublin.

> Is it that the problem is too hard for English statesman to solve? They pretend they can legislate for us better than we could for ourselves. And yet if we had but a free Parliament in College Green for the space of one single hour, this vexing question would be put to rest forever. It seems, indeed, that Englishmen, even the most liberal amongst them, with one or two notable exceptions, have never been able to understand the needs of Ireland properly.[10-1]

Eamon de Valera, Commandant of Dublin's 3rd Battalion, who fought and defended Boland's Mill during the Easter Rebellion, had correctly analysed the ongoing Anglo-Irish dilemma thirteen years before the Rising. England and the English did not understand Ireland

and the Irish. History was replete with examples and, once again, the British had erred on the side of overreaction. In putting down the uprising, England had antagonised the Irish citizenry who initially supported Great Britain's efforts in the First War and, more recently, in putting a stop to the fighting in Dublin. But England's cruel, impulsive and vindictive behaviour toward Ireland as a whole, not just toward the rebels, reversed national sentiments and further embittered the Irish people toward their English neighbours.

❧

The newspaper stories about the Rebellion crushed Aran. His mind raced back to the shed on the hill. He remembered the storm, the lightning and the thunder that had frightened and disturbed him so.

Was it just a coincidence or had it been some sign from above? Had the storm signified Pearse's earthly demise and spiritual assent? Was it some kind of Godly message sent to him on the wave of that huge clap of thunder?

He did not know what to think.

Brigid tugged at Aran's arm, pulling him back to the couch. Sitting them down together, she wrapped her arms around his spiritless body and held him close to her breast. After several moments, she sensed his gradual awaking to her caring presence. Neither of them, however, said a word. The young woman just slowly rocked the Irish Rebel in the warmth of her tenderness while gently stroking his tearstreaked face.

Minutes passed. Aran Roe O'Neill's mind was spinning. His body felt drained of all life.

As if to shut out reality's cruelty, Aran, with his eyes closed, imagined Pearse's wise and kindly face smiling down upon him through the foggy veil of emotional shock. He even fantasised he could hear Pearse speaking to him. The words were slow and measured. But gradually, the familiar voice of his teacher grew in strength as Aran imagined Pearse now standing before him. "Aran...when I was a child of ten...I went on my bare knees...by my bedside one night...and promised God...that I should devote my life...to an effort...to free my country. I have kept...that promise." [10 2]

Patrick Pearse's image faded and slowly disappeared. Gradually, human sensation flooded back, filling Aran's sense of emptiness. He became aware of Brigid's presence. He felt her strong, warm arms wrapped around his grief-strickened body.

As she brushed away his tears, her body rocked slowly...swaying to and fro like a bending branch on a breezy summer's day. His mind recalled the stately, initial-carved copper beech in Lady Gregory's walled demesne near his Gort home. He remembered the happy hours spent under its shady boughs with his friend Robert.

Quietly, Brigid began humming some musical refrain to soothe his terrible sorrow. Slowly, as the melody came to life, the notes grew in strength and conviction and the song spilled forth from Brigid's lips.

Almost at once Aran thought he recognised the tune and its words. It was something he had heard before... something... something... something by Thomas Moore. Yes, it was one of Moore's famed melodies... it was *The Minstrel Boy:*

> The Minstrel Boy to the war is gone,
> In the ranks of death you'll find him;
> His father's sword he has girded on,
> And his wild harp slung behind him.
> "Land of Song!" said the warrior bard,
> "Tho' all the world betrays thee,
> One sword, at least thy rights shall guard,
> One faithful harp shall praise thee!" 10-3

As Brigid finished the verse, Aran pulled himself free of her arms, sat back and looked at the woman. Her face was radiant...alive with emotion and feeling. As they faced one another, his eyes tried to probe her innermost thoughts.

Finally, with her emotions spinning as well, Brigid reached out and held his face in her trembling hands.

"I knew you must have been part of last week's Rebellion. You had the look of a warrior all about you. Though you picked your words carefully, I sensed freedom's burning passion within you. Ah sure, Aran, I too yearn for the day when this land of ours will no longer be enslaved by the English chains that bind us so..."

Aran smiled and closed his eyes again. As Pearse's last words echoed in his head, they were joined by hers. Suddenly, Aran Roe O'Neill realised something of significance was happening to him. Ireland's torch of freedom had been passed from Pearse's generation down to his. The flame of Irish hope...of Ireland's future...was now in his hands...in the hands of men and women like Brigid and himself. It was up to them to step forward now and assume the mantle of leadership left by the fallen heroes of Easter Week.

Brigid gently interrupted his thoughts. "When you are ready, I want you to tell me all about it. I want to know you, Aran. I want to know you...to understand you...to be part of your hopes and dreams. I want to be by your side and live those longings. I want to help you fight your battles. Oh, Aran...Aran..."

Aran Roe O'Neill could not fully comprehend everything that was happening to him. He felt as if he was floating on some magic carpet far above the earth. His mind and body became separated. His emotions were elevated to such a height that he imagined he was soaring on the wind like a bird in flight.

Aran wondered if this was what it was like to be in love or maybe dead...he had never known such feelings before in his life.

Brigid leaned over and kissed him. It was not a deep, passionate kiss, but a soft, gentle inviting one. Aran's lips responded to hers in return. Gently his hands wove their way through her tumbled hair that had fallen onto her shoulders framing her radiant face.

Just at that moment, something broke the spell he was under. Aran sensed they were no longer alone. Turning, he saw Gran standing by the cooker staring at them. The elderly woman seemed surprised and confused but said nothing.

With the two of them returning her gaze, Gran turned and walked back outside onto the porch.

Brigid stood up. It was time for her to collect the children. Their evening's tea was ready.

❧

Later, as they all sat around the table, Brigid told the children and her grandmother of the newspaper articles about the Rebellion. Up until then they had only heard vague rumours from Athy plus the occasional story from an infrequent passer-by. Now, everything became clearer as the newspaper painted a grim picture of the Rising and its gory aftermath.

The children wanted to know why the two of them had been crying. Brigid simply replied that Aran knew some of the people in Dublin who had been killed in the fighting. His sorrow at their death had caused the both of them to be very sad. She promised to explain everything in more detail soon. Tonight, however, they should each give thanks go God for Aran's safe deliverance. A second prayer might also be offered up for the souls of those brave soldiers who lost their lives fighting for Ireland's freedom.

❧

That evening, after the children had gone to bed, Aran told Brigid of his sudden decision to leave early the following morning.

Besides the newspaper's report of the leaders' deaths and some sketchy, biased details about the fighting, he had noticed a small article proclaiming, "REVOLT CRUSHED IN COUNTY GALWAY."

The story reported that a number of rebels had been routed from their headquarters near Athenry as their leaders were forced to go on the run. It mentioned the name of Liam Mellowes and stated that the authorities expected to arrest him in or around Limerick Town within a matter of days.

As Brigid and Aran sat by a slowly dying fire, he told her of his meeting Pearse, of his move to Dublin, of the fighting in the GPO and his escape into the Wicklow Mountains. She listened with wide-eyed amazement to his growing list of breathtaking adventures. With all there was to talk about, it was almost midnight before they said 'good night' to each other.

Prior to retiring for the night, Brigid filled his old haversack with food and decided he should ride Conor, the dashing chestnut stallion, to her brother's in Kilkenny. She wrote Andrew a short note introducing him and asked Andy to help Aran in any way he possibly could. Andrew would mind the horse and return it to her in a week or so.

The real reason, however, for Aran's going to Kilkenny was that some of Andrew's friends were postal clerks on the evening train to Limerick. With any luck, they might be able to smuggle him aboard the mail car without the conductor's knowledge. The British authorities were keeping a close watch on all rail stations throughout the country. If everything went just right, he would be in Limerick by late tomorrow night.

Before crossing to the byre to sleep, Aran and Brigid stood together on the back porch, holding each other close. Not knowing when they would see each other again, they dared not speak of the future. Instead, they pledged not to forsake one another while praying to God they would be reunited soon.

Looking up, they gazed at a heaven filled with millions of stars. Aran imagined that one of those twinkling lights was the burning spirit of Patrick Henry Pearse looking down on the two of them. Now with Brigid by his side, Aran envisioned he would be twice as strong and twice as able to carry through with the tasks Pearse had left undone. He vowed not to let his teacher or the others down...not Brigid...not himself!

❧

Before sunrise, the Irish Rebel was dressed, had the great horse saddled and was ready to depart. With the directions to Brigid's aunt's house safely tucked away in his head, Aran swung his leg up over the steed's broad back. Softly nudging his heels into its flanks, Aran rode out of the farmyard. Reaching the boreen, he turned and looked back at the cottage. There, framed in the doorway, was Brigid. Holding a candle in one hand, she waved and blew him a kiss with the other. He waved back, turned in the saddle, and galloped off allowing the fading darkness to swallow him up.

Having left the RIC's shotgun, Thomas's Colt .45 and his British Webley revolver, a sourvenir of the Brendan Road shoot-out, carefully hidden away in the byre, Aran felt naked and unprotected riding along toward Kilkenny. His weapons of war had been so important to him during his fortnight's struggle to stay alive. Now, without their comfort and protection, he felt defenceless. But, he and Brigid agreed there was more to fear from the authorities by carrying the weapons than there was to dread from not having them in his possession.

Not wanting to attract any attention, Aran rode carefully along by-roads and back lanes. This tactic, however, forced him to hold back his eager mount who wanted to race over the little used country roads. Conor seemed impatient and did not understand Aran's cautious tactics. A racing horse and rider would only have attracted unwanted attention.

Finally, just past noon, Aran found himself in front of the O'Mahonys' house just north of Kilkenny Town. Andrew answered his knock and, after carefully reading Brigid's note, invited Aran through into the dining room. His father's unmarried sister, known simply as Auntie O'Mahony, and Andrew were just sitting down to eat their noonday meal. They graciously invited Aran to join them at the table.

Adding some details to Brigid's letter, Aran described how he had spent a day and a half working at their old family farm, but now it was imperative he proceed on to Limerick without delay. A friend of his who had been involved in the 'troubles' last week needed his assistance. He felt it was his duty to go. Aran stressed that every discretion on their part was essential for his continued safety and their personal well-being.

The two O'Mahony's were wise enough to read between the lines of Brigid's letter and Aran's abbreviated explanation. They declined to press the Gortman for more details about his desire to remain under cover.

Andrew assured him a smuggled ride should not be difficult to arrange. He thought his friends could slip him aboard the train's postal car that very evening. At any rate, he would go to town immediately after dinner and try to make all the necessary arrangements.

Not knowing when their newcomer would be able to sleep again, Andrew showed Aran to a small bedroom on the first floor of the farmhouse and invited him to rest while he was gone. Andy hoped to be back before their evening tea.

"Aran, if everything goes smoothly, I'll take you into town tonight and my friends will slip you on board the ten o'clock train to Limerick. Ah sure, they'll be glad to have your company."

Andy gave Aran a reassuring smile. He slapped him affectionately on the back and said, "Aran, have no fear, you can count on the O'Mahonys to see you through."

Andrew remembered Brigid's letter telling him that the authorities were interested in questioning Aran, so please God, whatever you do be very careful about it.

Andrew trusted his sister's judgment. He would do everything in his power to deliver Aran safely to the Limerick train that evening.

Several hours later, Andrew returned with good news. "Everything is set for tonight. We'll meet my friends at half nine. You'll be grand so, Aran," promised Andy.

❧

As the three of them enjoyed their evening tea, the lads talked about growing up in rural Ireland. Auntie O'Mahony seemed content to listen. She passed only the occasional comment or query.

Though they had much in common, Aran was quick to discern that farming life in the west of Ireland was a good bit more difficult than here in the rolling rich soil of Leinster. The mere absence of stone walls in this part of the country told Aran that conditions here were not as harsh as they were back home on the small rocky plots of lands that many were forced to farm. Additionally, weather conditions in and around Dublin were not as severe. The strong winter winds off the Atlantic were much less formidable here than they were in the west of Ireland. But the biggest difference between the men was Andrew's dislike for the farming life that Aran loved. Andy had his heart set on being a successful businessman, which had no appeal to Aran whatsoever.

The evening passed quickly. Soon it was time they were off for town. It was a three mile walk and the weather was not cooperating one bit. It had turned into a dirty old night...one of the worse that spring.

As the two young men walked along in the rain, protected by their buttoned-up waterproofs, Aran told his host a few of the details about the Easter Rebellion. Purposely, he kept his involvement sketchy, but expressed his disappointment at its failure. He told Andrew that only time would tell if something good or positive would grow out of all the death, destruction and executions.

Andrew agreed with Aran. In turn he spoke about his great grandfather's brother who had fought and died at Wexford's Vinegar Hill during the Rising of 1798.

"Unfortunately, only more English repression followed that famous uprising," remarked the resentful Andrew.

Trusting Aran, Andy talked more about some of the events of '98. Andrew described how in the town of Tullow, just northeast of Kilkenny, Father John Murphy, one of the leaders of that famed Rising, had been captured by General Lake and his yeoman forces. In the town's square, the priest was half-hung and, while still conscious, British calvary forces placed his body in a tar barrel, then burned him to death.

"Another example of English justice and suppressive colonial government!" sneered Aran.

Once inside the old town itself, the two young men walked cautiously along its wet, narrow streets. Occasionally glancing into shop windows, Aran was surprised to see several pictures of Pearse and his rebel followers on display. The photos were surrounded by bits of black cloth or paper. Hand lettered inscriptions often adorned the photos. Several of the captions stated 'God Save Ireland and Its Heroes!' and 'They Fought and Died So Ireland Might Be Free.'

Posted in another window was a ballad sheet entitled *Easter, 1916.* Aran read the 'come all ye' to himself.

Easter, 1916

At St. Enda's School there gathers a group of men so fine,
Who talked and dreamt of Ireland's freedom unknown in their
lifetime.
For Britannia had decided so long ago to claim their land,
To tax and force the Irish to enrich her royal hand.
Thus with the start of World War I, a brotherhood did plan,
That soon an Irish rising would be heard throughout the land.
While England was now fighting so 'small nations might be free,'
Eireann's freedom fighters hoped to raise their harp of liberty.

And so on Easter Monday morning, a band of men marched out,
They declared a free Republic about which there was no doubt.
Some people laughed, some cried, "No!" while others paused to see,

Would dear old England finally allow little Ireland to be free?
But soon the Sassenach did arrive with its guns and bayonets,
To let the bloody Irish know who ruled lest some of them forget.
As bombs did fly and bullets rained, proud Dublin shook with fear,
But when the rebels felt death's bite, they all loudly raised a cheer.

Again a sacrifice of blood was asked so Ireland might be free...
To break the bonds that held her fast in hated slavery.
On Mount Street Bridge her men did vow, "No one will pass our
    way!"
And many a foreign soldier-boy did lie with death that day.
For along the River Liffey in bastions north and south,
All withstood the siege as death did pour from out the lion's mouth.
Six brave days did pass but all was lost, so Connolly, Pearse and
    Clarke,
Surrendered to the British Crown, yet freedom's fire was sparked.

Though Maxwell's pit of lime did wait for those that led the cause,
Their deeds and dreams and spoken words all give the people
    pause...[10-4]

The bottom portion of the ballad sheet had been folded over. Aran was unable to read the remainder of the tribute but it did not matter. The author of those words understood what Pearse and the rest of the IRB leadership had tried to accomplish. Unfortunately, their small military effort had been overwhelmed by the might of 25,000 British troops supported by waves of public opinion and an Empire's worth of weapons and military supplies.

As he walked away from the window, Aran again promised himself there would be another day and another opportunity to break the bond that tied Ireland to England.

❧

The train ride to Limerick was uneventful. Aran sat on empty mail sacks in the corner of the postal carriage watching the three-man crew stuff letters and packets into the several hundred narrow mail slots built into one side of the car's wall.

After a brief stop in Thurles, it was nonstop to Limerick. Throughout the ride, the three postal men talked above the train's rattle and roar. Most of their conversations centred around the Rebellion.

Aran knew that 'Bloody' Maxwell had recently extended martial law throughout the entire island. This restriction, along with the unpopular

executions of the Rising's leaders, was slowly turning the Irish population, especially Dubliners, against the repressive British authorities.

It was rumoured that ninety or more Irish republicans had also been
sentenced to death by various British military courts-martial trials. Seven
were already dead. How many more would be shot? What about the
Countess Markievicz? Would Maxwell execute a woman? And then there
was Eamon de Valera. Someone said the American President, Woodrow
Wilson, was trying to have de Valera's death sentence commuted. Something about his being born in the United States and having an American
mother.

The postal carriage was rife with stories, exaggerations topped off by
the growing resentment of England's heavy-handed rule and one-sided
brand of justice.

When the train was within a mile of Limerick station, it began slowing down. Not knowing what waited for him up ahead, Aran decided to
thank his hosts and jump off before it pulled to a stop.

Waving goodbye to his travelling companions, the Irish Rebel leaped
from the mail carriage. Landing safely on the grassy margin beside the
tracks, Aran quickly scrambled to his feet. Cautiously, he began making
his way through Limerick Town. Though he had visited here before on
several occasions and knew his way around rather well, it still took him
over an hour to bypass the city centre. Aran guessed that was where most
of the military patrols enforcing the curfew would likely be.

Earlier on the train, he had decided to head for Richard Doyle's
house. Doyle was the Area Commander of the Irish Volunteers. He had
met him briefly six months ago on a Volunteer training exercise.

Aran knew that Richard had fought in the Boer War with Major
McBride. He was an experienced officer and soldier. If anyone in the area
would know where Liam Mellowes was hiding, it would be Richard.

❧

Aran silently melted into the darkness of a garden wall directly across
the street from the Doyles' home. The cautious rebel waited a full twenty
minutes making sure he had not been followed or the house was not
being watched by the RIC. For all he knew Richard might already be
under arrest or on the run like himself.

A nearby church bell rang two as Aran slipped across the street and
around to the house's side door. The Doyle home was dark. The entire
neighbourhood was deathly quiet.

He knocked once and waited. He knocked again, waiting even longer.
Finally, just as he was about to walk around to the rear of the house, the

side door cracked open and a woman's voice sleepily questioned, "Who's there?"

"I'm an acquaintance of Richard's. Is he at home?"

"Identify yourself!" demanded the whispering voice from behind the partly opened door.

"Aran Roe O'Neill...former OC of 'C' Company, Gort, County Galway. I met Richard on exercises near Corrofin in early December last."

The door opened.

"I've heard your name before. Richard mentioned it once or twice. So inside with you now, but be careful. Walk straight ahead and down the stairs to the cellar."

Aran followed her instructions. Cautiously, he felt his way along the hall and down the darkened steps. At their bottom, he stopped, waiting for the woman to join him. The cellar was pitch black and he dared not go any further without a light.

Moments later, the woman, carrying a candle, came down the steps and stopped, facing him. The candlelight cast long shadows on the walls and the cellar's earthen floor.

"What do you want to see Richard about?" she inquired.

There was an edge of suspicious annoyance in her questioning voice.

"I was hoping he'd know where I could meet up with Liam Mellowes. I've come from Dublin so and read in the newspaper he might be hiding out around here," answered Aran in defence of his late-night visit.

"Richard's not here, but I can take you to him. What did you say your name was?" She held the candle very close to Aran's face. He blinked from its bright heat and turned his head away.

"Aran Roe O'Neill from Gort," muttered the young man, growing tired of having to repeat himself.

"Were you the one who went off to Dublin to that school of Pearse's?" queried the Irishwoman.

"Yes," smiled Aran, looking down at the curious woman.

"Richard has spoken of you. Did you know that Pearse is dead...along with several of the others?" she asked. A grim expression etched across her tired-looking face.

"Yes. I read about it in the newspaper. The English will pay dearly for everyone they shoot," declared Aran, his voice full of angry emotion.

"Not so loud! You'll wake the children," came her scolding reply.

"Stay put so. I must put on some proper clothing then we'll leave for Richard. I just left him three hours ago."

The woman turned to go back upstairs but stopped after several steps. Looking back down at Aran she said almost apologetically, "By the way, my name is Helen. I'm Richard's wife."

With that, the woman and candle disappeared up the stairs leaving Aran to the cellar's quiet blackness.

Patiently he waited, listening to her footsteps fade away as she went up to the top of the house. Then, a few minutes later, he heard her moving back down through her family home and, moments later, she was back beside him in the crudely carved out underground room. This time the woman carried a small oil lamp that cast a larger circle of light than had the candle.

Aran followed Helen across the damp cellar, through a flimsy wooden door and into a tiny storage pantry. It was partly filled with jars of home-made jam, bottled fruit, sacks of last year's potatoes and two baskets of freshly pulled onions.

She pushed aside half a dozen wooden crates stacked at the far end of the little room, exposing an opening to a low, narrow earthen tunnel. Helen, holding the lamp out in front of her, slipped through the hole with Aran right on her heels. They both had to crouch down to avoid hitting their heads on the hand-chiseled passageway. He marvelled to himself at the engineering feat required to create such a fine tunnel through Limerick's rocky soil.

He estimated they must have walked several hundred yards before the passage abruptly ended. At the terminus Aran saw several small wooden containers stacked on top of one another.
"Steps," he thought to himself.

After a moment's pause to listen for any unusual noises, Helen handed Aran the lamp, reached up and pushed aside a small trapdoor built into the top of the passageway. Mounting the crude stairs, she climbed up and peered around. With everything quiet, Helen lifted herself up and crawled out into the night air. Aran followed her example, leaving the extinguished lamp back in the tunnel.

Once above ground, the Gortman found himself in a small grove of trees almost a quarter of a mile behind the Doyles' home. The woman carefully reclosed the trapdoor making sure the covering of grass sods completely concealed the opening.

With no visible traces of the tunnel entrance left behind, the two quickly made their way through the trees, across several boggy fields and out into a narrow boreen. Without speaking a word to each other, they walked due west for over a mile. The woman stayed a step ahead of Aran as she led the way, asserting her position as the leader of their twosome.

Just as light was making its way into the eastern sky, Helen and Aran reached the outskirts of a small village. They headed for the first cottage on the right. Helen knocked four times on the door. Someone on the other side knocked twice. She knocked once more. With that the door opened and they hurried inside.

Curled up around the fireplace were the blanket-wrapped figures of four people. The man who had opened the door moved across the small room and gently shook one of the motionless forms.

"Richard...Richard, your wife is here...Richard..."

But before the guard could finish what he was saying, the reclining figure sprang to life.

Rubbing sleep from his eyes, the man mumbled, "Helen, is that you? You've returned! Are you all right? Something wrong with one of the children?"

"No, we're all right so, but I did bring a man to see you. His name is O'Neill...Aran O'Neill from Gort."

"Who the...well, if it isn't young Aran himself! I thought you were in Dublin...fighting for our freedom."

"Yes," Aran thought, "it was Richard Doyle all right"...and he must be in good form for he had heard that this experienced guerrilla fighter rarely teased or joked with anyone...a bit of a serious yoke he was.

"I was," whispered Aran not wanting to wake the others, "But luckily, I slipped through the Sassenach's fingers so. Now I'm after looking to speak with Liam Mellowes. Do ye know where I might find him?"

At that moment another ghostly figure stirred and sat up.

"I hope the English are having a wee bit more trouble locating me than you did!" said the man putting on his pair of pince-nez glasses.

It was Liam Mellowes himself!

By now the small cabin was coming alive with activity.

With more coded knocks and answered replies at the door, two other men entered the one room structure. They came in to report to Mellowes.

Aran listened and learned that the guards knew it had been Helen arriving at the safe-house. That cleared up the query in his mind as to why they were not challenged on their approach to the cottage. He had been unaware that the two of them had walked through a defensive circle manned by more than a dozen men. The cottage was secure and well guarded.

One of the new arrivals announced that the wagon would arrive shortly to take Mellowes and the others to a boat anchored out in the

River Shannon. The hooker was scheduled to depart with the noon tide.

Mellowes pulled Aran to one side. After inquiring about his personal well-being, Liam explained that Richard, himself plus two others were headed for Amerikay. "An old Fenian in New York has made arrangements to smuggle four of us out of Ireland and over to the United States. It might be months before it'll be safe for us to return home."

Then abruptly Mellowes changed the subject. "Now enough of this talk. What happened in Dublin? Sure, we haven't had any accurate accounts about what went on there."

While the two of them had been talking, Helen and one of the other men had made tea and were now serving eggs, sausage and buttered brown bread to everyone in the room. Several candles now illuminated the room for all the windows were shuttered and well covered with blackout curtains.

As they ate, Aran, with all eyes fixed on him, recounted his story of the Rebellion. He picked up the adventure from the evening Mellowes had bid goodbye to Pearse and the others on the steps of St. Enda's just a few days before Easter Sunday.

The more Aran talked the quieter his audience became. They all drew closer in an ever-tightening circle around the youthful Irish Rebel.

Mellowes was the only one to break the listening silence. Occasionally, he would clarify a certain point or ask a specific question about some particular place or person he knew.

When Aran finished his tale of rebellion, the room was still. Looks of amazement and admiration were fixed on him.

Mellowes broke the silence. "My friends, we are in the company of a real Irish hero. This young man is no bog-trotter from the west. He's a testimony to the quality and dedication Pearse often spoke of as being needed if we were to secure our freedom from England. Aran, we're proud to have you with us...proud to call you Irish."

As he spoke, Mellowes rose, walked over to Aran and shook his hand. The others, including Helen, all stood and followed Mellowes's lead.

Aran was embarrassed. He did not know what to say so he just said, "Thank you."

With the last of the tea poured, it was Aran's turn to ask a query. "I know ye didn't receive the German guns, so how did ye manage to mount an offensive here in the west?"

Mellowes answered for the group. "Yes, when the German trawler Aud went down with all our guns onboard in Queenstown Harbour

Holy Saturday morning things were desperate. I immediately left Limerick and returned to Galway. My men and I waited there hoping to receive some new directives from Pearse, but we received nothing."

Liam related how he and a group of one thousand poorly armed men waited impatiently in and around Galway Town. No orders arrived on Sunday either. Finally on Monday evening word came through from Pearse that the Rebellion was on. We were ordered to rise and take arms against the British.

As Mellowes continued speaking, he stopped pacing back and forth in front of the fireplace. Taking a chair, he sat down with his back to the fire, facing the little group.

"We left Galway as word reached us that the English were sending in a troop transport accompanied by a battleship. It was rumoured they intended to shell the town from their anchorage in Galway Bay.

"...and, as a matter of fact, the British navy did fire several of their big naval guns, but their efforts were unorganised and their gunners ineffective. Most of the shells were lobbed over the city proper and did no damage whatsoever."

Mellowes continued describing how he deployed groups of men in all directions. They secured the town of Tuam to the north, captured Ballinasloe in the east and occupied several small villages south of Galway.

"It was this east bound group that first engaged the enemy at a place called Carnmore Cross, five miles from Galway Town. A dozen English soldiers were killed and their lorries took flight in the face of our guns."

As he spoke, Mellowes' eyes shone brightly in the cottage's candlelight.

"For a short time we held most of County Galway, but our firepower was very limited and not extremely effective. Between the lot of us, we'd only a few rifles, some shotguns and a handful of revolvers. If we'd really and truly engaged the enemy, we'd have been slaughtered."

The others in the room nodded their heads in agreement.

Mellowes downed his last swallow of tea and continued. "On Tuesday, we retreated south from Oranmore toward the village of Clarinbridge. I was the last man out of Oranmore as five lorry loads of English poured in from Galway. Walking backward down the main street of the village I emptied my two revolvers into the enemy's advancing ranks. Several of their soldiers fells while the rest of them retreated back up the road out of sight...the cowardly bastards!

"Finally, the men and I left the coast road and marched inland to Athenry. We spent the night west of town on the Model Farm then took the village in the morning. We set up our HQ in the town hall but, realising we occupied a poorly defended position, retreated east to an old fortified building known as Moyode Castle.

"It was there on Thursday night that we faced up to the fact that we'd no chance at all for success. So, I ordered most of the men back to their homes. Afterwards, a few of us headed south and, with Richard's help, ended up here."

Mellowes paused for a few moments of reflection, then finished his story.

"Now, with our tails between our legs, four of us are heading off to Amerikay while things quiet down here at home. We'll raise money, formulate a new plan of attack and return as soon as possible.

"I plan on picking up the fight where we're leaving it today, but with better organisation, more weapons and a trained group of dedicated soldiers.

"This battle isn't over yet and, if it is true what you say Aran, the Irish people will be ready to join us in our fight before too much longer."

His words sounded so familiar to Aran. He saw the same intensity burning in Mellowes's eyes and heard the same determination in his voice that he had come to associate with Pearse and his dream of Irish freedom. Closing his eyes for just a moment, Aran thought he was back in Dublin listening to his beloved teacher planning the Rebellion all over again.

Aran's thoughts were suddenly interrupted by a knocking at the door. The coded answering reply was followed by more knocks, an opened door and a short, hushed conversation.

"The wagon will be here in five minutes. Time to pack up everything and get ready," came the warning command from one of Liam's scouts.

"Be right with you," called out the Dublin-cum-Galway man.

Aran noticed Richard and Helen had quietly slipped out the front door. He knew the couple wanted a few minutes to themselves before they were forced apart by time and circumstance.

Mellowes turned to Aran Roe and said, "I know there's not much time to consider this offer, Aran, but I would like you to come with us. We'll be on our way in a few minutes."

Aran was dumbfounded. He had looked forward for weeks to going home to his family and farm only a few miles up the road. Then of course there was Brigid...and what of Pearse's unfinished work? No, he just could not head off on such short notice. It was out of the question...impossible!

Liam broke the silence before Aran could decline his offer.

"Come, ride along with us in the wagon. We'll have an hour to talk. It will give you some time to think things over. What do you say?"

Out of respect to this loyal Irishman and not wanting to disrupt their carefully planned timetable any more, Aran agreed to ride out along the River Shannon with them.

They all picked up their meagre belongings and walked outside. The morning air smelled sea-clean and sweet as they took their places in the wagon. Liam Mellowes, again disguised as a priest, sat in the middle on the top bench. The driver was to his left while Aran occupied the right-hand portion of the front seat.

Richard and two other men jumped into the back of the wagon as the two horse team started up. They bounced along an old road toward the village of Cratloe and their scheduled rendezvous with the Irish sailboat.

The plan was to leave from Cratloe, head down the Shannon with its receding tide and strong current pushing them along and, finally, sail five miles out to sea beyond Kerry Head. At that point, Mellowes and his men would transfer from the hooker to a Brazilian steamship that would be stopped along the Irish coast for just one hour. The ship's captain had planned to stage a lifeboat drill as a covering manoeuvre while the 'special' passengers boarded the big vessel from the little sailing craft.

The powers that be in New York had said they would make all the necessary arrangements. It was a dangerous move with possible English warships and German submarines on the prowl. Supposedly, however, the necessary money was in the right hands and promises made of no problems.

As the wagon moved along the deserted byroad, Aran saw men on horseback in front of and behind their rig. They were acting as lookouts guarding the wagon's important occupants from any surprise enemy attack.

Aran thought to himself, "This was certainly a well orchestrated plan carried out by deadly serious and dedicated men. The outriders were risking their own safety to protect and defend the lives of four Irish soldiers on the way to Mheiricea."

Aran felt admiration and respect for Liam, Richard, Helen and the rest of this crowd. He was proud to be associated with the likes of them.

As they rode along, the Volunteer leader talked with Aran about the Rebellion. The Gortman, feeling a certain closeness to his companion, divulged some details of his final conversation with Pearse and his meeting Brigid. He briefly described the emotional bond that had suddenly developed between the Athy woman and himself.

As they drew nearer the Shannon, Liam Mellowes hurriedly outlined his reasons for leaving Ireland.

"In Amerikay, Aran, we'll have a free hand to plan and organise another rebellion. Men with your experience and dedication offer us a natural focal point around which other Irish nationalists can rally."

Mellowes talked of his fear that until the men taken prisoner after the Rising were released from their English prisons not much would happen in the way of rebellious activity. England had effectively deported too many of the revolutionary ringleaders.

Liam further emphasised that this trip to the United States would provide Aran with a golden opportunity...an opportunity to play an important part in Ireland's renewed quest for freedom.

Listening, as he was, to this persuasive Irishman, Aran's mind was awash with more queries than he knew how to answer. If Mellowes were Pearse, there would be no question about what he would do...he would go. But Pearse was dead. Sadly, he must adjust his loyalties and look to other men for encouragement. Was Mellowes capable of being one of Ireland's new leaders? His mind raced while it considered possible answers to all his questions. He just did not have enough time to think everything through. The Gortman felt pressurised and confused.

While Aran was sifting through all the complicated choices posed by the Dubliner, one of the rearguard riders raced up to the wagon crying, "Look out...the Limeys are coming! Ye all must take cover immediately!"

Responding to the warning, the wagon driver began pulling up on his team, but Mellowes cried, "No, no, no...drive on! Full speed ahead...go...go...go!"

The wagon slowed at first, then suddenly lurched ahead. The driver leaned forward on the bench urging his horses to run faster.

Guns had been hidden under the feed sacks stacked on the wagon's floor bed. With great haste, the men in back passed out the weapons. Mellowes reached for a new Lee-Enfield rifle while Aran grabbed a .38 Smith and Wesson revolver. Everyone quickly checked over their weapons.

With the enemy approaching, Aran, Liam and the driver, all positioned on the wagon's top seat, crouched down as best they could. Aran's heart pounded inside his chest. His thoughts flashed back to the time when the two British soldiers had broken down the Fannins' front door and had burst in on him and his two prisoners.

Though his emotions were racing, Aran's hand was steady despite the speeding wagon's swaying and bouncing. Aran realised that trying to hit a moving target under such conditions was difficult, but the enemy would have to cope with the same problem.

Looking back over his shoulder, Aran saw three, no four, horsebacked soldiers. Slowly, the English were gaining on the wagon and, as they drew closer to the rebels, the bloody blackguards began firing their revolvers at them.

The men in the wagonbed fired back at the approaching soldiers. Road dust flew up from behind the racing vehicle as the noise of gunfire filled the air.

Two of the British soldiers fell from their horses, just as one of the men in the wagon screamed, rolling over on his side...his face was covered with blood.

Aran only hoped Mellowes had stationed a few men along the roadside up ahead to cover them as they sped past.

Moments later, without warning, the driver suddenly dropped the reins and pitched off the left side of the wagon. Liam scrambled after the leather straps and tried to regain control of the racing animals.

From his position in the rear of the wagon, Richard Doyle rose up on one knee and started firing into a stand of trees off to the wagon's right.

"Redcoats on the right flank!" shouted Mellowes in Aran's ear.

Just as the Irish Rebel turned to fire, he felt a hot, dizzy sensation explode inside his head. Bright shooting stars clouded his view of the trees and the English soldiers on the far hill.

Aran tried to raise his revolver but his arm would not move. He felt as if he was floating. He could not understand what was happening, but he sensed he was losing his balance.

Realising that a fall from the racing wagon might be fatal, Aran did all he could to keep from pitching off the bouncing seat. But the more he tried to steady himself, the faster he seemed to fall.

Just before he slipped into a black void...soundless and deep, Aran felt a strong hand grab his arm.

❧

Aran Roe lost all track of time. He seemed to be drifting on an unending black sea. His head and body were no longer connected to one another. Aran felt nothing but, occasionally, he thought he could hear voices from a great distance away.

"Looks like a bad one. It's just above his left ear."

"Is there another wound near the top of his head?"

"Better leave him here. We'll find a doctor for him as soon as possible."

"No, lift him into the hooker."

"He's still bleeding pretty bad."

"He'll have just as good a chance on the ship as here."

"Are you certain?"

"Yes...Y.e.s...Y..e..s...Y...e...s..."

The voices faded away. Again, the darkness swallowed him up.

In the far recesses of his mind, Aran thought he must be dead. He tried to bless himself, but he could not move or feel a thing. Like a giant volcano, his head kept exploding in a shower of red flame and blinding white light. The sudden searing pain inside his head subsided only after his body seemed to defy gravity by floating free of its earthly bonds. Like a leaf being toyed with by a gentle sea breeze, Aran imagined himself floating and tumbling down...down...down. To his surprise the ride felt so soft...so smooth...so gentle...even painless.

Aran remembered experiencing a similar feeling before. He tried to remember when, but could not.

He fought to think through the shroud of fog now swirling around inside his volcanic head.

He struggled to remember back through time but his mind just would not cooperate with his determined will.

"Don't force it," thought Aran. "Just slowly let the memories come back...relax...relax...relax..."

Gently he floated, rocking back and forth. He felt so peaceful...so safe...so sleepy...

With all the strength he could muster, Aran tried opening his eyes. Through a hazy light, he imagined a face looking down at him.

"Yes, someone is staring at me...I can almost see their face floating in and out of focus...it's taking form again...it's becoming clearer...but...but who are you?"

Aran fought to remember.

"Yes...there it is...oh, it's you Brigid. Yes, I remember now. You're holding me in your arms. You're rocking me...holding me...wiping away my tears. Now you're crying with me. I didn't know you loved Pearse too."

Aran stopped trying to focus on Brigid's face. It was too much of an effort for him. He just wanted to close his eyes and fall deeper into

Brigid's womanly softness. He wanted to relish the comfort and warmth of her loving caress.

❧

"Aran...Aran Roe...Aran Roe O'Neill can you hear me? Aran, open your eyes and look at me!"

The Gortman heard the new voice. It annoyed him that it was interrupting his dream of Brigid.

"Aran, please, open your eyes!"

Aran's dreamy vision slowly disappeared. Brigid gradually drifted away and was gone. Reluctantly, Aran tried opening his eyes once more.

Looking up, he saw a strange face staring down at him. Behind the face was a huge brown wall.

Suddenly, he smelt it...heard it...felt it. It was the smell, the sound and the feel of the sea.

"Where am I?" queried the confused young man.

He tried to move, but it was useless. It felt as if someone had buried him up to his neck in wet sand. He was completely immobilised.

"Aran, it's Liam Mellowes. You've been shot in the head...once, maybe twice. In a few minutes, we're going to lift you up from this hooker onto a steamer. There'll be a doctor there to mind you...to care for you."

Mellowes cradled Aran's head in his lap and kept talking. "You're going to be all right. Don't try to talk or move. We'll take care of you. I know you have some more fight left in you yet. Ireland needs you. I need you. Don't give up now. We're almost there...besides, no one's heard a banshee in these parts for months."

Aran tried to say the words, "Home!" "Gort!" His lips moved, but no sounds emerged.

"Now...now, Aran. Don't try to talk. One of my men will tell your family. Don't worry about a thing. We'll take good care of you. That's a promise!"

Again, the darkness gradually swallowed up Aran.

He was back in Brigid's arms. She was rocking him. He saw her lips moving, but he could not quite hear what she was saying.

Deeper and deeper he drifted.

Then with incredible ease, Brigid lifted him up, holding his senseless body in her arms. She pressed him close to her breast, then laid him down on a cotton-soft cloud of white rose blossoms.

Aran was surprised that Brigid was able to lift him so effortlessly.

But, the feeling of lying on the delicate white cloud was wonderful.

Aran stopped questioning things. He simply laid back and savoured this new sensation.

❧

What was happening now?

He was back in Brigid's arms. She tipped her head and kissed him on the lips.

Aran wondered why he was not able to feel or taste her kiss? He wanted to relish Brigid's sweetness, caress her softness and sleep in her warmth.

Slowly, Brigid bent over and laid him on the couch...by the fire...inside the thatched cottage...on her Athy farm. Softly, she whispered, "My breast shall be your bed."

For one lingering instant, he smiled to himself knowing Brigid loved him too.

❧

When he opened his eyes again, she was gone.

He wanted to cry out, "Brigid come back! Please don't leave me! I love you, Brigid." But as hard as he tried, no sounds could he make.

He tried to speak...shout...scream, but it was too late. Brigid had faded from view. His unspoken pleas went unanswered.

❧

"I need some help over here. This man is badly wounded. Is he dying, doctor?"

"Quick...help me...do something!"

❧

Aran Roe O'Neill's wounded body had been hoisted aboard the waiting Brazilian steamship anchored off the Irish coast. Two other men and a priest were conveyed aboard as well.

As the Irish hooker moved away from the huge steamship, Aran was rushed below deck to the ships's surgery.

Though limited medical facilities and equipment were available, the doctor was skilled. Unbeknownst to the medical staff and the others onboard, an unseen angel hovered over this seventh son of a seventh son.

Was it possible, with God's blessing and present-day medical science, that this unconscious and badly wounded Irishman could be saved?

❧

Liam Mellowes and Richard Doyle paced back and forth in the next cabin hoping for some news about Aran's condition.

The time for making new plans and for carrying on Eireann's ancient struggle were on hold. They both waited for word that the Irish Rebel had survived the attack and would be able to help them in their continued quest for freedom from the Stranger's determined grasp.

PART II
Terror, Tragedy & Triumph

11. *Remembering*

"Long time ago" said the fine old woman
"Long time ago" this proud old woman did say
"There was war and death, plundering and pillage
My children starved, by mountain, valley and sea
And their wailing cries, they shook the very heavens
My four green fields ran red with their blood," said she.

Four Green Fields / Tommy Makem

*B*rigid Eileen O'Mahony stood alone in the cottage doorway staring into the empty darkness. The fading sounds of Conor's galloping hooves had melted away, returning dawn to its early-morning solitude. Only the beating of her sad heart and the chirping of a nearby bird were audible. Unconsciously, she blew out the candle in her hand.

Had Aran Roe O'Neill's short stay been real or was it a figment of a lonely, young woman's imagination? The events of the last two days swirled back and forth between some dreamlike state and warm reality. But, as a fresh May breeze began stirring the flowering chestnut trees separating the narrow lane from the farmyard, something inside Brigid told her Aran's visit had been real.

Pausing a moment longer on the front step, she stared up at a fading nighttime star. The young woman was suddenly filled with the feeling she had known Aran all her life. No, the events of the last two days were not some make-believe dream.

Brigid recalled every detail from the first instant their eyes had met in the little Athy church up to the very moment when Aran had ridden out of sight aboard Conor on his way to Kilkenny Town. During those few short hours, her life had been filled with an indescribable feeling of joy and happiness.

The moments of society enjoyed during their two days of living and working together ignited feelings of affection Brigid had only dreamed of in the privacy of her imagination. No man had ever touched her so profoundly and, just think, their friendship was only hours old. How could they have laughed and cried together so easily in such a short period of time? Then, the wonder of wonders, how was it possible to fall in love with a stranger so easily?

All this newness and emotional excitement seemed overpowering. She felt confused and uncertain about what to do next. Now his unexpected departure left Brigid alone to sort through her thoughts and feelings without his help.

Turning to close the door, she felt light-headed. The sitting room seemed to spin before her eyes. Reaching out for a nearby chair, Brigid steadied herself. After a momentary pause, she moved, almost automatically, over to the fireplace. Brigid knelt down and began the morning ritual of building the fire on the remains of last night's still glowing embers.

After carefully piling bits of wood and bark over the hot coals, she sat down on the hearth's hob seat. Transfixed, Brigid stared at the little tongues of yellow and orange flame that began dancing up to light the darkness of the room.

Without warning, feelings of sadness and forewarning swept over her. A strange and frightening wave of emotion suddenly enveloped her, blotting out the dreamy feelings of happiness. In their place was left a growing sense of desperation and doom. It seemed as if something terrible was about to happen and Brigid felt powerless to alter its coming.

This momentary spell of foreboding was broken by Gran's caring hand on her shoulder. Her grandmother's weathered face smiled down at her while Gran's strong hands pulled Brigid to her feet. The young woman and the mother of her dead father stood looking at one another. Suddenly, Brigid buried her tearful face and quivering shoulders in Gran's comforting embrace.

Neither of them spoke for the longest time. The room was silent except for the crackling and popping of the fire. Finally, Brigid pulled back. She looked into the gentle eyes of the person she loved and respected the most.

"He's gone Gran and I just have the feeling I'll never see him again. Why did he have to go just now? He seemed to care and believe in the same things that are so important to me. It frightens me, but I think I was falling in love with him."

Gran wiped Brigid's tearstreaked face with the corner of her apron. Smiling, she said in a soft voice, "I know. It wasn't hard to see that Aran was a fine lad. With any luck at all, he'll be back safe and sound."

There was comfort in her voice but Gran's eyes belied her words. They both knew Aran had set a dangerous course for himself and, if he was not careful, he could easily be consumed in freedom's flame. Aran's wheel of life was spinning fast. It was likely to run down before its time.

"Take your pause, child. I'll listen to your heart whenever you are ready. God knows I listened enough to your father's sad heart, may he rest in peace, after your mother died...and she with all her burden to carry after having to take to the bed as she did. Then who can forget all the stories of broken hearts and desperate lives crushed by famine, disease, immigration and exploitation. Yes, isn't He after giving us folk heavy burdens to carry?"

Brigid nodded in agreement and, taking Gran by the hand, together they walked over to the flagstoned kitchen. It was time to light the old blackened range and put the kettle on for morning tea. Brigid's three younger siblings would be up soon and there was breakfast to organise.

During the meal Brigid answered her brother's and sisters' questions about Aran's sudden departure.

Afterwards, instead of following his two sisters outside to their chores, Rory stayed back. He pulled Brigid out into the sitting room. He wanted to know if Aran's leaving had anything to do with yesterday's newspaper reports of the rebel executions in Dublin or with the fighting that had taken place there.

Brigid, swearing him to secrecy, told Rory that Patrick Pearse, Aran's headmaster at St. Enda's school in Rathfarnham had been one of the Rebellion's leaders. Aran had been with him in the General Post Office during the fighting and had willingly risked his life, along with hundreds of others, to help free Ireland from England's powerful grip. She explained to her young brother that luckily Aran had escaped British capture. He had fled safely into the Wicklow Mountains much as Michael Dwyer and his men had done after the disastrous events of the 1798 Rebellion. Fearing capture by the Crown's soldiers or the Royal Irish Constabulary, Aran had decided to head westward toward his family's home in County Galway. It was just by luck's chance they all happened to meet three days ago.

Brigid had often talked to her younger brother about Ireland's history, its often stormy relationship with Britain and how, down through the ages, small groups of Irishmen and women had attempted to break away from England. They had all wanted to reestablish their own free and independent nation.

This Irish thirst for freedom was nothing new to Rory. He had read books, heard stories, sung songs and sometimes even listened to his teachers describe Ireland's sad and storied past. But to have had a real live rebel in his own home was something new to him. His eyes opened wide with excitement as he listened to Brigid briefly describe some of Aran's adventures.

They interrupted their private chat only when the day's workforce began assembling on the back porch.

Another fine day was in full bloom. Brigid thanked the Ryan family and Sonny and his two sons for coming. An early crop of hay was only half cut while the rest of the late spring planting needed to be finished. All this work must be done prior to their annual 'saving of the turf' for next winter's fuel.

Brigid satisfied questioning looks with the news that Aran Roe O'Neill had decided to take advantage of the good weather and continue on his way home.

Brigid added, "Aran's two hands and strong back will be missed, but don't we have some of Ireland's finest standing right here? I say yes! So, let's get to work and ye all prove me right."

Everyone nodded, their curiosity seemed satisfied, but when walking past the byre for their tools, Peter Ryan remarked to Brigid, "I'll miss Aran's help and his hard-working ways. Will he be after returning this way again, Brigid?"

Brigid smiled to herself. After a moment's reflection, however, she shook her head replying, "I doubt it so, Peter."

After speaking those sad words, she quickly turned her head to hide the emotions that filled her eyes with tears and her heart with sorrow. Brigid did not want to expose her true feelings and possibly endanger Aran's safety with any details of his sudden departure.

❧

The rest of the day was filled with long hours of hard manual labour. Everyone kept to their own work, but during the dinner break just after one in the afternoon, Peter produced a harmonica. Everyone joined in singing a few of the old songs. The music seemed to give everyone's spirit a lift and made the afternoon's work pass more quickly.

It was almost dark when Sonny, his sons, the Ryan family and Brigid bid one another good night. As she made her way toward the whitewashed cottage, Brigid noticed rain clouds gathering in the western sky. Their churning mass gave the gathering twilight an unusually beautiful backdrop as shafts of lightning illuminated the approaching storm.

After evening tea, Brigid was too tired to sit by the fire and read. She excused herself and retired to bed earlier than usual.

The young woman fell asleep saying her prayers of thanks to God for her family, friends and now for Aran and his safe return to her.

❧

Later that evening, just before Gran blew out the candle and crawled into her own bed next to Brigid's in the loft under the thatched roof of the cottage, she looked over at her sleeping granddaughter. Though this extraordinary young woman had been coy about admitting her age to Aran, Gran knew the truth.

Crawling under her bed clothing and curling up for the night, Gran scrolled back through time, remembering events of the past twenty-one years. It was hard to believe it had been that long ago, for Gran remembered Brigid's birth as if it was only yesterday.

Brigid had been born on 31 January 1895, the eve of the feast of St. Brigid. Appropriately, she was named for one of Ireland's holiest religious figures. In fact, some of the early Irish poets even referred to Brigid as the mother of Christ. That made her the equal of St. Mary in some people's eyes.

It had been a cold winter's night. A lashing wind drove the rain through the cracks around every window and door. The small, two-room flat above a dry goods store in Kilkenny was all a young lieutenant in the British army could afford. The baby's father had recently been assigned to the 10th Irish Division stationed at the Curragh, County Kildare. Away on manoeuvres at the time, Gran and a midwife were charged with the responsibility of bringing the newest little O'Mahony into the world. It was just before midnight when Brigid joined Hannah, aged three, and Andrew, aged one, as the next member of their little family.

Mrs. O'Mahony's pregnancy and Brigid's childbirth proved to be difficult for the young mother. As a result, she never fully regained her former level of strength and good health.

The years passed. Gran remembered her daughter-in-law giving birth to two more children, Rory and Mary. Annie's arrival, however, was too much for Mrs. O'Mahony. She died giving birth to her sixth child in 1909.

Gran recollected the events marking Brigid's evolution from infancy into childhood. As the little child grew, life in Ireland improved for most folks. After the Local Government Act of 1898 and the Land Purchase Acts of 1903 and 1909, Irish communities were better able to govern themselves through the election of local county councils. Irish farmers were finally able to break the remaining bonds of landlordism and were actually allowed to purchase the land their families had worked and slaved on for generations.

But then with the death of Gran's husband, Brigid's grandfather, the recently promoted Captain O'Mahony moved his family from Kilkenny to the old family acreage just west of Athy in County Kildare. It was on that newly purchased land, once owned by members of the ancient O'Mahony clan, that Brigid and her siblings had grown up.

This land had once been worked by her ancestors hundreds of years ago. But with the coming of Oliver Cromwell and his land usurping policies in the early 1650's, Gran's ancestors were forced to move west beyond the River Shannon. By theft and by murder the Stranger again dispossessed the Irish. Under the harshest of conditions, the O'Mahonys were compelled to scrape out a living on the rocky, barren land of County Mayo. But, as the years passed, things finally began to change for the better. In the late 1700s, social and economic circumstances improved with the easing of the Penal Laws, a nearly one-hundred-year-old Anglo-Irish political system aimed at Irish societal destruction. These resulting ameliorations soon were followed by Ireland's union with England in 1801. Finally, the O'Mahony clan was able to move back to the Athy area. They worked as labourers, cottiers and lastly as tenant farmers on the land their ancestors once owned.

Eventually, Brigid's father purchased their present family farm from the departing landlord after the Wyndham Land Reform Act in 1903. He was finally able to restore a six-hundred-year-old O'Mahony Clan tradition of land ownership west of the River Barrow.

Unfortunately, Gran's son, Brigid's father, was killed in France during the early weeks of the First War. Tradition dictated that the land be left to Andrew, the oldest son. Andy, however, had no desire to manage the family farm. He wanted to become a businessman so he moved back to Kilkenny to live with his Auntie O'Mahony.

Lastly, Gran thought of Brigid's oldest sister, Hannah. She had emigrated to Amerikay in 1911. She now worked as a housekeeper for a wealthy Irish-American family living near Baltimore, Maryland.

The eldest O'Mahony smiled to herself, thinking how Brigid relished the responsibility and challenge of managing the farm. The young woman took a great interest in developing and improving the family business. With Peter Ryan's strong back and wise council, they made a great pair.

The three youngest children, with her help, kept a large vegetable and flower garden behind the cottage. The little ones, between going to school and doing their lessons, also assisted with the family's household chores.

Gran often wondered to herself how they ever managed, but Brigid was determined, proud, intelligent and hardworking. Their family was not only just getting by, they were prospering beyond everyone's expectations.

Now, looking over at the sleeping Brigid, Gran could only smile as her heart filled with loving pride. Every young man who lived in the townland had their eye on her. There was never a Sunday afternoon that one or more of them would not come calling. Brigid, however, always seemed too busy to spend any serious time with these bachelors. An occasional crossroads dance or a horseback ride along the river was the extent of her courting. She would much rather have the young man's afternoon help on the farm or spend a free hour reading by the fire in the sitting room. She was a free spirit with a mind of her own. This behaviour was quite a contrast to the other docile, marriage-hungry local women her age.

No, Brigid was different from the others in many ways. Her granddaughter was a staunch believer in Irish independence. For several years she had supported John Redmond and his Irish nationalist Parliamentary Party's efforts to obtain Home Rule legislation from Britain. But, with the rise of the Orangemen's demands and English Prime Minister Asquith's sidestepping, political chicanery, she changed her mind.

Fueled by a growing sense of continued English injustice toward Ireland, Brigid had begun thinking about older, less popular and more drastic measures to end Britain's seven-hundred-fifty-year-old dominance of her native land. The Fenians' physical force desire to change dreams into reality began to appeal to her.

Gran saw these changes in Brigid and it worried her. She feared Brigid's new, radical political sentiments might come back to harm the O'Mahony family and farm.

After more thoughtful reflection, Gran blew out the candle and pulled her warm patchwork quilt up around her. She said her prayers, thanking God for the good health and increasing prosperity of the O'Mahony clan. Gran closed with a prayer of thanksgiving to God for His blessing them with this wonderful and special twenty-one-year-old Irish lass.

❉

Now, just after seven in the morning, the overnight light rain had stopped. A warm spring sun emerged and the fresh clean smell of wet earth and sweet blooms filled the air. It spilled into the cottage through its open windows. Brigid and Gran dressed hurriedly. There was much to do before they would be ready to journey into town for church.

After waking the children, Gran climbed down and started preparing breakfast. Brigid went out to check on the animals. Passing by the byre, she glanced inside. Brigid was surprised to see Aran's truckle bed neatly made up in the corner. In all the busyness of yesterday, she had forgotten to tidy up and put away his bedding.

Going inside the wooden building, Brigid walked over and sat down on the side of the bed. She picked up Aran's pillow and pressed it to her face. The young woman breathed in his lingering presence. It smelled clean and strong, just like Aran. Suddenly, before she realised it, tears were rolling down her cheeks. The young woman's heart was breaking all over again.

Embarrassed by her own sentimentality, she dried her eyes and folded up the bed linen. It was then that she noticed a piece of writing paper lying on the bedside table. With excited, trembling fingers, Brigid picked it up. The letter was to her from Aran.

> Brigid, A Chara, Sure I haven't much time, but I wanted you to know how special you are. I've never met anyone like you...never! From the first moment our eyes met in the church, I had the strangest feeling...it's difficult for me to put everything down into words...but you seem to care and understand me so.
>
> I don't have much experience with women. All my life I've spent going to school with the lads or being around my family and other adults. That's not to say I haven't thought about the fairer sex...I have you know...but nothing of any serious consequence.

After Mass, when we met on the road and you invited me to dinner, I felt uneasy so. Partly because of the troubles and partly because of all the confused stirrings inside me.

You're a rare person...someone who, I think, understands me as I've wished from few others. So, it is with great reluctance I leave you today. Happily, though, I know you fathom my urgency. I must attend to the unfinished business Professor Pearse began in Dublin. I also fear Liam Mellowes is in danger. Pearse had great faith in him. With any luck, I'll find Mr. Mellowes and offer what assistance I can. The English have won this round, but many of us are unwilling to surrender any longer to their outrageous demands.

Brigid, you understand something of my growing resentment and mounting hatred of British injustice...of my thirst for our independence. I think you feel much as I do about the plight Ireland faces today.

Please God, don't forget me. With any luck I'll return and, hopefully, we can carry on. Please also pardon my letter writing...I haven't much experience in putting down on paper my innermost thoughts.

Bless you, Brigid Eileen. Know my thoughts and dreams are with you and of you.

Beannacht Leat, A Chuisle, Aran

Brigid's tears started anew. She clutched the letter to her breast and curled up into a ball on the bed. A thousand things raced through her mind. Her first impulse was to go after him, find him and tell him she loved him. But then her practical self took charge. In her mind Brigid ticked off innumerable reasons why she dared not leave.

While all of these thoughts and emotions surged through her head, Brigid was distracted by the sound of a motor vehicle driving into the farmyard. She could hear its engine and the sound of running feet out in the yard.

Still dazed and trembling from her discovery, Brigid made her way to the byre door and looked out. There in the front garden was an RIC lorry. From where she stood, she could see five policemen scattered about with their rifles at the ready.

Without realising that she still held Aran's incriminating letter in her hand, Brigid raced around to the front of her home and demanded to speak to the sergeant in charge.

On hearing her angry voice, a middle-aged Irish policeman, dressed in the uniform of the Royal Irish Constabulary, stepped out of the cottage door and saluted her. Brigid had known this man for the better part of five years and they had occasionally chatted about cattle and land prices.

"Sorry to disturb ye Brigid, but we had a report that there might be a wanted Sinn Fein Volunteer from Dublin in these parts. We just had to check things out...in case you were having a bit of trouble or whatnot."

"And who's to say we have such a person on our land, Sergeant McGee?" Brigid's face was red with outraged anger.

"Just rumours, ma'am...only idle talk."

"Now, who'd be filling your head with that kind of gossip?" lashed back Brigid.

"Don't rightly know, but someone said something in the King's Arms last night. This morning me captain ordered us to investigate the matter. I'm just doing my duty. As ye know, you can't be too careful with all that trouble in Dublin last week. Some of it might spill over here...you just never know."

Brigid's mind was racing. Who knew Aran had stayed here? Her mind checked off the list of possible suspects. Besides her own family there was Peter and his wife...no, they would never have said a word to anyone. Their two lads would not have said anything either. Besides, no strangers or travellers had passed by recently to see or hear anything. Wait a minute...maybe it was her neighbour, Sonny. He had dropped off the evening newspaper had he not? He had been to town...or what about his two sons? They had met Aran too. That's it! Probably one of the lads or maybe both of them were up town last night...having a few pints. Innocently or no they told of the stranger who had worked at the O'Mahony farm. Yes, that must be it. Just wait! I'll give them a piece of my mind next time I see them!

Collecting her composure and looking the RIC man straight in the face, Brigid replied, "Well, nothing is going to 'spill over' onto this farm without my knowledge or permission. Yes, we did have a young farmhand stay with us for two nights, but he is long gone...on his way back home to County Galway or Clare or somewhere down west. He even did me a big favour and took a horse up to my brother in Kilkenny. I'd been promising Andrew one since last autumn."

"Did he say where he'd been or what he was doing in these parts, Brigid?"

"Not a word of it and I haven't a bull's notion. You know me, Sergeant McGee. If it is none of my business, that's the way I keep it. He put in a good day's labour. I paid him, fed him and he was off on his way early yesterday morning.

"Now, if you and yis men have nothing better to do today, I've enough work around this farm to keep ye all occupied for a week. So, what do you say? How about lending me a hand today?"

"Begging your pardon, Brigid, but I've me own work waiting back home sure. Sorry for disturbing ye on this fine morning. We'll be after heading back to the barracks to make out my report. Sorry again for your trouble."

With that the embarrassed Sergeant McGee blew his whistle. The other men all hurried back into the front garden, saluted Brigid and piled back into the lorry. Carefully, it backed out of the drive and quickly drove off up the laneway.

It was not until the sound of the vehicle had died away that Brigid noticed Gran and the three children standing together by the front steps. They had not uttered a word to Sergeant McGee or his men. But, now with the lorry's departure, they all gave out in a shout and the children ran up to her.

"You told Sergeant McGee a thing or two," cried Rory in delight.

"Yes, Brigid, you were grand," echoed the girls.

As Brigid pulled her siblings to her, she became aware of the letter still clutched in her hand. Aran's letter! "Jesus, Mary and Joseph," she thought, "If that peeler had demanded to read Aran's note, we'd all be in gaol this very minute!"

Carefully folding the paper into quarters and tucking it into her skirt pocket, Brigid reminded the children, "Aran's business is ours and ours alone. You're not to be after telling others what goes on around this farm unless there's a good reason for them knowing it. You're not to mention to a soul anything about Aran's visit or his departure. He has important work to do elsewhere. No outsider has any business knowing about or interfering with his activities. Is that clear to ye all?" Brigid spoke in a soft but firm voice.

Then, without waiting for their answers, she continued, "If you've any questions about Aran, ye just ask me. He's special and, for the time being, we must stifle all urges to mention him to others, except in our prayers."

With that, Brigid reached down, hugged each of the children and whispered in their ears, "I love you." Then, administering a gentle slap to each of their bums, she sent her brother and sisters off to finish their morning chores and help Gran in the kitchen with breakfast.

❧

On the following Saturday, as Brigid Eileen readied her little brood for the trip to Athy's market, she was still preoccupied with thoughts of Aran. It had been a week to the day since he had ridden off to Kilkenny on his journey west. She had received no word from her brother, but that was not unusual. Brigid could only hope all was well.

The Ryan family pulled their horse and cart up in front of the O'Mahony cottage just before nine o'clock. The two families had planned heading off together to do their weekly shopping. The adults sat in the Ryans' trap while the children rode in the O'Mahonys' horse-drawn butt. This familiar journey to town was always a big occasion for Rory. Brigid recently had permitted him to drive their wagon while his sisters and the two Ryan boys served as his passengers.

With the adult's cart following Rory's, Brigid, dressed in a blue jumper and full-length black skirt, pondered Sergeant McGee's unexpected visit on Sunday last for the umpteenth time. Above the noise of the wagon wheels bumping and grinding along on the dirt and stony road, Peter and Carolyn listened quietly to their neighbour and friend's story once more. The entire episode had been an upsetting experience. The two families had talked of little else all week.

Brigid pleaded, "Are you positive you didn't speak to anyone about Aran?" She must have asked them that query a dozen times or more.

Mrs. Ryan patiently replied, "We didn't see or talk to a soul, Brigid, and that's the God's truth. Sure, that Sergeant McGee is the very divil...that ould bastard, please Mother Mary forgive me. He just likes stirring up the pot if ye ask me."

"Aye," muttered Gran, loosing the red shawl wrapped around her shoulders. The late-spring sun was unusually warm.

Clearing her throat, Carolyn continued, "He's just after giving you a hard time because he doesn't think a young woman should be running a farm and doing well at it to boot. He thinks you should be married, having childer and leaving the heavy work to the man. His pride can't stand seeing you succeed when he's such a miserable lout of a man himself."

Peter, wearing his good tweed suit and bowler hat, nodded his head in agreement with his wife but said nothing.

Brigid thought there must be more to it than that. "I agree with what you say, but besides old ways dying hard, McGee may have another motive. The fighting in Dublin two weeks ago could signal the start of a general challenge to English and RIC authority in this country. Besides the obvious physical dangers that the Rebellion posed, Professor Pearse and his followers longed to change the system. They wanted the people to wake up from their years of political slumber and economic preoccupation with all the daily problems of surviving and getting your crust."

Brigid's three travelling companions thoughtfully nodded their concurrence.

Silence momentarily wrapped itself around the adults, but Brigid's mind was whirling. There was more to be said but she thought it wiser to hold her tongue. She understood that Pearse meant to uncover the real root of Ireland's problem...England and its coercive, hateful and self-interested obsession with ruling Ireland. If we were truly independent, reasoned Brigid to herself, Sergeant McGee and many others like him would lose their power, prestige and monthly wages. Yes, there were a lot of selfish Irishmen who wanted more control of their own concerns but who were not willing to scrap the system and throw out the English. There was just too much to lose...and besides, hadn't Ireland's history always been told in a sea of tears? And sure, if I'm any judge of things, she thought, there will be a few more shed before all this is said and done.

Peter finally broke his silence. "You may be right, Brigid. All those arguments over the last three or four years about Home Rule brought matters to a head. It's clear the Unionists in Belfast aren't going to give up their wealth and power willingly. Unfortunately, if they don't, it could mean civil war here on our own island."

His wife quickly interjected, "The only thing that has stopped the arguing and united most of the people has been that bloody war in Europe!"

"Aye," acknowledged Peter. A grim expression was etched across his face.

Gran, who usually kept her thoughts to herself, added her own observation, "...and now the Sinn Feiners want to stir things up and catch the Stranger off guard with all their eggs in one basket. Mind you, the law has always been dispensed by England and inflicted upon Ireland. Now, some want to change all that. I fear we're all in for some hard times...ye mind my words."

Brigid wondered if Gran's troubled words were an omen of things to come.

❧

Their talk shortened the ride to town. Upon arrival, the two families tied up their rigs next to the market house. Splitting up, the Ryans and O'Mahonys headed off in different directions to do their shopping and visiting.

Athy, a small rural town, was alive with people. Carts and stalls were positioned around the 1740 two-story, stone market house in Emily Square. Farmers and tradesmen displayed and sold their homemade and Dublin-imported foodstuffs and wares to a crowd of eager shoppers. Besides the usual variety of potatoes, cabbages, onions and other assorted veg were women selling eggs, prints of butter, homemade loaves of bread and currant cake, jam jars filled with fruit preserves and several types of locally produced cheese. Bolts of dyed linen, hats for both men and women as well as large jars full of colourful candy humbugs to satisfy the desires of excited children. There was even an old man selling religious medals and strings of handmade rosary beads.

Across the square in front of the former British military barracks, now Athy's courthouse, was a group of men haggling over small milling knots of cattle and sheep. From the tone of their bargaining, it seemed as if there was more talk and less buying going on among the assembled punters.

Observing all the market-day happenings, Brigid thought, "Yes, one immediate and positive benefit of the war abroad was that everyone seemed to have a few more bob in their pockets than in bygone days."

After all their purchases were made, Brigid and Gran stopped off at the church to say their prayers and light a candle. Brigid asked God to bless and keep Aran. She also vowed to do all she could to keep Patrick Pearse's spirit alive in her heart and somehow help continue his work of freeing Ireland.

After gathering up the children, the O'Mahonys stopped off for a cup of tea and a sandwich at the Leinster Arms before heading back home. While they were in the hotel, two of the RIC policemen who had visited their cottage last Sunday walked in. From where they sat, they gave Brigid the once-over. These two were not local men. No doubt they had been reassigned from another barracks to reinforce the Athy post due to the recent trouble in Dublin. Brigid could see them talking to each other in hushed tones. They punctuated their guarded conversation with occasional glances in her direction.

"It's hard to tell if those lads over there are making honey in their hearts after your good looks," whispered Gran.

"Somehow I doubt it," answered Brigid. "They seem more like troubled souls caught between earth and water."

❧

There was more than a day's worth of work left for the O'Mahonys back at the farm, so they loaded up the cart with their purchases and headed home. The Ryans would follow in their own good time.

The afternoon was spent cleaning the cottage, doing chores, making butter and washing clothes. Everyone had their jobs to do and, while she worked, Brigid's thoughts were filled with wonder about Aran and what her future might have in store. If Gran was right, some hard times were just around the corner.

The Ryans came down that evening and all joined in a sing-song and storytelling by the O'Mahonys' fire. Peter contributed a jar of homemade Connemara poitín he had bought off a cattle trader from County Galway. All the troubles of the day seemed to melt away by the light of the fire, the warmth of the conversation and the shared friendship.

Later that night, after everyone had left and all were safely tucked away in bed, Brigid lay awake under her white eiderdown covering in her old metal bed. Again, her mind swirled with thoughts of Aran and what had happened over the last ten days.

She closed her eyes and envisioned Aran lying next to her. She imagined herself curled up and fitted snugly against the curve of his body while his arm and shoulder cradled her head. She could almost hear his breathing and taste his kisses. She had never been with a man before, but any fears she might have had in giving herself to him were washed away by the waves of love and excitement he aroused in her.

Aran was strong yet sensitive...proud and determined but wise and thoughtful...driven by high-born principles, respectful of family and its time-honoured traditions yet willing to listen and consider the opinions of others. Brigid only hoped and prayed she would have the chance to know and love Aran...but that was something only time could buy.

Brigid knew Aran was almost four years her junior, but that did not seem to matter. He was older and wiser than his years.

She snuggled closer to him in her imagination. His six-foot frame seemed to swallow her up and she fantasised she could feel the strength and power of his taut muscles and smooth skin. His thick curly hair was almost the same colour as hers with maybe a little less red and a bit more blond in it. His coal-black penetrating eyes had a sparkle and shine to them. What a handsome couple they would make!

Brigid remembered Aran telling her on their last night together, while they stood outside looking up at the starry heavens, "Don't worry about me. I'm the seventh son of a seventh son. God is watching over me. Thanks be to Him for my chance of birth. I have a special guardian angel protecting me."

Holding her face in his hands, Aran had whispered, "Brigid, if we're born to be hanged, we won't drown...so there's no need to be troubled. We just have to do the best we can and not to worry about things beyond our control. God will keep us safe as best He can so."

Brigid fell asleep imagining Aran warming her in the narrow metal bed.

❧

Sunday morning dawned grey and soft. The lightly falling rain had little bite to it, but after a few minutes outside, everything would be wet. Dark billowing clouds were gathering in the west for a right blow, but Brigid felt compelled to saddle her black mare and ride to church in Athy. Gran and the children could go into town for the evening Mass as they sometimes did.

Wrapped in her oilskins and wearing high leather riding boots, Brigid raced out of the farmyard on her horse's back. No feminine English saddle for her. She prized her American-made, hand-tooled western saddle that had been her father's pride and joy.

She threw back her head and let the wind pull at her hair. The horsewoman urged her mount on with encouraging words and gentle kicks to its side. Racing along on the back of her high-spirited animal gave Brigid a great feeling of pleasure. The usual sense of risk and danger was soothed by the knowledge that her fast-riding skills, developed over the years, were to be enjoyed, not feared.

After flying through the outskirts of town, she galloped through

William and Duke Streets, rode up over the arched stone bridge span-
ning the River Barrow and past White's Castle. Slowing down, she
moved up along Leinster Street. A left turn into a side street put the
market house and Emily Square behind her. She trotted along the narrow roadway toward St. Michael's.

With the village church in sight, Brigid was surprised to see a group
of British soldiers standing about in the street. From their uniform
insignias she knew they were Royal Horse Artillery men from nearby
Newbridge. There, in front of the pack of Redcoats was one of the
RIC men who, with Sergeant McGee, had visited her cottage a week
ago. He was also one of the same two men who she had seen in the
hotel restaurant yesterday.

She did not know the policeman's name nor had she ever set eyes
on him prior to the RIC inquiry at the farm. But on this Sunday morning, the rozzer seemed angry and in a desperate mood. Brigid could
not tell if the cavalry men were trying to restrain him or if they were
slagging the new peeler.

In any event, as she rode by, the Irish rozzer recognised her. He
called out for all to hear, "There goes that little Shinner bitch,
O'Mahony...the dirty scut."

The other soldiers, all except one, laughed. He saluted and apolgised
saying, "Please pardon him, ma'am. He's a bit lumbered. Your man is
after having a drop too much of the drink in him."

"The hell you say I'm screwed," roared the peeler. The RIC policeman fired a hateful look back at the courteous soldier.

With that, the drunken one spun around and, after nearly stumbling over his own two feet, belched out, "It's lot like you that will be
the ruin of this country. You Taig women just don't appreciate that the
English are the force in this land and there's nothing ye can do about
it...God Save the King, God Save the King I say, God Save the King!"

The man's northern Irish accent was clearly discernible as he spewed
forth his venom.

During this verbal battering, Brigid's horse came to a full stop not
five feet from the belligerent. Sitting tall in her saddle and facing this
offensive little beast of a man, Brigid's pent-up rage grew in intensity.
Finally, she could not contain herself any longer. Her emotions erupted.

Standing up in her stirrups, Brigid verbally lashed back at the group.
"Is this the kind of man ye throw up to us Irish as examples of English
honour and British responsibility? It's a bloody shame you wretched
blighters and layabouts don't have anything better to do than to pick

on a woman. Ye bring shame on yourselves, your regiment and your country sure."

Brigid's unexpected verbal volley seemed to embarrass the soldiers. They collected their drunken associate and hustled him off down the street, away from Brigid and the small group of surprised villagers who had been attracted by the commotion.

Disturbed and upset, Brigid rode her horse over to the main entrance of the little church. She dismounted, tied the steed to a tree and entered the cool recesses of the chapel. The quietness and beauty of its interior had a calming effect on her inflamed emotions and seeking the comfort of prayer, Brigid gathered herself and relaxed.

Later, as she left the church after Mass, Brigid noted the sky was even darker than before. It was raining quite hard now. She pulled her oilskin cape close around her and fitted its hood tightly over her head. The soft Irish morning had turned into a right dirty day. It would be good to get home. She looked forward to warming up with some of Gran's homemade potato soup and brown bread. It was one of life's little pleasures—drying out by the comfort of the sitting room's fire with Gran's cooking inside her.

With her vision largely obscured by the waterproof and intent on returning home as quickly as possible, Brigid failed to notice the three horsemen who followed her out of town. She was well past the bridge and almost to the spot in the road where Aran had overtaken her rig ten days ago.

It was there, without warning, that the two soldiers and the drunken RIC policeman overtook her. Their abrupt emergence caught Brigid by surprise. Startled, she first noticed them out of the corner of her eye. Turning her head, Brigid clearly saw their lathered mounts. Above the rushing wind, she heard them yelling and fear knew her name.

Realising who they were and the danger she was in, a bolt of terror shot through her. Brigid's body stiffened. She lowered her head and spurred on her horse.

"Get that papist witch off that horse now!"

Brigid could not tell which man was doing the shouting. There was mass confusion with all four mounts racing hard at such close quarters. For the moment, however, she focused all of her attention on trying to stay atop her frightened mare.

"Grab the reins and pull her down!" came another frenzied command.

"Bloody hell, I'm trying to, but the little swine won't cooperate!"

After that first moment of shocked surprise, Brigid recovered her composure. She began exhorting her powerful horse to run even harder.

She thought to herself, if it's a fight ye want, well, let's see what ye can do when I am in full control of my senses.

The four riders raced down the narrow dirt road almost as one. A horseman closed in on either side of Brigid while the third man brought up the rear.

Slowly Brigid's fine horse began pulling away from the others. She could hear them shouting oaths of anger as they realised she might beat them at their own game and escape their clutches.

Gradually, her horse inched ahead. Then, just as she was about to break free of their trap, Brigid felt a huge weight thrust upon her horse's back. One of the men had leaped off his animal and jumped onto hers. He clung desperately to her as his hands and arms grabbed at and encircled her. Brigid could smell his foul, liquored breath. His whiskered face scraped against her cheek.

"You dirty hoor of a woman...stop this horse now or I'll kill ye!" By now Brigid was as mad as a fighting cock. She had no intention of giving in to this drunken sod.

It seemed to Brigid that her assailant was barely hanging on for dear life. So, with all the force she could muster, Brigid shot her right elbow backwards into the man's ribs.

She knew she had made contact with his solar plexus for the brute let out a mighty groan of surprise and pain. She felt his grip on her loosen. Brigid Eileen was vaguely aware of his slow slide off the back end of her horse...but that was all. The next thing she knew, she too was flying through the air.

When Brigid's attacker fell backwards off her horse, his falling body struck one of her mare's rear legs, tripping the frightened animal. As the horse stumbled and fell, Brigid was unsaddled and also thrown violently to the ground.

By the time the two soldiers had brought their horses to a stop, turned themselves around retracing their steps, the drunken RIC policeman was lying motionless in the roadway.

Brigid too was sprawled on her back. The thin trickle of blood now oozing from her mouth slowly began to increase in volume. Her fine mare was standing on only three legs. It tried to maintain its balance while painful whinnying sounds emanated from the panting beast's mouth.

The two British soldiers panicked. With wild-eyed expressions, they looked at one another. Without pausing to dismount or offer aid to the fallen victims, they galloped back towards Athy.

In the sudden silence, the sound of thunder began rolling out of the black clouds overhead. A bolt of lightning flashed across the leaden sky. The rain fell even harder than before.

Brigid's mare hobbled over to its fallen mistress. The faithful animal nuzzled the bleeding woman's neck and shoulder. Instinctively, the animal knew something was terribly wrong.

12. *Escaping*

"What did I have?" said the fine old woman.
"What did I have?" this proud old woman did say.
"I had four green fields, each one was a jewel,
But strangers came and tried to take them from me.
I had fine strong sons, they fought to save my jewels,
They fought and died, and that was my grief" said she.

Four Green Fields / Tommy Makem

"Still no change, but at least he's sleeping comfortably, Doctor," reported the ship's duty nurse.

The doctor was pleased. "Hopefully, the worst is over. We'll just have see what time and the good Lord are able to do for the lad. He was lucky the bullet didn't go any deeper. Now that the bleeding is under control, we'll just have to wait for the swelling to subside before I can assess the real damage."

With the nurse looking after the patient, the doctor walked out of the ship's surgery. Wearily, he made his way down the narrow passageway toward his quarters. He paused briefly at the open doorway of the makeshift reception area that doubled as a waiting room. He peered inside. The two men were still there. One was slumped over asleep in a wooden captain's chair. The other, lying on the floor wrapped in a blanket, was wide awake.

On seeing the doctor standing in the corridor, the reclining figure raised himself up with his elbows and asked, "How's he getting on?"

"Still too early to tell, but at least he's resting comfortably. As for your other friend, Mr. Kelly, the bullet only nicked the bone in his arm. Barring any unforeseen infection and, assuming he allows the cast and nature to do their work, he'll be as good as new in four weeks."

The man on the floor nodded, smiled and thanked the medical man for all he had done.

Curling back up on the ship's floor, Liam Mellowes thought to himself how lucky they were. This doctor was no amateur. From the initial looks of Aran's wounds and from the amount of blood he had lost, it was truly a miracle he was still alive. On the other hand, Danny's arm appeared far less serious. Even Danny, the master of understatement, had said the bullet felt more like a bee sting than a piece of English lead that had come close to killing him.

With the doctor gone, the man from Dublin-cum-Galway pulled the blanket more closely around him. He pushed his back against the wall trying to compensate for the ship's constant side to side movement.

Liam Mellowes was not a sailor. The relentless motion of the vessel slowly ploughing through the waters of the North Atlantic made him sick. He had already thrown up everything in his stomach but still his head kept spinning to the rhythms of the Brazilian steamship's pitching and rolling. Unless the seas became heavier, he could perhaps grow accustomed to the unfamiliar instability of his constantly moving world. A few more hours or, at the most, another day of misery and he would be back on his feet...or so he hoped.

For the moment, however, lying down and trying to sleep was the only proper antidote for his agony. Sitting up or moving around just compounded his ill feeling and renewed his urge to throw up. Besides, he had nowhere to go. He wanted to be near the young rebel lying near death in the next cabin.

From his position on the floor, Mellowes looked up through his pince-nez glasses at the man sleeping so peacefully in the chair opposite him. For a baker and landlubber, Richard 'Shadow' Doyle seemed right at home at sea.

Shadow was only in his mid-thirties but his powerful, low-sized frame was topped with a fine crop of grey curly hair. His face had a well lived-in look about it while the lines radiating from the corners of his eyes told the careful observer that this was a kind person given to smiling more often than not. His nickname 'Shadow' was well deserved. During the Boer War in 1899, he was a nineteen-year-old junior staff officer assigned to an Irishman, Major John 'Foxie Jack' MacBride. Doyle had been a key, behind-the-scenes organiser assisting in the formation of a small Irish pro-Boer Brigade in the South

African Transvaal. Consisting of about 300 men, many of them American, the unit saw limited action during the one year of its existence. Over Shadow's objections, the brigade was disbanded in September, 1900 by the Afrikaners themselves. By his own recollection, Shadow guessed they had only fought in something like twenty engagements.[12-1, 12-2]

During one of those encounters, MacBride was elevated from second-in-command to Brigade Commander when the unit's OC, a colourful American named Colonel Jack Blake, was wounded. Later, at the Battle of Tugela River east of the Transvaal, Shadow took two bullets in the back while he single-handedly dragged his injured friend, MacBride, to safety.

His reputation as a brave and courageous soldier continued to grow among the Irish after Shadow joined a second pro-Boer Irish Brigade formed under an Irish-Australian by the name of Arthur Lynch. This group, however, composed mostly of Afrikaners, Germans, French and Irishmen, was soon dispersed toward the end of the war.[12-3] Doyle had often openly expressed his disappointment that this second unit had only engaged the British in limited combat, most notably the Boer retreat toward the Natal border in March, 1900.

Mellowes knew well how Shadow enjoyed talking about that turn-of-the-century conflict. He had heard Richard lecture others about how the political climate in Ireland and in parts of England was strongly pro-Boer. Irish moderates joined British liberals in their support of the Dutch farmers' fight against English imperialism. These sentiments, however, were in sharp contrast to the thousands of Irishmen who were fighting against the Boers in various Irish units of the British army. When the conflict finally ended, hundreds of Ireland's finest had given their lives in support of Queen, Crown and British colonialism while the real plight of the native black African Bantu, especially the Zulus, was never really understood or considered by either side. In reality, this indigent population had been dominated and suppressed for many years by the Dutch and English just as the Irish had been oppressed for centuries by the British.

MacBride's Brigade, created to fight Englishmen and fellow Irishmen, was another symptom of the confused and divided political, economic and social conditions existing in Great Britain at the time.[12-4]

Mellowes continued his reminiscences of the now innocent looking Irishman asleep in the chair across from him. Shadow had been instrumental in the formation of the Irish Volunteers in counties Galway and Clare. For the past three years Doyle had given unselfishly of his soldiering skills. He had often risked arrest in his efforts to support the plan to organise and train a fighting force that would assist Pearse and the IRB's Easter Rebellion plans in the west of Ireland.

Fighting nausea, Mellowes thought of how on Thursday night of Easter Week, with his forces retreating and in danger of being surrounded, Shadow Doyle, Danny Kelly and the rest of them decided to call it quits. Sadly but wisely, he had to send his men home. Despite the disappointments, his men parted feeling proud of their efforts but deeply dissatisfied at the results.

And so it was that he, joined by a handful of his closest friends, headed south into County Clare. They sought the security of Shadow's safe-house outside of Limerick while final plans were made for their escape to Amerikay.

✺

Shadow woke from his long nap. With nothing better to do he began pacing up and down the cabin floor. After inquiring about Aran's condition, he offered to scrounge up something for Mellowes to eat. Liam shook his head, turned his green face to the wall and moaned a thanks but no thanks reply.

An hour later, a satiated Shadow returned with a pot of weak tea, honey and toast for his friend. Surprisingly, the nourishment stayed down. Gradually, Mellowes began feeling human again.

As the two sat facing each other across the room's table, Liam asked Richard to analyse what had gone wrong with their escape plan.

After a few moments of reflection Shadow answered, "Nothing and everything!"

"What do you mean by that so?" queried Mellowes.

Shadow knew his OC loved to dissect each plan of action they had ever undertaken together. Besides formulating new schemes, Shadow knew this reviewing process was important to Liam. It seemed to satisfy his leader's need for checks and balances.

"Well Liam, didn't we make plans weeks ago with our friends in New York and London to have this ship cruise up the west coast of Ireland, just five miles off Kerry Head, in case we needed to make a run for it?"

Mellowes nodded and smiled. "A truly brilliantly conceived and executed plan, especially in light of the dangerous sailing conditions created by the war. Yes, it was a real coup."

Shadow paused, allowing Mellowes to savour the sweetness of the moment before he continued.

"Remember, Liam, how Devoy and the other powers-to-be in New York made all the arrangements. They smuggled over the travel documents and departure details. The necessary bribes were in the right hands and we were promised there'd be nothing to worry about."

"Well, so far you're right, Shadow. Those Yanks certainly held up their end of the bargain!"

As he continued, Shadow lowered his voice in case the walls had ears. "Everything was fine until those bloody lousers ambushed us just outside of Cratloe. Liam, the only thing I can think of is someone in our group tipped them off. How else would they have known where to position their troops?"

Mellowes interrupted his friend. "I've been making a mental list of those who knew our plans and I will deal with each one of them when we get back home. If I can find the sodding blighter who informed on us, he'll wish he'd never opened his gob. Our history is too replete with traitors and informers. Sure, those greedy Irish agents and English spies have, all too often, rendered our efforts for freedom useless.

"Shadow, do you realise that down through the ages, these Judases have been one of Ireland's greatest weaknesses and England's biggest strengths. If I can only ferret out the punter who did us in, it will be his last act of treachery...you can bet on that!"

Mellowes paused, reflecting on his own words. He thought back to his own capture by British authorities just two months ago. As a known Sinn Fein organiser, he was on Britain's list of wanted men. With luck and careful planning, however, he had evaded capture. Then, in early March, while staying with friends in Tuam, he was arrested and deported to England. Luckily though, he was not placed under close arrest, but merely warned not to return to Ireland unless he wanted to end up in prison for the next ten years of his life.

Knowing the Rebellion was scheduled for Easter Sunday, he ignored the warning, disguised himself as a priest and, with the help of his brother, returned to Dublin via Glasgow and Belfast. He stayed a short time with Pearse at St. Enda's before returning to Galway to coordinate the Rising in the West. It was there at Pearse's school just before Easter that Pat had introduced him to Aran Roe O'Neill.

Now once again dressed in his priestly robes and collar, Mellowes spoke to his friend, who had resumed his pacing. "Shadow, do you think Tommy will make it?"

"He was hit pretty bad. I tried to locate a pulse while we were banging about in the back of the wagon, but things were too wild and happening so fast. I just couldn't be sure if he was with us or not. He had a pretty serious head wound. There was blood everywhere. Hopefully, the lads back home were able to find a doctor who'll patch him up. Maybe, he'll be as lucky as Aran has been.

"Just imagine, Liam, finding a doctor on this bucket of nuts and bolts, who worked for six months patching up wounded men from Gallopoli. Sweet Jesus in Heaven, Aran couldn't be in better hands if he was back home in Dublin or in London."

Both men fell silent as each remembered the running gun battle with the English forces...some on horseback and others firing down on them from a hill just outside Cratloe.

Suddenly, Mellowes interrupted Shadow's reverie. "Are you after recalling my orders to Aidan and Colm as we lifted Aran onboard the hooker?"

"Just before we set sail down the Shannon?"

"Aye."

"You instructed them to locate Aran's family and give them the news of our departure. I distinctly remember you said, 'They live somewhere near Gort.' Is that what you're referring to, Liam?"

"Yes, but now I'm after wondering if it was enough."

"What do you mean?"

"What I mean is...Aran told me about a lassie he'd met near Athy. From his brief description, it was evident he'd grown sweet on her."

"Would that be the 'Brigid' he kept calling out to as we headed for open water?"

"That it would so!"

"Now, if I can guess what you're thinking, Liam, it might be months before we could get word back to that woman."

"Ah sure, you're right, Richard. So, maybe, if we're all lucky enough, Aran himself can have the honour of writing to this Brigid lass. From what he told me, I'm thinking he'd like to make her a permanent part of his life."

"Jaysus, Liam! If he doesn't make it, that woman will be after eating the both of us when she finds out who talked the kid into riding out to Cratloe."

"Right so, Richard. There's nothing worse than a woman's anger, except maybe the noose-end of an English rope!"

Talk of Aran had reminded the two men of their narrow escape. As if hypnotised by Shadow's pacing to and fro in the small cabin, Liam lapsed into thoughtful silence.

Finally, the veteran guerrilla fighter sat down once more. His doing so seemed to break Mellowes's trance. "Richard, the wind, the tide, everything was perfect for us, wasn't it?"

"That's what I meant, Liam, when I said everything and nothing went right with our plan...smooth as silk yet rough as a rocky road if you please.

"Look at us...here we are high and dry like the ould kings of Ireland sitting atop the Rock of Cashel. But on the other hand, Tommy's been shot and maybe dead, Aran's on death's doorstep and the three of us, Danny, you and me are after hightailing it out of Ireland...away from our families and friends...on the run from the English for who knows for how long sure?

"The Rebellion's in shambles and the British are executing and deporting our comrades at a merry clip. Ah sure, 'tis all a pretty desperate situation if you ask me."

Liam Mellowes could only agree with his friend. Their hard work and careful planning had suffered the same fate as Dublin's once-grand General Post Office which now lay in smoldering ruins. Its destruction had become a grim testimony to the rebels' failure despite their noble ideals, determined will and deep sense of patriotism.

❧

Their journey to Amerikay would take them ten days to cross the wide Atlantic, often referred to in days of old as 'the sea of tears.' In those days the 'coffin' ships willingly and unwillingly transported millions of Irishmen and women to new beginnings or to lonely, watery graves beyond the loved hills of their ancient homeland.

For the first three of those ten days both Liam and Richard kept watch over Aran from the waiting-room cabin next to the ship's infirmary. During that time, Mellowes finally found his sea legs.

Nothing, however, seemed to bother his friend Shadow Doyle. Richard's only complaint was that he thought he was putting up some weight from all the food he was eating.

Danny Kelly's arm finally stopped throbbing and he was growing accustomed to his cloth sling. This twenty-two-year-old, fair-complexioned young Irishman from the little seaside village of Spiddle in County Galway was a quiet lad but possessed a fierce temper when angered. He had dark, deep-set eyes, a thin face and small yellowish teeth that had wider than usual spaces between them. One of Danny's special talents was his ability to spit tiny but powerful streams of liquid from between his teeth at friends and foe alike. His favourite target was the back of the neck of an unsuspecting mate. But despite this annoying habit, Danny was a fine marksman, a brave soldier and a very loyal friend.

As for Aran Roe O'Neill, the one Mellowes began calling the only real Irish rebel in their midst, there was little news, good or bad, to report. The doctor stated he was resting comfortably, his brain swelling was beginning to subside and there were no signs of infection in or around his wounds. But despite those positive signs, he was still in a coma. The medical man assured Aran's three companions that this was entirely normal for one suffering from severe skull and brain trauma.

From time to time one, two or all three of them would visit Aran as he lay in the ship's small hospital ward. Though he did not respond, they continued talking to him about their recent adventures. Additionally, they would read to him or just simply sit and offer Aran as much comfort as possible.

In reality, though, Aran was a stranger to them all. They had not grown up together nor had they worked as a team during the planning and training phases of the Rebellion. But, this lack of unity was compensated for by the fact that each of them shared one deep, abiding and burning interest. All four men wanted to see their land free of the British blight that had polluted and infected it for over seven-hundred-fifty years.

❧

On the fourth day at sea, Liam and Shadow moved in with Danny Kelly to the quarters that had been reserved and paid for by Devoy's Clan-na-Gael/Irish-American money. It was a comfortable cabin with a porthole for admitting fresh sea air.

It possessed two sets of bunk beds, a chest of drawers filled with underclothes, toilet articles and four Luger automatic revolvers with twelve clips of ammunition. Hanging in the closet were four new suits with waistcoats, braces, shirts with accompanying hard collars, neckties, tie pins and a half a dozen pairs of various sized hobnailed boots.

They even found four waterproofs and four soft felt hats to finish off their wardrobe. Their new rigouts were even grander than their things left back at home.

The boys in Amerikay had not missed a beat and, as the three rebels paraded around in the cabin in their new things, they vowed to repay their American cousins as soon as they were able.

❧

During most of the journey, the three Irishmen remained in their cabin and avoided calling any unnecessary attention to themselves. They only left their quarters to take late night walks on the ship's deck or to visit the still unconscious Aran and help with his tube feedings. During this time, a steward faithfully delivered their meals to the cabin.

Three days prior to the ship's scheduled docking in Baltimore Harbor, the men were unexpectedly awakened by a late-night knocking on their cabin door. First fearing Aran had taken a turn for the worst, the three Irishmen were relieved to find the ship's captain, not the doctor, standing in the passageway.

Asking to be admitted, the weathered old seaman said he had just received a special message for Liam Mellowes from his 'Uncle Paddy' in New York. Thanking the captain and wishing him a good night, the three men fell to work decoding the short message.

❧

With only forty-eight hours to go before landfall, a small miracle happened...Aran Roe O'Neill regained consciousness for a few minutes. Shadow was alone with him at the time in the hospital ward.

"Doctor, nurse, somebody...come quick...he's awake!"

Moments later the doctor was standing next to Aran's bunk.

"Don't try to talk, son...my name is Doctor Thompson...you've received two nasty head wounds, but now everything seems to be under control. One of the bullets only grazed you. Its impact must have been something akin to a pebble bouncing off a piece of granite rock."

Shadow could not help but laugh and Aran tried to muster a weak smile.

"Now, there ye go...I see you're coming back to life a bit at a time," grinned the medical man.

Quickly, though, the doctor's expression changed. He grew more serious.

"Aran, your other wound is more involved but we've made great strides in patching you up. That second bullet entered the back of your skull just behind your left ear. But instead of going straight through your cranium and into your brain, it travelled along the curve of your skull. It probably passed very near the surface of your cortex. It came to rest just under your hairline above your left temple. I was able to remove the bullet quite easily. I've even saved it. I thought you might fancy the souvenir.

"Your wounds have been cleaned, dressed and there are no signs of infection, at least at this point. All the bleeding has been stopped and the swelling of your injured tissues is on the decline.

"You're going to have a sore head for a while and I would be surprised if your memory wasn't affected, at least temporarily. But as long as you take it easy for the next several months, I'm confident it'll return. You should make a complete recovery."

Shadow was uncertain whether or not Aran heard or understood all of the doctor's comments for the wounded man's eyes closed again while the doctor was still talking.

The physician turned to Shadow Doyle and said, "Hopefully, if he heard me, Aran should take comfort in what I said. He's really a very lucky young man. In my field hospital back in Gallipoli, I've seen men die of head wounds that weren't as serious as his. He must have a guardian angel watching over him!"

Shadow nodded, thanked the doctor for the thousandth time and hurried back to tell the others the good news about Aran's return to the land of the living, at least momentarily.

Liam and Danny were delighted to hear the report, but were still concerned with how they were going to move Aran without further damaging his injured head.

As things stood now, the four of them would transfer at sea to a fishing boat and then be taken the last twenty miles to shore in the smaller craft.

The powers-to-be in Amerikay felt it was too risky trying to slip them in through the regular customs and emigration channels. At the moment, America was expressing many strong pro-British/anti-Irish sentiments. All this because the United States War Department felt the Irish Easter Revolt was a German inspired, planned and supported affair.

In light of present feelings, trying to bring in four Irishmen without proper passports and documentation would only arouse suspicion. Immigration officials might easily view them as part of some pro-German conspiracy to infiltrate the United States with undercover agents. Then, to top off matters, if the American authorities discovered that two of the men were suffering bullet wounds, there would be no question that they would all be denied entrance. The four Irishmen would be detained, then shipped back home to England's waiting arms on the next available vessel.

Therefore, in order to avoid detection and American border problems, Devoy and his people had sent Mellowes a coded letter, via an imaginary 'uncle,' describing how the rebels would be brought into the country.

At three o'clock the next morning, their steamship would slow to a stop and rendezvous with a fishing boat twenty miles from the mouth of Chesapeake Bay. From there they would be transported into the Bay, up the Potomac River and offloaded at the tiny fishing village of Leonardtown. At that point, the four lads would be met by other Clan-na-Gael members and taken by motor car to safe-houses.

The ship's captain and doctor had assured the anxious Irishmen Aran could be safely lowered onto the fishing boat, but he would be without medical supervision for the two days it would take them to reach land.

"But," as Shadow said, "what choice do we have?"

So, it was settled. The necessary plans had been made and now all they could do was wait.

❧

The pending boat transfer and the danger involved in avoiding the American authorities seemed to excite the three rebels, though Mellowes was not looking forward to the rocky journey in the fishing boat. Even after nine days at sea, his stomach still had not entirely settled down.

The men had grown complacent and bored aboard ship. But now, faced with a new, challenging situation that could prove dangerous, their adventurous appetites were whetted.

At Mellowes's suggestion, the three men huddled one last time. Prior to catching a few hours of sleep, they went over the details of their deboarding the ship.

The Volunteer OC ran through a verbal checklist with his comrades. In addition to the new clothes on their backs, each of them was taking waterproof packets containing thirty American dollars and some well-worn papers describing them as Irish farm machinery salesmen. The German Lugers, carefully secured in their small holsters, were strapped across their chests. Each gun hung just below its owner's left armpit.

In addition, Shadow had bundled up Aran's things and placed them in a small duffel bag purchased from one of the ship's crew.

"Richard, Danny...I've come to a decision about how we should proceed once we've reached land. But when all is said and done, we're going to have to trust the Yanks to keep us out of trouble.

"I've after several appointments to keep plus I want to spend time with Devoy and the others. I must be free to move around so. Unfortunately, Aran will only tie me down. Therefore, I'm going to ask you lads to split up. Richard, I want you to stay with Aran until he's on his feet again. Do whatever you need to do to help and safeguard him. Cover for him if necessary. Danny, I'm after wanting you to stay with me. Your assistance will be most invaluable."

Doyle and Kelly looked at each other, then nodded approvingly at Mellowes.

"Shadow, we'll keep in contact through Devoy's office. Toward the end of the summer, we'll see what the situation at home is like. If it looks safe enough, we'll plan to meet and make our way back to Ireland so. In any event, I want a minimum of one letter a month from you, Richard. You can expect the same from me. Are we agreed, no?"

Doyle answered in the affirmative, being careful to hide his disappointment at not being asked to accompany his friend.

"Any last minute details that need going over?" queried Mellowes.

Shadow answered for the two of them, "No, I think everything is clear. I just hope our good luck holds over here."

❧

With their plans finalised and only time between them and their departure, the three rebels lay down and tried to rest.

From his top bunk, Shadow gazed across the dimly lit cabin down onto Liam Mellowes's bed. His commanding officer was stretched out on top of his blanket and was snoring lightly.

Doyle's first thought was how innocent and peaceful Liam looked in repose. His OC's childlike appearance contrasted dramatically with the intelligent, dynamic and charismatic leader he was during his waking hours. The two men had been friends for several years. Shadow's admiration and respect for Mellowes knew no bounds.

Born in 1892, Liam, like Richard, was a republican through and through. The older man smiled to himself as he pictured Liam, tousled hair and all, dressed in his usual three piece outfit of waistcoat, trousers and jacket. In that innocent looking rigout, Mellowes could easily be mistaken for a simple shopkeeper or humble civil servant instead of the armoured knight he was.

The thoughts of dress reminded Shadow of one of Liam's trademarks—his leather gaiters. His modest appearance took on a more militaristic look when he strapped on the leather puttees that covered his lower legs from just below the knees to the tops of his polished boots.

The two other Mellowes trademarks that defined his uniqueness were his smile and his pince-nez glasses. Shadow often wondered if Liam's smile was born of personal delight or because he was always squinting through the glasses fastened to his nose while he tried focusing on the person speaking to him or upon the object he was scrutinising.

Mellowes's smile-formed dimples, high forehead, gently receding hairline topped off with wispy, sandy coloured locks painted a picture of someone who you would like to know and could easily trust. Shadow certainly did.

Finally, Doyle thought that his friend's rather short and slightly stocky frame truly understated the giant of a man Liam Mellowes was.

For all those reasons and more, Shadow delighted in being his loyal assistant. He was proud to be associated with the man whose love for Ireland and whose desire to see her free were unremitting and uncompromising.

❧

Later that evening, when Danny was out of the cabin checking on Aran, Mellowes called Shadow to his side and looked his friend straight in the eye.

"Shadow, it's not an easy task I've saddled you with. Being responsible for Aran and looking after his well-being will be a challenge. As soon as he's able, I want you to begin showing him the ropes...the little ins and outs that help make you so valuable. Teach him to be more like us. If I'm not mistaken, there's going to be a proper war back home very soon and we'll need all the quality men on our side we can find. Aran has the potential of being a great one. Do your best, keep him safe and train him well."

As the two men shook hands, Mellowes put his arm around

Shadow and momentarily squeezed his shoulder. A bond of deep friendship and common respect linked the two together, a bond so strong that only death could break it.

❧

The night was dark but the sea was calm as Liam Mellowes, Shadow Doyle and Danny Kelly made their way along the wooden deck to the ship's stern. Following the three Irishmen were two sailors carrying Aran cradled in a sheet and wrapped warmly in several blankets. It was just as well he was unconscious. The pain from moving him might have caused Aran to cry out, drawing unwanted attention to their late night activities. The ship's doctor walked behind Aran and kept a watchful eye on the little procession.

When they had reached the appointed spot, the ship's captain and two other sailors emerged from the deck's shadows. The seamen had rigged up a canvas stretcher with ropes attached to its four ends. Carefully, Aran was deposited in the elongated conveyance. Several straps were tied around his sleeping body, ensuring that he would not slip out of his cloth hammock.

As Shadow looked over the ship's railing and down into the water, he saw a stubby fishing boat with its tall mast waving in the night approaching the big vessel. In addition to Aran's contraption, one of the crew had tossed a rope ladder over the side of the ship.

Mellowes thanked the captain and doctor for all their help. They had saved Aran's life and in the process had earned the three Irishmen's undying gratitude. The ship's officer signaled the converging craft as the doctor pulled Mellowes and the two other rebels aside. He spoke to them in quiet tones. "I didn't mention this before, but my mother's from County Cork. Her father was on board the *Indomptable* with Wolfe Tone as the French fleet waited in Bantry Bay for General Hoche's flagship to arrive in December, 1796. Ye know the rest of the story and its sad ending. Hoche didn't arrive in time and with the wind blowing from the east, Tone's fleet couldn't land. Another chance for Irish freedom was lost."

The three Irishmen glanced at one another in veiled amazement.

"Now, I wished I'd said something earlier," continued the doctor. "Though I'm English, I just couldn't stomach what we did to all those young men in the Dardanelles last year. It was a terrible slaughter and a senseless waste of fine human beings.

"Britain's thirst for military domination needs to be arrested and if you three lads are able to right the wrongs England has visited on

Ireland...well, more power to ye. May God watch over each of you, especially Aran.

"And speaking of Aran, I think he'll be all right. With his improved state, you can eliminate the tube feedings. But mind that head of his and have a doctor look at him after you land."

With that the medical man shook each of their hands, turned and disappeared into the night back along the decking.

"Steady lads...slow and easy does it."

It was the captain's voice directing Aran over the side and down onto the fishing boat.

Climbing up and over the railing, Shadow was the first to head down the rope ladder. Danny was next. But with his arm in the sling, his descent was laboriously slow. Shadow stayed close in case he needed a supporting hand to keep him from falling.

Mellowes was the last one over the rail and, as he disappeared below the ship's deck, Liam saw Aran's empty sling being hauled back up from below. Liam knew the Irish Rebel was safely aboard the fishing boat. Please God, he thought, if they could just avoid any storms and the American Coast Guard, his little band of freedom-fighters would soon be on dry land.

Continuing to descend, Mellowes said a prayer of thanksgiving asking God to continue watching over them all.

Finally, with his feet squarely on the deck of the little boat and his rope lifeline disappearing into the night, Liam could feel the dwarfed vessel's engines rev up and surge to life. Slowly the distance between the fishing boat and the huge Brazilian steamer grew wider.

Mellowes lingered at the railing and watched the big ship slowly move off into the night. Its lights continued to twinkle like stars on the water for the longest time.

A voice at his elbow disturbed his thoughts. Liam turned and saw a smiling face grinning at him. The man thrust a cup of something hot into his hand saying, "Welcome to Mheiricéa, Mr. Mellowes. I'm Gabriel McCracken. Some of my friends call me Gay while others prefer Gabby. As for me, it doesn't much matter...just take your pick. My brothers, Lawrence and Dominic plus the two mates who own this tub are here to take ye ashore.

"...and oh, by the way, just in case you're wondering, my mother's American but my father came over from Westport in Mayo during the land wars in the early 1880s...but more of that later.

"You and your men are in safe hands. As you might have guessed, we lads all work for the Clan and Mr. Devoy.

"When you are ready, come below, meet the others and change into some proper nautical gear. We've a good two days of fishing and sailing before we're home. Ah sure, each of us needs to be looking like we're really sailors in case of an inquiry.

"Again, very glad to have ye on board, Mr. Mellowes. Yes sir...mighty glad!"

13. *Healing*

When all beside a vigil keep
The West's asleep, the West's asleep
Alas! and well may Erin weep
When Connacht lies in slumber deep.
There lake and plain smile fair and free,
'Mid rocks their guardian chivalry.
Sing, Oh! let man learn liberty
From crashing wind and lashing sea.

The West's Asleep/ Thomas Davis

$\mathcal{T}$he black Model T Ford made slow but steady progress on its way inland from the little Maryland fishing port of Leonardtown.

The sun was just rising, lifting an early morning fog to expose a lush rural landscape. Richard 'Shadow' Doyle, wedged in with two others on the rear seat of the motor car, was enjoying his first look at Amerikay through the side window of the Ford.

He remembered feeling this same sense of excitement years before when his father took him to Cork for his departure to South Africa in 1897. At the time, he was only sixteen but hoped to seek his fame and fortune working in the diamond mines near Johannesburg. He planned on living with his uncle who was a crew boss for one of the big excavations there. Everything worked out well for the first couple of years but things quickly changed when the war broke out.

In 1899, he met Major John MacBride, an Irishman from Westport, County Mayo. He willingly joined the newly organised Irish Brigade and fought with the underdog Boers against imperial England.

Three years later, during the final weeks of the war, he was badly wounded for a second time, but luckily survived. Much like Aran, he had received some unexpectedly fine medical attention at a Dutch-run hospital in Pretoria.

While recovering, Shadow was arrested for conspiring against the British government and was placed under house arrest along with dozens of other pro-Boer Irish soldiers. After his wounds healed, he was deported to England and spent ten months as a guest of the English government in London's Clerkenwell Prison.

Stories still circulated through the old gaol about the Irish Fenians' 1867 rescue attempt to free Richard Burke, a rebel armaments buyer. A large explosive device had been placed on the footpath next to the prison's stone wall. The resulting blast blew open part of the outer protective perimeter that enclosed the prison's exercise yard. But, due to a mix up in communications, Burke was not where he was supposed to be at the appointed time and the attempt to free him failed. Tragically, twelve innocent Londoners were killed and several dozen others were seriously wounded in the explosion.

This raid, coupled with the September attack on a police van in Manchester by independent-minded Irish rebels, woke up British public opinion to the widespread seriousness of Irish discontent. Previously, the English citizenry seemed to lightly regard 'distant' Ireland and her desire for freedom as something foreign and unimportant. But now, the problem was dramatically alive in their own back garden. Its sudden and deadly presence shook England and frightened its suddenly concerned English public. [13-1]

It was in this same historic penal institution during 1903 that Shadow received his first formal education in Irish republicanism and radical Fenianism.

Reflecting back on those days, he often smiled to himself as he recalled how Irishmen over the years, arrested for 'crimes' against the state, entered British prisons as politically tepid and naive men. But with the passage of time and the exposure to other embittered, radicalised and disaffected activists, an innocent prisoner emerged months later as a dedicated revolutionary.

The English never seemed to learn that their gaols had become the universities for a republication revolution that sowed the seeds of rebellion and discontent throughout Amerikay, Ireland and other British holdings around the world. A classic example had been Tom Clarke. As a recent 'graduate' of Portland Jail, he had instilled, inspired and incorporated his die-hard Fenian philosophy of 'England's difficulty equaled Ireland's opportunity' into the planning of the 1916 Easter Rebellion.

Shadow mused to himself, as he rode along though the unfamiliar countryside, that again England hopefully would sufferer another round of embarrassing and destructive consequences when the 1916 internees were freed from their imprisoned institutions of rebel education.

Shadow continued his solitary musing. After his 1904 prison release, he remembered returning to his native Limerick. He took over the responsibility of managing the family bread and baking business from his ailing father. As the oldest son, he was charged with providing for his mother, father and four younger siblings.

With a natural talent for business coupled with his untiring hard work and backed by a loyal staff, the family business boomed. The bakery grew in reputation and prosperity.

Additionally, Shadow married a childhood sweetheart in 1910 and fathered three beautiful children who, he always maintained, favoured his attractive wife, Helen, rather than his less handsome self.

As his business success grew, Shadow had more time for other interests. His long desire to see Ireland free of English authoritarianism, which had been spurred by his recent war and prison experiences, caused him to join a new political 'club' called Sinn Fein. His administrative skills soon vaulted Richard to the top of Limerick's local executive.

It was at these meetings that he became acquainted with Liam Mellowes, a key Sinn Fein recruiter in the west of Ireland. Their friendship grew and deepened. Mellowes began counting on Shadow to shoulder more and more of the party's organisational responsibilities. Then, with the formation of the Irish Volunteers in November, 1913, Liam recommended to the Dublin executive that Shadow become Limerick's commanding officer.

Following his OC appointment early in 1914, Doyle was sworn into the secret, oath-bound Irish Republication Brotherhood. Later he was called on to help Mellowes with the regional planning for the 1916 Easter Rebellion in Connacht and Munster.

Now, because of that disappointing and disastrous defeat, the four of them were here in Amerikay. Three thousand miles was a long way to run from the revengeful hand of English injustice!

❀

As their road journey stretched out, Shadow gradually began feeling very uncomfortable. His body was poured into the rear seat of the small vehicle and his legs had nowhere to move. It seemed as if most of Aran Roe O'Neill's twelve stone weight was pushing the Limerick man into the side panelling of the motor car. But, he dared not move for fear of reopening one of Aran's wounds.

The third man squeezed into the narrow confines of the Model T's back seat was Dominic, one of the three McCracken brothers who had picked them up at sea from the steamship three nights earlier.

Dom was the youngest, looking to be in his mid-twenties. While his two older brothers had darker complexions, Dom was fair skinned with a fine crop of curly red hair. The tallest of the three at just over six feet, Dom had broad shoulders and a muscular physique. He looked to be as strong as a bull. Though outwardly self-assured, Shadow had noticed the youngest McCracken seldom expressed a personal opinion. He usually let one of his brothers do his talking for him. But, despite his seeming lack of self-confidence, Dominic possessed a lovely baritone voice and gladly joined his two brothers in singing songs of Irish freedom.

Speeding along the uneven, Maryland country roads at thirty miles an hour only increased the uncomfortableness of the ride. As they bounced from one pothole to another, the driver, Larry, seemed unconcerned about the possibilities of damaging a wheel or breaking a leaf spring.

It seemed that Lawrence McCracken was the risk-taker in the family. The oldest at thirty-three, he stood about five feet nine inches tall and had a slightly Mediterranean-looking complexion. Shadow thought that his southern Celtic blood must run deeply. Larry's long, curly black hair almost touched his shoulders while the man's love of life was evident in his usually beaming brown eyes and habitually optimistic worldly outlook. Broad of beam like his brother Dom, Lawrence was a man of action, though in Shadow's mind, he seemed a bit impulsive. But despite any misgivings Shadow might have had about Larry, the Yank possessed one distinctive characteristic that he trusted and respected...and that was rough hands. They spoke volumes in Shadow's book. Any man with hands like Larry's was not afraid of hard work. That meant a lot to the Limerick man. It was those calloused paws of the oldest McCracken lad that reminded Shadow of his old friend and commander, Major 'Foxy Jack' MacBride, the Transvaal Rebel.

"Any chance of opening a window up there? The air back here's very close...I'm feeling a wee bit sick to my stomach," complained Shadow.

Gabby, sitting in the front next to his brother Larry, cranked the handle, lowering the door's window. Gratefully, Shadow pulled in several deep breaths of sweet-smelling fresh air.

Gabriel turned around to see how the three in the back were getting on. Smiling, he could not help teasing Shadow. "You Paddies probably don't have all these modern conveniences back in the 'ould country,' do ye? I mean like cars, roads and all our many other newfangled comforts."

"Never even knew what one was until we crawled into this creature a couple of hours ago. Sure, I must be the first 'real' Irishman to ever have gone so far, so fast in such a short time!" rebutted Shadow.

Everyone laughed except Aran. He still drifted in and out of wakefulness and, for the moment, was fast asleep. Aran's two weeks of inactivity and limited food intake were having an effect on his usually vital and muscular body. His six-foot frame was visibly thinner. The Gortman's normally tanned cheeks now had a pale, yellowish cast about them. A dullness had replaced the usual sparkle and intensity of his coal-black eyes. What little hair he had left after his surgery was stringy and unkempt. A bandage still protected part of his slowly healing head.

It continued to be a struggle to bathe him, brush his teeth and get him to eat and drink at mealtimes. But, he was definitely improving, thanks in large measure to the attentive care of his three comrades.

Aran now spent several hours a day awake and sitting up. Though he spoke little, Aran had started recalling some events of his recent past. Vague memories of Dublin burning and of meeting Brigid were beginning to emerge from the hidden recesses of his battered head.

Shadow was pleased with Aran's improvement though he looked forward to the time when a doctor could evaluate the Gortman's condition. Having a professional confirm Aran's progress would put the older rebel's worrying mind to rest.

The mid-May morning was warming up. Shadow carefully shifted Aran's body over onto Dom for a few minutes in order to take off the heavy woollen jumpers he and Aran had donned when they first boarded the fishing boat. The four Irishmen had changed clothes at the McCrackens' suggestion in case their boat was stopped and boarded by the Coast Guard. The nautical look was all part of their cover story.

Motoring along under such crowded conditions caused Shadow to grow more and more uncomfortable. He was not used to the oppressive heat and humidity that greeted their arrival in Amerikay. It was now over eighty degrees with very high humidity. With the sun rising in the sky, the conditions both inside and outside the car grew more oppressive. It was never this hot back home...even in the middle of summer on an unusually fine day.

Gabriel seated in the front seat, seemed impervious to the rising temperature. Taller and thinner than Larry, this middle brother, aged thirty, was the leader of the McCracken trio. Gay's handsome features were highlighted by short-cut brown hair, a thin pointed nose and finely etched lips. Clean-shaven and meticulous in appearance, Gabriel's keen observations and friendly chatter were a constant source of entertainment to those around him. It took less than a day of being together on the fishing boat for the three Irishmen, Liam, Shadow and Danny, to realise that Gay was an exceptional person. He was someone who could easily fit into their recruiting plans.

The family demon of sibling rivalry seemed to have no place in the McCracken household. Despite their individual differences, it was apparent, even to a casual observer, that the three brothers loved and respected each other. Their mutual admiration was never more apparent than during their family music sessions. With Gabby's guitar playing, Larry's fiddling and Dom's singing, the three talented brothers often collaborated to celebrate their love of music, their family and the land of their forefathers—Ireland.

But for now, the Limerick man tried to take his mind off the heat by comparing the American countryside to that of his homeland.

The terrain outside his window was flatter than the rolling hills of County Clare. Everything was certainly green here but it lacked the contrasting shades of green that were so famous back home. He noticed the farm fields were much larger and fenced in with wire instead of the dry stone walls and thick hedgerows that enclosed the small plots of ground he had grown up knowing. The farmyards in Ireland were small and usually dominated by a neat whitewashed cottage. The outbuildings, if any, were simple, often thatched stone structures. As they drove on, Shadow saw two-story, wooden-framed farmhouses with huge barns and other assorted sheds and storage bins. Most of the farms appeared much more prosperous than those back in Ireland. Wood and brick had certainly replaced the irregular shaped stones used in so much of the rural Irish architecture found throughout the west of Ireland.

They were driving northwest up a wide peninsula toward the twisting Potomac River and the ferry crossing near Mount Vernon, the old family home of America's first President, George Washington.

Just before arriving at the river, they pulled off onto a side road, stretched their legs, relieved themselves and ate the sandwiches Dom had packed while still on board the fishing boat. They had decided this would be a safer strategy then stopping to eat at a restaurant along the way where they might draw unwanted attention to themselves.

Aran was awake again and actually took a few steps on his own though he was very weak and shaky. Throughout the morning the young Irish Rebel kept asking where they were and when they would be home again.

Shadow kept reassuring him that everything was fine and under control. He should just stop worrying about home and begin enjoying his life as an international traveller.

※

It was almost ten in the morning when they drove aboard the little cable-guided ferryboat that took them the hundred or so yards across the river.

After landing on the opposite bank, they had another two-hour drive to the McCracken farm near the village and civil war battlefield of Manassas, Virginia.

It was Gabby who reminded the car's passengers that nearly 200,000 Irish and Irish-Americans had fought in the America Civil War, mostly on the northern, anti-slavery side during the early 1860s. Over a quarter of them were wounded or lost their lives in the conflict that proved to be an important training ground for future Irish Fenians.

Finally, after what seemed an eternity, they pulled into a tree-lined avenue and drove up to an attractive two-story, white, wooden-framed farmhouse.

As they piled out of the Ford and climbed the porch steps, they received a warm welcome. The first to greet them was a middle-aged, smiling woman who wore her greying hair tied up into a neat bun pinned to the back of her head. Gabby introduced her as his mother and the 'lady of the house' who was to be obeyed at all costs, that is if you valued your life. The woman's broad smile, twinkling blue eyes and happy disposition belied the warning and lessened the severity of the admonition. She wore a dark blue skirt and white blouse with a checked apron tied to the front of her. Larry formally introduced her as 'Mother' McCracken.

Gabby explained that their father was away on a cattle buying trip in Richmond, Virginia and would return home at week's end.

The second woman to welcome them was young and striking in appearance. At twenty years of age, she appeared more pretty than beautiful. The five-foot, eight-inch tall brunette with flashing blue eyes was standing halfway down the stairs as the men entered the house.

After introducing his mother, Gay turned and invited his sister Sarah Anne to come down, meet everyone and give them a hand. She smiled and with a bouncing air of confidence and athletic grace, descended the remaining steps, came over to Aran and, with Shadow's help, led him into a small bedroom located behind the staircase toward the rear of the farmhouse.

Shadow helped her remove Aran's boots, trousers and plaid shirt. Then, as the young woman sponged off his face with a cool damp cloth, Aran Roe smiled and asked, "Shadow, where are we and who is this lovely vision?"

"You're on our family farm in northen Virginia," answered Sarah. "Beside my parents and my three brothers, who you already know, there's me, the youngest and the only sister those lucky lads have." Her eyes twinkled like Gabby's and her mother's.

"I guess you'll be after telling me what happened to you before too long. But for now, Mother has some soup on the range. The two of us here would like to put a little of it into your stomach and then see you get some real rest."

Saran Anne disappeared down the hallway only to return a few moments later with a steaming ceramic container.

Aran nodded and lifted the small bowl of homemade vegetable soup to his lips and drank. It tasted very good and he asked Shadow if he might not have a bit more.

With the soup gone and Aran tucked into bed, Shadow and Sarah joined the others in the front parlour.

The boys had just brought their mother up to date on the details of their adventure. Larry was talking as Shadow walked in on them.

"We pulled into Leonardtown just after four this morning. Everyone, except Aran, helped unload the catch and tidied up the boat. After a few quick goodbyes, Liam and Danny drove off to Washington with the two lads down from New York who had come to collect them. Mellowes thought it best to split up, especially with Aran in the shape he's in."

Dom chimed in with, "Then, we headed for home ourselves. Everything went smoothly and nobody asked any embarrassing or prying questions. All went just as planned. Devoy should be pleased as punch with the way we handled this job!"

Mother turned to Shadow and asked, "How long do you think you'll be staying with us?"

"That all depends, but considering Aran's present condition, if we could stay a couple of months that would be grand."

Mother nodded and glanced at Gabby. "What do you think?"

"Finding room is not a problem and I'm sure Shadow will be after helping around the farm...Aran too when he's able."

"Absolutely...I wouldn't want it any other way," replied Doyle. "In fact, I'd go crazy if I didn't have something to do. It'll be my pleasure to lend ye a hand. As for old Aran in there, I know he grew up on a farm and, as soon as he is well enough, I can think of no better therapy than farm work to help him get back on his feet.

"Oh, speaking of Aran," continued Shadow, "is there a doctor nearby that you trust who'd have a look at the lad?"

"Larry's already gone to get Dr. Anderson. He's a good man and can be counted on to keep his mouth shut," answered a reassuring Gay.

After a momentary lull in the conversation, Mother McCracken glanced at her two sons then turned to Shadow saying, "I know you've told the boys all your news, but both Sarah Anne and I would like to know of the circumstances that brought you two so far from home. Maybe after you've settled in and had something to eat, we can all sit a while on the front porch and you can tell us your story."

"It would give me no greater pleasure and besides, I'm anxious to hear the latest news from home. It's been almost two weeks since I've read a paper or heard any news reports," answered Shadow.

Mrs. McCracken looked down at the floor for a moment, then spoke. "As far as Ireland is concerned, the news we have here for you is not very good. But things are beginning to turn around. A long time ago I learned that time heals all wounds and this one seems to be mending quickly."

On that note, Mother with Sarah following, disappeared into the kitchen while Dom and Gabby took Shadow upstairs and showed him to his room.

❧

As Shadow Doyle thought back over the summer, he realised the months of June and July on the McCracken farm had disappeared into a haze of fond memories and hard work.

Sitting alone on the front porch of the farmhouse as night descended, he rocked back and forth in an old cane-bottom chair enjoying the gentleness of a refreshing evening breeze. This was his favourite time of the day. With his spent muscles glowing from his day's labours, he loved watching the fireflies commence their evening ritual of lighting up the growing darkness with their incandescent bodies. The whippoorwills and bats filled the air with song and squeaks as they swooped and dove for unsuspecting insects.

There was nothing more satisfying than enjoying a restful pause after a hard day's work. Aran, Dom, Father McCracken and he had spent the day mending fences and beginning the construction of a new corral that would serve as the milking herd's winter home.

That was the way the last two and a half months had gone. One job seemed to lead into another as they days blended into weeks and the weeks melted into months.

Shadow had never spent such a wonderful summer in all his life. If only Helen and the girls could have been with him...it would have been perfect.

The weather had been grand. Lots of sunny days and warm evenings. The Limerick man even moved his bed out on to the porch and, with the protection of some mosquito netting, had spent many a peaceful night. Thanks be to God, nighttime breezes made the humidity more bearable. He was getting used to the heat and had even stopped complaining about it.

The rain, when it did come, arrived in thundering blasts of gusting winds, dramatic lightning bolts and often torrential downpours. But the storms soon disappeared, leaving a cool calmness behind. As far as he could remember, they had only two all day rains to remind him of Ireland. Secretly, Shadow wondered how he would again manage the dismal 'soft' days that seemed to drag on and on back home in Limerick.

Aran and Mr. McCracken, however, were the real story of the summer. Father, as everyone called him, took the wounded Irish Rebel under his wing and nursed him back to health almost single handedly.

The two of them spent hours together 'walking the land,' working in the garden or just sitting on the front porch. They talked of Ireland's storied past, its prospects for a new beginning and how best to realise freedom's dream. Father told Aran stories of his family and growing up in Mayo that reminded him of his own grandfather. Aran also retraced the threads of his life. Nothing was left out. Few details were omitted. The Irish Rebel told Father of his friendship with the Gregorys, his first encounters with Patrick Pearse and school days in Dublin. With emotional pride, he described his involvement in the Rising and his meeting Brigid. He opened his heart to the older man and, in return, received Father's unconditional acceptance, wise counsel and unspoken love.

From a weakened and melancholy young man, Aran sprang to life on the farm. Gradually, his memory and strength returned. His hair grew over his wounds and you had to look closely to see the scars. A healthy colour crept back into his face. A new vigour and delight marked his daily intercourse with everyone on the farm. Only occasionally, during the quiet of the evening, did Aran's mood become pensive and sad. Shadow knew he was grieving for his dead heroes. He understood the homesick ache in the Gortman's heart for his family back in Ireland and his growing desire to be reunited with Brigid. The Limerick man knew and understood Aran's feelings all too well. These same emotions were engulfing him, opening his heart and soul to life's painful realities.

On another somber note, the two Irishmen learned soon after their arrival at the McCracken farm of the continued executions of the Rebellion's leadership. Besides Aran's beloved teacher, Patrick Henry Pearse, and the handful of other men whose fate he had read about prior to leaving Athy, there were more names to add to Ireland's roll of martyred dead. The names of the 'murdered' Easter Week heroes read like a litany of Irish Saints...Clarke, MacDonagh, Pearse, Plunkett, Daly, O'Hanrahan, MacBride, Ceannt, Heuston, Colbert, Mallin, Kent, Mac Diarmada, Connolly, Patrick's blameless brother Willie...and the revenge was still going on. Just last week they had learned that the English government hung Roger Casement in London's Pentonville Prison.

Sixteen of Ireland's finest, all dead at the hands of a bitter, defiant and ignorant England, but their sacrifice was not in vain. The dream of awakening the Irish people was coming true just as Patrick Pearse had hoped it would. Ireland's initial public outrage toward the rebels' Rising was turning around. The people were lining up against Great Britain and her policies of repression. It was still too early to tell what the final outcome would be, for England was keeping a tight rein on the country, but dynamic forces were at work throughout the land. Something dramatic seemed bound to burst forth soon.

As they worked together on the farm, Father talked of similar times back home during the late 1870s. He remembered standing in front of the speaker's platform on a June day in 1879 when Charles Stewart Parnell spoke to the assembled thousands. The stately Irishman from Wicklow demanded 'fair rents' for Ireland. Later that same year, Michael Davitt chose Parnell to lead his newly formed National Land League of Ireland. [13-2] Davitt's objective was to nationalise the land and return it to the Irish people, but Parnell sought more politically complex and comprehensive ends.

Two years later, the Land Act of 1881 had granted the Irish tenantry their long sought three F's of fair rent, fixed tenure and free sale, but the political extremists in Amerikay and Ireland were not satisfied. Not only did they want land reform for the people of Ireland, they also wanted total separation from England. They demanded the realisation of Eireann's long sought dream of complete independence from Great Britain.

As time went on, Parnell, Ireland's National Parliamentary Party leader, and William Gladstone, England's Liberal Party Prime Minister, continued to argue and bargain with one another about land reform, rent controls and nonviolent parliamentary power. In the end, many felt Parnell, often called 'the Uncrowned King of Ireland,' gave away too much. The result was renewed agitation, defiance and conflict that saw unresolved social issues foster greater political bitterness. Emerging Irish nationalistic feelings caused the English government, the Anglo-Irish landlords and the Irish tenant farmers to clash in often hateful and bloody encounters.

As a result of this unrest, Father, his two brothers and their sister left Ireland in 1882 for Amerikay. If they had remained, they faced possible imprisonment or transportation to Australia for their seditiousness.

The brothers found work building roads and railways along the east coast and westward toward Chicago. But within a year, their sister had died of an illness brought on by long hours of overwork in a Massachusetts textile mill.

Finally, with the small savings they were able to accrue, the three brothers bought a piece of land in Virginia and began farming and raising cattle. Father prospered unhappily. His eldest brother decided to return home when he inherited the family farm after their father's death in 1889. Then, two years later, his younger brother was shot and killed in a card game. He had been accused of being a 'Catholic' cheat. Later, a jury found him innocent of the charge, but life could not be breathed back into his cold body. The gunman was sent to prison and Father had to go on alone without his brothers.

Soon afterwards, however, Father's life took a change for the better. He met and married Mother and their little family soon grew to include three sons and a daughter.

The farm also increased in size and wealth. The meagre thirty acres now numbered three hundred and twenty-five. Along with sixty head of dairy cows, Father now raised a fine herd of beef cattle, grew corn and hay, plus slaughtered over fifty hogs a year.

Dressed in his usual bib overalls, blue denim shirt and high topped boots, Mr. McCracken, a distant relative of Henry Joy McCracken of 1798 fame, was considered a distinguished and successful northern Virginia farmer. He was tall, muscular though slightly stooped from years of manual labour. His wavy black hair was thick and showed no signs of thinning. He seldom smiled or spent his time in idle talk. He simply allowed his warm grey eyes to speak for him. Father had a talent for seeing through people's self-interests and often made embarrassingly honest appraisals of things. Aran thought his new mentor reminded him of his own father. The McCrackens' neighbours frequently looked for Father's advice on a range of farming matters much as Aran's father was sought out back home.

Under this veneer of respectability, however, Father was a died-in-the-wool republican. He had raised his children to passionately love Ireland and to support its cry for independence. He taught them to speak some Irish, insisted they study the history of their ancestral homeland and he chose to retain many old Irish customs in his new homeland. Father was a frequent contributor to John Devoy's Clan-na-Gael fund-raising efforts and encouraged his sons to participate in Clan meetings and activities. It was because of their active membership in this Fenian organisation that they were chosen to help the four Irish rebels illegally enter the United States.

※

Shadow and Aran kept in touch with Liam and Danny through Clan offices in New York. Letters were forwarded back and forth keeping the duos abreast of each others' activities.

While farm life kept Aran and Richard busy, their two Irish countrymen were active in raising money for the purchase of arms and supplies in the event war should break out in Eireann. Additionally, Liam and Danny participated in recruiting campaigns seeking volunteers willing to fight for Ireland's freedom back home on 'Paddy's green shamrock shore.'

※

As autumn approached, Mellowes wrote Shadow that Danny and he were planning to visit the McCrackens' Virginia farm between the twentieth and twenty-fifth of August. They wanted to renew their friendships, assess the situation and discuss plans for going home.

The political climate in Ireland was continually changing. Though the British military kept a close rein on the people via strict law enforcement, Catholic Mass and public demonstrations supporting the ideals of the martyred Easter leaders were growing in popularity. But it was not the Fenian extremists or the Sinn Fein politicians who were proving to be the catalysts. It was England's ill-advised wish to impose Home Rule on a partitioned Ireland that was turning public opinion around in favour of the separatists.

The Irish people's strong desire for a country united by the Home Rule legislation approved of prior to the First War was dissolving into a fierce anti-Home Rule following based on England's proposed intention of politically dividing Ireland into two parts. A larger southern government would be established in Dublin while a smaller northern administration would be installed in Belfast.

With the reality of the partitioning of their small island staring them in the face, the Irish people were redirecting their thinking toward the republican goal of a free, united and independent nation devoid of English authority altogether.

Of the approximately three thousand Irish who were rounded up in the military and RIC sweeps after the Rebellion, a thousand had been released in the past month, but well over fifteen hundred were still imprisoned in England. Many of those who were being held had never been charged with any crime against the government, much less tried and convicted of any criminal offence. The British only 'thought' they were dangerous and 'might have been' involved in some plot to overthrow the English government.

To top matters off, England was having a difficult time of it in Europe. The war had bogged down and had become an entrenched stalemate. England's men and material resources were being stretched to the limit. Because Britain badly needed American help and additional Irish soldiers to defeat Germany, the Crown began easing its harsh Irish policies imposed after the Rebellion. She backed off from imposing partition, released a few more imprisoned Easter Week men and continued to encourage greater Irish enlistment in the British army.

❧

Two of Devoy's men delivered Liam Mellowes and Danny Kelly to the McCracken farm at the beginning of the fourth week in August.

It was a great reunion. They all relived some of the tragic adventures and personal highlights surrounding the Rebellion and their traumatic escape to Amerikay. They shared the limited news they had about their families at home. They discussed the political changes that the Easter Rising had wrought and talked about going back to Ireland.

As the evening wore on, their spirits rose, buoyed up by platefuls of

Mother's good cooking, by glasses of American whiskey and by the warmth of their shared friendships. All seemed to be in fine form except Liam Mellowes.

After the evening meal, everyone moved into the family parlour for tea or coffee laced with some of Father's good homemade brew. Outside the farmhouse, a gentle rain fell as a cool blast of Canadian air turned summer into autumn.

Looking out of the window at the rain, Aran was reminded of Ireland and its soft weather. Soon he would be home again. It would be his family and Brigid sitting around a turf fire instead of his adopted Irish-American family and rebel friends as were gathered here tonight.

When everyone was settled, Mellowes stood up and walked over to the fireplace. Its flames cast a warm light and cozy glow on the room and the assembled party. Everyone could sense the soberness of his mood.

"I'm sorry to disrupt this little affair, but there is a serious matter I must discuss with all of ye."

The room grew silent as a serious Liam Mellowes continued. "Devoy has received reports of a secret, radical pro-Allied war group whose agents are operating in this country with the express purpose of threatening, terrorising and, even in some extreme cases, murdering Americans, Germans, Irish...anyone expressing strong opposition to the United States joining the Allied war effort in Europe.

"Without question this crowd is risking a possible anti-involvement backlash by people already supporting Yankee war participation, but Devoy seems to feel their lot thinks the possible negative risks are worth the likely positive outcomes.

"Of course these multinational terrorists are operating entirely outside the law and, if caught, would be prosecuted to the legal limit by the American authorities."

After an initial expression of "oh's" and "no's", the parlour again fell silent.

Mellowes continued, "It probably was foolish for Danny and me to come here today. Our visit may have tipped off others to ye and this farm. Sure, we just don't know who these people are and how deeply or widely spread their intelligence network goes.

"Then, to top matters off, Devoy's heard rumours that the British would love to get their hands on all four of us. There are supposed to be warrants out for our arrests as traitors to the Crown. All in all, it looks like we could be facing some very threatening and dangerous times ahead."

Mellowes came over and took a seat next to Shadow.

"Shadow," said Liam to his friend, "do you still have those German Lugers we took off the steamship?"

"They're upstairs hidden away in the back of my dresser," replied Richard.

"I think it might be a good idea if you kept those on ye at all times. You just never know when they may come in handy," warned a cautious Mellowes.

"In fact, ye all might take warning and be on guard. It's better to be safe in these matters than sorry. We all know the grief Ireland has known from the likes of spies and informers."

Father jumped up, looked around the room and abruptly spoke in an authoritative voice, "We'll just have to get organised around here. I'll have no strangers coming on to my land with murderous intentions in mind.

"My family knows how to use a gun and we won't hesitate to use force if we're threatened by some dirty scut. I remember what the English military and Irish peelers did to defenceless farmers in Mayo during the land struggles. Those outrages won't be repeated here...not on your life they won't!"

The news of possible enemy intrusion disturbed and alarmed everyone. In a general burst of chatter, the family began talking and making plans about how they would go about protecting themselves from a possible attack.

With everyone's attention occupied, Mellowes motioned for Aran to follow him out onto the porch.

After they were seated on the swing, Mellowes reached over and put his hand on Aran's knee.

"Ah sure, I'm very sorry to have to bring you some troubling news, Aran."

Immediately, the Gortman's mind flashed back to his home, to his parents and to his aging grandfather.

"Something wrong at home?" he queried.

"No, everything is fine there, at least as far as I know."

"Well, what is it then?" Aran's mind quickly sorted through the possibilities. "Does it have something to do with St. Enda's or maybe Brigid?"

"Yes, it's about Brigid. She was in a riding accident. The lass fell off her horse and struck her head. She was unconscious for several days and then, back on the twelfth of May, I'm sorry, to say, she died."

Aran was struck dumb. His body went limp. His head swirled in dizzy confusion. A lump filled his throat and tears welled up in his eyes. The unexpected death and loss of Brigid left him totally numb and empty.

His arms reached out and he buried his face on Liam's strong shoulder. Mellowes put his arm around the sobbing young man. He tried to comfort Aran with reassuring pats on the back and quiet words of compassionate understanding.

But, after a few moments, Aran broke free of his friend's embrace. He walked down off the porch and out into the gentle rain. He headed off across a pasture toward a small stream that ran through some of the farm's acreage.

As the first shock of Brigid's death began to sink in, his thoughts raced back through time to the moments the two of them had spent together. He remembered the evening they had cried in each other's arms after learning of Pearse's death. He recalled their standing side by side as they looked up at the night sky prior to his departure for Kilkenny. He thought of the letter he had left for her by his bed in the byre and wondered what her reaction to it had been.

These memories were quickly followed by the rush of his many imagined plans for their future together. She was the woman he had planned to spend the rest of his life with...to have children with...to love until death. Now, all was lost. His reason for living seemed void of all meaning.

Walking through the wet grass with the rain soaking him through to the skin, Aran wished he too were dead. He wanted to throw himself down on the ground, hoping the earth would open and swallow him alive. The pressure of grief was smothering him and he was helpless to struggle from its grasp.

With darkness descending, Aran sought the support of an old elm tree growing alongside the stream. He sat with his back to the rough bark and watched the rain-swollen creek flood out of its banks. Its gushing current carried leaves, sticks and muddied water away in a roaring rush.

❧

He was not sure how long he had sat under the tree's leafy protection, but the next thing he knew Mellowes and Shadow were by his side. They had brought a blanket to shield him from the light mist that was still falling. His two comrades pulled him to his feet, wrapped him in the warm cover and led the Irish Rebel back toward the lights of the farmhouse.

Shadow spoke first. "Aran, sure I know your grief is deep, but there are some things you should know about Brigid's accident. In the first place, it wasn't really an accident."

Aran turned his head and looked at his friend.

"What do you mean it wasn't an accident?"

With that, Mellowes unfolded the story of Brigid's encounter with the soldiers and the inebriated RIC man. He recounted their jealously-inspired insults and their hateful, drunken attack on the defenceless woman riding home from Sunday Mass. To compound the atrocity, Liam told how the soldiers tried to hide their guilt and shame by not reporting the accident to the proper authorities. Instead, the two men just rode off as if nothing had happened.

"Bloody conspirators those two sodded divils," muttered Aran.

Mellowes continued his tale, recounting how the two British soldiers left Brigid and the drunken RIC policeman lying on the roadway. Several hours later, after the peeler had regained his senses and fled the scene, a passerby discovered Brigid's body on the road. After finally locating a cart, he rushed her to a doctor. The strong woman lingered in a coma for five days before death took her. Brigid never regained consciousness or felt any pain. Her family was at her bedside when she died and many a folk in the Athy community mourned her death. Even that fine horse of hers had to be destroyed because of the broken leg it suffered in the attack.

Rage and anger pushed out some of his sorrow and grief. His friends could see it written all over his face.

Noting it, Mellowes continued, "We know who the RIC man was that attacked Brigid. The IRB has identified the yoke and they're keeping an eye on his whereabouts. The two soldiers involved were recently reassigned. For the moment, they're in England but, sure I wouldn't be surprised to learn of their being shipped to France before the year is out.

"When we return, we thought you might like to have 'a word' with the copper who caused Brigid's death. True to their tradition so, the English authorities have swept the entire matter under the carpet. Ye might know it, they're pretending nothing happencd."

Ignoring Mellowes' thinly veiled offer of revenge, Aran asked, "How is the O'Mahony family getting on without her?"

"We've heard that Brigid's elder sister, Hannah, who was living here in the States, moved back to the farm. Andrew, her brother from Kilkenny, the one who helped smuggle you aboard the train, also returned home to help," answered Mellowes.

Yes, Aran thought, that family would pull through with Gran's wise counsel and the Ryans' generous help.

"Liam, how did you come to hear of all this so? My father failed to mention it in either of his two letters. As you might have guessed, I wrote and told my family all about her. Ah sure, I wondered why I hadn't received anything from Brigid...but in light of the Rebellion's aftermath and my sudden departure, I thought, 'Well, all right, there's nothing strange there to worry me head about.'"

To Aran's query, Mellowes replied, "some local Volunteers and IRB men learned of the attack and through Devoy they contacted me. In case you didn't realise it, your wounding by the River Shannon and journey over here is common knowledge among some circles back home. They have kept me apprised of events a'happening in Ireland. I thought it better for you to find out the news from me rather than in the post. I hope you understand, my young friend. Please God, appreciate everyone's deep concern for you and of my decision, as your comrade, to tell you myself?"

Aran's only reply was a soft, "Thank you, Liam."

❧

When Aran finally returned to the farmhouse, the McCracken family was waiting with open arms and warm hearts. Again, they welcomed him like a member of their own family. They reassured him of their willingness to help him deal with his sudden and unexpected trouble.

He gratefully accepted their heartfelt concern for his loss. Through Aran's conversations over the past several months, all had grown to know Brigid and had learned of his desire to marry her.

The McCrackens and his three rebel friends realised Aran had just been dealt another set back. But this time it was an emotional blow rather than a physical one. They all knew another healing process must begin and be allowed to take its natural course. Everyone was optimistic that the courageously resilient young Irishman would survive this newest trauma dealt him. They all believed Aran would again learn to experience life with the zeal and enthusiasm that was his way. They were all there to help him as best they could, for they all thought of Aran as a friend and brother.

Down through the years, life had taught the Irish what it meant to hold on and help one another during the weal and the woe. Once again, another Irishman was being put to the test and, please God, he would make it through.

Aran was unable to sleep that night. His thoughts were filled with images of Brigid...of her lying there in the roadway alone and dying...of Gran and Brigid's family...of the drunken RIC man and his two bleeden caffler mates...of her flower bedecked coffin being lowered into the ground...of the grief he shared with so many others...of the twelfth of May. For it was on that day that Brigid Eileen O'Mahony, Sean Mac Diarmada and James Connolly all died tragic deaths at the hands of the Sassenach intruders.

14. *Fleeing*

And if, when all a vigil keep
The West's asleep! The West's asleep!
Alas! and well may Erin weep
That Connacht lies in slumber deep.
But, hark! a voice like thunder spake,
The West's awake! The West's awake!
Sing, Oh! hurrah! let England quake,
We'll watch till death for Erin's sake!

The West's Asleep/Thomas Davis

$\mathcal{L}$iam Mellowes and Danny Kelly spent three days at the McCracken farm before departing for Chicago. They were scheduled to speak on Sunday at a large Irish-American rally in Grant park along the shore of Lake Michigan. Larry and Gabby drove them to the train in Washington, D.C. and saw them off.

Before they left, however, Liam and Shadow carried out a private ceremony. The two rebels swore Aran Roe O'Neill into the Irish Republication Brotherhood. After much thought, Aran had decided it was something he wanted to do. Both his friends were pleased to oblige, knowing he would be an able and dedicated member. After his return to Ireland, Aran planned on joining a local parish circle and start playing an active role in IRB activities.

In taking the secret society's oath of allegiance, he acknowledged that the president of the IRB was, in the eyes of its membership, the president of the Irish Republic. Additionally, its members viewed the IRB's Supreme Council as the sole and rightful government of Ireland with the exclusive authority to make treaties, declare war and negotiate terms of peace. [14-1] Thus, the IRB was regarded by its diehard republican membership as the legal and rightful vehicle for achieving Ireland's long sought freedom and independence.

The 'Brotherhood' or 'Organisation,' as it was sometimes called, had been reorganised beginning in 1908 by Thomas Clarke, Sean Mac Diarmada, Bulmer Hobson and a handful of others. As the senior member, Clarke took control, assuming the mantle of leadership for its revitalisation. As the revered 'living connexion' between the older 'bold Fenian men' of a past generation and today's rejuvenated separatists, Tom Clarke had become the Easter Rising's father-figure. He had certainly paid his dues. From 1883 to 1898, Clarke had endured fifteen years of tortuous English imprisonment. But after a brief spell in Amerikay, he had returned to Ireland in 1907 to rekindle its neglected partisan fires.

Because of its clandestine nature, few people knew that Clarke had declined the IRB's presidential chair. So, because of his oratorical abilities, Patrick Pearse had been chosen president of the IRB's Supreme Council on Easter Sunday, 1916. As a result, Aran's headmaster had become the first president of the soon-to-be declared Irish Republic. The intentions of this new government were outlined in Pearse's and Connolly's *Proclamation* which Pearse proudly read aloud to the Irish people from atop the steps of the GPO on Easter Monday.

❧

Watching the McCracken car disappear down the avenue, Aran missed his two departed friends already. Having Liam and Danny around seemed to take away some of the sorrow and bitterness he felt about Brigid's death. Their visit reminded him of the pain and disappointment they all were living with.

During his visit, Liam had discussed with Aran his deep sense of disappointment and feeling of personal loss that the failed Rebellion had caused. The death of so many of his close friends and the reason for which they died was not easily forgotten. Mellowes placed much of the blame on the shoulders of Eoin MacNeil and his lieutenant, Bulmer Hobson. Their refusal to rally the Irish Volunteers to Connolly's, Clarke's and Pearses's cause was a major factor in the Rising's failure. Their deliberate refusal to join forces and support the IRB's plans made a difficult situation untenable. Their decision helped guarantee the Rebellion's failure before it even began.

Aran remembered Mellowes rising from his chair on the McCrackens' front porch one evening to make his point. The Gortman clearly recalled how the agitated Volunteer commander paced back and forth while he talked. Liam's utterances made sense to Aran. "I certainly recognise that the IRB and Connolly's Citizens Army behaved recklessly. They acted alone and without the support or approval of the Irish people. But sooner or later, someone had to step forward and strike a blow for Irish independence. If it wasn't Pearse and the others, then somebody else would have had to seize the moment if our freedom was ever to become reality. Many blamed Pearse for the Rebellion's failure, but he was just the scapegoat."

Liam had reminded Aran that unlike their Irish revolt, American revolutionaries had the support and approval of many of its people prior to their declaring war on England in 1775. In Ireland, things were just the reverse. The Irish Republication Army had declared war on England without the backing of the people. It was only now, after the Rebellion's failure, that Ireland's citizenry began believing in Pearse's dream.

In Aran's mind, it was almost as if the Dubliner was still there. The Gortman imagined Liam sitting in one of the McCrackens' rockers with his arms folded across his chest. His pontifications echoed in Aran's ears. "Ireland's initial sense of selfish embarrassment has turned to anger in light of England's heartless executions of our leaders. I wonder if we will ever know the success Amerikay has had as we continue the struggle for our independence?"

Shadow Doyle understood Liam's and Aran's sharp sense of loss and frustration. With the execution of Major John MacBride after Easter Week, he too had lost a dear friend and important teacher. MacBride's death, coupled with the military failure to overcome the power of the Sassenach was a devastating blow. Shadow knew that only Irish independence could take away the sting of defeat and justify the terrible loss of life that once again had to be endured.

It had been reported that MacBride had cried out, "Mind the flag!" just before his execution in Dublin. Shadow had promised himself that he would 'mind the flag' in his mentor's absence.

❧

Knowing that work was a positive outlet for his grief, Aran threw himself into the demands of the farm with renewed vigour. The manual labour and his growing closeness to Shadow and the McCracken family provided Aran with a natural release. They all listened to him with sympathetic compassion while he worked through his sorrow. But of all the McCracken's who empathized with the Irish Rebel, it was the twenty-year-old Sarah Anne who reached out to Aran with a woman's sensitivity mature beyond her years.

From the first day of his arrival at the farmhouse, Sarah had fancied him. She was not exactly sure what it was that attracted her to him, beside her physical desires. After frequent reflection, Sarah concluded it was not just one thing but a combination of forces...Aran's reputation as a brave soldier, his desire to give himself to a noble cause, his thoughtful kindness to all the members of her family, especially Father, his loyalty to Brigid, his quiet reflective nature...and the list seemed to go on and on.

She had been and still was jealous of Brigid, but it was her growing and deepening respect for Aran and his beliefs that stopped Sarah Anne from trying to lure him into a superficial, romantic entanglement. It was a difficult decision for her to make, but she was proud of the way she chose to handle it.

Putting aside all her womanly desires, Sarah tried to soothe Aran's grief with heartfelt understanding and womanly compassion. She offered her kindness openly and without any ulterior motives. She was learning to value Aran as a friend and wanted to help in any way she could.

Aran too was attracted to Sarah. However, he always dismissed any romantic thoughts from his mind, knowing that Brigid was waiting for him at home. Now, in his hour of sorrow, Aran was able to gratefully accept Sarah's comforting kindness in the innocent way it was offered. He would have to endure a period of mourning before he could ever entertain the thought of another serious feminine relationship.

❧

With the departure of Mellowes and Kelly, the McCracken clan decided to take Liam's warning seriously about the possible presence of terrorists in Amerikay. If these men were practicing their own special brand of mayhem, they truly must be warped and desperate souls. Any sane person could only conclude that the desire to silence activists opposed to America's entry in the war was simply motivated by unbridled self-interest and not by rational thought.

Respecting Mellowes's warning, Shadow and Aran strapped on the German Lugers provided by Clan-na-Gael. The Irishmen felt a bit more secure with their pistols tucked safely away next to their skin. Additionally, the men and Sarah all carried a rifle or shotgun whenever they were working away from the farmhouse. It may have seemed a bit over-reactionary, but Irish history was replete with stranger happenings.

One morning, several days later, as everyone sat around the breakfast table, the conversation turned to the possibility of the terrorists' presence in Virginia. Father reminded them all that past Irish revolutionaries had concocted and carried out some pretty sinister plots themselves. He retold the story of the six radical Irish National Invincibles who assassinated two British officials in Dublin's Phoenix Park in May, 1882. Five of the six were eventually tried and hung in Kilmainham Gaol. The surviving member was rumoured to have betrayed his comrades to Dublin Castle, the seat of English authority in Ireland. Eventually, the man fled the country by ship, but was murdered while at sea. As it turned out, he was killed by one of his own comrades seeking revenge for the hanging death of the other five. It was not until much later that this sixth man was found to be totally innocent of any collaboration with the British...but, by then, it was too late...he was dead.

As Father continued to regale his captive audience, the light in the old man's eyes began to shine more brightly. This was his favourite pastime. Father McCracken loved to rehash the ups and downs of Ireland's traumatic history with any willing listener.

With all eyes on the old rebel, Father continued, "Then, there were all the Irish peasants, who in 1880 and 1881, took matters into their own hands. They rebelled against their greedy landlords for all the heinous deeds that Ireland's poor had been forced to endure."

Continuing, he asked, "...and what should the landlords be after expecting from an enslaved nation of proud people? Jaysus, there was the tenantry who had no political leverage or military power to help them in their plight. So what did they do? They resorted to the only weapons available to them...they withheld their rents and refused to harvest the landlords' crops.

"The landlords were outraged at the peasant impetuousness. They felt their only recourse was to, once more, visit violence upon the masses. So, new rounds of harsh measures were designed to show the common folk who was boss and that the lawbreakers would not go unpunished. Ah sure indeed, the soldiers arrived with their rifles and the land agents descended with their crowbars and battering rams. The authorities, urged on by the landed gentry, knocked down the cottage walls, burned the thatch roofs and threw the crying children and their elders out into the ditches to live or die. Some survived but many didn't. Ireland's proud people died by the side of the road just as they had during the famine of Black '47. It was a terrible time to be alive! I know! I was there!"

With that, Father cleared his throat, took a sip of his tea and leaned back in his chair. Looking over at Mother, he smiled and continued,

"But the Irish people were not always passive in their resistance to land-lordism. Years before Davitt's Land League, many of Ireland's underclass were also not satisfied living with the status quo. During their days, some daring souls, the good Lord have mercy on them, took the offensive by inflicting economic vengeance on the 'master.' They burned his crops, killed or crippled his cattle and even attacked the 'big house.' These roving bands of men, known by such names as the Whiteboys, Ribbonmen, Rightboys and Defenders, sought their own kind of revengeful justice for the bitterly hateful treatment they had received at the hands of landlordism.

"Yes, we Irish have taken our turn at committing evil in the name of freedom and righteousness on more than one occasion...and who's to say who was right and who was wrong. I guess we'll just have to leave that pronouncement to the historians, philosophers and, yes, to God Almighty Himself."

With that, Father pushed back from the table, stood up and declared, "Well, lads, shall we have at it? There's work aplenty for us all and it's after getting past the time when we should be bending our backs over it. Besides, it's just too fine a day to be sitting around this table talking so much."

❧

Trouble arrived three days later. It showed up just after the family's midday dinner.

Shadow and Larry were off rounding up some fattened Black Angus cattle Father planned on selling the next day at the cattle market in Alexandria.

Father McCracken was having his usual afternoon catnap.

Dom was digging fence holes for the new corral out beyond the barn.

Gabby and Aran were inside the barn cutting fence posts. Above their chopping and sawing, both heard the sound of a car racing up the driveway. Gabriel remarked, "Those old cods must be in a big hurry flying in here like that!"

Suddenly, they both looked at one another and ran to collect their rifles stacked against a stall railing. With his weapon slung over his shoulder, Aran raced to the ladder leading to the overhead hayloft. He sprung up the wooden slats nailed to one of the barn's huge square uprights. Ten giant tree-trunk like legs rose almost thirty feet into the air, supporting the large barn's metal roof. With a mattress of hay under his feet, the

Irish Rebel took a dozen silent, bounding strides until he stood behind one of those massive beams. From his new vantage point, he could look down onto the yard below through the ventilation gaps in the barn's wooden-panelled siding.

Staying below, Gabby dropped to the ground behind the pile of wooden posts they had been cutting. From this ground level position, Gay also had a good view of the farmyard as both of the barn's huge doors were wide open.

No sooner had the dusty car pulled to a stop not twenty yards from Gabby's prone position than Dom came marching around from behind the barn into the yard with a stranger holding a shotgun at his back. The youngest McCracken son had his hands in the air and was shouting, "Hold your fire, lads...hold your fire!"

Aran could not believe his eyes at the scene unfolding below him. In a flash, thoughts of the Easter Rebellion atop the GPO flooded his mind. He also remembered firing down on a surprised enemy manning the Moore Street and Moore Lane barricades from his Saturday-morning rooftop position.

With those thoughts racing through his head, Aran had to pinch himself to clear his mind and refocus his attention upon the scene evolving before him.

The attacker's car was parked in the middle of the McCracken's large farmyard, halfway between the barn and the side of the house. Its three occupants had jumped out of their vehicle and were using it as a barricade to hide behind, safe from any possible attack from the barn.

From his lofty perch, Aran saw two more men taking up positions at the near end of the farmhouse's front porch and another two were now visible standing by the corner at the rear of the house.

The young Irishman realised that this was no random raid but a well planned and carefully coordinated attack. He wondered if some of the invaders might not have entered the house and detained Father, Mother and Sarah Anne. Such an action would effectively neutralise any possible help he and Gay might expect from that quarter. As Aran surveyed the yard, everyone was behind some sort of protective barrier except Dominic and the man holding him at gunpoint.

Suddenly, the hushed quiet was broken. One of the men crouching behind the car yelled out," We mean ye no harm, McCrackens. All we've come for is the Irishman, Richard Doyle, and the O'Neill lad. Give them up now and we'll be on our way. No one needs to be hurt."

Hearing his name called out topped off by the attacker's Irish accent made the hair on the back of Aran's neck stand on end. So Mellowes was right! Some kind of freelance terrorist squad was operating over here. By their carefully planned attack, the Gortman knew they meant business. Once again, Aran realised that the power of the British Crown was stretching its deadly tentacles, hoping to ensnare more victims. First Ireland, then the Americas, India, Africa, an untold number of defenceless islands and today, it still had its clutches on the United States. In jest, Aran had often referred to this English abuse of might as the 'Rule of Ruleless Lawlessness' or just simply the 'Rule of Non-Law' for short. [14-2]

"What do ye say mates? We have ye well surrounded. The old man, his wife and daughter are under our guns. Send out the two we want and we'll be on our way with nobody harmed."

Another Irish voice, thought Aran...but this one's from Ulster...probably Belfast from the sound of him.

Though they had obviously planned their operation carefully, it was clear the invaders did not know who or how many were in the barn. They also probably did not realise that Larry and Shadow were off working away from the house. As things stood now, it was a bit of a stalemate.

"Bring that McCracken lad around to the front of the house," shouted a Yankee voice from the porch.

With that, the man standing behind Dom prodded him in the back with the barrel of his shotgun. "All right mate, it's off you go but don't make any sudden moves. My trigger finger is itching to unload this thing and you'd be right in the way."

This man spoke with an English accent!

Begad, thought Aran, it is a real international effort to be sure...Irish, American and now English. This was no fly-by-night operation. They were deadly serious and would probably stop at nothing to get the two of us. They all must be possessed of the divil himself, mused Aran.

As he watched Dom disappear around the front end of the porch, Aran thought he saw movement and a flash of metal along the tree line some sixty yards in front of the house. He did not know whether it was friend or foe, but someone was lurking behind those big elm trees that hid the house from the main road about a quarter of a mile away.

Another minute passed. No one moved or said a word.

Aran wondered if Gabby was in a good position to return fire if it was required. As for himself, he felt his position in the barn's loft was a great spot from which to engage the enemy...that is, if things came to that.

With Dom out of sight, the Irish Rebel wondered where the invaders might have taken him. Maybe they had herded him into the house with his parents and sister or simply held him under guard on the front porch.

Another silent minute passed. Aran could catch an occasional glimpse of the three men hiding behind the motor car. They seemed to be huddled together in hushed conversation. He guessed they were talking over their next move.

With the momentary pause in the action, Aran looked down at the rifle Father had loaned him. It was a familiar friend...a heavy Lee-Enfield .303 rifle with its clip of ten rounds snugged up into the breech just in front of the trigger guard.

Over the past two weeks, they had all spent several hours sharpening their marksmanship skills by shooting at targets set into a hill below the barn. Aran liked the sweet acidic smell of gunsmoke and the feel of the rifle's kick as he squeezed one round off after another. He had not lost his touch and was the best shot of them all, though Shadow gave him a good run for his money.

Suddenly, the warm September afternoon's quietness was shattered by the crack of a single rifle shot. Aran's entire body tensed. He instinctively dropped down to one knee behind the wooden pillar. He could feel his heart thumping and his pulse pounding at his temples. Aran's fingers grew white as the force of his grip on the rifle squeezed the blood out of them. His tongue felt swollen and his mouth became as dry as cotton-wool. A sudden bolt of fear gripped his chest in a viselike hold.

"Wait just one bloody minute, Aran," he said, scolding himself. "Remember, you've been in a few dangerous situations before. Get a hold of yourself, you bleeden eejit!"

Aran pulled in several deep breaths of air and slowly exhaled. This helped him to relax. Almost immediately, he felt calmer and more in control of himself.

For just an instant, his mind flashed back to the GPO. He remembered General James Connolly dressed in his smart Citizens Army uniform complete with Sam Browne belt, puttees and a slouch hat. The perfect image of an officer and soldier ready to do battle with the enemy.

With that thought in mind, he glanced down at his own rigout. He looked more like a farmer than a warrior, but that was all right...he was a farmer! His blue denim bib overalls were covered with sawdust and bits of hay. In addition, Aran wore a white shirt without its stiff collar, good hobnail boots graced his feet and a broad-brimmed straw hat sat on his head to keep the warm autumn sun out of his eyes. Yes, a lot of Irish farmers down through the centuries had fought for their rights.

Aran did not need a uniform or military rank to do what in his heart he knew was right.

Gathering his confidence, he reminded himself that it would take more than a few trespassers to flush him out into the open. They were not going to scare him like some frightened rabbit if he had anything to say about it.

Aran looked around, wondering who had fired the first shot. From the sound, the discharge had come from a rifle fired some distance away. He scanned the tree line in front of the house hoping to catch a telltale wisp of smoke or see something move...but there was nothing to see.

The sound of moaning and excited voices from the farmyard below caused him to look down.

One of the men who had been hiding behind the parked vehicle was doubled over beside the car. He clutched at his stomach with both hands while writhing on the ground in the dusty farmyard.

"For Christ's sakes, John, I'm hit. The sons-of-bitches have shot me. John, John, do something...I'm bleeding bad."

It was one of the Yanks. He had taken a round...no doubt shot through the lower back or ribs. The bullet probably tore through his abdomen and exited near his navel. The shot must have come from the row of trees in front of the farmhouse. Maybe it was Larry and Shadow...probably Shadow...who else could it have been?

With their mate wounded and screaming for help, the other two men shielded by the car panicked. One started to crawl under the vehicle while the other stood up and ran for the rear of the house.

The Irish Rebel shouted down to Gabriel, "You cover the car, Gay. Sure, I've got the bloody barnyard!"

A second later, Aran and Gabby fired simultaneously, as if they had rehearsed the scene often.

From his ground level position, Gabriel had a clear shot at the man scrambling under the car as he tried seeking better cover.

Gay's first shot pinged off the car's running board, but his next shot must have hit the man who let out a loud scream of pain. His roaring lasted only a few moments. Gabriel's third shot silenced the man forever.

Aran had a larger target but it was a moving one. His first shot ploughed into the side of the McCracken house. His second, however, pounded into the running man's hip. The unsuccessful escapee sprawled forward, landing in one of Mother's well-maintained flower gardens that bordered the side of the building. The man lay motionless, spread-eagled on the ground. His cries for help were lost in a sudden volley of gunfire that erupted from all directions.

With no enemy targets in sight, Aran bounded over to the ladder and called down to Gabriel, "Gay, are you all right?"

"Fine as can be, my friend. Some shootin' don't you think? We're two for two, but what about Dom and the others in the house?"

"I'm going to try and have a look. You stay here and cover me. I'll circle around from behind and come up on the back of the house. Stay alert and watch for my signal. I may want you to join me in case we need to storm the place."

Gabby whistled in reply and resumed his watchful guard over the farmyard.

Taking one of the heavy ropes used to lift bundles of hay and straw up into the barn's loft, Aran lowered himself through an opening in the floor. He landed safely in one of the empty cattle stalls.

After a quick look outside, the Irish Rebel slipped through the outside fencing that surrounded one of the pig sties. He ran directly away from the house and farmyard, being sure to use the barn as a screen to hide his movements from any observant farmhouse occupant.

About a quarter of a mile from the barn was a shallow stream that ran through a three-foot deep, washed out gully. Using the creek's bank as cover, Aran worked his way around to his left and back toward the house.

Crawling up out of the eroded ditch, he carefully made his way through a field of Father's prized sweet corn. There were still a few ears left on the six-foot-tall stalks.

Leaving the protection of the high garden foliage and bending low, Aran raced across twenty yards of open ground, coming to a stop behind the safety of the little shed that housed the McCrackens' Model T.

Now, lying flat on his belly, Aran peered around the corner of the wooden structure. With no one in sight, he carefully strapped his Lee-Enfield rifle across his back and slid the Luger automatic out from its holster under his shirt. Quickly rolling to his feet, he ran across the grassy back garden, over the stone footpath behind the dwelling and up to the farmhouse's rear door. He peered through the screened opening. The kitchen was empty.

"Those stupid eejits!" thought Aran. A multinational gang of desperadoes has carefully planned this ambush, captured the farmhouse and its occupants but yet they have thoughtlessly allowed their rear flank to remain unguarded. They must not have any experienced soldiers in their ranks. Their sloppy leadership has left them vulnerable to counter-attack.

Aran could still hear the sounds of sporadic gunfire coming from the front of the house. He paused and tried to imagine how many of the enemy were in the house. The Gortman knew the three by the car were out of commission. He had seen at least two on the front porch and two at the rear of the house. Additionally, there was the man who had captured Dominic...that made five plus there could be several others...he was not sure exactly how many of the enemy there were.

He also had to think about the safety of the four McCrackens being held hostage. The situation seemed impossible.

Crouching low as he passed under the kitchen window, Aran moved to the corner of the house nearest the barn. Seeing no one in the side yard except the two wounded men and the dead third one wedged under the car, he motioned to Gabby to take cover behind the stranded vehicle.

With his pistol in hand, Aran stepped out from behind the building's corner and covered Gabriel while he made his dash safely from the barn to the motor car.

So far so good.

A moment later Gabby sprinted the remaining thirty yards and came to a flying stop behind his family's home. With his breath coming in short gasps, he took up a position beside Aran who was now crouched down beside the rear wall of the house.

Quietly, the two men discussed what they should do next. It was decided that Gabriel would enter the house through the back door and take up a station behind the big black range. Its metal frame would stop any bullet and Gabby would have a clear view down the hallway toward the front of the house. The narrowness of this passageway guaranteed that no more than one man at a time could attempt to rush him. Gabby's rifle truly guarded the 'Bearna Baoghal.'

Gay's parting words to Aran before he took up his position in the kitchen were, "...and for God's sake, don't you go breaking any of Mother's good china, will ya now Aran?"

They smiled at one another before Gabriel slipped into the kitchen through the screen door. Aran covered his move through the window.

After seeing that Gabriel was safely in position, Aran intended to move along the outside wall of the house. He would try to assess the enemy's strength by peeping in through the dining room and parlour windows.

They had agreed that Aran would make his move after the next outburst of shooting that periodically emanated from the front end of the house. Shadow and Larry were doing a fine job of keeping the sodding buggers inside the house busy.

Aran did not have long to wait...four, five, six shots rang out almost as if they were a single volley.

Bending low, with his Luger poised for action, Aran proceeded cautiously along the side of the house.

Both of the wounded agents lying in the farmyard were motionless. They must have passed out or were dead. Mindfully, he stepped around the man he had shot from the barn's loft. The gunman was lying amongst Mother McCracken's roses. Aran guessed she was going to be upset about that. He carefully sidestepped the bloom-laden bushes.

A moment later, Aran Roe glanced in through the dining room window. He saw two men sitting at the big table. Their rifles were lying on top of its oaken surface. One of the men was talking loudly and motioning dramatically with his hands. The other man frowned and shook his head while his partner ranted and raved. Aran was privileged to each frantic word through the open window.

The angry man accused the other of leading them all into a dangerous and foolhardy situation. The accusations, indictments and rebuttals were flying hot and heavy.

Aran had no other choice but to put these two men out of commission. He wanted to even up the odds and unnerve the remaining members of the gang. Whereupon the Irish Rebel took a step backward, raised his weapon and fired his Luger automatic through the screened window.

He hit both men in the chest with the two rounds he squeezed off. One man slumped over onto the table while the second gang member rolled off his chair and fell to the floor.

Again ducking down below the window ledge, Aran counted eight, nine, no ten more shots erupting from the porch-end of the house. A moment later, he heard shouting and the sounds of running feet coming from inside.

Standing up and looking back in through the window, Aran saw the blurred forms of two men running down the hall. They flashed past the open dining room door and were headed toward the back of the house. Seconds later, a volley of gunfire erupted from that quarter. The shots quickly dissolved into desperate cries for help. Two, maybe three men were screaming out in pain.

With his heart in his throat, he yelled out, "Gabe!"

Much to his relief Aran heard Gabby's voice bellow back, "Everything's under control back here so."

Aran almost yelled a 'yahoo.' He could picture Gay standing over the downed terrorists with smoke still curling up from the barrel-end of his rifle.

"We may make it safely through this after all," thought Aran to himself.

Again, ducking low, Aran Roe O'Neill moved to the parlour's side window. One peek inside confirmed his hope that the enemy was beaten. From where he stood, he could see only two other gang members left to offer any resistance. One was crouched below the sitting room's front window with the tip of his rifle sticking out through the broken glass. The other, holding a shotgun, was frantically pacing around lounge like a trapped animal. Dominic was tied to a chair in the far corner of the room.

"Drop those weapons and put 'em up!" Aran shouted through the window screen. "Do it now you bloody lousers or ye'll never take another breath of this life's sweet air."

Two guns fell to the floor and the panic-stricken men raised their hands high in the air.

"Gabriel...come to the parlour quick...the wretched blighters have had it," shouted Aran at the top of his lungs.

A moment later, Gabby entered the room. He roughly pushed the two captives up against the wall and searched them carefully.

Aran turned, sprinted around the corner of the house and bounded up onto the front porch. Hearing familiar shouts from behind him, the rebel turned around. Running toward him up the front garden's grassy slope were Shadow and Larry.

"It's over, Shadow. It's over and the bastards have been beaten! We've done it...we've done it! Can you believe it...we've done it!" shouted a jubilant Aran.

Larry was yelling and making some crazy noises that reminded Aran of what a banshee was supposed to sound like.

Shadow was more composed. Leaping up the porch's front steps, he smiled at Aran. "Ah sure indeed...and what did ye expect so? We saw them park their second car down below and watched them slip up toward the house while we were rounding up the cattle.

"Larry and I just took our ould sweet time and came up behind them. We stopped to take cover behind the elm trees down in front of the house."

The three jubilant men confidently strolled into the parlour with the swagger of conquering heroes.

Larry gave his brother a hand with the two captured gang members. Aran untied Dom.

"Are there any more of this lot in the house, Dom?" asked Aran.

"I don't think so but ye better check. Anyone seen Mother, Father or Sarah Anne?"

Shadow rapped the butt of his rifle on the floor to get everyone's attention. Taking command, he ordered, "Grab a weapon, Dom and let's check the rest of the house. Aran and Gay...you two see about the wounded." Shadow was in his own element again. He had on his best OC voice and was giving orders in a crisp military fashion.

The dining room survey yielded one dead and one badly wounded. Aran's bullet probably punctured the wounded man's lung. He was having great difficulty breathing.

Both men lying on the hallway were alive. One was shot in the groin while his mate had taken two rounds in the stomach.

"Mother is going to have a fit when she sees this mess. Her lovely home is a wreck. There's blood everywhere and the front of the house looks like a piece of Swiss cheese from all the bullet holes. We'll never hear the end of this," moaned Gabriel.

"That's true, Gay, but at least we're all still alive and kicking," answered Aran. He could not help it that a little smile of satisfaction stole across his face.

"The house is clear and everyone's all right!" shouted Shadow as he came back down the stairs.

"Now, how the hell are we going to explain this scene of death and destruction to the authorities?" questioned Larry from the bottom of the steps. The three freed McCrackens filed down the stairs behind him.

Sarah was crying...more out of relief than fear.

Father's eyes were flashing with anger as he surveyed the ground floor devastation that greeted his return to freedom.

Mother just began mumbling, "Oh my...oh my..." as she looked at the terrible state of things from her vantage point in the hallway.

"Larry, take the car...get Sheriff Watson here this minute. We'll also need Dr. Anderson and don't forget to bring Father Michael too." The elder McCracken was as mad as a bag of cats.

"Wait a minute," said Shadow in a firm voice. "What are ye going to say to your man Watson?"

"The truth! No one's coming onto my land with their guns blazing.

The days of crowbars and thatch burning are over here, by God, and they better be soon over back home as well!"

Shadow did not have any logical rebuttal to Father's emotional reasoning, but he felt certain that Aran's and his presence were going to come under some close scrutiny very soon.

Upon their arrival, Father had introduced them as sons of the McCracken Clan from back home in County Mayo. He explained that they had decided to come over, work on his farm for awhile and see what they thought of living here in Amerikay.

Father was well liked and respected in the community and no one questioned his story then. But, after this pitched battle with Irish, English and Yankee strangers, Shadow knew that the ensuing investigation would raise many difficult and unwanted questions.

Who are these two new Irishmen? Where did they come from? What are they doing here on the McCracken farm? How did they get into this country? Why was the McCracken farm attacked by this band of outlaws?

Then, of course, who could predict what the wounded terrorists would say to the authorities and what their identities and backgrounds might reveal?

Shadow knew it was time they must be leaving the McCracken farm and strike out on their own. It was in everyone's best interests.

Shadow pulled Aran and Father out onto the porch. In a low voice Shadow told Father that he and Aran had to leave immediately. It was the only sensible thing to do in light of what just had happened. "Give us five minutes to pack a bag. The terrorists parked a second car down at the bottom of the lane next to the main road. We'll take it and head out."

Aran spoke up, "Father, do ye have any suggestion as to where we might go?"

Father started to object, but Shadow issued a firm, "No, it's the only way."

The elder McCracken thought for a moment then replied, "Eoin Black. He has a sheep farm just outside of Frederick, Maryland. It's only a three-hour drive from here. He's an old friend and a longtime Fenian. He'll help you out and give you a place to hide. Just tell him I sent you and be sure to describe what went on here today. Sure, ye can put your trust in Eoin."

With that, Richard Doyle stuck out his right hand to father and they shook hands warmly. But, when Father turned to Aran, the Irish

Rebel knew a handshake would not be enough. He threw his arms around the old man's rounded shoulders and hugged him. He whispered into the elder McCracken's ear. "Thank you, Father. You've saved my life more than once. You've been a wise and loving friend these past months. I'll never forget you as long as I live...and you can be sure that the next time we raise the harp without the crown above the GPO, your name will be in my heart and on my lips. Take care, mind yourself so and God bless you and your family."

Aran pulled back from his embrace and, with tears in his eyes, asked Father, "Will you tell the others we're going? Let them know where we've gone when it's safe. I only hope and pray we can all meet again, at least once more, before we leave for home."

Father nodded yes and the two men hurried upstairs to pack.

"The lads are leaving, aren't they Father?" asked Sarah from the front doorway.

"Yes, I'm afraid so, my dear." His reply was somber. Sarah Anne started crying again. She felt her heart breaking.

After a moment of sad reflection, Father gathered himself and regained his composure. He had seen many mournful partings in his day and this was just one more in a long line of goodbyes. He had learned to steel himself against the heavy weight of a breaking heart. Despite everything, he knew he and his family had to go on with their lives and put this new grief behind them.

Father stalked back into the house. He swallowed hard, cleared his throat and told Larry and his brothers to help sort out the dead from the wounded and captured. "Lay out the bodies on the front grass, make the wounded as comfortable as possible on the porch and tie those other two blackguards to the front railing. Sarah, go help your mother clean up this mess. Shadow and Aran are heading off for safer surroundings.

"As soon as they're gone Larry, you make your trip to collect the sheriff, doctor and priest."

❧

As Shadow and Aran hurried down the long shady avenue to the abandoned gangmembers' car, they turned and looked back at the McCracken farmhouse. Three dead men were laid out in front on the sloping grass. Gabby and Dom were fussing over the four wounded gang members on the porch. They could also see the other two terrorists tied up to the front railing.

Father was standing on the flagged walkway. His hands were on his hips. It was clear he was overseeing the entire goings on. Mother and Sarah were at the top of the driveway.

The McCracken men must have heard Father say something for suddenly they all looked up. Aran and Shadow could see broad smiles on their faces as everyone saluted the departing Irishmen.

The raiding party had left the key in the ignition. Aran cranked the Ford's handle. On the second turn the engine kicked over. Aran jumped in the front seat, Shadow threw the machine into gear and they roared off down the dusty dirt road in silence.

With father's directions in their heads, the two Irish rebels headed toward the Maryland line and Eoin Black's farm.

With a few miles of cushion between them and the shoot-out, Shadow turned to Aran. The tension of the last several hours had magically disappeared from the older man's face. He winked and declared, "If luck is on our side, please God, we'll make it before dark, my young rebel friend."

15. *Waiting*

I wander her hills and valleys
And still through my sorrow I see
A land that has never known freedom
And only her rivers run free.

Only The Rivers Run Free/ Mickey MacConnell

*T*he Model T bounced along the rough dirt road. Eoin Black was at the wheel. Aran Roe O'Neill sat next to him while Richard 'Shadow' Doyle drifted between sleep and wakefulness in the back.

Beside its occupant, the rear seat and boot were filled with bags of supplies, haversacks of food, bedrolls, tools, a small tent, two Lee-Enfield rifles, a twelve gauge shotgun and two cartons of heavy winter clothes. The two retreating Irishmen were heading for the safety and seclusion of the Allegheny Mountains.

Riding along, Aran reflected on all that had transpired since the farmyard attack. The drive from the McCracken's to Eoin Black's farm was uneventful, but it had taken longer than planned. The two foreigners lost their way several times as the roads were poorly signposted and Father's directions were a bit vague.

Deciding to error on the side of caution, they refrained from asking directions along the way for fear the locals might remember them. Luckily, the car's tank was full so there was no need to stop for petrol.

Shadow felt that their distinctive accents would make an impression on the rural farm folk. With some careful police work, the coppers might be able to narrow down their whereabouts and actually ferret them out.

As the two fleeing rebels drove toward Frederick, they passed near the eastern edge of the Blue Ridge Mountains. The setting sun over their tree-covered slopes made for a breathtaking evening. This venerable mountain range, worn down by time and rounded off by the elements, reminded Aran of the silhouetted topography of western Ireland and the gentle Wicklows south of Dublin. With the evening's high humidity and fading light of day, the old mountains appeared to be bathed in a blue mist.

Despite the beauty and majesty of their surroundings, Aran felt sick. A singular, haunted feeling gnawed away at the pit of this stomach. It made him feel like retching.

The afternoon's gun battle at the McCracken farm had upset him. Though he knew he had little choice in today's confrontation, the killing of another man ran counter to his innate sense of morality and respect for human life.

On reflection, though, Aran realised that most of the men he had held in his gun sights over the past months had willingly placed themselves in harm's way. They had made the decision to engage Ireland and, therefore, himself in battle. Aran felt that they had chosen to make war against him...against his family and friends...against the values and beliefs he held in high esteem...against his country's right to be free and independent from the unbridled domination of a foreign agent. But the feeling of horror and remorse he felt after killing another man was not easily forgotten despite all his intellectual gamesmanship and logical justification.

"Face it, Aran," he thought to himself, "you're just not a born killer. Though you have had to kill, it is something you just cannot and will not become accustomed to despite all your high-minded reasoning."

With these troubling thoughts, Aran closed his eyes and said a prayer.

❧

Eoin Black was a low-sized man in his late fifties or early sixties. Almost entirely bald, the overweight man was rarely seen without his black bowler hat on, both outside and inside the house. Eoin's face had a haunting appearance created by the several small, dark, fleshy semicircles of loose skin that rippled out from under his deeply set eyes. These swarthy, unhealthy-looking pools created the impression that he was an unfriendly, unhappy and depressed person. He was not.

Fortunately, the rest of his face offered the viewer a positive contrast. His tanned complexion, jolly laugh and flashing gold-capped teeth provided a more accurate view of this good-hearted and contented man.

Eoin Black was a tireless worker, a devoted family man and one of the most generous human beings Shadow and Aran had ever met.

At first introduction, Eoin appeared a bit suspicious, but over time their heavy Irish accents and their intimate knowledge of the McCracken family eased Eoin's fears.

He listened wide-eyed to their description of last May's secretive arrival into Amerikay and of today's terrorist raid on their friends' farm. But, what seemed to impress Mr. Black the most was Shadow's brief description of their involvement in the Easter Week Rebellion.

Eoin was a died-in-the-wool republican and dreamed of the day when Ireland would have her freedom. He was an active supporter and tireless fund-raiser for Clan-na-Gael. It was for these and other reasons that Eoin Black was held in high regard by the Clan's ruling elite.

"Leave the details of your relocation with me. I will handle everything. I know just the spot where you'll be safe from prying eyes and police inquiries.

"I'll need seventy-two hours to put everything together. In the meantime, my wife and I would be most pleased to have ye as our guests."

The Blacks were first generation Irish-Americans. Eoin's father had emigrated from County Down through Canada and finally to the United States before the great famine years. Both Eoin and his wife, Martha, were Scot-Irish Protestants. They had grown up, met and wed in upper New York State. After their marriage, the couple lived with his parents for a year before they moved to Maryland.

Eoin and Martha had managed to scrape together a few hundred dollars and with the bank's help bought a piece of land and some sheep. Over the succeeding years, their animals' wool and meat had gained a much deserved reputation as some of the finest along the east coast.

After rearing and educating three girls, the Blacks were looking forward to turning over the responsibility of the farm to their second daughter and her new husband. Currently, the newlyweds lived in a small cottage behind the main house. They spent their days learning the ins and outs of sheep farming from Eoin himself.

The Blacks were also very proud of their eldest daughter who was teaching school in Baltimore and their youngest one who was currently studying French at the University of Montreal.

Martha directed the lads to a large bedroom on the upper floor of their modest two-story farmhouse. Two canopy-topped beds dominated the sleeping chamber. The quilt-covered beds were separated by a table decorated with two basins and a large ewer of water for washing and shaving. In addition to a comfortable rocking chair, a large table featuring a handsome oil lamp topped with a red glass chimney, the room boasted a big cupboard for their clothes and a small writing desk with a wooden, cane-bottom chair.

After putting away their things and washing up, Shadow and Aran were treated to a fine meal of boiled lamb stew, buttered potatoes and great mugs of tea.

Ever the consummate hostess, Mrs. Black had hung the kettle on the crook for making tea only minutes after she had heard them drive into the farmyard. The reheating of the family's evening meal had taken her only a bit longer to ready after she had learned the newcomers were staying the night.

❧

True to his word, Eoin had everything organised in his promised three days.

During their second day at the sheep farm, two men from the Clan arrived and collected the terrorists' Model T Ford. In exchange, they gave Shadow and Aran an envelope containing two hundred dollars. It was a lot of money and the though of carrying it around with them made Aran nervous.

The Clanmen pledged to take the rebels' just composed letters back to New York. They promised to see to it they were delivered to their families back in Ireland.

It was Aran's third letter home to his family since his arrival in the United States. He assured them he was fine but gave little detailed information about his activities or whereabouts. If the British were still after him, he could not be too careful in case the letter fell into the wrong hands.

Shadow was equally as cautious with his attention to detail in his letter to his wife, Helen, back in Limerick.

The New York men could not be sure when or by whom the envelopes would be personally delivered, but they felt sure they would arrive before Christmas.

❧

It was decided that the two Irishmen would spend the winter in an old prospector's cabin deep in the Allegheny Mountains. It belonged to the father of a Clan member and was occasionally used as a hunting lodge during the spring and fall months.

With Eoin's help, Aran and Shadow made a list of supplies they would need for spending the winter in the isolated West Virginia mountains. They would use part of their new-found wealth for the purchases and, upon departing the retreat in the spring, the two Irishmen would leave the hardware items behind for the next occupants to use. It would be their way of thanking the Clan for all the help they had provided during these past months.

Not wishing to draw any unwanted attention to themselves, Aran and Shadow thought it best they stay out of sight. Thus, Eoin and Martha drove over to Hagerstown to purchase the necessary provisions.

Later that afternoon, after the couple had returned from their shopping excursion, the Irish rebels felt like little boys on Christmas Day. What great sport it was unloading and inspecting all of the supplies stacked in the back of the Black's motor car. Aran Roe and Shadow Doyle were looking forward to the pending adventure with more anticipation than regret.

❧

After stopping for petrol in Winchester, Virginia, the three men drove on toward Petersburg, West Virginia. Eoin knew an outfitter who could be counted on to help them. He was a good man who knew how to keep his mouth shut even if there was some sort of a police inquiry. Eoin had worked with the man on several occasions and found him to be entirely trustworthy.

Their plan was to use a string of three pack mules to haul the gear and supplies up to the cabin. After unloading everything, they would release the animals, letting them make their own way back to the outfitter. Having worked with mules on his father's farm near Gort, Aran knew they were smart animals and, in a day or so, would find their way home. The beasts would retrace their steps, knowing that food and shelter were waiting for them back in Petersburg.

From memory, Eoin drew a crude map detailing the location of the cabin. Upon leaving the village of Petersburg and its famous Gap, Aran and Shadows would hike north by northeast for four to five hours. It wold be slow going as there were few roads and, to complicate matters, they would be climbing about fifteen hundred feet in elevation.

After reaching a long narrow S-shaped lake, Eoin instructed them to head due east and continue climbing a heavily timbered slope for another two miles. Once on top of that eastern rise, they should proceed north along the ridgeline for a mile or so. If everything worked out just right, they would find a log cabin situated in the middle of a small clearing.

Proudly, Eoin stated, "Look carefully, lads...you'll see the Irish word 'Innisfree' burned into a wooden shingle that's hanging just above the front door."

Grinning from ear to ear, Eoin promised there would be plenty of trees waiting for them to chop into firewood. In a more serious vein, he said, "I envy all the great times you'll have hunting and fishing. The woods are full of deer, rabbits and squirrels plus the lake below the cabin is teeming with fish."

"I know ye'll have the time of your lives toughening up your bodies, sharpening your hunting and survival skills while you enjoy the adventure of living in the great American outdoors. I hope you lads will grow to appreciate what some of our early pioneer settlers experienced as they opened up this country a hundred years ago."

Eoin went on to say that, unfortunately, he was too busy with his farm responsibilities to come along with them even for a few weeks. There was just no way he could take the time off.

Then, with a twinkle in his haunting eyes, Eoin said, "I'm sorry to disappoint ye, but I've a bit more bad news. Up there on the mountain lads, there's not a pub or the opportunity for female companionship to lift your spirits through all those cold, lonely winter nights."

Both Aran and Shadow smiled at Eoin. They assured him that his company would be sadly missed but, by sacrificing the other two pleasures, it would only help them with their conditioning and training...both physically and mentally.

"Seriously lads," continued Eoin, "if there is much snow, you're biggest job will be finding enough food to eat...and from the way you two cleaned up Martha's tableplates back home, I'm guessing you'll go through all those spuds in that bag before the first snow."

Shadow assured Eoin he would keep an eye on Aran and not let him grow too fat or complacent.

❧

Eoin, Shadow, Aran and the outfitter named Joseph plus his family spent a great evening together under the shadow of Orr's Mountain. Joseph's wife, Susan, and their two daughters served a beautiful meal of brook trout, homegrown vegetables and new potatoes. The feast was topped off with freshly-baked, red raspberry cobbler and steaming cups of strong black tea.

Later, Joseph cracked open a jug of some home brewed whiskey and the cozy evening spent in front of the roaring fire faded away into a sweet blur of music and conversation.

It was no wonder that early the next morning Aran found it difficult to drag himself out of his warm bed. The thought of sleeping rough on some mountaintop caused him to pull the blankets up around him while he snuggled down under the warm covers. He knew the next six months of living in the log cabin was going to be a challenge. He was homesick for Ireland. He missed his family very much and knew these past months spent away from home in Amerikay could never be reclaimed. He said his prayers again and fell back asleep wondering what would become of his budding relationship with Sarah Anne.

His life's recent sadness, its loneliness and present uncertainty all weighed heavily on him. He felt like the world was spinning along and leaving him behind.

Lately, he realised he had been running away from all the things that were important to him, rather than facing them straight on. He was growing impatient with the waiting and wanted to get on with his life. He was tired of wasting these precious moments. It was time he moved forward in his quest for his own happiness and for seeing Ireland achieve its long-denied freedom. He was tired of treading life's water.

After a number of wake-up calls, Shadow finally had to pull Aran out of bed saying, "Sure, and it's time we were making a day of it, my fine young Irish friend!"

As he stood partially dressed outside the outfitter's house, Aran cupped his hands and splashed some icy water from the wash basin onto his face. The resulting shock of cold seemed to clear his head and helped him purge his persistent feelings of depression and self-pity.

It was another fine day and, after taking several deep breaths, the morning's clean mountain air filled his lungs with energy and vitality. It felt good to be alive and he was again eager to tackle the challenge of living off the land with Shadow. It would be good training for what he hoped lay ahead.

❦

The three pack mules were roped together in single file and loaded down with supplies and camping gear. Aran walked ahead and Shadow followed, holding the lead animal's rope in his hand. After a few steps, they both stopped, turned around and waved good-bye to Eoin, Joseph and Susan.

The three returned their salute from the outfitter's front porch. Once more, Shadow and Aran turned and headed out of the little settlement of Petersburg.

The two Irish rebels began hiking up a winding three-foot-wide trail that snaked its way up along the side of Orr's Mountain.

After walking for twenty minutes or so, they stopped and looked back down into the Gap. For hundreds of years, Indians and later the white man had used that passageway to move back and forth across the Allegheny Mountains. During the American Civil War, the village had been a Union outpost along the disputed North-South border. There were even intact sections of the earthworks that Yankee soldiers had built to protect the settlement from southern rebel attacks. But, even more striking than these last century fortifications, were the ancient Indian drawings carved into sections of the mountain's face. Aran imagined he could make out animal shapes on the mountain wall across the narrow valley from where he stood. The ghostly figures gave him a haunted feeling, as if the two of them were walking back into some timeless past far removed from the political, economic and social troubles of their present-day, Anglo-Irish-American world.

Aran Roe imagined himself returning to an earlier age, two thousand years ago, in a quest to rediscover his Gaelic roots. Walking along the mountain trail, the Gortman's thoughts drifted back to a wild and forested imaginary Ireland. He closed his eyes and tried to visualize things more clearly. In doing so, however, his foot slipped on the rough path and he almost fell. Quite abruptly, the embarrassed young Irishman was jolted back to the realities of the present.

Aran righted himself, adjusted his trusty Lee-Enfield rifle Father had given him before they had fled the McCrackens' farm and pushed on up the trail.

The autumn sun was warming the air and the world around him was alive with living things...birds, grasshoppers, rabbits, bees. The green leaves on the surrounding trees were beginning to transform themselves into brightly coloured harbingers announcing autumn's arrival. Even the musty woodland scents and the odor off the pack animals smelled good.

As he walked along ahead of Shadow and the mules, Aran was forced to do battle with several nasty horse flies that constantly kept trying to carry off bits and pieces of him to wherever such vicious insects live.

"Ah...the pain and pleasures of the outdoors," thought Aran to himself.

❧

The cabin was simple but comfortable. The furniture was home-made from pine boughs. The six chairs and the three bunk beds were constructed of branches four inches in diameter bolted together. Smaller pieces of pine bough were used to reinforce the critical weight-bearing joints. Rope webbing formed the seats and backs of the chairs. They substituted for the beds springs and mattresses. Cross-cut sections of logs acted as stools and foot rests. Two large tables dominated the single room...one for eating on and sitting around while the other served as a kitchen counter. A dozen or so books were stacked on the huge beam that doubled as a mantle above the stone fireplace. The tomes were mostly nineteenth century English novels, but there was a worn copy of John Mitchel's *Jail Journal,* much to Aran's delight.

He staked his claim to the book by announcing to Shadow that it was one of the books he had always wanted to read. He intended to begin pouring over its yellowed pages immediately.

The walls were made of pine logs notched at the ends to form snug-fitting corners with the other beams. The seams in the walls had been filled with a mud and plaster mixture that seemed to keep the room free of cold drafts. A door and two windows had been cut out and properly finished off. There was even heavy glass in each of the windows.

The roof was formed from split timbers that were tightly fitted together and covered with a layer of grassy sod. It turned out to be quite watertight even in the heaviest of rains.

Finally, the flooring was made of additional sections of hand-split pine but its surface was rough and uneven. Shadow and Aran both had to learn the hard lesson that heavy socks or boots must be worn indoors at all times to protect their feet from painful splinters.

With sunlight entering the cabin during daylight hours and with their nightly fire augmented by candles, the cabin proved to be quite a cozy and comfortably warm place to live.

In addition to their living quarters, a simple wooden-railed porch dressed up the structure's westward-facing front door. There was also a dilapidated shed for storing wood and smoking meat at the southern edge of the clearing.

The other necessities of life were also rustic but certainly not unpleasant. A fine little mountain spring yielding sparkling fresh waster bubbled up about two hundred yards down the eastern face of the mountain. The rocky trail leading down to it from the cabin, however, made walking unsteady. The return trip, lugging two water-filled wooden buckets was even more of a struggle, especially in the dark of night. Even so, the reward of a cool drink at the end of the trip made the journey worthwhile. Though the autumn had been unusually dry, the little spring gurgled merrily forth, reassuring the lads they would not go thirsty.

Life's other necessity, a lavatory, was satisfied by a pine board placed between two tree stumps. A hole had been sawed in the wooden panel and it was situated directly over a pit dug in the ground. With an ample supply of leaves, the Irishmen were comfortably accommodated though answering nature's call on cold winter days proved a chilling experience for all exposed body parts.

❧

The two Irishmen spent the remaining weeks of warm weather exploring their new environment, cutting wood for winter fuel and hunting. Not only was there an ample supply of deer, rabbit and squirrel, but Shadow had managed to bag a large, wild-tusked boar.

The two men had trailed the seventy-pound beast for several hours one morning. Fearing the pig might escape, Aran circled around in front of it and turned its path toward a steep rocky slope. Thinking it was trapped, the boar turned on Aran and charged.

The seventh son of a seventh son's fortune again smiled on him as he made a frantic dash for a low hanging tree limb. Aran pulled himself safely off the ground just in the nick of time.

Between laughing and trying to steady his rifle, Shadow was finally able to squeeze off two shots and dropped the beast.

Later that day, they built a sturdy spit over a shallow pit and each took turns rotating the roasting boar over a bed of hot coals. Its sweet, delicious meat combined with some fire-baked potatoes and fresh watercress from the lake below provided the lads with a meal they talked about for months.

Their other big project of the autumn was the shooting, cleaning and smoking of two large bucks. Aran nailed the hides to the outside of the cabin and proudly added their racks of eight and ten points to the small collection already displayed above the fireplace.

But, of all the work and pleasure they shared together that fall, the times they spent fishing were the most memorable.

Occasionally, they hiked the three or so miles down to the lake in the early afternoon. After setting up their two-man tent and organising their campsite, Aran and Shadow fished till sunset. By the light of their fire and twilit sky, the two men pan-fried their catch. Often the trout or bass were combined with some boiled rice and fresh watercress all topped off with tin cupfuls of hot tea.

Falling asleep with full stomachs and dreams of home, the two Irish rebels would sleep peacefully through the night. However, at dawn's first light, they would be up and spend the next several hours lost in more fishing.

He enjoyed the challenge of fishing but Aran's real pleasure in these excursions were the long periods of relaxed conversation he shared with Shadow. They talked about themselves and their families back home...about their loves and hates...about their dreams and nightmares...about their innermost thoughts and fears. They took personal risks and opened up to each other. They talked about their secrets, their life's embarrassing interludes and their silly, vain frailties. In doing so, they felt a special bond of friendship grow between them.

It was during these hours of fishing or of idling the evening hours away by the stone fireplace in the cabin or of sitting outside at night staring up at the star-filled heavens that Aran Roe O'Neill and Richard 'Shadow' Doyle became close friends. Their admiration, respect and trust for one another created a brotherly connexion of uncommon strength.

In addition to their personal disclosures, the two men talked of Ireland and how they wanted to continue their fight for its freedom. They speculated about the Irish people's desire for real independence from England. If the current feelings of separation back home continued growing and strengthening, maybe the IRB and Volunteer movements might come together and work toward a common end. To be effective, this combined effort would have to discover ways of supplying Ireland with the weapons and manpower necessary to stage an all-out fight against England.

As they continued spending their days working and playing in the wilderness, this thought of an Irish War of Independence was always in the back of their minds. They never forgot that all of their hunting, hiking and working together was strengthening their bodies and conditioning their minds. They were acquiring the skills needed by a soldier to successfully wage war against the Sassenach.

Long discussions would ensue regarding how freedom's war should be fought. They both agreed that the tactics employed by Shadow and Major MacBride in South Africa were the ones to use if any fighting was to be done in Ireland. It just was not possible or imaginable that Ireland could ever scrap toe to toe with mighty England. Eireann simply lacked the men, the training, the experience and the weaponry of the Crown. However, Aran and Shadow both knew, from firsthand experience, that small groups of well trained and equipped men could inflict physically damaging and psychologically embarrassing losses on a much larger and more formidable enemy force.

This outdoor adventure they were now living in the West Virginia Mountains would help them prepare for such a guerrilla life.

On occasions, they even fantasised about organising and preparing for combat a small band of guerrilla fighters here in America. When they were well armed and trained, they would set sail for 'the Holy Ground.' Shadow called them their little 'Army of Liberation.' It reminded Aran of James II's attempts to re-establish Catholic Old English control in Ireland in 1689. This time, however, he hoped for a different outcome.

❧

Time passed more quickly than either imagined.

Luckily, the weather stayed fair so Joseph was able to pay them his planned visit in mid-November. One day he just walked into camp trailing three mules behind him. Joe reported all was well with his family and that the three freed mules had safely returned home. In fact, he had brought two of them with him on this trip.

Since the two Irishmen had arrived at the cabin too late in the season to plant and harvest anything before winter, the animals were loaded down with additional staples...potatoes, rice, flour, sugar, salt, tea, apples, onions and small containers of butter, cheese and jam. Thoughtfully, Joseph's stores included two jugs of his lovely homebrewed whisky, ten boxes of .303 shells plus several cartons of shotgun cartridges. The boxes of ammo reminded the lads that they had not fired their Luger automatics since leaving the McCracken farm September last.

Joseph stayed for two days. The three man enjoyed some hunting and fishing together, but what Aran and Shadow liked most of all was having another face to look at and another voice to listen to. His visit provided a refreshing change to their simple, quiet and sometimes lonely life on the mountain.

❧

In mid-December, they cut a small Christmas tree and brought it into the cabin. The two men relived many childhood holiday memories while decorating the tree with pinecones, holly berries, and sprigs of mistletoe. They carved a few simple figurines from wood and Shadow fashioned a cross to sit atop the little evergreen.

Aran had brought along a harmonica given to him by one of Joseph's daughters and he had taught himself to play some tunes on it. Sitting before the cabin fire, sipping the outfitter's whiskey, Shadow sang a few Christmas carols while Aran accompanied him on his mouth organ. Afterwards, they knelt on the wooden floor, said the rosary together and thanked God for his many blessings. They both prayed they would be reunited with their families by this time next year.

Two days after Christmas they celebrated Aran's eighteenth birthday.

❧

The first heavy snow of the winter did not arrive until mid-January. One morning they woke up to a white world that was three feet deep.

Wearing the snowshoes that hung on the cabin's wall, the men took turns digging paths to the spring, woodshed and toilet.

With their leaf supply buried, the lads discovered that snowballs were a fine substitute for lavatory paper though the chilling experience was a bit of a shock to the privates.

They continued to busy themselves with their little routines of cooking and eating, washing the odd bits of clothes, taking the occasional sponge bath, hauling water and making tea, cutting firewood and saying the evening rosary. They read all the books in the cabin plus the five or six they had brought up the mountain with them.

Each day, after their chores were finished, the two Irishmen went hunting, hiking or worked on building a small animal stable on the far side of the clearing. It was fun planning, cutting and building the log walls and roof. They delighted in seeing the building grow from the ground up. The two men knew others would use the shelter for many years to come and would appreciate their hard work. They certainly felt that way about those who had built the cabin and smoke shed they so enjoyed using.

When it was nearly finished, the two of them carved their names and the date into the wood above the framed entrance. The inscriptions would remain a lingering remembrance of their efforts and time spent in the Alleghenys.

But, of all the things they shared together, their made-up game of hide and seek was the overwhelming favourite. Aran had dreamed it up one evening after recalling the fun he had as a child playing it with his brothers at home.

They made up their own rules along the way but there were two variables they always agreed to abide by before their play began. The first rule was that the person hiding could only do so within a prescribed quadrant or a specified distance from the cabin. The clock was the second qualifier. The time given to hide from the seeker and the time allocated to find the hidden one were faithfully respected.

It was a great activity requiring patience, imagination, tracking skills and intelligence. They played two or three involved and lengthy games a week. Aran was the most creative of the two at finding hiding places but Shadow was the best tracker. They both felt the game added to the soldiering skills they were trying to develop and sharpen.

❧

In late February, the snows turned to rain and it stayed wet for the next three weeks. But despite the dirty weather, Aran and Shadow, wearing their rubber ponchos, stayed active outdoors.

They put the finishing touches to the stable, continued their hunting and began taking long hikes through the mountains that required sleeping rough for several nights in a row.

They each carried only one haversack and their rifle. On several occasions when the weather was particularly desperate, they almost gave in and turned back. But, just at the last moment, they changed their minds, knowing that they would not have that luxury in wartime. They simply knuckled down and toughed it out despite their desire to head for the warmth and comfort of the cabin.

These long overnight hikes provided great physical and mental training. The lads had to rely on their own imaginations to solve problems that civilians never confront in a peacetime world.

❧

Seeking more diversion during a string of fine days toward the middle of March, Aran Roe and Richard decided to play one of their 'war games.' They hiked down the eastern side of their mountain and reconnoitered the village of Moorefield. They had never been there before and thought it would be great sport to see if they could survey the little mountain community without its residents being aware of their presence.

It took them most of the day to reach their target. They spent that evening and part of the next morning playing their 'war game' of spying on the unsuspecting villagers.

At the conclusion of their exercise, Aran and Shadow longed to walk into town for a proper meal and a glass or two of beer. Unfortunately, doing so might raise more questions than they wished to answer. It could also compromise their privacy and the location of the safe-house.

Heading back toward the cabin, Aran and Shadow laughed out loud as they speculated on what the local town's folk would have thought if they had seen or learned of their 'unusual' doings. No doubt they would have been judge to be as crazy as nine shilling notes.

❧

As they finally neared the cabin, they heard the sounds of horses...three maybe four, but they could not be sure. Taking the cautious approach, they split up. Aran slipped up to the clearing from the north and crawled in behind the newly finished stable. Shadow took the southern route and used the smokehouse for cover.

They could hear voices coming from inside the log cabin. One sounded Irish and the other had an accent, but it was difficult to pinpoint from a distance.

Aran was waiting for Shadow's signal to advance when he heard his friend let out a yell. The next thing Aran knew, Shadow was running across the clearing shouting, "Liam...Liam...Liam..."

Sure enough...out of the front door popped Liam Mellowes as pretty as ye please.

By now, a surprised but delighted Aran was on his feet racing Shadow to the cabin porch.

Shadow made it first exclaiming, "Jesus, Mary and Joseph! Liam Mellowes you're a sight for sore eyes. Only just yesterday, I was telling the young rebel here it was about time to make some plans for going home."

Before the last words were out of Shadow's mouth, he had his arms around Mellowes and was lifting him off his feet.

"Begad, from the looks of ye, you've turned into a mountain man...at least your arms are as strong as one sure."

By now Danny had joined the three on the porch. The questions and answers flew hot and heavy.

Shaking his other friend's hand, Shadow asked, "Danny, what happened to the two of ye after yis left the McCrackens?"

"Certainly nothing as exciting as what happened to ye two. We heard all about the raid from the Clan and Eoin. Apparently the devastating blow ye dealt those terrorists did them in. Nothing more was ever heard from the likes of those lousers. Probably locked up somewhere I'd imagine.

"No, Liam and I actually spent a quiet winter in one of Chicago's western suburbs surrounded by working-class Irish-Americans. We just kept a low profile and stayed out of trouble."

Without letup, Danny Kelly continued, "Ah, dear Mother of God, from the looks of you two and the ruggedness of these mountains, I'm sorry to report we led a pretty soft life. I must say, though, I'm a little jealous. I think I'd rather have been here with yis enjoying life on this mountaintop."

After the initial excitement had died down, Aran and Shadow took their visitors on a tour of their encampment. They pointed out the trees they had cut down, the shed they had built and the supply of cured game they had stored in the smokehouse. Aran and Shadow talked about taking their friends fishing, hunting and maybe they would even teach them how to play their version of hide and seek.

Mellowes and Kelly were impressed with the way their two friends had managed to survive the winter in such an isolated place. But the biggest delight was the obvious bond of friendship that had grown between the two.

After finishing the tour, they went back to the cabin. Shadow started a fire while Aran sliced up one of his loaves of homemade bread. With a few hunks of smoked fish and Shadow's tea, they all settled down for a good chat.

"Yes, Liam," said Aran, "we've really tested ourselves up here, grown stronger and learned how to live off the land. Sure, we've disciplined ourselves to be tough. We're better men and soldiers because of it."

"Now, speaking of soldiering, what do ye hear from home and

family. Any new developments?" demanded Shadow.

"Helen and your girls are all fine. So's your family, Aran. You'll also be happy to know that the O'Mahonys seem to be getting on well too."

Turning to Danny, Liam directed, "Fill them in on the news from England."

Danny cleared his throat and began. "England's war in Europe went badly throughout all of last autumn. Westminster finally grew tired of Asquith's bungling mistakes. They threw his government out of office. David Lloyd George has taken his place and, as a goodwill gesture, he released over five hundred Easter Week men just before Christmas.[15-1] These were mostly the men who were being held without any formal charges or criminal convictions. Aran, some were your mates who fought with ye in Dublin. The others had played no part in the Rising but had simply been swept up by the British in the days and weeks after Pearse's surrender."

Mellowes interrupted, "Lloyd George's motives for the release were more pro-American than pro-Irish. He continually tries to entice the United States into entering the war. He hoped the prisoner release might favourably influence the Yanks."

"Be sure to mention Plunkett's win in Roscommon," prompted Danny.

"I was just getting to that. Count Plunkett, Joseph Mary's father, won a by-election in North Roscommon.[15-2] As Sinn Fein's first, post–'16 election candidate, he simply ran as the father of an executed Easter Rebellion hero. Ever the political opportunist so, he pointed out in his speeches that he'd two other sons still being held as Rebellion prisoners in England. Arthur Griffith wanted him to campaign on the platform that, if elected, he'd abstain from taking his seat in Westminster but, for some reason, Plunkett didn't. Besides the Rebellion angle, the Count advanced his name as Ireland's representative at any forthcoming, postwar Peace Conference held in either Berlin or London. He wishes to champion Eireann's rightful claim to becoming a free and independent state regardless of who wins the war.[15-3]

"Griffith, your GPO friend, Michael Collins, and other newly released prisoners threw themselves into the campaign and Plunkett won the seat for our side. John Redmond's old Parliamentary Party man didn't have a chance.

"Let me add one more thing," said Danny, shifting his weight in the homemade chair. "Earlier this month, Lloyd George declared that the partitioning of Ireland was the only way to solve the 'Irish Problem.'"[15-4]

Mellowes interjected, "I think the battle lines are being drawn, even as we speak. Mark my words lads...the two issues of Ireland's partitioning and Ireland's independence will be the most important questions our country has ever had to face. Their outcomes will, no doubt, determine our nation's future for generations to come."

There were no signs of lightheartedness or optimism in Mellowes's voice. He was deadly serious.

After hearing Liam's and Danny's news, Shadow and Aran knew it was time they made plans for going home. Things were hotting up back in Ireland...the people were waking up and beginning to flex their political muscles. A major confrontation with England could not be too far way. The mountain refugees wanted to play a part in determining Ireland's future. They did not want to do it from this side of the Atlantic. It did not matter to either of them if the settlement was political or military or both. All that mattered was that Ireland received her freedom and that they played a part in its settlement.

"Liam," said Aran, "sure, it seems to me it's time we were all heading back to Ireland. What do ye think?"

"Ah, you've taken the words from my mouth so!" replied Mellowes.

With that, the Dubliner stood up and walked over to the fireplace. Putting his mug of tea on the wooden mantle, he turned and addressed the trio. "Based on good information, the United States will enter England's war in the next couple of weeks. Some think the announcement will come as early as the 6th or 7th of April. That's less than two weeks away.

"When it happens, there'll be a great flurry of activity. All kinds of ships will be leaving the east coast heading for England...men, supplies and the like.

"'With its connexions, Clan-na-Gael can arrange for all of us to hire on as seamen. No doubt we'll end up in some English port and have to make our own way to Ireland, but that shouldn't be a problem.

"Apparently, the English have given up on trying to track us down. Seems they've bigger fish to fry. They're trying to put our Easter Rebellion behind them and deal with matters of more immediate importance.

"Now with Sinn Fein winning an election, the English are more concerned with political issues than viewing a demilitarised Ireland as a viable threat. In their stupidity, they've even begun arresting Irish nationalists who are speaking out in favour of Griffith's party.

"There's also talk of passing some kind of conscription legislation throughout Great Britain. If that happens, Ireland may just stage a national revolt the likes of which England has never imagined in their wildest dreams.

"So, my friends, let's spend a few days enjoying ourselves in this mountain hideaway and on Saturday we'll all head down to Petersburg. The Clan has arranged for cars to meet us. They'll take us straight to New York. We'll stay under cover in the city until our ship is ready to sail."

Mellowes's announcement had an air of finality about it. Aran was struck with two conflicting emotions. His first reaction was that of pure joy and excitement at the prospects of going home. Sadly, though, a wave of melancholy swept over him. The special time that he and Shadow had shared over the past six and half months was over. A huge lump of sorrow welled up in his throat. He looked over at Shadow. Their eyes met. Aran realised Shadow was feeling the same mixture of emotions he was. The two men smiled at each other, nodded and slowly raised their mugs in salute. It was a silent acknowledgement that their time together had been special and would never be forgotten.

❧

The few things they were taking with them were all packed and stacked out on the little wooden porch. Liam Mellowes and Danny Kelly were outside saddling up the four horses. Shadow and Aran Roe stood alone in the cabin. They were having a last sentimental look around. The two were leaving many wonderful memories behind on this mountaintop.

After making sure the fire was out, Aran turned to his friend. "Shadow, I'll never forget the wonderful times we've shared together here sure. You've taught me so much about life...about what it is to be a friend and a soldier. I'll always cherish these months we've shared so. But, I know this is not the end...it's only another beginning. We're going home and, please God, we'll organise our little guerrilla band and carry the fight for freedom to their fetid King and Crown...and if God so chooses, we'll live to see our country free."

Shadow walked over, put his arm around the younger man's shoulder. Cheerfully, he replied "...and that we will my young Irish Rebel...and that we surely will."

Liam Mellowes gave a shout, "Let's be off, lads!"

Following Aran outside, Shadow pulled the door of the cabin closed behind him.

16. *Returning*

Soldiers are we, whose lives are pledged to Ireland
Some have come from a land beyond the wave.
Sworn to be free, no more our ancient sireland
Shall shelter the despot or the slave;
Tonight we man the bearna baoghal
In Erin's cause, come woe or weal;
'Mid canon's roar and rifle's peal
We'll chant a soldier's song.

A Soldier's Song/ Peadar Kearney

A small reception party was waiting for the four Irishmen on Joseph's front porch.

"Bagad, Gabriel...Sarah...what a grand surprise! I can't tell you how many times Shadow and I have thought of you two and your entire family during the past seven months. How've you been keeping...and what in heaven's name are ye both doing here?"

Aran was flabbergasted as they all took turns greeting one another and shaking hands.

"Shadow, what do you think? Gabby and Sarah Anne are here to greet us! I just can't believe it!"

"Ah sure, it doesn't surprise me one little bit. Didn't I tell you she fancied you," answered Shadow, nodding his head in Sarah's direction.

Aran's sun-browned face turned red. The Irish Rebel's eyes darted around the little group hoping someone would rescue him from his embarrassment.

Finally, Mellowes came to his aid. He spoke up cheerfully saying, "We thought yis might be pleased to see a couple friends. Now, ye can never say that your ould mates weren't minding you so."

"Wait just a minute, Liam. Who are you after calling 'ould' around here?" retorted Danny. "Remember, I'm just twenty-three."

"Just a figure of speech, my friend...and don't you go denying that this whole idea was yours in the first place," countered Mellowes.

In reality, Liam Mellowes was only twenty-five himself but, as Commander of the Irish Volunteers in the west of Ireland, everyone respected Liam. People thought of him as being older and wiser than his years might indicate.

"All right you two...I can see ye both were cooped up together far too long in Chicago," interrupted Shadow.

Having spoken, Richard, the elder statesman of the group at thirty-six, looked around the little gathering and asked, "Would someone be after telling me what's going on here anyway?"

"All in good time, Shadow. All in good time," laughed Mellowes.

After all the good-natured teasing and the volleys of harmless incriminations had stopped, Joseph invited the jubilant lot inside the house.

Shadow and Aran's entrance sparked another round of welcoming greetings from the outfitter's family and the Clan-na-Gael men who had driven down from New York to collect them.

After all the formalities had been attended to, the group adjourned to the dining table for some of Martha's delicious country cooking.

Aran sat opposite Sarah. As he glanced at her between forkfuls of food, he could not get over how attractive she looked. Sarah Anne was taller and slimmer than he had remembered. She wore her brunette hair in a single plait tied up in a bun at the back of her head. Her flashing blue eyes had little specks of white in them that flashed and danced with an intensity that excited Aran. She wore a bright yellow jumper over a white blouse with a tan, ankle-length muslin skirt. Brown riding boots graced her feet.

During his seven months of isolation, Aran had almost forgotten how delightful and enchanting a woman's figure could be. At their reunion outside, the Gortman had to consciously remind himself not to stare at Sarah's feminine form when they were standing around in Joseph's front garden. When the group had finally moved indoors, his eyes wanted to follow her every move. Without being obvious, he watched her climb the steps and walk through into the dining area.

Now, at the table, Aran was caught off guard by his surging feelings. On the one hand, he felt a persistent loyalty to his lost Brigid, but on the other, he knew life must go on. Aran wanted to share his life with a woman. Sarah McCracken seemed to possess many of the qualities he sought in a wife. She was intelligent yet sensitive; strong willed but considerate of others; attractive though not full of herself.

Once during the meal, he looked up to find her staring at him. Again, a fire seemed to ignite his cheeks and his heart thumped madly inside his chest. Aran dropped his head, looked down at his plate and shifted positions in the straight-backed wooden chair. In doing so, his foot accidentally bumped against one of Sarah's legs hidden away under the table.

It was as if a bolt of lightning had shot up through his body. His loins suddenly glowed with excitement. Looking up at her, he involuntarily uttered, "Sorry."

Everyone else at the table glanced over at him.

In defence of his unseen clumsiness, he forced a laugh and replied, "Guess I've been away from civilisation too long. I've forgotten how to sit properly at the dinner table."

No one quite understood what he meant, but Sarah did. She smiled and pressed her foot down on top of one of his boots. "You're forgiven, Aran, but you've probably done permanent damage to some of my tender little toes."

Aran felt another surge of excitement light up his face. The touch of her foot seemed to electrify him.

"I guess it will take me a while to become civilised again," mumbled Aran.

Hoping to draw everyone's attention away from himself, Aran turned to his mountain comrade, "Shadow, why did you let me abandon all the social graces my family had instilled in me during our wilderness outing?"

"Sure, I didn't realise you had any to lose," teased Shadow in return. Then, in an effort to soften his bediviling remark, Richard Doyle leaned over to his right and lovingly rubbed the back of his young friend's head.

As the normal chatter of conversation returned to the table, Aran knew he must reconcile the romantic conflict that swirled around inside him. He heard his inner voice saying, "I know Brigid would have wanted me to lead a full, rich and satisfying life with or without her by my side. Sure, I would have wanted the same for her. Now, I must find a way to resolve my feelings of disloyalty to Brigid and start making a new life for meself. It's the only way I'll ever be happy so."

Aran knew he must somehow summon up the courage of his convictions if he was to live the life his conscience demanded. It was a difficult balancing act. To honour the bonds of family, friends and loved ones, to turn Easter's failure into a Pearcian triumph, to be true to himself at all times...these were the Herculean challenges he had set for himself.

Aran had talked with Shadow about these issues on many occasions during their winter together. He had openly discussed his budding love for Brigid and his romanticised plans for their future that now was never to be. The Irish Rebel could rationally talk about life and love but his emotional uncertainty regarding another romantic relationship with a woman was far from resolved.

Aran puzzled about these issues while finishing his meal. He hoped he might have the time to speak with Sarah Anne about these haunting ghosts that so often occupied his thoughts.

❧

Aran Roe O'Neill and Richard 'Shadow' Doyle stood side by side against the railing on the big ship's starboard deck. They watched intently as the little tugboats guided their freighter into its Bristol Harbour berth.

"This crossing was a bit different from the one we all took over to Amerikay last year wasn't it, Shadow?"

"Aye, it certainly was, Aran. Back then sure we didn't know if you were going to live or die."

Looking out over the busy harbour, Shadow continued his thoughtful reflections. "As I think back upon that crossing, I often wonder what happened to Dr. Thompson and that wonderful assistant of his. No, Aran, there isn't any doubt about it in my mind so...those two saved your life. We're all very fortunate the pair of them happened to be aboard that ship."

Aran had only the vaguest of memories about their sea voyage and the fishing boat that took them ashore. Sometimes he doubted if he really remembered anything at all about the journey. He wondered if he had not simply painted a picture of it in his mind after all the things his three friends had told him of it.

In contrast, this crossing of the North Atlantic had been uneventful despite it being filled with long hours of hard work.

Aran gazed down at the waters where the Bristol Channel merges with the estuary of the River Severn. He watched the distance between the ship and the quay grow smaller and smaller. Once more, he reflected on all the unbelievable events that had occurred since Shadow and he had ridden down out of the mountains with Danny and Liam.

It all had started with the unexpected appearance of Gabriel McCracken and his sister, Sarah, who were waiting to greet their return to the outfitter's home in Petersburg.

After spending the night with Joseph and his family, their little group headed for New York in two cars. The plan was to wait in the city until passage was secured for them on a ship sailing for England. As usual, Clan-na-Gael was taking care of everything. There was nothing to be done except to follow their orders...and that's exactly what they all did. But, several things happened prior to their ship's departure that took Aran completely by surprise.

Liam, Shadow, Sarah and a Clanman, Christy, took one of the cars while Danny, Gabriel, a northern Virginian named Turlough Molloy plus himself followed in the second motor car.

They were heading back to Eoin Black's farm to spend the night before driving on to New York the following day.

Gay and Danny asked Aran tens of questions about his time in the mountains. In turn, Aran asked Gabriel all about the things that had happened to the McCrackens since the September shoot-out at the farm.

They were almost to Eoin's farm when Gay dropped the first of two bombshells on Aran.

Gabriel turned to Aran, patted him on the knee and said, "We have a little surprise for you, my Luger-toting friend."

"What's that Gabby?" queried Aran.

"Well, you know that little band of rebel fighters you and Shadow talked about forming while ye were up there in the mountains?"

"Aye..."

"Well, you are looking at some of them right now."

Aran thought Gabby was having him on. "Gay, what are you talking about...looking at what?"

"As difficult as it is to believe, you're looking at two of your much discussed guerrilla fighters this very minute."

After several moments of disbelief, the gravity of what Gabriel was saying hit home.

"Do yis mean..."

"Yes, that's exactly what we mean. The two of us are joining you, Shadow, Danny and Liam on your trip back home. If it comes to it, we intend to take up arms against England and fight for Ireland's freedom along with you and your comrades."

Aran was speechless. He just sat staring at the thirty-one-year-old McCracken son. He never in his wildest imagination dreamed Gabriel or this stranger, Turlough, would be joining them.

"It's really very simple, my friend," continued Gabriel. "Ah sure, one of the things that Mellowes had always hoped to accomplish here in America was the recruiting of groups of well trained men who'd be willing to journey to Ireland and fight for her independence."

Aran nodded his head in agreement. He had heard Liam talk about this idea on numerous occasions.

Gay continued, "After you and Shadow left for your winter in the mountains, Larry, Dom and I began thinking. Father had always wanted the three of us to go back and live for a time in Ireland. But, between school and working on the farm, we never seemed to have the time. Then, when the war in Europe broke out, we had to put those plans on hold. Don't you remember...we all talked about going over on several occasions while we sat around the kitchen table together."

Aran nodded and went on listening to Gabby with keen interest.

"Your visit and talk of having a good slap at England peaked our interest. The farmyard shoot-out only whetted our appetites even more. Within days of your departure, Larry, Dom and I approached Father.

"After hours of discussion, he finally agreed that one of us could go. You see, Father's youngest brother, Peter, and his family own a pub in the village of Cahir, County Tipperary. There's always been a long-standing invitation to move in with them. As you can imagine, an extra pair of hands or two at the pub would always be welcomed."

Aran could sense Gabriel's growing excitement. He could see it in his eyes and hear it in Gay's voice.

"Aran, would you believe it...Father said he'd speak with Devoy and, if the Clan could work it out to get one of us over, he'd give one of us his blessing."

Aran could hardly contain his delight. "But Gay, how's it you're coming and not Larry? Since he's the oldest, I'd imagine he'd first choice, no?"

"Hold on, you're getting me ahead of myself. Yes, needless to say, we all wanted to go so we decided to draw straws. You'll never guess who was the lucky winner?"

Gabriel grinned and paused to catch his breath. "Well, what do you have say about that, Aran, my friend?"

I'm glad it was you that pulled out the short one, Gabby. As you might have guessed...from the very first, I thought we got on well together. Our thinking and way of doing things just seemed to mesh."

Gabriel nodded his head in agreement.

"Sure, Gay, but if things go according to plan, life in Ireland isn't going to be some Saturday night ceili at the crossroads. It's going to be a life and death struggle...to the victors will go the spoils. The ould divil will be let go and God only knows who he'll be after dancing with," cautioned a sober Aran.

"Ah sure, don't you be going on like that. You sound like Mother all over again. I know full well what I may be getting myself into. I've read some of your same books and talked to a good few people over here as well. There may be three thousand miles between us and the Holy Ground, but Ireland's fire of freedom burns brightly on this side of the Atlantic too. No, Aran, I can only imagine what's in store for us and I can't wait to taste the blood and smoke of it all."

After a moment of reflective meditation, Gay leaned forward and tapped the driver on the shoulder. Changing the subject, he said, "Turlough, maybe you should tell Aran a thing or two about yourself. You know all about him but he doesn't have a clue about you."

The man behind the wheel turned his head and looked back in Aran's direction. Aran had already tried sizing up Turlough Molloy after they were first introduced back in Petersburg.

Molloy was in his late twenties or early thirties. Besides their age, both Turlough and Gabby had similar builds. The Clan-na-Gael man was just short of six feet in height and weighed about twelve stone. He was fairer skinned than Gay and possessed a fine crop of wavy black hair. His facial features were finely etched, much like his friend's, but he was not as talkative as the middle McCracken son. However, when Turlough did speak up, his baritone voice had a musical ring to it. Aran wondered if his family might have come from County Cork. There was still a bit of that distinctive singsong Munster lilt.

Turlough's words interrupted Aran's thoughts. "Me father and his younger brother came to Amerikay after the aborted Rising of 1867. They managed to buy their passage over just as the Constabulary was about to pounce down upon them. If their sailing date had been de-layed, they'd likely have been arrested then transported in irons to Aus-tralia.

"Together, with a lot of hard work and God's good luck, they man-aged to make a success of it here. The two of them are now retired, but for years they managed the stockyards in Alexandria, Virginia. That's where I met Gay, his brothers and Father McCracken. We've all known each other for more than a dozen years now. I've been a member of the Clan since '14."

Keeping one eye on the road ahead, Turlough continued talking, "It's no secret where my family loyalties lie. So, when Gabby approached me with the idea of joining Mellowes's little outfit, I'd no trouble in making up me mind."

※

Watching some navvies tie up the freighter, Aran recalled Gay's other startling announcement during their motor trip from Petersburg to Eoin Black's farm. Not only had his friend announced that he and Turlough were going over with the four Irishmen, but Sarah Anne would be joining them.

Thinking back on that day six weeks ago, Aran still could not believe Gabriel's news about his sister's intentions of sailing with them. He had never heard of such a thing in his life...a woman hell-bent on leaving home, travelling some three thousand miles and no doubt becoming involved in a war. Sarah's apparent well thought through decision still boggled his mind. Though he was secretly pleased, Aran somehow felt responsible for her presence. He definitely needed more time to sort out his thoughts and feelings regarding Sarah Anne in his life.

Liam, Danny and Shadow agreed with Aran that it was a crazy idea, but they offered no objection. Sure, the four of them had known women who had joined the Cumann na mBan and who had made valuable contributions to freedom's cause during the Easter Rebellion. On numerous occasions the Gortman had marvelled at their heroic level of dedicated service and incredible bravery during the week of GPO occupation and ensuing street fighting.

Turlough liked her spirit of adventure and said she was old enough to make up her own mind.

Gabriel too was one hundred percent behind his sister's desire to go to Ireland. He even took credit for suggesting the idea in the first place. Gay knew of her keen sense of adventure and her romantic interests in Aran. He told her that if she wanted to find out if Aran was the man for her, she would have to go to Ireland. Gabby knew Aran planned on returning home. The Irish Rebel had no intention of staying in Amerikay any longer than was absolutely necessary.

The real obstacle lay in convincing Father and Mother McCracken. But, in the end, they gave in to her strong-willed determination after she promised to stay with Father's brother, Peter, and his family in

Cahir. Gabriel helped copper-fasten the deal by giving his solemn promise he would look after his only sister. Before his parents, he swore to God that he would keep her out of harm's way.

Secretly, Father admired his daughter's enterprising spirit and her heartfelt desire to see her ancient land freed. Mother McCracken, however, was not as easily convinced. Her American upbringing outweighed her Irish loyalties. No amount of talking was going to convince her that Sarah Anne should be traipsing off to God knows where. But, Father's word was final. So, Mother just shook her head, pulled out another handkerchief from the sleeve of her dress and tried to hide her feelings. Predictably, her silent tears had little effect on her daughter's romantic notions or her husband's hard-headedness. Sarah loved her mother, but wanted to follow her own life's plan, not someone else's.

And so it all came to be...the seven of them set sail from New York Harbor on the twenty-fourth of April, 1917, one year to the day after the Easter Rebellion had begun in Dublin.

Aran Roe O'Neill was going home to hopefully help conclude the struggle that Patrick Henry Pearse and the others had undertaken twelve months ago.

His only regret in leaving was that he had not had a chance to say goodbye to the other McCrackens, especially Father. But Aran promised himself that he would keep the dear old man's spirit of Irish freedom alive and well in his heart.

Leaning against the ship's railing, Aran blessed himself, closed his eyes and imagined Professor Pearse's and Father McCracken's smiles of approval at his desire to keep the 'Green Fire' of Irish independence burning brightly.

❧

The freighter they had all come over on was loaded with medical supplies and ammunition for the desperate English. Though their stores of men and materials were running dangerously low, Britain's fighting spirit was greatly buoyed up by America's entry into the war in Europe. Soon the Yankee military war-making machine would be pouring across the sea to help take the burden off the beleaguered British.

As their ship was labelled a floating death trap with all its lethal munitions stored onboard, it was relatively easy for the Clan to pull some strings and have Shadow, Aran, Danny and Turlough signed on as temporary crew. The four of them were assigned to the boiler room below deck and were responsible for keeping the ship's furnaces well fed and stoked.

Wanting to draw as little attention to Sarah's presence as possible, the other two decided it would be safer for them to dress as members of the clergy. Liam donned his familiar priest's disguise and Gabriel joined him. Sarah Anne retained her identity as Gay's sister while dressing in the habit of a newly vowed Sister of Charity.

Each of them realised that a nun travelling by herself was unusual but they hoped that the war's confusion would mask the anomaly. Additionally, they hoped that brother Gabriel's and Liam Mellowes's priestly presence would discourage any suspicious questioning about her being onboard the ship.

Their cover story had them going to England as an advance party for the purpose of establishing and organising a Catholic support agency for incoming American military personnel.

Additionally, their religious facade made a perfect cover for the three cases of guns, ammunition and equipment the group hoped to smuggle into Ireland.

Under the guise of religious literature, missals and hymnals, the Clan had supplied them with thirty three-naught-three rifles, thirty Smith & Wesson New Century revolvers with accompanying holsters, several thousand rounds of ammunition, six pairs of high-powered binoculars, haversacks, bandoleers, Bowie knives, high-topped boots, clothing and other incidental necessities.

Several Fenians living in England were to meet Liam, Gay and Sarah with a lorry at the quay in Bristol. They would then transport them and their precious cargo to Birmingham where the three would spend the night. On the following day, the undercover agents would put the religious troika and their belongings aboard the train for Holyhead. Late that evening, they would take the mailboat across the Irish Sea to Dublin. Upon their arrival, members of the IRB would meet the trio and transport them to a safe-house in Dublin.

By contrast, Aran and his three travelling companions planned to go directly from Bristol to Holyhead with a change of trains in Birmingham. Once in Dublin, they would go to Vaughan's Hotel at #29 Rutland Square.

Aran knew the location well as it was on the opposite side of the square from the Fannin house where he had rested on Saturday after fleeing the burning GPO Friday evening. It was from that same house at #3 Rutland Square that he had barely managed to escape with his life.

Aran still remembered the two British soldiers standing in the front doorway firing their weapons at him. He would never forget his two prisoners either as they all dove for cover in the house's narrow hallway.

A tugboat's insistent horn jolted Aran back to the realities of the present. He thought that if everything went according to plan, all seven of them would be together again in Dublin in less than forty-eight hours. But, this time their little reunion would be special. They all would be standing on Irish soil...three of them for the very first time.

❧

"Jesus, Mary and Joseph...sure if it isn't the Irish Rebel himself!"

Aran could not believe his eyes...it was Michael Collins in person.

The Gortman hardly recognised the handsome, youthful captain. He looked so businesslike dressed in a dark brown suit, matching waistcoat, white shirt with stiff collar and a tightly knotted dark-green tie. Collins's little mustache danced on his upper lip when he spoke. His left hand busily brushed back a dangling lock of curly brown hair that kept falling down onto his forehead.

The sign on the door had said M. Collins, Secretary, Irish National Aid and Volunteers' Dependents' Fund.

Back in New York, Aran had learned from John Devoy himself that after Michael's release from Frongoch's prisoner-of-war internment camp, just before Christmas last, the County Corkman had paid a short visit to his family home, Woodfield, near Clonakilty.

In early January, after a good taste of Irish homecoming and cooking, Collins left West Cork and moved to Dublin. With the generous help of Thomas Clarke's widow, Kathleen, and some of his newly freed friends from Frongoch, Michael was appointed the fund's secretary. Its purpose was to offer financial help to the families of those killed, wounded or imprisoned because of their Easter Rebellion participation.[16-1]

Now, as Aran and his three companions filed into Collins's little Dublin office in Mary Street, the handsome Corkman bounded out of his chair, dashed across the room, grabbed Aran Roe and tried throwing him to the floor.

"How about a bit ear, you bloody Yankee adventurer?"

Before Aran could object or defend himself, Collins had him down on the floor, trying to take a bite out of his right ear.

Quickly recovering from the unexpected attack, the Gortman rolled over onto his stomach, reared up on all fours, lowered his head to his chest and pushed off the floor with a powerful kick.

The resulting somersault caught Collins off guard. The next thing he knew, Aran was on top of him.

With the strength earned from a winter of demanding physical activity in the Allegheny Mountains, topped off by a dozen days of shovelling coal on board a Yankee freighter, Aran Roe O'Neill positioned himself squarely on top of Michael Collins's chest. With his strong hands, Aran pinned the Irish Volunteer captain's arms to the floor.

As he knelt over the prostrate body of his former military superior, Aran lowered his head and defiantly spoke into one of Michael's unprotected ears only inches away from his own gnashing teeth, "Sure, now, who's after going to have a bit of ear, Captain Collins?"

"You fecken little bastard...how'd you get to be so strong and so quick on your feet? I guess your gallivanting abroad has taught you a thing or two, my fine young friend."

"That it has Mr. Collins or is it still Captain Collins?"

"The name's Michael and if you ever refer to me by either of those titles, I'll really have a piece of your fookin ear."

With that, the two combatants burst out laughing.

Aran pulled the powerfully built man up onto his feet and they embraced like long lost brothers. Both men paused momentarily to catch their breath.

Collins broke the silence, "Ah sure indeed, I can't tell you how good it is to see you again. That dive of yours off the quay wall into the Liffey was bloody unbelievable. The British lackeys never had a chance."

"I'd some help and a lot of luck. God was really smiling down on me that day, Michael," replied Aran.

"He certainly was and from the reports I've been receiving from Devoy and the Clan in Amerikay he still is. I guess there is something to that story of a guardian angel watching over the seventh son of a seventh son."

Aran smiled shyly, turned and introduced his three friends to Collins.

"This is Richard Doyle but everyone calls him 'Shadow.' He was Mellowes's second-in-command in Counties Galway and Clare during the Rising. He helped save my life, nursed me back to health and spent last winter trying to make a soldier out of me so."

Collins raised the index finger of his right hand. "Ah sure, I've heard several members of the Organisation speak most highly of you, Richard. Everyone says you're a first rate soldier. Welcome back home."

Aran continued, "...and this is Danny Kelly, a longtime friend of Shadow's and Liam's. He was out with them during the Easter Week fighting in Galway and can put a candle out at ten paces with his peerless spitting."

Everyone laughed, even Danny. Collins smiled and nodded his head.

"Finally, I'd like you to meet Turlough Molloy. He's an Irish-Yankee who's over to help us even the score with the British. His father's family is from Macroom...not too far from where you grew up so, Michael. Do you know any of his people?"

"I know a Dan Molloy from Newcestown...any relation?" questioned Collins.

"Yes, as a matter of fact," replied the surprised Molloy. "He's an uncle of mine...my father's youngest brother. I was hoping to stay with him...at least for a while."

"Turlough, sure if there's one thing you'll have to learn over here, it's the fact that this is a small country. People have a way of knowing each other more often than not. Sometimes that's good and sometimes its not. Most often, though, it works to your advantage...unless you've something to hide," warned the man from Sam's Cross whose nickname was the 'Big Fellow.'

Collins had earned that nickname during his days spent as a prisoner in Frongoch prison camp near Barra in North Wales. Though the man acted older and appeared wiser than his years might indicate, Michael Collins was only twenty six when Aran introduced him to his friends that May day in 1917.

After the pleasantries were finished, Collins motioned his guests toward some chairs arranged before of his desk. With everyone seated, the Corkman proceeded to go over the plan for tomorrow morning's meeting. "Your other three travelling companions will be there and besides, I'd like to have a look at that 'equipment' ye smuggled over here from from Amerikay.

"Sorry lads, we can't get together any sooner but I've made other plans for tonight. "Everything fine at Vaughan's?" Collins looked straight at Shadow.

"No complaints...first rate accommodation," replied the Limerick man. He had heard Aran talk about Collins but this was the first time they had ever met.

Acknowledging Richard's reply, Collins added, "The night man's a good friend of mine. He'll mind ye like his own."

Michael Collins lowered his voice. His four guests were forced to draw their chairs in closer to the Big Fellow's desk. For the next few minutes he talked and they listened. "If Ireland's going to make a real break from England...to once and for all win back our lost freedom...it's going to require a kind of national crusade...for God and for the Irish people. But, instead of some Holy Grail, our quest is for true independence from the bleeden Limeys' rule. Our journey is going to be much more difficult than the one undertaken centuries ago by the knights of old."

Waving his index finger in the air, Collins warned, "The days and months ahead, though filled with excitement and adventure, will be fraught with terrible danger and lots of hard, thankless work. But, despite everything, I want ye to know what a great comfort it is to me to have ye fighting for Eireann's cause...comrades together in arms...that's what we'll be. When its over, Ireland will either be consumed in freedom's flame or emerge victorious. I for one am willing to risk it all." Collins's face looked as if it had been etched out of granite rock.

Jumping to his feet, he slammed his fist onto the desk and shouted, "Are yis with me or not?"

In unison, as if the scene had been rehearsed, his four guests jumped to their feet. Before anyone could speak, Aran spoke for them all, "Saoirse, Miecal! Saoirse agus Eireann go brach!"

With the Irish Rebel's words ringing in his ears, Michael Collins was out the door and off on his bicycle. A meeting in another part of the city demanded his attendance.

❧

Aran and Turlough were the first to arrive at the address scratched on the little piece of paper...#5 Mespil Road. It was just down from the Leeson Street Bridge which spanned the narrow Grand Canal, the narrow finger of water that curved around the southern perimeter of Dublin.

It was early in the morning and the streets were coming alive with merchants opening their doors for business and eager shoppers trying to get a head start on their day's activities.

Michael Collins's key admitted them to the nondescript, brick two-story building that included five other narrow houses divided by common walls. Aran's mind was racing. He was only a few blocks from Thomas and Anna's house in Wilton Place. They had opened their home to him, a complete stranger, in his hour of need after the Easter Week Rising.

He thought of the revolver that Thomas had given him. He remembered the secret place where he and Brigid had hidden it a few days later. As soon as he could, Aran wanted to revisit the O'Mahonys on their farm west of Athy.

He was also less than a mile from Ballsbridge, the scene of the Brendan Road shoot-out with that squad of British soldiers. That's where he had met Willie Ronan and the Walsh brothers, the defenders of Clanwilliam House and the protectors of Mount Street Bridge. Those three had known some of the Rising's bloodiest and most deadly fighting.

He wondered how Willie and Tom were getting on today. He thought how he would like to go back to Brendan Road and pay the Ronan family a visit.

Aran's mind was jolted back to the present with the arrival of Shadow and Danny.

Fifteen minutes later Liam, Gabby and Sarah Anne came through the front door still dressed in their religious trappings. Three members of the Brotherhood followed close behind, lugging the wooden crates of smuggled military goods from Amerikay. They had parked their innocent-looking delivery lorry at the curb.

The seven friends were still greeting one another when Michael Collins bounded in through the rear door of the house. He greeted Liam warmly and was introduced to Gay and Sarah.

Everyone could see he was surprised by the presence of a woman, but he treated her with dignity and respect.

Collins invited everyone to sit while he paced up and down the parlour floor.

Continually pushing at a lock of curly brown hair that kept falling down onto his forehead, Michael Collins addressed the little group. "Meetings like this are being held all over Ireland these days so. It's only been a year since the Rebellion, yet we're after making steady progress in organising a network of dedicated men and women. Many have already begun working behind the scenes for Irish freedom.

"Count Plunkett won a seat for Sinn Fein in February and just a week ago we had Joe McGuinness, still an Easter prisoner in Lewes Gaol, elected to the Imperial Parliament from South Longford."

Collins's voice and approach reminded Aran of some military briefings he had taken part in with the Volunteers during the run-up to Easter Week.

The Corkman's staccato singsong continued without a pause. "Besides these recent political successes, Rory O'Connor and other Irish republican supporters staged a modest celebration commemorating the first anniversary of the Easter Rebellion last month.

"Though groups of our men are still being held in English prisons, sure, they're beginning to exert some embarrassing pressure on their warders and gaol officials. Through a series of violent and nonviolent actions, they have staged their demands to keep public attention focused on their plight. Because of these efforts and other recent developments, I'm after thinking all of our prisoners still being held in England will be out soon.

"The nation's mood is beginning to swing away from the old Parliamentary Party's way of doing business. The political extremists in Ireland, like us, are beginning to influence more and more of the moderates. Gradually, we're bringing them over to our way of thinking so. The idea of a separate and independent Ireland is gaining strength daily. Padraic Pearse's idea of a free Irish Republic is alive and well, thanks be to God. Now, if we can just bring along some of the conservatives, Britain will have to sit up and take notice of our demands."

With his little speech concluded, Collins momentarily stepped out of the room. Upon his return, he carried a large crowbar.

"I don't have much time for talking today. I'm due over at Sinn Fein headquarters in Harcourt Street within the hour."

Shifting the bar in his hand, Collins walked over to one of the crates. As he pried open its lid, Michael said, "I know the Clan sent over this 'equipment' with ye. If there's no objection, I'd like to divide it up. I've some men who are in desperate need of these supplies."

The Corkman presumptuously continued, "If it's agreeable with you, Liam, let's split up the contents. You and your group take half and I'll take half. What say ye?"

Mellowes stood up. In a firm, confident voice he replied, "I need equipment and supplies for eighteen men. You're welcome to the rest, Michael."

"Done, my friend," replied Collins.

With that the eleven republicans set about dividing up the weapons and gear.

When they were finished, Collins reloaded one of the wooden boxes with part of his share and stuffed the rest into two large canvas bags he had pulled out of the press from under the stairs.

"I'll have some men collect these things tonight," said Collins. "Liam, where should your two boxes be sent?"

"Deliver them to Shadow's family bakery in Limerick. It's in Nicholas Street between the King John's Castle and St. Mary's Church."

The Big Fellow nodded and glanced around the room. From his manner, it was apparent he was anxious to leave.

"I must be going," voiced Collins, glancing at his watch. "So yis know, Liam and I met earlier this morning. I want him to keep in touch with me. He'll fill you in on all the details."

Just before Collins headed out the rear door of the house, he pulled Aran to one side and whispered, "Keep fit and stay ready...I'll be needing your help before long."

With that, the Big Fellow was gone...out the door and off down the lane on his bicycle. Dressed in his best felt hat, suit of navy-blue serge and overcoat, Michael Collins blended into the crowd of people making their way to work or to market that Dublin morning.

☘

The two Volunteer leaders' plans were simple. Liam's little band of seven would disperse and go their separate ways. They were to blend back into their home communities and family circles with as little fanfare as possible.

Mellowes or Shadow Doyle would contact them if the political or military situation changed for better or for worse. In the meantime, each of them should plan a visit to Shadow's Limerick bakery during June. Their share of the smuggled equipment would be waiting for them there. Additionally, each man was to maintain a high level of personal fitness and should participate in local Irish Volunteer training and drilling sessions. Finally, Mellowes would try and organise a reunion for their little group in late summer. He had not had time to work out the details but he would be in touch with each of them soon.

Before leaving, they helped the IRB men reload Liam's share of smuggled supplies into the back of a covered lorry full of fresh veg and baskets of eggs.

With their weaponry disappearing out of sight down the road, Liam, Shadow, Danny and Aran were not completely unarmed. They still had their German Lugers safely squirrelled away among their duffel-bagged clothes back at Vaughan's.

With their moment of departure at hand, Aran found it difficult saying goodbye to his friends. Silently, he prayed to himself, "Please God, keep them safe. Mind and protect them till we all meet again."

Shadow was heading for Limerick and a reunion with his wife, Helen, his three daughters and the entire Doyle family. Turlough was going to Cork and then on to Newcestown where he would stay with his uncle's family. Gabby and Sarah were bound for Uncle Peter's pub in Cahir, County Tipperary. Liam and Danny were heading for Galway and reunions with friends and family.

All seven of them had been given fifty English punt apiece by the Clan before they had left New York. Additionally, the four stokers had their ship's wages too. They all would have no difficulty in finding and paying for transportation to their various destinations. The English authorities had finally relaxed their controls on the civilian population. Most Irish citizens were again experiencing a great degree of personal freedom. Things were much like they had been before Easter, 1916.

As they all shook hands before leaving the house on Mespil Street, Aran presented each of his friends with a small metallic Easter-lily badge he had had made by a New York City artisan.

"May these badges remind you of the ideals of Easter, 1916. May they serve as symbols of our trusted friendship for one another and as tokens of our commitment to the common cause that binds us all together...and to Ireland."

The six were so struck by Aran's gesture that they were speechless. Instead of words, their eyes expressed their love and thanks to the Irish Rebel.

Silently, they left...Turlough, Danny and Shadow by the front door while Liam, Gay and Sarah Anne headed out the back.

As he followed the two McCrackens, Aran stopped Sarah and took her by the hand.

"Ah Sarah, I love you. Those few weeks we shared together in New York City... 'twas a wonderful time, no? We've opened our hearts to one another so...I've come to know you, to want you, to love you. Please God, just give me a bit of time. I'll be down to visit you and Gay soon. I want to be after making plans with you about our future together. Will you be all right for a short while?"

"Oh, yes, yes, Aran, but I'll miss you so. We've found something very special...you and I. I knew it from the first moment I saw you back at the farm. Now, these last weeks together have only confirmed it. Aran, you are my precious one...I love you, too."

With that the two young people hugged each other tightly. Aran could feel her body trembling against his as their lips met in a long, slow loving kiss.

Pulling back, she turned and joined Gay and Liam who were waiting just outside the back door. In a matter of moments, she was gone. Aran stood alone in the kitchen. His heart was torn between wanting to follow her and going back to his family in Gort. But, he knew what he must do. With God's grace, there would be time for Sarah Anne McCracken very soon.

❧

Before he left Dublin, Aran had several things to do. He wanted to linger and renew some old acquaintances. He stayed on at Vaughan's Hotel while he pedalled around the city on a borrowed bicycle, making his visits.

First, he paid his respects to Mrs. Pearse and her two daughters at St. Enda's School. Then, he dropped by Thomas and Anna's home to thank them again for helping him when he so desperately needed it. Next, he visited Willie Ronan and the Caseys. He wanted to see how they all were getting on during the past year. He also learned from Willie that Tom Walsh was well and still living in Wicklow Town. Next, he called in to the 'old Rebel' and his wife. They lived near Croke Park and had sheltered him for several hours on the Saturday night Pearse had surrendered to the English. Finally, he visited his St. Enda's classmate's home in Drumcondra. Marty was away at school but Aran wanted to thank his family for his friend's brilliantly engineered plan that had allowed him to escape the chains of English imprisonment.

Dublin's main thoroughfare, Sackville Street, was still showing off the devastation it had suffered from the British bombardment last spring. All the rubble had been cleared away, but the English government felt it could not divert money and materials from its war effort to repair the destruction England had inflicted on this beautiful city. As a result, the lion's share of the rebuilding expense had fallen on the shoulders of the private entrepreneurs whose businesses were destroyed by Britain's fury.

The still-gutted iron skeleton of the GPO loomed up before Aran as he rode down Sackville Street. It filled his heart with waves of sorrow, grief and pride as he reminded himself of his promise to raise the Irish harp without the crown above its fire-blackened facade when Ireland's freedom had finally been achieved.

He walked up little Moore Street and stopped at the spot where he had hidden from the British machine guns and where Seamus had died. The dark stains of his friend's blood were still visible on the cobblestones.

Aran peddled over to Beresford Place and climbed through the ruins of Liberty Hall. Just a few days ago on the 12th of May, a group of Irish Labourites had hung a large banner from its first floor windows. Inscribed on the white canvas were the words, 'James Connolly, murdered by the British on 12 May 1916.'

Despite the controversy it had created, the declaration was still proudly flying over Liberty Hall.

Aran parked his bicycle and entered the deserted bombed-out building. He carefully descended its broken steps. There in the basement wall under the stairs was the old coffee tin still wrapped in its potato sack. Safely out of reach of the enemy's artillery shells were his four secreted copies of Pearse and Connolly's *Proclamation* to the Irish people. The sheets boldly declared the Provisional government's intention of forming a free 'Republic.' Aran's dedicated hands had helped print the documents on Easter weekend and his fighting courage had tried to make its pronouncements become reality.

The dream of a free Irish Republic was still a fantasy. But, with the passage of just a single year, Aran realised that a bright new hope was slowly forming. The birth of a new nation was gradually taking shape in the hearts and minds of many Irish men and women...both in Ireland and around the world.

Aran carefully placed the sheets in his haversack and rode back to Vaughan's Hotel to collect his things. Three hours later Aran was in Kingsbridge Rail Station waiting to board the Cork train for Marysborough.

Upon his arrival there, the Irish Rebel spent the rest of the day taking the long, sad journey to the O'Mahonys farm and Brigid's grave.

Gran, the children and Brigid's sister, Hannah, welcomed him with tears and open arms. The farm was still doing well, thanks to the Ryan family's loyal help. Everybody was in good health and brother Andrew had returned to Kilkenny to live with his aunt and pursue his vocation.

Aran was surprised by how much the three children had grown in just a year, but Gran, bless her soul, had not aged a day in his absence.

Together, they spent the evening exchanging news and remembering their Brigid. They all decorated her grave in the family plot with freshly cut flowers.

Gran told Aran about Brigid's 'accident' and about the subsequent RIC and military cover-up. She even brought out her granddaughter's jewelry box. Inside its little wooden cavity, carefully folded up, was Aran's letter. Gran said she had discovered it under Brigid's pillow after her death. Beside the letter, the box contained several small mementos that had belonged to Brigid's mother who had died giving birth to little Annie.

As he fell asleep by the fire on the eiderdown quilt Gran had laid out for him, Aran's heart was breaking, but he knew it was good he had come.

Early the next morning, before he departed, Aran went out to the byre where he had slept during his two-night stay at the farm. Still hidden under the flooring of the building were Thomas's Colt .45 and the British Webley revolver, a souvenir of the Brendan Road shoot-out. They were exactly where he and Brigid had secretly placed them. He removed the guns from their oilcloth wrappings and slipped them into his little travelling case.

While Aran returned to the house for breakfast, Rory tackled old Sean to the trap.

With the family lined up to wave goodbye, Rory clicked his tongue at the horse and the two of them headed west out of the farmyard toward Stradbally and Marysborough.

Nearing their destination, Aran promised the twelve-year-old lad that he would visit them all again as soon as he could.

With his heart filled with sad yet warm memories, the Irish Rebel waved to Rory and walked into the Marysborough Rail Station.

With his long-delayed journey home finally coming to an end, Aran boarded the train for Limerick Junction. He had not seen his family since early spring last year. So much had happened to him in those fifteen months that he had no idea where he would begin retelling the tale.

❧

Aran arrived home just as the summer sun was setting over his loved Kilmacduagh and its ancient, leaning round tower.

He was looking forward to spending time with his family and catching up on all their news. He, in turn, had many things to tell them. Though there was much to remember, the Irish Rebel felt some strange stirrings deep down inside him. Something told him there was an even greater adventure waiting just around life's next corner.

The surprised shouts of his two sisters greeted Aran's ears. "Mama, Mama...come quick! It's Aran, it's Aran...he's home!"

Moments later the family's seventh son was surrounded by loving arms and smiling faces as three generations of O'Neills welcomed home their wayfaring warrior.

17. *Rebelling*

When boyhood's fire was in my blood,
I read of ancient freemen,
For Greece and Rome who bravely stood,
Three hundred men and three men;
And then I prayed I yet might see
Our fetters rent in twain,
And Ireland, long a province be
A Nation once again!

A Nation Once Again/Thomas Davis

*T*he hair on the back of Aran Roe O'Neill's neck felt like it was standing on end. Crouched behind the dry-stone wall, he thought what strange
reactions the human body produces when it is faced with high
drama...excitement, fear, danger and death.

Kneeling on the uneven grassy surface of the field, he peered through
the gaps between the stones. As he patiently waited for the other squad
to move into position, his thoughts travelled back to another place and
another time just three years ago. Aran still vividly remembered the 1916
Easter Rebellion and occupation of Dublin's General Post Office.

Taking several deep breaths to settle his emotions, Aran glanced back
over his shoulder at the five men under his command, who were crouched
in single file along the wall behind him. His Volunteers appeared calm
and prepared. For most of them, however, this evening's operation was
about to be their first real taste of combat.

With the night's silence enveloping the countryside, Aran's thoughts
flashed back to his first 'battlefield baptism' during the spring of 1916.
Sometimes that week of fighting seemed so long ago and at other times
it was as if it had happened only yesterday.

Tonight, while waiting under the cover of this County Galway stone wall, Aran thought about the barricade he had squatted behind atop the GPO during the Rising. Instead of the carefully stacked limestones that hid him tonight, Aran had spent most of that week hunkered down behind a hastily constructed barricade of mailbags and overturned wooden tables. He and his fellow Volunteers had been assigned to rooftop observation and sniping duty.

Aran remembered the rush of emotions that had flooded his body on that first evening when he looked out over the rooftops of Dublin. Except for the Lancers' mounted charge down Sackville Street Monday afternoon, the British had not had time to organise a counter-attack on their rebel stronghold.

Aran remembered the prideful excitement he felt when Pearse read the *Proclamation* declaring Ireland's independence from England while his professor and James Connolly stood in the shadow of the General Post Office's imposing portico. Those moments of elation, however, were soon followed by a growing sense of fear and trepidation as the British began shelling the city and encircling the GPO. The poorly equipped and ill-trained Irish Volunteers, trapped inside the three story granite-stone structure, had been unable to defend their headquarters.

Now, three years later, things were different. Yes, he still felt those emotions of fear and excitement, but tonight his being embraced other sensations. He was looking forward to having it out with the enemy on a more even footing. His body ached to put a dent in the RIC's ring of stone barracks that dotted the Irish landscape. From their modest fortresses, the police kept Ireland's civilian population under its ever-watchful eye and well-sharpened heel. Its twelve thousand Irish policemen, mostly Catholic by religion, were all on England's bloody payroll. They had been assigned to barracks throughout the country to enforce Britain's law in Ireland.

Aran had changed since that first taste of war three years ago. Time and circumstance had made him less idealistic about dealing with the obstacles obstructing freedom's path. Brigid's senseless death, the multinational assassination team's vicious attack at the McCracken farm, the long winter of learning to be a soldier in the Allegheny Mountains and, more recently, his deepening friendship and involvement with the dynamically resourceful Michael Collins had cured his innocence.

The former Volunteer captain and then secretary of the Rebellion Prisoners' Fund had called Aran back to Dublin in September of 1917. Thomas Ashe, the new President of the IRB, had been arrested in August for making a seditious speech in Ballinalee and, in protest for not being granted prisoner of war status, Ashe had gone on a hunger strike.

Collins, Aran and several other men had planned to stage a gaol break in hopes of freeing Thomas, but increased prison security crushed their plans at the last moment. At the end of September, before they could reorganise and plan another rescue attempt, Thomas Ashe, the 1916 Easter Rebellion hero of the Battle of Ashbourne, died after his warders thrust a feeding tube down his throat. Instead of Ashe's stomach receiving the nourishment, his lungs filled with the liquid and he suffocated to death alone in his jail cell.

Collins was grief stricken and the entire country mourned the cruel death of this brave Irishman. To make matters even more heartbreaking, Ashe and two others, Eamon de Valera and Thomas Hunter, were the only three Easter commandants who had survived a British firing squad.[HN-7]

At Collins's request, Aran remained in Dublin for several weeks after Ashe's funeral. During that time, the two men began planning how they might organise and train a specialised team of men who would use guerrilla warfare tactics to attack selected enemy targets in the west of Ireland. Soon the 'West Briton authorities' would realise that the 'Irish natives' had again slipped the leash!

Hardened by the brutality of Thomas Ashe's death and influenced by his growing friendship with Michael Collins, Aran's perceptions changed regarding his role in Ireland's fight for freedom. He realised that the only way to win the pending war with England was to be uncompromisingly dedicated to the principles of Irish independence and unafraid to answer British violence with Irish retaliation. It could easily result in a life and death confrontation but that was what Michael and Aran felt would be required if Ireland was ever to be free of Britain's rule. The years of Ireland's talking and negotiating with England about its own freedom had always proven fruitless.

Collins had impressed upon Aran that fear and weakness were England's allies and that they would have to turn the tables on the British if Ireland was to succeed in its quest for independence. The consequences of the use of violence must be a friendly ally and not their dreaded foe.

Aran knew Collins believed that throughout the course of Anglo-Irish history, diplomatic and parliamentary manoeuvring had been rendered useless by Britain's blatant disrespect and long-held contempt for her island neighbour. The facts of the matter supported his contention.

No, if Ireland was going to bring England to the bargaining table, it would not be with brandy and cigars but at the point of a gun. It seemed that force was the only language the British Empire respected and understood. Collins felt that this dramatic and assertive approach was the only way Ireland would ever gain Britain's attention and consideration.

❧

Months after Ashe's funeral, Michael Collins called upon Aran for help in the anti-conscription campaign. In May of 1918 most of Sinn Fein's leadership had been arrested and deported to England. The English authorities were becoming frightened of this new political party's popularity. Fearing another Irish revolt over the imposition of conscription, Britain decided to eliminate Sinn Fein's political influence by rounding up all its party officials and banishing them to English jails. Luckily, Collins and a few others learned of the pending raid and escaped capture. The Big Fellow had also warned the Sinn Fein leadership of the Castle's plans. Gambling, however, that the political fallout from any such arrests would only gain the sympathy of Ireland's citizens and strengthen their hand in the eyes of the world, Ireland's political chiefs chose to ignore Collins's warning.

The pro-British authorities, after carrying out their plan, stated that the arrested men had been involved in a plot to aid Germany's war efforts. This simply was not true. The Sassenach had tried to disguise another of its draconian attempts to stunt Ireland's growing desire for its own democratic government. England used the alleged 'German Plot' as a convenient cover-up to undermine the Irish anti-conscription movement that was being organised throughout the country.

When Aran discussed the matter with Shadow several weeks later, they both laughed out loud. The British authorities in Dublin Castle had really shot themselves in the foot this time over the arrests. They had interned the more conservative and moderate elements within Sinn Fein who were represented by men such as founder Arthur Griffith and current President Eamon de Valera. In their place, a more radical element championed by Michael Collins and Cathal Brugha, who also had managed to evade capture, were forced by default to begin assuming the mantle of party leadership. Without Sinn Fein's more cautious administration to protest, Collins and his associates were free to implement their own stronger revolutionary ideas.

With the First War finally over in November, 1918 and with most of its leadership still behind bars, Sinn Fein won a resounding victory at the polls during the December British general election. England had won the war in Europe but had lost a crucial political battle at home.

Ireland's victorious Sinn Fein candidates refused to take their seats in Westminster and organised their own parliament, Dail Eireann, which held its inaugural meeting at Mansion House in Dublin on 21 January 1919. Only a third of the elected membership was present as most of the remaining representatives were still in English prisons charged with sedition.

It was during the late winter of 1919 that Collins again needed Aran's help. The Corkman was making plans to rescue de Valera from Lincoln Gaol in England. Michael wanted to bring him back to Dublin for the sake of party unity and Irish solidarity.

So, in February of 1919, Michael, Aran, Harry Boland and others freed de Valera and two of his prisonmates from their English confinement. They hid them in English safe-houses prior to smuggling them back into Ireland.

This escape plan worked so well that they repeated their efforts a month later. This time they successfully managed to free Robert Barton and twenty others from Mountjoy Jail, which was located right in the heart of Dublin Town itself.

During these successful adventures, Aran had to use his Luger automatic twice to cover their retreating footsteps. Though he had fired in self-defense, Aran had shot to kill instead of merely trying to wound his attackers.

On those occasions, as Aran fled into the night with the escaping prisoners depending on him for protection, Michael Collins's words rang in his ears. "It's time Ireland stood up and fought for her rights...unfortunately, the time's come to kill or to be killed...it's time for an enslaved people to rise up in righteous indignation and strike a blow for freedom...if we don't fight now, another generation of manacled people will be backed up against the wall and, with our hands raised in surrender, we'll be compelled to kneel and kiss the ring of the greedy, mindless Stranger!"

Michael often concluded these little emotional tirades with, "Aran, isn't it better to die on your feet than live a lifetime on bended knees?"

❧

Sergt. Donleavy's hand on Aran's shoulder jolted his thoughts back to the matter at hand beyond the stone walls. It was late June, 1919 and the warm night air smelled sweet with the scent of freshly mown hay.

The Laburnum trees with their bright yellow clusters of grapelike flowers dotted the landscape. Joining them in their floral splendor were hedgerows of lavender-brushed rhododendrons, teardrop-shaped blossoms of crimson fushsia and, overrunning the rock-strewn ground, brightly-yellowed knots of prickly gorse. Topping off this botanical display were the twisted yet grandiose flowering white thorn.

Despite the blooming beauty surrounding them, Aran's little company of men were on a deadly mission that required their ignoring Ireland's rural grandeur. They had only several hours to complete a potentially dangerous job that had been assigned to them by the IRA's leadership in Dublin.

Soon morning's early light would creep into the sky and by half four one could sit out on the front porch reading a newspaper without the aid of a candle or oil lamp.

As Green Section Commandant, Captain Aran Roe O'Neill had divided his detachment of twelve men into two squads of six each. Under his direction were Sergeant Caoimhin Donleavy, Section Engineer Desmond Burke, Section Driver Turlough Molloy and Volunteers Neil Dempsey and Christopher McKee.

Moments earlier he had heard the sound of Gay's low whistle. This signal meant that the other squad of six were safely in position behind the stone wall that lined the opposite side of the narrow byroad that separated the insurgents.

The man overseeing this second squad was Green Section Vice-Commandant, Lieutenant Gabriel McCracken. Strung out behind him were Sergeant Nicholas Robinson, Section Quartermaster Frank O'Leary, Section Driver Pat Grogan and Volunteers Damien Casey and Jimmy Carroll.

During the autumn of 1918 and the winter of 1919, Michael Collins, Liam Mellowes, Richard 'Shadow' Doyle and Aran Roe O'Neill had organised a cross-county company of fifty men from Galway, Clare, Limerick and Tipperary. They called themselves the Flying Gaels. On their uniform jackets, each man had a small green pike-head lovingly embroidered on the underside of his right-hand, breast pocket flap. The symbol was a tribute to the men of 1798 who had fought for Ireland's freedom with simple wooden staffs each crowned with deadly hand-forged steel blades.

Major Doyle was the Gaels' overall Commanding Officer. He also doubled as White Section Commandant. Captain Danny Kelly commanded another of the column's units, the Orange Section. Addition ally, the Connemara man acted as Shadow's Adjutant and the Gaels' second-in-command. Aran headed up the third unit which was dubbed the Green Section. Furthermore, as was IRA custom, he had been elected third-in-command behind Shadow and Danny. Their military organisational leadership had Major Doyle reporting to General Liam Mellowes, who retained overall responsibility for the Flying Gaels' activities. Finally, Liam coordinated the group's movements with the Volunteer's Director of Organisation, Michael Collins.

Mellowes occasionally met with Collins who now held several key positions within the newly formed Irish Government, Dail Eireann. With Ashe's tragic death, Michael had been chosen to head the Supreme Council of the Irish Republican Brotherhood and thus, unofficially, was President of the Irish Republic. Additionally, Collins had been appointed Minister of Finance for the Dail and Adjutant-General of the Irish Volunteers.

The individual members of the Flying Gaels usually trained with their local Volunteer units, which had lately changed their name from the Irish Volunteer Force to the Irish Republican Army. Recently, however, the Gaels had spent two concentrated periods of time training together as befitted their own unique unit. They had gathered for a week in the Galty Mountains of Limerick and Tipperary during February of 1919 and had reformed for another week last month in the Slieve Aughty Mountains west of Lough Derg in County Galway.

Together, Liam, Shadow, Danny and Aran had handpicked the men. Most of them were country lads who had been raised on farms and knew the value of hard work. They were in their late teens or early twenties. As a prerequisite, each man must be physically fit, know how to handle a weapon and be unswerving in his dedication to rid Ireland of the English blight that had infected their land for so long.

The company, divided into three sections of twelve to eighteen men each, depending on the assignment and personal circumstances, had been active throughout the spring and early summer of 1919.

By the fall of 1918, the British had effectively cut off all weapon shipments into Ireland. As a result, the men of the IRA had few avenues open to them for obtaining additional firepower. They could buy a rifle or revolver from an English soldier if they had the money and could find a willing seller. They could raid an RIC barracks and capture police equipment or they could 'requisition' the desired weaponry from their fellow Irish citizens. This meant invading Irish homes and taking privately owned rifles and ammunition from their fellow countrymen and women. It was a distasteful option but the IRA had little choice. They justified their actions as being necessary for the good of the country, but their behaviour flew in the face of the democratic principles espoused by Pearse and Connolly in their 1916 Easter *Proclamation*.

When such a raid occurred, the soldiers always left a receipt for the goods taken, but usually it did not ease the resentment and anger generated by such a brazen tactic.

As a result of the IRA's insatiable need for more weapons, Liam Mellowes and Shadow Doyle had approved of and helped plan tonight's raid. It would be the Flying Gaels' first major military operation since the unit's creation six months previous.

For some unfathomable and illogical reason, the British authorities had planned to ship a large supply of military hardware into the port of Galway. It would then be transported overland to their principal artillery base in Athlone.

When the IRA learned of the convoy's intended destination, they guessed that the British army was laying down a challenge to the Irish rebels. They were hoping that an armed confrontation would end in a republican military defeat and a resulting public embarrassment. Furthermore, the Sassenach were seemingly trying to assert their military dominance and control over Ireland's roadways. Their prideful egos had been damaged by several localised IRA successes and it was time to assert their might in light of mounting English public and political criticism.

Collins felt this was likely another calculated attempt by the Crown authorities to drive a wedge between the IRA and the Irish people, to discredit and stunt the growth of his growing army and to employ their age-old technique of 'divide and conquer.' This time, however, the British Army was offering up a prize worthy of the risk. As a result, Dublin's GHQ decided to field test the metal of the Flying Gaels.

During the week prior to the shipment's arrival in Ireland, Liam Mellowes had received an advanced intelligence report. It suggested that if the transport column was delayed for any reason, it might well stop over and spend the night in the village of Craughwell, Longhrea or Ballinasloe. The English did not want to risk travelling at night and encountering an IRA raiding party under conditions that would be less than favourable for their heavily armed escort party.

With this information in hand, Shadow called out all three sections of the Flying Gaels, Green, White and Orange, to cover each of the three possible layover points. In case the convoy failed to stop at any of the three villages, another unit of IRA soldiers from County Longford would intercept the convoy outside the village of Cornafulla just prior to its arrival in Athlone.

A British vessel was scheduled to off-load the guns at the quay in Galway Town just past noon on Saturday next. The crates of weapons then would be loaded onto lorries and driven under heavy guard to Athlone.

However, British military planning went awry. Lady Luck seemed to be on the side of the republicans. The cargo ship was late in arriving and two of the six Crossley transports had experienced mechanical problems on the way from Galway's Renmore Barracks to the quay. Because of these delays, the convoy did not leave Galway until almost nine o'clock Saturday evening.

Unknown to the authorities, the IRA had observed their unloading activities and through the use of dispatch motor bike riders had alerted the waiting Irish army units of the delay.

Shadow had assigned Aran's Green Section to the village of Craughwell. Aran and his men were disappointed with their area of responsibility. As it was the closest of the three villages to Galway, it would be the least likely spot for the convoy's overnight stay. But, despite their disheartening location, Aran, Gabriel and Caoimhin Donleavy spent two days staking out the barracks and surveying the village for any patterns of daily life that would prove useful in planning their attack on the RIC headquarters or the British military convoy.

The three men stayed together at the farm of a fellow Volunteer between the villages of Craughwell and Athenry.

One by one, these three Flying Gaels walked or peddled bicycles in and out of the village as they observed the RIC base and talked with some of the villagers.

They learned that the barracks was usually manned by six men...a sergeant and five policemen but on Saturday nights, one or two of the RIC would often bike into the village for a few pints and a bit of craic.

Through some discreet questioning, Aran was disappointed to learn that the local Craughwell police appeared to have no knowledge of the British military convoy or its possible plan to bivouac in their town on Saturday night.

In addition to its close proximity to Galway, no doubt the undersized Craughwell RIC barracks would be another influential factor negating a British army decision to choose it as a suitable overnight resting place.

Though the building itself was constructed of stone and had walls several feet thick, it was only a single-story structure and had no sleeping accommodations for the three dozen or more soldiers that certainly would accompany the motorised vehicles.

This combination of factors served as a great discouragement to Aran and his two comrades while they finalised their attack strategy on Friday evening.

For planning purposes, Gabriel had drawn a map of the village and the roads leading to and from it. Additionally, he had made an outline of the barracks property itself.

Besides the single-story floor plan with its limestone-rock construction, the building had six front and six rear windows all with attached metal shutters. But, according to the local people, the metal plates were rarely closed and locked at night. Stone chimneys dominated both gable ends of the little fortress. Its gently sloping roof was covered with slate tiles. There was also a heavy metal front door with a sliding plate covering the spy hole. Finally, local informers reported the building's rear entrance was seldom used.

In order to provide an additional level of protection, the barracks was the sole occupant of a two-acre field and was surrounded by a substantial stone wall.

Topping off matters, the building was situated at the top of a T-junction along the main east-west Galway Road. Directly in front of the walled building and abutting the highway was a smaller single-lane road that ran due south toward the villages of Ardrahan and Gort a few miles away.

A three-foot-high stone wall lined both sides of this little byroad and, at the main intersection, was joined by two other stone walls that stretched in opposite directions along the southern edge of Galway Road.

Unlike its counterpart on the other side of the highway, the stony barrier surrounding the barracks was over four feet in height. Its chiseled limestones had been cemented into place for added strength. This protective partition wrapped itself around the building, creating large front, side and back grassy garden areas.

An entrance opening had been cut into the wall and a metal gate was used to secure the aperture at night. Fortunately, this swinging gate was fastened with only a single sliding bolt. The peace and calm of village life decried the necessity for locks.

Two dozen houses, three pubs and several shops dotted the main roadway four hundred yards to the west of the barracks and the byroad intersection. One of the public houses doubled as a small grocery and village post office.

Aran, Gay and Caoimhin were still considering all the possible contingencies when they were joined at the farm by three of their section mates early on Saturday. This morning group arrived in a horse-drawn dray whose load of hay concealed most of the section's rifles, ammunition, several gallons of paraffin oil, tins of petrol and sticks of gelignite. Desmond also brought along some of his newly constructed 'bombs.' It would be the first time they had ever used the crudely made devices.

Desmond had collected tin cans that were sized to fit comfortably into a man's hand. Into the canisters he poured alternating layers of viscous concrete and scrap metal around a wooden core. After the concrete had dried, the wooden centre was removed, making room for the insertion of an explosive charge. Finally, by attaching a detonator and fuse, the hand bomb was armed and ready for use.

The men were impatient to test one of the new grenades but refrained for fear of attracting unwanted attention.

Later that day, the remaining six men cycled into the temporary camp. By three o'clock the Green Section was eagerly awaiting the evening and their wished for encounter with the enemy.

During the afternoon, their hopes were raised when a motorcycle dispatch rider arrived with news that the convoy had been delayed in Galway. The man stated that he would notify them of the convoy's actual departure time as soon as it was known.

While they waited for the messenger's return, they busied themselves constructing two ladders, cleaning their weapons and going over their battle plan. Regardless of whether the convoy stopped in Craughwell or not, the squad planned on attacking the barracks. Its likely store of weapons was too valuable a prize to pass up.

Aran's squad would leave the farm first, skirt around the perimeter of the village and take up a position behind the two easternmost stone walls that formed a right angle with the narrow byroad and the main highway.

Gabriel's group would depart fifteen minutes later and take a westerly approach around Craughwell. His men would come up on the other side of the byroad directly opposite Aran and his men. Both groups of soldiers would be hidden from the barracks by several low rises of land and the stone walls bordering the Galway Road.

At half eight, the IRA messenger arrived with the news that the convoy planned to leave Galway at about nine that evening. It would probably pass through Craughwell around ten o'clock. The dispatch rider guessed that the lorries would be travelling more slowly than usual. Some of the vehicles still appeared to have unresolved mechanical problems.

After taking a final equipment check and handshakes all around, Aran and his five men headed out of the barn toward the village. They stayed off the roads and cut across country using the natural cover provided by hills and woods to mask their movements.

It was mid-June. The evening light would linger in the western sky until almost half eleven. Then, only four hours later, morning's light would begin dissolving the nighttime darkness.

Unlike their comrades, Aran, Gabriel and Turlough were well equipped for combat. During the summer of 1917, they had visited Shadow's bakery and collected their share of the Clan-na-Gael equipment they had smuggled into Ireland that May. On this occasion, the three brandished new .303 Lee-Enfield rifles, Smith & Wesson revolvers, Bowie hunting knives and a hundred rounds of ammunition each.

The other men in their Green Section were not as fortunate. On tonight's raid, they carried an odd assortment of rifles, shotguns and revolvers. Finding modern rifles and ample supplies of the proper ammunition was a constant problem. To date, however, Michael Collins had been more than generous with the Flying Gaels. They were better equipped than most fledgling IRA units.

Besides their weaponry, each man in the unit wore either a slouch hat or tweed cap. They all wore a short military coat over their usual white shirt and tie.

The rest of the men's uniforms were an odd assortment of tweedy trousers, riding breeches, boots, Sam Browne belts and bandoleers. Some sported leather holsters for side arms.

On this particular evening, Desmond and Caoimhin wore packs containing carefully separated and wrapped sticks of gelignite, fuses, detonators and six of Desmond's hand bombs. Besides their rifles, they also carried short sections of the homemade ladder needed for climbing up onto the barracks's roof. Aran and the other three men took turns lugging cans of petrol, paraffin oil and the ladder's third section.

It was slow going with all their gear. It took them over an hour to cover the two miles from the farm to the rendezvous point three hundred yards south of the T-junction. They quickly sheltered down behind a low hill that shielded them from the barracks itself.

No sooner had Aran and his squad arrived than Volunteer Damien Casey, an advanced scout assigned to Gay's team, crawled down off the hillock and greeted them.

"Sure, I never thought ye'd ever get here," whispered Damien.

"We didn't receive news of the convoy's departure until half eight," replied Aran. "Besides, it was slow going with all the gear.

"But, enough of that...are there any signs of activity or the lorries?" asked Aran.

"Nothing to report except I doubt if your rozzers know anything about the British coming through here tonight. Just thirty minutes ago, three of their lot cycled off toward town," answered the soldier.

"That's disappointing. If they'd known the convoy was stopping, I doubt whether they'd been given the time off," speculated Aran.

"Aran, sometimes I wonder if the English trust the RIC with their secrets," quipped Damien.

"You're probably right," retorted Aran.

It was growing darker. Aran knew the convoy would be passing through Craughwell at any time. Wanting to have a closer look at the barracks, Aran decided to move forward and keep his own vigil.

The Gortman informed his men that he was going up ahead to check things out for himself.

"Damien, I want you to cross the byroad and wait behind the opposite wall for Gabriel and our other men to arrive. My guess is they'll be here in about fifteen minutes. Keep them back until I return.

"The rest of ye stay put, relax and keep out of sight. I'm going up to watch for the lorries. Remember men, no matches or smoking...someone might see the light. Caoimhin, you're in charge here during my absence."

With his bootlegged American field-glasses in his haversack, Aran, on all fours, crawled up along the stone wall toward the T-junction and the barracks.

Carefully, he moved forward until he was within fifty yards of the main Galway Road and well hidden behind a large clump of furze. From his new position, Aran had a good view of the stone RIC building.

Looking westward, Aran could see several of the outlying village houses dotting the skyline before they disappeared below a hill as the road dipped down and swung around to the right. All that was visible in the other direction was farmland, stone walls and the occasional glimpse of Galway-Athlone Road before it disappeared on its meandering path toward the village of Loughrea.

Five minutes passed. The warm sweet-scented air was soft and motionless. Bright streaks of pale pink, faded blue and soft white tinged the western sky. All seemed so peaceful. Even the birds had bedded down for the night.

Gradually, the hush of twilight was disturbed by the sound of motors. "They're coming!" thought Aran. His watch had just gone half ten.

At first the machines made a low rumbling drone. But, as they grew nearer, the putt-putt-putt of the engines became more distinctive until their roar engulfed the night air. The world around Aran seemed to vibrate. He even tasted the convoy's petrol exhaust in his mouth.

As the vehicles came up the little rise out of the village and approached the T-junction, Aran could tell all was not well with two of them. Steam poured out from under one of the motor's bonnets and the fifth Crossley tender in line was towing the sixth one with a stout rope.

As the procession pulled up in front of the RIC barracks, an agitated army captain jumped down from the lead lorry. He brusquely ordered his troops to line up on the road with their rifles at the ready.

From Aran's hiding place, he could hear every word being spoken. It was apparent from the captain's tone that things were not going well for him or his convoy. He swore profusely and in a semicontrolled rage, ordered some of his men to begin unloading the last lorry.

By now, the RIC sergeant had emerged from the barracks. In the dim light, Aran focused his field-glasses on the rotund man. He could see the middle-aged Irishman trying to tuck his loose shirt-tail into his trousers while he hurried down the path toward the front gate.

"Sergeant, you and your constables help my men unload two of my ficken vehicles," barked the captain, pointing to the fourth and sixth lorry in the convoy.

"Sure, it's just meself and two others at the moment, sir," puffed the policeman who was now standing in the roadway saluting the officer.

"Shut your gob! Never mind how many there are of you...just get to work! I'm behind schedule and must press on immediately!"

The sleepy policeman still failed to grasp the captain's urgency. This infuriated the Englishman even more. "Can't you stupid Irish ever understand anything?" shouted the officer. "Sometimes it's hard to know which side you lot are really on! If I'd my way, I'd drive all you bloody prats into the sea and start over with a decent, intelligent, law-abiding crowd."

Elevating the volume of his voice, the captain continued, "I'm leaving thirty crates of supplies here with you. I'll assign four of my men to stay behind and help you look after them tonight. Tomorrow, I'll arrange for a vehicle to come by and collect the lot. Is that understood, Sergeant?"

"Yes, sir," answered the RIC man. He saluted the captain once more.

"Stop that fecken saluting and get your men out here on the double,

Sergeant!" shouted the captain. "I must be in Athone by midnight to-night not tomorrow night, you stupid lout."

Suddenly, the sergeant seemed to regain his senses. With a few crisp shouts, he had his two men and several of the British soldiers moving the elongated cases from the two lorries into the barracks.

The unloading took only ten minutes.

After assigning four of his men to stay behind with the crates, the captain remounted his vehicle. The rest of the soldiers scrambled into the back of the four remaining Crossleys and the convoy roared off down the road. The two disabled tenders were left abandoned by the side of the road in front the RIC's building.

As the four military motors droned off into the distance, Aran thought to himself how he would like to meet that Englishman some day. "I'd give him a thing or two to think about regarding British military intelligence and English manners." Aran regretted the convoy's departure for no other reason than he would miss the opportunity to confront the captain and, hopefully, teach him a lesson or two.

The sound of the barracks's metal shutters being slammed shut brought the Irish Rebel's attention back to the matter at hand. Moments later, he could hear them being bolted and locked from the inside.

The unsuspecting sergeant, however, did not station a guard in front of the building. Aran imagined the policeman thinking, "Craughwell is such a quiet little spot. I've never once had any problems with those rowdy IRA troublemakers in my village!"

Aran wondered what the abrasive and pompous British army captain would have said about the peeler's careless omission.

With the convoy gone, Aran crawled back to where his squad waited for him in the near darkness. Caoimhin informed Aran that Gabriel and his men were across the way in the next field.

"Good! Slip over the wall and tell Gabriel to join us here," instructed Aran.

A few minutes later Gay was sitting on the grass next to Aran and his men.

Aran reviewed the good news/bad news developments. The good news was that the convoy had been forced to leave behind thirty crates, probably containing rifles. They also had to abandon two of their lorries. The bad news was that the rest of the convoy had moved on, leaving four British soldiers behind to help with guard duty. That made seven men inside at the moment with the three pub-goers due back before long. Aran knew there was no telling what state they would be in when they returned...the drunker the better thought Aran.

"Gay, nothing has happened to change our plans, so it's business as usual. Any last minute questions?" queried Aran.

His Irish-American friend whispered a negative reply, shook Aran's hand and disappeared back over the wall.

After Gay's departure, Aran carefully moved his men and equipment up toward the intersection using the stone walls as cover.

Gabriel would bring his men up on the other side of the little road in an hour. In the meantime, they would act as backup in case Aran's group was discovered or challenged. Conversely, Aran's men were in position to cover Gabriel's squad in case they were surprised.

Just before midnight, Gay moved all his troops except two up into position. This duo moved off in the opposite direction down the byroad one-hundred-fifty yards or so. Once the first shots had been fired, their job was to finish chopping down three large trees growing beside the side road. They had been three-quarters of the way cut through by Aran, Gay and Caoimhin the day before. The felled trees would prevent any enemy vehicles from racing up the narrow roadway and attacking the partisans from the rear. With their five minute cutting assignment completed, the two Volunteers would then promptly rejoin their comrades behind the rear wall that encircled the barracks.

Aran heard Gabriel's low whistle indicating his team was all set and ready to go. But, Aran continued to wait. He did not want their attack to be interrupted by the three pub-going policemen.

Twenty minutes later, the rebels heard the peelers returning to the barracks. From the sounds of their singing, they must be well slashed and feeling no pain.

The policemen were having difficulty staying up on their bicycles and one of the men actually crashed his bike into the closed metal gate in the barracks's wall. It was often left open but, in his present state, the man could not see well enough to notice that tonight it had been closed and bolted shut.

The three drunks wisely decided to lean their bicycles against the barracks's outer wall for the night. With some difficulty, one of them managed to open the gate and together they all staggered up the front walk singing some unrecognisable song.

After pounding on the door several times, shouting to be let in, the sergeant obliged his drunken men. Dressed in his nightshirt, the man opened the front door and ushered his jarred constables inside.

Aran reasoned he should wait another thirty minutes to let the men in the barracks fall back to sleep.

Finally, at five minutes before one in the morning, Aran decided it was time to move in and requisition the contents of the barracks.

Leading his men over the low dry-stone wall, Aran slipped across the main Galway Road and up to the front wall surrounding the RIC's fortress. Gabby's men followed suit. The two abandoned lorries, parked to the left of the barracks' gate, served as an additional screen obscuring their presence.

Moments later, everyone was safely strung out along the outer perimeter of the barracks' wall. After pausing a moment and allowing everyone to catch their breath, Aran gave a short whistle. The Flying Gaels swung into action.

With the front gate standing wide open, thanks to the inebriated coppers, Aran Roe, Desmond Burke and Christopher McKee advanced through the opening. They carried one of the reassembled ladders and two zinc buckets filled with a mixture of petrol and paraffin oil. Silently, on cat's feet, the trio moved around to the rear of the building. Gabriel, Pat Grogan and Jimmy Carroll, similarly burdened, disappeared around the lefthand side of the barracks.

With Caoimhin in charge, Turlough Molloy and Neil Dempsey stayed back, fanned out behind the stone wall. Their assignment was to cover the front of the barracks and keep a watchful eye out for any approaching vehicles on the main Athlone-Galway road.

Sergeant Nick Robinson circled around behind the building, taking up a position opposite the rear door. His task was to stop anyone escaping from that quarter. The four-foot-plus high wall surrounding the house offered excellent protection from any shots fired in Nick's direction from inside the police station. He would soon be joined by Damien and Frank O'Leary, after they had completed their roadblocking assignment.

With their rifles strapped to their backs, the two teams of men at the rear corners of the building positioned their ladders against the roof. Cautiously, Aran and Gay climbed up the homemade devices with one hand on the rungs and the other carrying buckets full of the volatile accelerant. The ladders were shaky but, with someone steadying them from below, they held together.

When they had reached the low roof, the two men placed their buckets on its gently sloping surface. Warily, they swung themselves over onto the slate shingles. Righting themselves, each carried his pail up to the chimney at his end of the building.

After balancing their containers on top of the stone openings, the two separatists returned to their ladders and received a second filled bucket that had been brought up to them by one of their squad members.

Returning to their chimney, Aran and Gabriel straddled the roof's peak. With one bucket securely wedged between their feet and the other in their hands, the duo was ready.

Aran gave out a short low whistle. Responding to the signal, Desmond slipped around front and planted a gelignite bomb up against the thick metal door. Holding his breath, he lit its thirty-second fuse.

The seconds ticked away but nothing happened. The device had failed to explode. Retracing his steps, Desmond ignited a second home-made device. Seconds later...BOOM! The powerful blast nearly shook Aran and Gabriel off their rooftop perches.

Regaining their balance, the two men dumped first one bucket of petrol and oil down the chimney and then the other.

As Aran finished pouring his second pail of flammable liquid into the bricked cavity, a white-hot ball of flame exploded upwards from the floor below. It almost knocked him off his feet. He managed to drop to his knees and was able to steady himself against the stone chimney.

Pulling himself upright again, the Gortman withdrew a homemade bomb from his jacket pocket, struck a match and chucked it down the flaming hole. Quickly, he executed a retreat down from the roof. On the other end of the barracks, Gabriel was mirroring his actions.

Swinging his legs around, Aran bounced down the ladder and was over the four-foot side wall of the barracks in less than ten seconds. His other two comrades raced after him. They too vaulted over the stone barrier.

With his attention riveted on his assignment, Aran had little time to witness what was going on around him.

Their little plan had worked to perfection. The effects of the surprise attack had devastated the barracks. It had caught the RIC policemen and British soldiers completely off guard.

After the two rooftop teams were again safely behind the perimeter wall, Nick hurled a lighted bomb up against the barracks' back door. The explosion nearly blew the door off its hinges. Immediately afterwards, Nick began pouring precious rounds of rifle fire into the open gap.

Behind his wall, Aran tried to control his excitement. He realised his mixture of petrol and oil must have hit the hot coals of the evening's cooking fire. It had exploded with a blast of fiery orange-red light. The intense heat must have turned the room into a flaming inferno.

The Irish Rebel had guessed his hand bomb must have bounced out of the fireplace, skidded across the floor and exploded against the building's forward wall. It's detonation had blown one of the front room's shuttered windows wide open.

Gabriel's two buckets of lethal liquid reacted differently. Because of the warm weather, no fire was lit in the second fireplace. As a result, when Gay's fluid was poured down the chimney, there were no hot coals to ignite the deadly potion. It simply flowed out onto the surrounding floorboards and was set alight by his hand bomb's explosion.

The trapped men inside the barracks had no place to retreat except out through the front door. Its partly unhinged metal barrier was quickly thrown open. From it, a British soldier emerged with his rifle blazing. He had taken only two steps outside when Caoimhin and his two men cut him down.

The other inhabitants of the barracks took a more sane approach. Led by the sergeant, they rushed out with their hands in the air shouting, "We surrender...We surrender...For God's sakes man, don't shoot...We give up!"

The men hurriedly filed out of the now burning building. They were promptly ordered to lie down on the grass with their arms and legs extended. Aran and his men along with Gay and his two accomplices leaped back over the stone perimeter to cover and disarm the captives.

Gabriel took a quick count of the prone prisoners. One dead and eight on the ground. That meant there was still one inside.

Thinking that the missing man might have been one of the drunken peelers, Gay, with his pistol drawn, ran in through the front door.

Neil Dempsey and Turlough followed right on his heels. Thirty seconds later, the three re-emerged pulling a kicking, coughing man out behind them.

In the meantime, Aran had raced around to the back of the building only to find Nick and his two men carrying British rifle cases out through the rear entrance.

The four of them managed to save eleven of the thirty crates before the burning building became too hot and dangerous to enter.

By now Gabby and Desmond had come around to the back of the barracks and were helping their comrades lift the wooden boxes over the back wall and away from the heat of the fire.

Minutes later, the rest of the Flying Gaels joined the others in the back garden. Turlough announced that all were present and accounted for. He also proudly reported that not one of them had received so much as a scratch during the operation.

"Thanks be to God!" exclaimed Aran.

Caoimhin proclaimed that the nine captives had been bound hand and foot and were safely away from the burning structure.

Chris McKee concluded the report by saying that the two disabled British lorries left by the side of the road had been set on fire and were merrily burning away.

Aran knew that the barracks's conflagration, the explosions from their hand bombs, the rifle fire and the two blazing vehicles would soon attract unwanted attention.

"Men, it's over the wall with ye. Let's open and distribute the spoils of our victory. We haven't a moment to lose!"

The words were hardly out of Aran's mouth when the barracks was rocked by several loud explosions.

"Must be some munitions the rozzers had stored inside," shouted Aran. "It's time we got a move on and fast!"

With knives and rifle butts, the wooden crates were quickly opened. By the light of the burning barracks they divided up the contents. Seventy-two new short Lee-Enfields, forty-eight Webley and Scott .455 revolvers, more belts of ammunition than they could possibly carry plus several dozen newly manufactured British hand-grenades.

Each man filled his haversack with as many revolvers, boxes of shells and grenades as would fit. Quickly, they all swung four or five rifles over their shoulders and topped everything off with several belts of ammunition.

Though it broke the rebels' hearts to do so, the remaining weapons were piled up on top of the crates and their protective wooden shavings set alight. If the IRA could not take all the weapons with them, then the enemy must be denied their use as well.

Realising that it only would take minutes for the bonfire to begin exploding with deadly consequences, the twelve men of the Flying Gaels fanned out and headed due north toward their farm hideout.

With morning's early light beginning to steal away the darkness, the men chose as their escape route a little-used road that passed within a mile of their rural staging area.

Despite their heavy loads and fatigue, the men made good time...their lives depended on it. Nearing a well-scouted wooded area, Aran directed everyone off the narrow lane and into the seclusion offered by the grove of trees.

Safely out of any passer-by's field of vision, Aran instructed each man to take a revolver, two grenades, ammunition and a new rifle for his own.

After Frank O'Leary and Pat Grogan had made their selections, they raced back to the farm. There they tackled the two horses to the dray, loaded up the bicycles and brought the rig back to their waiting comrades.

Again, with the load of hay serving as a disguise, both new and outdated weapons and surplus ammunition were stuffed in canvas bags. All were secreted under the newly harvested animal feed.

The two drivers headed northeast toward the village of New Inn. There they would dump the canvas bags in a safe place for subsequent distribution to other members of the Flying Gaels and their needy neighbouring IRA comrades.

At half three in the morning, the remaining ten men, boldly bearing the spoils of their victory, split up into groups of two or three and headed off in different directions. Most were going straight home. They did not want the authorities questioning a dubious absence. The IRA men wanted to appear innocent and above suspicion.

As for their part, Aran and Gay cycled south toward Limerick. They planned to stay in Shadow's safe-house and report to him about their night's success when he returned. After things had calmed down, Aran would accompany his Yankee friend back to Uncle Peter's pub in Cahir. It had been three months since Aran Roe had last seen Sarah Anne. He missed her very much and longed to spend some quiet time in her company.

※

Two days later, Shadow reached the safe-house with the great news. The British army and the RIC were as mad as a sackful of cats over the dramatic Constabulary raid and the convoy's subsequent destruction.

For not only had the barracks at Craughwell been totally destroyed, but the IRA detachment near Cornafulla had blown up the other four Crossley tenders. Six of the enemys' ranks were killed and the remaining twenty-six British soldiers were disarmed.

It was reported that the convoy's commanding officer, a fiery, out-of-control captain was blindfolded, gagged and tied backwards on an old plow horse. This insult was in repayment for the vile oaths and deadly threats that repeatedly spewed forth from his venomous mouth. His Irish captors relished with delight the reproaches he would be forced to endure at the hands of his livid superiors.

Prior to the IRA's destroying the four British military vehicles, every piece of Sassenach weaponry was carefully off-loaded onto waiting farm wagons. It was then dispersed in all directions to needy undercover Irish soldiers who resided in the nearby countryside.

To date, it had been the greatest rebel coup in the west of Ireland since General Humbert had landed his French troops at Killala Bay in August, 1798. Local republicans would remember and commemorate its anniversary for years to come.

No longer would the RIC leave their barracks so unguarded and so vulnerable to enemy attack. Additionally, the British army stopped transporting lorry loads of weapons during the evening and nighttime hours. They also doubled and tripled their armed escorts when they did have to travel by day.

In Dublin, Michael Collins was ecstatic about the news of the Flying Gaels' raid, though his close friend and confidant, Harry Boland, did not share the Big Fellow's unrestrained enthusiasm.

After being tackled and wrestled to the floor by an exuberant Collins, poor Harry was lucky to escape with all of his body parts intact...except, that is, for the small trickle of blood that dripped from his right ear.

Late that evening, Boland was seen retreating from Vaughan's Hotel with a hand cupped over his battled and bloodied ear. From an upstairs window came the Corkish voice of Michael Collins shouting, "Come on Harry, old friend...just one more bit of ear...just one more, for ould time sake..."

18. *Torturing*

At Boolavogue as the sun was setting,
O'er the bright May meadows of Shelmalier,
A Rebel hand set the heather blazing,
And brought the neighbours from far and near,
Then Father Murphy from old Kilcormack
Spurred up the rock with a warning cry:
"Arm, Arm!" he cried, "For I've come to lead you,
For Ireland's Freedom we'll fight or die!"

Boolavogue/P.J. McCall

The small village and simple stone-walled, whitewashed thatched cottage was just as Aran remembered it. Since his only brief early-morning visit to Shadow's safe-house in May, 1916 little had changed. A few homemade chairs, a crude cupboard, a roughly constructed table and three metal beds dotted the modest hideout.

A large stone fireplace dominated one end of the single-room cabin. From its opening a red-hot turf fire cast a warm glow on the room. Reflected flecks of flame danced on the floor and surrounding walls. Three men sat around its stony hearth drinking cupfuls of strong tea. It was a cold wet day for the end of June.

Major Richard 'Shadow' Doyle, OC of the newly organised Flying Gaels, was finishing his narration about the Galway-Athlone convoy ambush of two weeks ago.

"Once again, I can't tell ye how proud and delighted I am about the whole affair sure," purred an ecstatic Shadow.

Listening, Aran thought to himself that that's the fifth time in the past twenty minutes his dear friend had expressed his great delight at their column's recent success.

The Irish Rebel almost laughed out loud. He found it difficult containing his own sense of satisfaction while reveling at his usually reserved leader's repeated words of enthusiastic joy.

"In the three-plus years I've known Shadow," reflected Aran to himself, "my strong-willed but quiet friend has not changed very much. Sure, his grey curly hair seems a bit whiter and less curly. Yes, there is a small but expanding bald spot at the back of his head where before none had existed. Well, maybe, it's just my imagination but aren't there a few more lines etched into that tanned face of his? Or is my memory simply playing tricks on me? I can't be sure."

One thing Aran did know was that the stresses and demands of the past three years were taking their toll on everyone. Even he was feeling the effects of the struggle on his own seemingly indestructible constitution. From time to time, they had each been nearly off their heads with strain.

Captain Aran Roe O'Neill has no longer an innocent, naive youth of sixteen. It seemed ages ago that his father had falsified his age on the Irish Volunteer's enlistment papers.

Now, physically mature at twenty, Aran had tasted the dangers and hardships of life that were becoming commonplace among young men throughout Ireland. For those lads who had chosen to take up the cause of Irish freedom, many seemed to be aging before their time.

The rigours of living on the run through long days and dark nights filled with danger and death were beginning to take their weary toll on the minds and bodies of Ireland's youth.

Life's normal emotional stresses were magnified and intensified by the constant fear and untold hardships of waging a guerrilla fight against a vastly more powerful foe. This unholy way of living had a devastating effect on the human psyche as war's harsh realities coupled with its stark economic deprivation and desperate physical demands continually haunted every Irish republican. Finally, these hardships were amplified by the constant threat of capture, imprisonment, torture and even execution for the British had spies and informers planted everywhere. The old saying that more Irish republican graves had been dug by mouth than by the gravedigger seemed truer than ever!

Contrary to English propaganda, Aran's lot were not some aggressive and intrusive band of malcontents plotting the overthrow of a great foreign power. No, they were simply ordinary Irishmen and women who were essentially waging a defensive battle on their home

soil. They were trying to wrestle back their land and national freedom usurped centuries ago by their greedy, power-hungry, colonial-
minded neighbour.

The blight of the Sassenach had been felt in the Land of Erin for
too long. Regardless of the cost, it was time to drive this foe from
the shores of Ireland.

Along with Shadow and Aran, the third man seated around the
fireplace was an Irish-American. Lieutenant Gabriel McCracken had
just celebrated his thirty-third birthday. In the two years that Gay
had been in Ireland, he had adapted to the Irish ways as if he had
lived in County Tipperary all his life. No one had to tell him about
the 'Green Fire.' It had burned in his breast from the day he was
born. It had been nurtured by his Irish-born father and fed over the
years by his participation in Clan-na-Gael activities in Amerikay.

So, with his and Sarah Anne's arrival at their Uncle Peter
McCracken's pub in the village of Cahir, the transition from American to Irishman was an easy one for him. Gay's Irish-speaking skills
had improved dramatically and the increased musical lilt in his voice
removed most traces of his former soft Virginia accent. No, Gabriel
was as much an Irishman as any of the lads who daily risked their
lives for the fulfillment of Eireann's ancient dream.

As Aran sat listening to Shadow's words of praise and excited
rejoicing, he felt a strange sensation of sadness and sorrow creep into
the pit of his stomach. He had first become aware of this feeling on
his train ride back from Dublin to Galway after freeing de Valera,
Barton and the others from prison. It was something akin to the
emotional upset he remembered experiencing in the Wicklow Mountain shed on that stormy morning after Pearse's execution in May,
1916.

Similar feelings had come and gone over the past three years,
but now a stronger, more pervasive gnawing in his stomach was becoming a constant, unwanted companion.

Aran was not sure of its cause but, in the back of his mind, he
knew it was somehow tied to the feelings of hatred, revenge and death
that now seemed to consume his life. Usually he was able to rationalise
the horrors that he and his comrades lived with and experienced but,
as time went on, it required more of an effort on his part to deal
with these disturbing feelings.

Aran wished he was again back in the West Virginia mountains
with his friend Shadow. That peaceful time they had spent there to-

gether was the perfect setting to discuss and, hopefully, understand the troubling feelings he was experiencing. He missed the closeness, the friendship and the shared trust he and Shadow had known back then. Aran wanted to take time out from his troublesome life. He desired to reconstruct something akin to what he and Shadow had known in Amerikay. Unfortunately, however, time and events had changed things. Despite his troubled, aching heart, Aran did not know how to go about recapturing the past he longed to embrace once again.

Lost in his own unsettled thoughts and haunted feelings, Aran was abruptly brought back to the present by Shadow's insistent voice. "Aran...Aran...Aran Roe O'Neill! For God's sakes son, sure, are you all right? Are you even after hearing a word I've said?"

"Absolutely, Shadow. I'd just drifted off for a moment. All these short nights and long days must be catching up with me."

"Ah, ye can say that again!" chimed in a sympathetic Gabriel.

Recovering his mental focus, Aran rose and refilled his cup with more tea, milk and a spoonful of sugar.

"Shadow, what other news are you after hearing from Mick?" queried Aran.

"Because of our recent success, the Big Fellow has decided to officially declare war on the Royal Irish Constabulary. IRA units throughout Ireland are to make life as difficult as possible for our fellow Irishmen who've chosen to work for the English. If these 'West Britons' are going to take the Saxon shilling then they're going to have to answer for it. Whenever possible, we're to attack their barracks and relieve them of their arms and ammunition. We're to do everything in our power to convince them to give up their commissions and resign their appointments.

"Mick has outlined some of the same strategies Michael Davitt and Parnell used during the Land Wars of the 1880s. He wants the RIC and their families ignored, shunned and given the silent treatment. It will be our responsibility and that of other IRA units to spread the word. We must do all we can to see that the general population cooperates and supports his boycott.

"If we're successful, the English will be forced to either close their outlying RIC barracks and pull back their forces into the larger towns or assign regular British troops to occupy the vacated positions.

"When and if the Sassenach do send in their troops, many more people will come over and support our side. It'll be a major political coup for us that might well spell disaster for the bleeden enemy."

Shadow stood up to refill his cup.

Gabby McCracken tossed several more sods of turf onto the fire. Returning to his chair, Gabby added, 'I've read that the English are divided in their support for an all-out campaign of violence and war against us here in Ireland. They've had their fill of hardships and death after fighting it out with the Germans in Europe for almost five years. The prospect of dispatching more troops here, risking more casualties and sending more of their lot home in wooden boxes doesn't have much support among the common folk or with their political representatives in England.

"Besides, the English are perfectly keen on having Irishmen fill the ranks of the RIC. They'd much rather have 'Paddy' serve in harm's way than have their own soldiers police us, the troublemakers!"

With the day's chill creeping in under the door, the three belligerents pulled their chairs closer to the fire. They began discussing the various ways the Flying Gaels might disseminate and enforce the Big Fellow's orders.

Suddenly, Shadow jumped up exclaiming, "I almost forgot. The Dail has decided to organise two new schemes. First, they plan on launching an Irish fund drive to raise a quarter of a million pounds in twelve months to help finance our struggle. It'll be officially launched in a month or two...and guess who they've chose to head it up? That's right...Michael Collins himself.

"With Sinn Fein President de Valera in Amerikay trying to raise another quarter of a million for our cause, Collins, who's the Dail's Minister of Finance, was selected to coordinate things at home.

"If ye remember your history lads, both the Fenians in Ireland and Amerikay used similar strategies to raise money going back as far as Davitt's time.[18-1]

"One other thing. The Dail is also in the process of setting up something they're calling 'arbitration courts' to settle land disputes and to identify our country's national economic resources.[18-2]

"Don't ye get the feeling lads that Collins, Griffith and the rest of them in Dublin are hell-bent on getting things organised. I think we're finally going to make a nation out of this dreadful old place yet. What do you say?"

They all laughed...more because Shadow had made a bit of a joke than at what he actually said. For Richard Doyle was a man of few words and he seldom poked fun at anyone or anything. This slight deviation from his usual ways was a noteworthy occasion easily recognised by his two close friends.

❧

With their rifles, haversacks and uniforms safely stowed in a secret compartment under the floorboards of Shadow's bakery lorry, Aran and Gabriel sat back against the cab of the bouncing vehicle, enjoying the warmth of the summer sun. They had found comfortable spots atop the empty flour sacks that were being returned to a granary by the River Suir near the village of Cahir.

Though the flour mill was almost forty miles from Shadow's Limerick bakery, his father's family had owned and operated that milling enterprise for several generations. The fine quality of grain grown in the Golden Vale near Tipperary Town, coupled with the expert processing it received at the mill, was one of the secrets behind the Doyles' fine cakes, biscuits and breads.

Besides replenishing his supply of flour, Shadow's lorry provided a convenient way of discreetly transporting men and weapons between counties Clare and Tipperary.

Unfortunately, the roughness of the road between Limerick and Cahir made travel slow even for a modern motorised vehicle. The narrow road was unpaved, muddy and full of potholes. Occasionally, the two men had to hang onto the sides of the open-bed truck for dear life or else they would likely have been bounced out onto the roadway.

After one particularly violent tossing about, the driver yelled back through the lorry door's open window, "Are ye two still with me?"

"Only by the grace of God we are!" came the echoed retort as the two soldiers, rolling around in the back of the vehicle, tried to regain their balance. But most of the time Aran and Gay were able to carry on a normal conversation and enjoy the ride.

"I'm a little confused, Aran. Explain to me how the RIC came to be such a powerful force in this land?" asked Gabriel.

"Well, sure, it all started around 1836. British Prime Minister Robert Peel had been successful in organising and establishing an unarmed police force in England several years earlier. You probably know the name 'Bobby' is a British nickname taken from Peel's given name."

After another violent bump, Aran resumed his answer. "Though his government fell from power in 1835, his influence in Westminster remained strong. Then, a year after losing his high office to the Liberals, Peel, the Conservative Party leader, organised a second uniformed but armed police force...this time in Ireland. It was all part of the Catholic political reform movement that Daniel O'Connell was spearheading at the time...one which Peel supported.

"At first, the police or 'peelers' were called the Irish Constabulary. They were established as a nonsectarian entity and, for the first time in Irish history, I think, the day-to-day practice of law enforcement stopped being a Protestant weapon of discrimination against Catholics."[18-3]

"All that doesn't sound so bad. When did things change?" queried Gay.

"It was a slow process, but gradually the mostly Catholic Irishmen hired to police their own became entangled in a web of what I simply call 'Englishness.' The British government, with her long-established political and military power base firmly ensconced within the walls of Dublin Castle, became the Irish Constabulary's overseer. They hired, paid and controlled Irishmen to support and look after their own self-interests."

"As an example, the peelers were only permitted to marry after they'd served the Crown for seven years...and what's more, Dublin Castle even dictated who they could and couldn't marry. Imagine, government officials making it a practice of screening prospective brides!

"So slowly, Gay, the IC became an institution in this country. Employment in the Irish police force became as much a tradition as sending a son off to the priesthood or going over to work in England or Amerikay.

"Sometimes the law was administered fairly and sometimes it wasn't. But, the main point was that this police force was charged with no only keeping the peace in Ireland but safeguarding England's interests as well."

Suddenly, the lorry passed over a particularly rough patch of road. It took all of Aran's and Gabriel's strength to hold on to the sides of the lorry. Finally, things smoothed out again and Aran continued his story.

"A major turning point in Constabulary history occurred in the spring of 1867. The Fenian leadership in the United States and Ireland organised a revolt...a Rising against English authority here at home.

"Gay, that's the Rising your father was so keen on telling us about.

How many times have you and I heard him say how proud he was that his father was 'out' in '67? But, like so many other Irish rebellions, this one was poorly planned, inadequately equipped, half-heartedly supported and betrayed by spies and informers. You know the old story...more Irish graves dug with mouths...

"During that brief conflict, the rebels were only able to capture a few police barracks in County Cork and a couple along the coast south of Dublin. Not surprisingly, very few men lost their lives in that Rebellion as all the fighting was quite localised.

"All in all, the Rising of '67 was a total failure. Many of the Irish separatists were arrested and, you guessed it...they were sent off to prison in 'jolly old England.' More, of course, were transported to Australia. Thankfully, though, there were no mass executions like there had been after the Rebellion of '98. This time the British authorities wisely took precautions against precipitating any possible Irish backlash, which most likely would have occurred if England had followed its customary practice of brutal, retaliatory reprisals.

"As a reward for its role in successfully defending their police barracks and defeating their rebellious countrymen, the Constabulary was honoured and renamed. The word 'Royal' was added to their official title."[18-4, 18-5]

"Aran, it's hard to understand why Irishmen would turn on their own. But then, given the passage of time, the rewards of power and the economic security of employment, I guess a downtrodden people might place their own and their family's interests ahead of national causes...a classic example of England's age-old policy of divide and conquer. It's too bad that practical solutions so often win out over idealised ones."

"Yes, Gay, they often do," replied Aran.

Gabriel's comment reminded him of this beloved teacher, Patrick Pearse. He had often quoted one of Lord Arthur Balfour's infamous Irish rebukes. Arrogantly, the man observed, 'Irish nationalism was born in a peasant's cot, where men forgive, if the belly gain.'

After a brief pause, the Gortman continued, "Oh, the English authorities tried to take some of the pressure off the locals by assigning constables to barracks away from their home villages or towns but, at the end of the day, the RIC were often seen as British dupes used to suppress political freedom and prop up Ireland's decaying landlord system...all for England's benefit. As a result, there was and still is today a climate of festering emotion and hidden resentment simmering away just beneath the surface of social respectability toward those men who've chosen to take 'the Crown's shilling.'

"Yes, in the final analysis, England's been able to control and direct their own interests through the hired help of Irishmen. So, today, throughout the cities, towns and villages of Ireland sure, some twelve thousand RIC policemen keep the peace and watch over us...all from behind the security of their stone-walled, British-backed barracks."

After a thoughtful moment, Aran added, "Just as an aside, Gay, the English call their own law enforcement headquarters 'police stations' but 'police barracks' here in Ireland. Doesn't that give you a little insight into how the British view the different state of things in our two countries?"

Aran stopped talking...lost in contemplation.

A few moments later, he turned and looked over at his friend. Gay's lips were pressed into a thin, straight line. His eyes flashed with a glint of stern determination.

"You know Gay...all this reminds me of something Mick said to me recently. As he looks back through history, Ireland was never actually invaded in the true military sense of the word. No, our neighbours across the Irish Sea took another tack. They slowly worked their way into the very fabric of our society. In support of this theory, Collins firmly believes that England's seven hundred and fifty years of peaceful penetration has been more dangerous and more morally debilitating then any military domination by Britain's army might ever have been."

Aran was just concluding his remarks when the bakery lorry came over a rise in the road near the outskirts of Oola, a small village northwest of Tipperary Town. There, waiting for them, as if by invitation, was a roadblock manned by both British soldiers and RIC policemen.

"Looks like trouble up ahead lads," shouted back the driver. "It's a roadblock and seems like they have us in their sights."

Looking back over their shoulders through the lorry's front windscreen, the two men could see ten or twelve uniformed figures milling about while an armoured Rolls-Royce partially blocked the roadway.

"Aran, we'd better hide our revolvers or we're done for," warned Gay.

"Right you are. Here, slide them into one of those empty flour sacks and pile some of the other bags on top. We'll just have to take our chances...remember, we're just ordinary help-staff from the bakery," instructed Aran.

Quickly and with remorse, Aran slid his old friend, the Colt .45 and his Luger automatic into one of the empty bags. He carefully spread a dozen or so flour sacks over the top of the incriminating evidence. Finally, he pushed the entire lot over to one side of the lorry and slid it halfway down the vehicle's open transport bed with his boot.

Gay followed suit with his Webley and Scott .455 revolver.

After taking several deep breaths, they both settled back, tried to relax and waited for God only knew what to happen.

A minute later the lorry driver pulled his machine to a stop in front of the roadblock. Aran heard an English voice ordering everyone out. "On your feet lads...stand at attention...hands up over your heads...hurry up and be smart about it!"

As he dismounted from the bed of the lorry, Aran had a start. There, directly in front of him, was the British army captain who had been in charge of Galway-Athlone convoy he and his fellow IRA soldiers had destroyed two weeks ago. Luckily for Aran, the captain had not laid eyes on him that evening.

The Gortman wondered if the officer had been reassigned here as a punishment for his failure to deliver the shipment of weapons or whether manning roadblocks was part of his normal military duty.

"Stretch 'em high boys and only speak when you're spoken to," ordered the pug-nosed captain.

"Johnny, Allen, Anthony...search these poor blokes and you two Paddies see what's in the lorry." The captain sounded annoyed that they had come along and disturbed his day's peace and tranquillity.

The British officer standing before Aran was tall and thin. His beady black eyes bulged from their sockets almost as much as his Adam's apple projected from his elongated neck. The man's skin was ivory white in colour and he had unusually long thin fingers for a man. Aran wondered if he might not have been a concert pianist at one time. The Englishman's uniform was immaculate. His stance was stiffly erect in a somewhat haughty, vaguely regal way.

"Nothing on these three," reported the one called Anthony.

"All clear up front in the cab, sir, but I'll have to look in back," replied one of the policemen.

The Irish constable lifted himself up over the low side of the lorry. He began poking around the truckbed with the barrel end of his rifle.

Aran and Gabriel stood watching while holding their breaths. It would be all over for them if the weapons were discovered.

The two rebels waited while the policeman now jabbed at the flour sacks with his foot.

Suddenly, the man stopped. He acted as though he felt something with the toe of his right boot. Quickly, he dropped down on one knee, put his rifle down and began feeling through the piles of flour sacks with both hands.

"Find something?" called out the captain.

"Sure, I thought so for a moment, sir, but it's just the empty bags all knotted up there on the floor of the lorry. No, Captain Hawkins, everything's after being in order here. Permission to jump down, sir."

"Permission granted," replied the captain.

With that, Aran and Gay slowly breathed a sigh of relief. They both knew how lucky they were. The two realised that the RIC constable might well have saved their lives by not disclosing his find.

The policeman jumped down off the bed of the lorry. As he passed by the two IRA men, he winked his eye and gave a slight nod of his head. Both Aran and Gay gave a quick return nod in grateful acknowledgement of their countryman's discretion.

"Now, lads, since we know you're not armed, tell me what you're both doing out here so far from Limerick?"

The captain strutted back and forth in front of his three captives.

Gabriel, not wishing to alert the soldiers to his real identity, kept silent.

Aran took up the challenge and answered the captain's query. Pointing to the business name printed on the side door of the lorry, he explained that they were employees of Mr. Doyle's. The vehicle was on its way to Cahir to collect flour from the mill.

The driver confirmed his story in an overly grovelling and humble manner that made Aran doubt where his true loyalties lay.

After conferring with two other soldiers and the Head Constable, the captain ordered the driver back into the lorry. The captain told him he was free to continue on with his journey.

After the vehicle departed, the captain's mood changed. He issued a brusque order. Aran and Gabriel's hands were roughly handcuffed behind their backs. Hawkins then ordered his captives into a new Model T Ford parked by the side of the road behind the Rolls-Royce.

"There's been a lot of nasty business around here lately...as far back as last January...a place called Soloheadbeg Quarry. Two policemen were shot dead there for no reason by some pathetically misguided Irish troublemakers. You wouldn't happen to know anyone like that would you?" questioned Captain Hawkins.

But before Aran or Gay could reply, Hawkins answered rhetorically, "No, of course you wouldn't know or associate with anyone like that...would you?"

In their defence Aran stated, "Ah sure, we're from Cratloe in County Clare. We've been working for the Doyle family for the past year and a half."

Looking over at Gabriel, he continued, "We're not familiar with these parts. In fact, I've only been to Cahir once before in me life...that was only to collect more flour."

"Well, we'll just see about that," retorted Hawkins.

Aran guessed that the Galway-Athlone convoy's failure had made Hawkins the laughing stock of his unit, especially among the enlisted men. He realised that the British officer's career could not withstand two humiliations in a row. The man was on the spot. He simply could not afford to make another mistake.

❧

Twenty minutes later the Ford and its motorcycle escort pulled up in front of the RIC barracks in Tipperary Town. The wide main street set into the rolling landscape was filled with Saturday afternoon shoppers. Tipperary was an important dairy centre and its weekly market was doing a thriving business in the town square. All the assembled carts, horses and people gave a festive air to the former hotbed of Land League agitation during the last quarter of the nineteenth century. It was also the hometown of two famous former Irish rebels, Charles Kickham and John O'Leary.

More recently, rebels like Dan Breen, Seamus Robinson, Sean Tracey, Sean Hogan and Michael Brennan were carrying on the tradition of 'Rebel Tip' in the hearts and minds of their fellow Irish neighbours.

Though Aran had never met any of these modern-day Tipperary freedom-fighters, he knew of their exploits and of their growing reputations.

After being hustled inside the large, two-story stone police building, Aran and Gabriel were thrown into a sturdy iron-barred cage built out from the wall of the main RIC office.

As he turned to leave the room, the captain's parting words to them were, "We'll soon see just how innocent you both are!"

With that, the officer slammed the door shut, leaving his two captives alone in their cell.

An hour later, fifteen people filed into the room to have a good look at the captain's two prisoners.

Gabriel knew to keep his mouth shut. Fearful his Americanised accent could get him into more difficulty, he planned to mutter any replies he might be forced to make. Aran knew the lion's share of the talking must fall on his shoulders.

As the assembled eyes stared carefully at the two jailed Irishmen, it became obvious from Captain Hawkins's questions that the British soldiers, RIC policemen and civilians had been witnesses or victims of recent IRA attacks.

Neither Aran nor Gabriel had ever spent any time in Tipperary Town. The two felt they had little to fear from the identity parade. Additionally, the village of Cahir was just too far away for the locals to have seen Gay working in Peter McCracken's pub.

Unfortunately for Captain Hawkins's ego or advancement, no one was able to identify Aran or Gabriel who stood watching the inquisitive group from inside their cell.

After the invited guests were led from the room, Captain Hawkins flew into an ungovernable rage. Again, his military judgement had come into question. Even if the witnesses had not identified his prisoners, these two were just the kind of men who might be mixed up in some kind of seditious activity.

Throwing open the cell door, maybe in deference to Gay's age, Hawkins grabbed the younger man by the hair and pulled him out into the room. With the aid of two other British soldiers, Hawkins sat Aran down and securely tied his upper body and legs to a straight-backed wooden chair. The captain then ordered his men to lash Aran's wrists to the table that was pulled up before him. This particular piece of furniture had a specially designed set of iron manacles securely fastened to its wooden surface. After Aran's wrists were locked in place and his fingers immobilised by two small metal plates, the table was securely bolted to brackets installed on the floor. Restrained as he was, the Gortman could not even move so much as a finger.

With fear filling his heart and hatred flooding his eyes, Aran watched Captain Hawkins methodically draw his revolver and carefully engage its cut-off. With is eyes flashing, the British officer firmly grasped his weapon by its barrel. The man's gun butt suddenly assumed the divilish characteristics of a hammer.

With a deepening fury, the captain started shouting questions at Aran while he banged the handle of his .32 revolver on the table. Slowly, after each repeated blow to its wooden surface, the deadly hammerhead inched its way closer to Aran's outstretched and helpless fingers.

"Once more...are you a member of Sinn Fein?"

"No!" answered Aran.

A loud bang rang throughout the room as the butt of the gun crashed down onto the table.

"Do you own a gun?"

"No, I don't!" lied the Irish Rebel.

Bang...the sound of the revolver butt rang out again as it struck the wood.

Staring up at the man standing so threateningly before him, Aran tried to remain calm. He did not know if he should try conning the captain out of doing him physical harm by begging for mercy or if he should remain stoic and possibly gain the man's respect for his show of courage.

The decision, however, about what role he should play for the captain's benefit was to abstract for Aran to deal with at that precise moment. It was all Aran could do to fight back the growing urge to scream out in self-defence. But his feelings of terror were occasionally interrupted by thoughts of how he would deal with this lunatic, if he was ever to survive. Aran forced himself to maintain some semblance of composure before the raging British officer.

Gabriel stared out from his cell at the unbelievable scene unfolding before him. It was like something out of Henry VIII. He remembered reading the horror stories about imprisoned souls tortured to death inside the Tower of London. To his way of thinking, Hawkins's methods were nothing more than crude torment, gross intimidation and represented the most despicable behaviour he had ever seen.

Gabriel's mind recoiled at the thought that he would be this deranged man's next victim. He felt like bellowing out in Aran's defence, hoping his stentorian roar might startle the out-of-control officer back to reality.

Suddenly, out of sheer frustration, Gabriel screamed at Hawkins, "Stop it, you bloody blackguard...we've nothing to do with you and your lot!"

The words that exploded from Gay's mouth startled everyone in the room including himself. It was as if some imaginary being had cried out in Aran's defence from Gay's solitary cell.

"Shut up you stupid Irish idiot...I'll have a piece of you when I'm good and ready," screamed the enraged captain.

And, as if to show everyone in the room who was in charge, Hawkins brought the grip-end of his revolver crashing down on the little finger of Aran's right hand.

The violence and suddenness of the attack caught everyone by surprise. Aran had no time to brace himself against the blow.

For a moment, the crunching of bone and Aran's involuntary scream of pain echoed and re-echoed around the room.

The Irish Rebel's first few seconds of intense pain were immediately followed by a momentary numbness marked by the total disbelief that his hand had been badly damaged.

Seconds later, more huge waves of blinding pain raced back up his arm and enveloped Aran. An uncontrollable flood of vomit erupted from his mouth. It splashed onto the table. It streamed down the front of him, contaminating his clothes. Violently, Aran tried to pull his hands from the shackles holding them but he could not break the grip of the metal clamps or dislodge the table from its brackets.

"Now, you son-of-a-bitch, I want to know the truth or I'll break every bone in both your hands." The captain's slitted eyes glowed red with hate.

The other two soldiers in the room looked at each other. They realised their officer was out of control but felt powerless to do anything about it.

With his pain so unbearable, Aran felt himself slipping into the arms of unconsciousness. His head drooped to one side but his shoulders could not slump forward because of their bindings.

"Don't you think he's had enough, sir?" ventured one of the two British soldiers in attendance. "He's just a simple Mick...too dumb to take on the RIC or us."

"That's just what he wants you to think, soldier," retorted their OC.

...and with that, Hawkins brought the butt of his .32 down on Aran's right ring finger.

"Splat!"

Even in his semiconscious state, Aran reacted to this second blow. His head snapped back and he screamed out again.

By now, blood covered his entire hand. It was beginning to trickle across the table toward the captain.

"Stop that this instant!" blurted Gay from behind the bars of his cell.

"The hell I will!" shouted Hawkins. "...and I want you to know right now, you're next. So button up that lip of yours or you'll never live to tell about it."

Aran's screams of pain and Hawkins's cries of rage brought several more British soldiers and two RIC constables into the interrogation room.

Quickly sizing up the situation, the older of the two constables stepped in between the captain and the table. "Looks like he's had it, Captain Hawkins. What do you say? Let's let him sleep it off. He's no good to you in this condition anyway. How about it, sir?"

For a moment, Hawkins started blindly at Aran's mangled hand and the growing pool of blood on the table. Abruptly, his eyes clearer, Hawkins stepped back.

"You may be right. I never did think this Paddy knew anything. Just a simple muck savage with half a mind. I've seen hundreds like him in Dublin, Athy and Athlone."

The word 'Athy' momentarily registered with Aran, but that was all.

Regaining his military composure, Hawkins ordered two of his soldiers to untie Aran and chuck him back into the cell.

As the metal-barred door swung open to make way for Aran's motionless body, Gabriel lunged at the officer.

His powerful fist landed a glancing blow along the side of Hawkins's face. Immediately, blood began gushing from the man's nose. It spilled down onto his clean, carefully-pressed military uniform.

Rage returned to Hawkins's eyes. He raised the revolver that was still in his hand, pointed it at Gay and tried to pull the trigger. Fortunately for Gabriel, the cut-off was still engaged.

Furious that his weapon would not fire, Hawkins swung it down in a sweeping motion with all the force he could muster. The resulting 'whack' snapped Gay's left collarbone. The sharp crack sounded like a dry limb breaking away from a dead tree in a wind storm.

Despite his own pain, Gay took one more half-hearted swing at the British officer, but his fist failed to connect.

This second, ill-advised swing caused Gabriel to lose his balance. He fell in agony against the bars of the cell.

Hawkins brought the full force of his knee up into Gay's unguarded groin.

A rush of air exploded from the Irish-American's mouth. He slowly crumpled into a screaming heap on the barrack's cold stone floor.

Never missing a chance to hit a man when he was down, Hawkins swiftly brought the toe of his military boot up and into Gay's exposed side.

Again, the sound of breaking bones was audible as two of Gabriel's ribs were shattered from the force of the Englishman's kick.

With that, Captain Hawkins, clutching his nose to stem its flow of blood, marched out of the cell, ordered it relocked and warned those assembled in the room, "If one word of this incident is ever spoken of again, that person will have to deal with me...personally!"

❧

Six hours later, the two mangled IRA soldiers were quietly released from their cell. They were unceremoniously pushed out the back door of the RIC barracks and warned never to show their sorry faces in Tipperary Town again...that is, if they knew what was good for them.

Aran, with part of his bloodied shirt wrapped around his crushed right hand, helped guide a battered Gabriel up the laneway toward the main street. Gay's testicles were so swollen and painful that he could not stand upright or walk without great discomfort. Any sudden movement caused his broken ribs to cut into him like tiny knives. Anything more than shallow breaths made Gabriel recoil with excruciating pain.

As they rounded the corner of the barracks and stepped out onto the footpath, they almost tripped over a man on his way home from an evening at a nearby pub.

At first the man wanted nothing to do with the two battered strangers. Aran spoke to him in Irish, begging him for help.

Cautiously, the man gave the two of them a second look. Were these really fellow Irishmen pleading for assistance? With the RIC barracks looming up overhead, the man suddenly put two and two together.

"Quick, this way lads. My horse and trap are just up the street."

With great effort, the two Flying Gaels struggled into the little tubular cart. Hanging on with what little strength they had left, the partisans were quickly driven away from the town centre.

Thankfully, after a few minutes, the conveyance stopped bouncing. The humanitarian had pulled his horse to a stop in front of an attractive, two-story stone house with a wooden porch stretching across its front.

The driver ran up the front walkway and knocked on the door. After some repeated pounding and hushed conversation, a heavyset man with a waterproof pulled around him and a woman in a flannel dressing gown rushed out of the house and down to the cart. Carefully, the three strangers helped the two wounded men inside.

The cart driver turned to Aran. "This is Dr. O'Toole and his wife, Mary. They'll take care of ye and see you're properly looked after. God bless yis both. God Save Ireland."

With that, the man turned and hurried out of the house, leaving Aran and Gabriel in the hands of the O'Toole's.

❧

Late the following night, just as the first light of dawn etched it sway across the eastern sky, a two-horse wagon loaded with freshly cut hay drew up to the rear entrance of Dr. O'Toole's surgery. After a few moments of handshaking and words of grateful thanks, two bandaged and beaten Irish republicans slipped out the back door. They gingerly climbed into the wagon and buried themselves in the sweet-smelling harvest.

As a token of appreciation for the risk and help the O'Toole family had provided Aran and Gabriel, the wagon driver hung a freshly slaughtered and dressed pig from a hook affixed to a ceiling beam under the roof of the O'Tooles' back porch.

The man driving the wagon, Thomas Grogan, was a close friend of the McCrackens. His son, Pat Grogan, was a member of the Flying Gaels.

As the story later unfolded, the morning after Aran and Gay were brought to the doctor's home, the medical man sent word down to Cahir detailing the men's injuries. Immediately, friends and family made hurried arrangements to collect the lads that very night. Soon, they would be safely away from Tipperary Town and could begin recuperating in the seclusion of the Galty Mountains, high above the lush green Glen of Aherlow.

Aran's and Gabriel's families, friends and the Flying Gaels were all nearby. They would see to it that the two were well looked after. But, in addition to the caring provided for them, Aran longed for Sarah Anne's much-missed company and fondly remembered nurturing.

❧

It was a warm, almost summery autumn afternoon. Sarah Anne McCracken, hands full after an hour of marketing, was struggling to find her key to the front door of her Uncle Peter's public house.

"Ah sure, it looks like you might be in need of a helping hand there, miss." The man had appeared out of nowhere and surprised her by his unexpected offer.

Turning, Sarah said, "Thanks very much. You're grand to offer, but I'll manage just fine."

"Ah, if I'm not mistaken, you're Peter McCracken's niece, Sarah Anne from Amerikay."

"And who might be after asking?" queried Sarah.

"Sean Treacy, ma'am. From Tipperary Town. I know of your brother's and the O'Neill lad's troubles from the summer. 'Twas an awful business, indeed, but I hear they're getting on well."

"Sorry, sir, you've me confused with someone else. I don't know what in the world you're talking about."

"Mick said you'd be on the lookout."

"Lookout? You're going to have to do better than that. As you can plainly see, I've me hands full of packets. Now, if you don't mind, I'd like to be after getting on with my chores. This pub opens its doors in twenty minutes and I've more to do than a dog has fleas!"

Gabriel had talked to her about always keeping her guard up. She also remembered Aran's warning, "Sarah, you can never be too careful about what you say, especially to strangers."

The young woman finally located the pub's key in her purse. Turning her back on the stranger, she quickly unlocked the door and hurried her purchases inside. But before she could turn to close it, the man had followed her into the pub.

"I beg your pardon, sir. We're not yet open!"

"It's not the drink or the comfort of a public house I'm after," he replied.

"I haven't a clue what you're about. So, if you don't leave this instant, I'll be after giving a shout for someone who'll show you the way out!"

Sean thought to himself, "Sure, this colleen's only been living here for a little over two years and already she's picked up our ways."

"Miss McCracken, I don't mean to alarm you. I believe you know Michael Collins. He's asked me to call in on you for a favour."

Sarah Anne surveyed the good-looking man standing in front of her. He was in his early to mid-twenties, slim, fit, and wore a pencil-thin moustache. His well-groomed hair and nearly pressed three-piece suit befitted the man's confident demeanour. He spoke with an educated voice and had a disarmingly attractive twinkle in his eye.

"Who'd you say you're after delivering a message from?"

"Michael Collins from Dublin. You remember. He first met you and the lads in his Mary Street office after ye arrived from Amerikay two years ago."

Sarah was deciding what to say next when her Uncle, Peter McCracken, walked into the pub's lounge. "My God, Sean Treacy! What in the world brings you to these parts?"

"I was just telling your niece here, Peter, Mick Collins sent me down here, but she's having none of it."

"You know yourself, Sean, you can't be too careful with all the trouble we've been having."

The man called Sean smiled knowingly.

"Sarah Anne, I want you to meet one of the heroes of Soloheadbeg. Your man here, along with Dan Breen, Seamus Robinson, Sean Hogan and some others, lit a fire under this country of ours back in January."

Nodding in Sean's direction, Peter added, "...and just in case you haven't guessed, my dear, Sean here's a wanted man. Sure, the authorities in these parts would love to get their hands around his neck so."

Tilting his head to one side, Sean allowed the faintest of smiles to invade his usually tight-lipped countenance.

With her confidence restored, Sarah McCracken relaxed. "'Tis a pleasure to meet you, Mr. Treacy. I mean that so. I was just being cautious. You understand, no?"

"You're all right, Miss McCracken." The rebel outlaw smiled.

With her hands on the tall wooden back of a nearby chair, Sarah said, "Please, take a seat here. It's our family's table. I'll go put the kettle on and organise some tea."

That was the beginning of it. A week later Sarah Anne was in Dublin. The Big Fellow had arranged for her to stay with the elderly Irish historian Alice Stopford Green. After the Easter Rebellion, this well respected Irishwoman had decided to move back home from London. Her Dublin residence, a comfortable terraced house at #90 St. Stephen's Green, had become an intellectual centre for other like-minded individuals with strong anti-imperialist views. Facing the fabled 'Stephen's Green' with its twenty-two acres of tree-lined footpaths, ornamental lake and attractively groomed flower gardens, this inner-city park had witnessed its share of the Easter Week violence.

The day after her arrival in Dublin, Sarah met Michael at #6 Harcourt Street, Sinn Fein headquarters. It was only two blocks away from where she was staying. Armed with the forged documents Sean Treacy had left behind, Sarah Anne had assumed the role of an International Red Cross representative. Her brief was to tour the country, inquiring into whether British or Irish prisoners of war were being treated according to the rules of international law. Treacy had also given her an official-looking folder and a list of important people, both in England and in Ireland, who would vouch for her. Collins had not missed a trick in establishing her new identity.

Sitting across the table from Michael Collins, the Irish-American expressed her eagerness to become involved in Michael's organised fight for independence. Sarah casually brushed aside the IRA leader's warning of danger. She felt her femininity, counterfeit credentials and American accent would insulate her from any serious British retaliation. But she was honest when she told Collins that her two greatest fears were of being deported from Ireland and of suffering Aran's wrath over her patriotic adventuresomeness. For the moment, though, she had postponed his possible objections by deciding not to tell him of this unexpected Dublin rendezvous.

As a young American with strong Irish republican feelings, Sarah Anne was not content performing the passive, supporting role currently assigned to her by her more tradition-minded family. If Aran and Gabriel could play active roles in Ireland's struggles, then why not herself as well?

The wise Corkman carefully outlined the possible dangers of her becoming a courier during wartime, but Sarah did not bat an eye at the deadly picture Collins painted. No, her mind was made up. She was eager to get on with it.

The next morning Sarah Anne McCracken, dressed in a heavy, ankle-length skirt, white blouse with high laced collar, tailored jacket and a dark overcoat with an International Red Cross insignia sewn into its sleeve, boarded the Dublin to Belfast train. Strapped beneath her underclothes was an oblong leather pouch containing a handful of important IRB documents. They outlined General Michael Collin's plans for Ulster's continued involvement in Ireland's War of Independence.

Despite her bravado yesterday with the Big Fellow, fear was her travelling companion today. She felt as if every passenger's eye was fixed upon her. Sarah imagined that each innocent glance was, in truth, querying her every move. She fantasised that the customary polite nod or the smallest comment was clandestinely aimed at exposing her hidden secret. The Cahir woman quickly came to realise that some things are certainly easier said than done...especially when your very life is possible at stake. Collins had been right. This business of being a spy was a deadly game requiring steely nerves and clear thinking. Sarah Anne now knew that it would take a little longer than she had imagined to grow accustomed to her new role.

After safely delivering her documents, she refilled her pouch with a thousand pounds of 'donated' English notes. They would be used to buy much needed rifles for Collins's new 'flying columns' in the south of Ireland.

Sarah stayed the night in Belfast, then took the morning train for Athlone. She was scheduled to meet with Collins's friend, Sean MacEoin, an IRA commander from County Longford. After delivering the secreted bank notes, the Blacksmith of Ballinalee, as MacEoin was affectionately known, arranged for a motor car to return her to Cahir.

On her final leg back home, the McCracken woman decided to tell Aran what she had been up to for the past five days. Sarah only had to find the right time for her disclosure while praying he would understand.

❧

The last half of 1919 was memorable. Much happened during those final six months. Aran and Gabriel recovered from their beatings. Both men were almost as good as new.

Gay's shoulder mended perfectly but his broken ribs still bothered him when he did any heavy lifting or hard running. Happily, however, he took delight in reporting that his 'manhood' was still intact. Gabriel's pending springtime marriage to Pat Grogan's eldest sister, Aine, seemed destined to be a blessed and fruitful one.

Aran, on the other hand, suffered nagging bouts of shooting pain in his right hand. His two crushed fingers had healed imperfectly. They often became swollen after the least amount of use. This, coupled with the premature onset of some aching arthritis, compromised his right hand's usefulness and flexibility. But, he too was able to find a bit of humour in it all...little did Captain Hawkins know that Aran was left-handed. His letter writing, weapon handling and other fine motor skills were luckily unaffected by the revolver-butt beating.

During those infrequent days when his right hand felt fine, the ugly sight of his two permanently missing fingernails and gnarled digits were a remembrance of Captain Hawkins's brutality. The injury was a constant reminder to Aran of England's hated presence and Ireland's thirst for freedom. Yeats's prophetic words, "Too long a sacrifice can make a stone of a heart!" had special meaning for the Irish Rebel.

There was one other bit of good fortune to come out of their Tipperary episode. Aran's and Gay's three dumped handguns had been returned to them. After Shadow's driver was given permission to continue on with his journey to Cahir, the lorry driver proceeded directly to the McCrackens' pub. He informed Peter of what had transpired and gave him the hidden hardware plus the gear secreted away under the flooring of the lorry.

By the time Dr. O'Toole's news had reached them, Peter and his friends were in the process of organising a raid on the Tipperary RIC barracks to free its two captives.

Aran remembered how Peter, Sarah Anne and the whole McCracken Clan were waiting for them when they reached their mountain hideaway. The publican and his wife were thoughtful enough to bring their 'equipment' up from the pub. They had it all laid out on a table as a welcoming surprise.

Aran had felt heartsick at the thought of losing his Yankee Colt .45. Its sudden reappearance helped make the journey down the road to recovery a little bit shorter and sweeter.

☘

Aran did suffer a mild setback in early November. This one was emotional rather than physical. Sarah Anne told him of her Dublin meeting with Michael Collins and her short but successful venture into the underworld. The Irish Rebel's first reaction was utter surprise quickly followed by outrage and betrayal. "How could Mick put your life in such danger, especially after what had happened to Brigid?"

But after some calm discussion and thorough airing of Sarah Anne's desire to play some role in Gabriel's and his fight, Aran relented. He knew of other women in the Cumann na mBan, in particular, and many brave Irish civilians, in general, who were daily risking everything for God and country. Sarah would never forgive him much less herself if the hostilities ended tomorrow, for better or worse, and she had not made her contribution.

Aran Roe agreed not to interfere with his friend's courier requirements for his beloved. His only request was that Michael keep him informed, if at all possible, about the Corkman's need for Sarah Anne's help. The Irish Rebel thought that if he knew something in advance, maybe he or his friends might somehow provide an extra cushion of protection or safety.

☘

As autumn turned to winter, the Flying Gaels carried on several small, isolated raids for weapons. Unfortunately though, nothing equalled the success they had experienced at the expense of Captain Hawkins and his military convoy the past summer.

Michael Collins again called on Sarah for help delivering some important documents, this time to London. Upon her return, she transported another large sum of money collected by IRB members in Scotland, England and Wales. No one paid her any serious attention and she returned to Cahir and the Galty safe-house none the worse for her efforts. Despite the dangers, Sarah Anne's short ventures into the arms of the unknown challenged her, excited her and left her feeling exhilarated. She knew she was making a real contribution in Ireland's struggle for independence.

Nationally, the country was in a constant state of flux. First, the IRA had begun putting more pressure on members of the RIC to resign. Then, Liam Lynch, OC of the 2nd Cork Brigade, raised the level of guerrilla hostilities a notch when he and his men attacked a parade of British soldiers in Fermoy as they sought to capture more weapons for their own use. In a counter move, the British government suppressed Dail Eireann, driving the newly elected Irish government underground in early September. Two months later, British soldiers flexed their muscles once again. They looted and burned parts of Patrick Street in Cork City. Finally, on December 22nd, the British House of Commons, under the direction of Prime Minister David Lloyd George, introduced his Better Government of Ireland Bill. It proposed to partition Ireland by establishing two separate par-liaments...one in Dublin for Ireland's twenty-six, mainly Catholic, southern counties and one in Belfast for Ireland's six remaining, predominantly Protestant, northeastern counties.[18-6]

❧

Winter's first snow added a special luster to the O'Neill family's planned Christmas festivities. Aran eagerly looked forward to the short reunion. In addition to the Irish Rebel making a secretive flying visit home, Sarah and Gay were expected to join the Gort family for a day. Everything seemed to signal a joyous Christmas and happy twenty-first birthday for Aran. The Irish Rebel and his family could only hope that 1920 would finally mark the arrival of Ireland's long-awaited independence.

In reality, though, pessimism rather than optimism was the order of the day. Despite Michael Collins's plans to step up pressure against the RIC and British army of occupation, it seemed as if the cards were stacked against those committed to the separatist ideal. The Flying Gaels were well aware that in response to increased IRA activities, the British army had upped the level of troops stationed in Ireland to forty thousand. One-third of those forces were posted to County Cork.

This military influx was a reaction to the past year's successes orchestrated by Collins, Liam Lynch, Sean Treacy, Thomas MacCurtain and others. Together the republicans were prosecuting a successful guerrilla campaign against the Sassenach in selected parts of Ireland. As a result, it was time for the British to up the ante.

Another ominous signal was sounded as 1919 came to an end. On December 19th, a special IRA unit, under the direction of Tipperary's Dan Breen and supported by Michael Collins, narrowly missed assassinating Field-Marshal Lord John French, Ireland's Lord Lieutenant and Governor-General, at the Ashtown railway station near his residence in Phoenix Park, Dublin.[18-7] Lord French was the epitome of what British imperialism stood for in Ireland. He represented all the influence and forces that Irish republicans were trying to drive out of the country. He was the figurehead of 'Englishness' the IRA wanted dethroned.

Any number of those in the IRA's and IRB's inner circle had often remarked, "French wasn't just a man, he was a bloody institution and his time to go had come!"

Often a target for elimination, once more the Field-Marshal had successfully dodged death. One IRA volunteer, however, was not as lucky. Young Martin Savage met his death that December day as Ireland's War of Independence hotted up in earnest.

19. *Fighting*

At Vinegar Hill, o'er the Pleasant Slaney,
Our heroes vainly stood back to back,
And the Yeos at Tullow took Father Murphy,
And burnt his body upon a rack.
God grant you glory, brave Father Murphy,
And open Heaven to all your men,
The cause that called you may call tomorrow,
In another fight for the Green again.

Boolavogue/P.J. McCall

*T*he situation was rapidly deteriorating. What had begun as a special training exercise was turning into a life and death struggle.

Aran Roe O'Neill, Gabriel McCracken, Danny Kelly and Michael O'Sullivan, a member of the hosting 3rd West Cork Brigade, were sheltered behind a stone outcropping up on an exposed flank of the Boggeragh Mountains.

Five lorry loads of British army troops and RIC forces were moving up along the narrow road below them. Unless the rebels retreated back up the mountain, their position was in danger of being overrun. To make matters even worse, a dozen members of their IRA training team were below in the village. Their comrades were in the path of the enemy and in immediate danger of being captured or killed. For Aran and his companions to abandon their mates by fleeing over the mountains to safety was not an option even worthy of consideration.

The dozen or so whitewashed houses of Ballynagree dotted the green grass and grey rocky mountainside four hundred yards below them. Further down on the glen floor, the River Laney curled its way southward toward the Sullane River and the town of Macroom.

This third and final day of their mountain training had suddenly came to an abrupt halt. The idea for the joint effort had been suggested last autumn by Michael Collins but seven months had passed before it was finally implemented. By June, 1920 all the plans had been finalised. Official approval had been issued.

Under the leadership of Liam Mellowes, Richard 'Shadow' Doyle and Liam Lynch, selected members of the Flying Gaels and men from County Cork's three brigades had assembled in a secluded valley in the heart of the Boggeraghs.

For Aran and the other fifteen men of their flying column, the journey to the meeting site was an ordeal in itself. The Gaels from Counties Galway, Clare, Limerick and Tipperary had assembled in Mallow on June 15th. From there, small groups of men took circuitous routes along the River Blackwater and up into the surrounding mountains. Some rode bicycles, two came by horse and trap, four risked driving a lampless old motor car under cover of night, but most walked. It took Aran, Gay and Danny a day and half to reach the little farmhouse near Nad.

Volunteer Tommy O'Reilly's barn had been converted into a military barracks and classroom for the specially invited thirty-five IRA soldiers.

Major Shadow Doyle and twenty-two-year-old Tom Barry were in charge of the camp. Shadow, now close onto thirty-nine, was an experienced soldier and guerrilla fighter while his fellow instructor had seen three years of action in France as a member of the British army. Barry had just moved to West Cork from Bandon Town, south of Cork City. The British had become suspicious of his activities and political leanings. Tom, wanting to avoid arrest and possible deportation to England, had moved in with family friends living near Millstreet.

This whole idea of some advance training had been the result of the earlier successes experienced by the Gaels. Their flying column, serving as an elite guerrilla fighting force, had proven its worth to the General Headquarters Command in Dublin. Now, plans were underway, at least on paper, for the creation of flying columns in many of Ireland's other counties. Soon the men gathered at the O'Reilly farm would play key roles in the organisation and training of these new fighting units.

The outlawed Irish government had little choice in the matter if it expected to successfully continue waging war against England. There were not enough trained men or available guns and ammunition in Ireland to take on the might of the British army. If Irish freedom was to be won, it would have to be bit by bit in isolated attacks against the enemy rather than engaging their opponent via conventional military tactics. The IRA would have to pick its spots and dictate the terms of battle if they were to inflict any telling blows on the Sassenach.

The exercises scheduled for the camp had proceeded flawlessly until this afternoon, their third and final day of training.

During the three days, the mornings had been spent in the barn listening to lectures about military strategy, use of weaponry, analysis of British army tactics and how to live rough off the land. These discussions where followed by practical exercises in the surrounding mountains and nearby glens during the afternoon and evening hours. The men practiced organising ambushes, attacking manned positions, reading terrain maps, plotting nighttime raids and rehearsing outdoor survival strategies.

But now with the enemy in sight, the artificiality of training was over. It was time to put into action some of the strategies they had been rehearsing.

Through his field-glasses, Aran was able to count twenty-four British soldiers, five RIC policemen plus ten or twelve of the special English coppers Britain had recently sent over to terrorise Ireland. These 'Black and Tans,' as they were called by the people in these parts, were a force to be reckoned with indeed!

Michael Collins's and the IRA's efforts to intimidate the RIC had grown successful. During the past year, hundreds of policemen had resigned and more continued to do so every week. Some of those remaining on active duty had refused to bear arms against their fellow countrymen. Several magistrates and Justices of the Peace were beating a hasty retreat and resigning as well. Recently, most of Ireland's population seemed unwilling to challenge the growing might of the IRA or the dictating policies of the Dublin Dail.

The continual resignations of RIC personnel had created huge holes in Britain's ability to govern and spy on the Irish people. Their highly developed network of informers was beginning to tumble like a house of cards collapsing overnight. Because of its damaging political overtones, the British government had refused to assign Crown forces to fill the growing void of resigning policemen. Instead, Westminster had begun recruiting former First War soldiers, who were paid ten shillings a day, to fill the RIC vacancies.

To everyone's recollection, the first detachment of these 'new rozzers' had surfaced in the village of Upper Church, County Tipperary during early March of 1920. Since there was a shortage of regulation RIC bottle-green uniforms, the new English recruits were outfitted in mismatched dark-green tops and khaki trousers. From a distance, the men's green shirts and light-brown britches appeared to be black and tan in colour.

By some strange coincidence, there were several packs of local hound dogs in this particular part of Tipperary that had similarly shaded two-tone, coloured coats. For years these hunting animals had been nicknamed 'Black and Tans.'

Thus, before long, these new recruits were being referred to as Black and Tans by people throughout the immediate countryside. By mid-summer of 1920, the nickname had spread and was in common usage throughout Munster. The Tans' growing reputation for violence and uncontrolled behaviour toward the Irish citizenry was becoming legendary.

Many accused England of raiding their jails and prisons as they sought recruits for these new positions, but that was not the case. The enlistees were mostly former First War soldiers seeking adventure and the handsome pay they were promised.

In Britain's determined rush to crush their neighbour's latest uprising, these new 'policemen' were sent over to Ireland without proper supervision and training. These inadequacies, coupled with the men's thirst for thrills and violence, led the Tans to commit many heinous and outrageous acts against the Irish people. Though the Black and Tans were not criminals when they arrived in Ireland, many returned to England untried but guilty of terrible crimes against their fellow human beings.

On 16 March, Thomas MacCurtain, the newly installed Lord Mayor of Cork City and local IRA commander, received a written death threat. Four nights later, a party of armed men with blackened faces, entered the Lord Mayor's home and murdered MacCurtain in front of his wife and daughter. The men in the assassination party appeared to be dressed in 'unusual' uniforms. Afterwards, it was widely believed that this 'job' was the first official act carried out by the Tans. A subsequent legal inquiry returned a verdict of murder against the RIC and the British government, but no one was officially arrested or indicted for MacCurtain's murder.

This cold-blooded event, coupled with the IRA's stepped-up policy of intimidation and occasional assassination of cruel, vindictive and traitorous RIC policemen, elevated the intensity of the conflict between the two belligerent parties. Collins and the IRA were determined to rid Ireland of British spies, informers and dupes while the English refused to be frightened into withdrawing. The new Sassenach administration in Dublin Castle headed by Chief Secretary Sir Hamar Greenwood was more than willing to answer coercion with coercion...terror with terror...murder with murder.

Innocent Irish civilians were being pulled into the growing conflict on a daily basis. Local residents who had taken no part in the fighting and violence were being singled out by the Black and Tans and forced to pay for the actions of their IRA countrymen. With little justification, these new 'peelers' began treating both the IRA and the civilian population as its enemy. As a result, the Tans' acts of vengeance against law-abiding members of Irish society helped create a growing, united nationalistic feeling among the Irish people.

Now, however, as puffs of white smoke and the distant sound of rifle fire began filling the air, Aran put aside his reflections on the state of the nation. He readied himself for battle.

Positioned four hundred yards above the little hamlet, Aran's and his mates' rifles were virtually useless. But, if the IRA lads positioned in the village chose to withdraw back up the mountainside, their weapons would provide important covering fire.

The four men, crouched behind a large granite outcropping, huddled to review the situation. After careful deliberation, they decided to stay put and see what the enemy was about. One element in the equation, however, concerned them. The troops massing below must be coming from Macroom. If the RIC or British decided to send in a wave of reinforcements from their barracks in Millstreet, they and their IRA comrades in Ballynagree would be trapped in a deadly crossfire.

To protect their rear and guard against such an eventuality, Gabriel was chosen to unobtrusively work his way back up the mountainside to the top of Musheramore. From there he would have an excellent view of the two roads that ran southeast from Millstreet on which reinforcements would advance to encircle the village and their hillside location.

The IRA's avenue of escape depended on Gay's signal. After firing several shots in the air to get his three comrades' attention, he would signal to them the direction from which the danger was approaching. If he held his rifle above his head with his right hand, the enemy was taking the right-hand road. If his weapon was in his left hand, they were coming in from there. If he held both hands high in the air, they were in big trouble because additional troops were approaching from both directions.

Aran only hoped that the enemy would not commit all of their available forces to this one area. He was gambling that they would not stage a massive three-pronged attack to deal with such a small Irish force. The Gortman felt that the enemy would act conservatively. He hoped the commanding officers of both districts would choose to protect their own barracks in Macroom and Millstreet from being isolated and possibly falling victim to a rebel counter-attack.

With Gabriel's departure, Michael O'Sullivan assumed the role of spotter. He kept a lookout in Gay's direction, watching for a sign from Lt. McCracken. If someone did not keep a sharp eye out, they could easily miss his warning shots and signal from above.

The twelve IRA men in Ballynagree could see the enemy approaching. Quickly, some took up defensive positions inside several of the houses flanking the roadway. Others chose to hide behind some of the natural cover on the steep hillside directly behind and above the little hamlet.

As the lorries of soldiers and Tans motored up the valley, the partisans began firing at them, hoping to turn them around. Rather than retreat, however, the enfilade only forced the enemy to stop their advance, using their vehicles as protective cover.

The Irish soldiers had only a limited supply of ammunition at their disposal. They would be unable to hold out indefinitely against the larger and better armed enemy force.

Even as Aran and Danny eyed the fighting below through their Yankee binoculars, they noticed some of their mates leaving the safety of the houses. Seeking a more advantageous position from which to carry on the fight, the Volunteers started working their way back up the mountainside.

As they stared down at the battle going on, the two Gaels recognised some of the retreating men. Crawling on his stomach through an open patch of ground was Nick Robinson...and there, just to his left, was Caoimhin Donleavy.

Apparently, they had worked out a two-man retreating strategy. Sergt. Donleavy would run low to the ground or in some cases crawl until he had reached a place of cover while Sergt. Robinson kept up a covering fire at the enemy. They would then reverse roles. Nick retreated upward while Caoimhin held the enemy at bay.

Far to the right and closest to the lorries were Neil Dempsey and two of Michael's County Cork comrades. They too would advance upwards, stop and fire, then pull back once more.

While this was going on, the British soldiers and Tans had started to move out from behind their lorries. Because of their lofty position, Aran could see the enemy, using stone walls and isolated boulders as protection, begin to slowly advance and overrun the village.

From the sound of things, firing had intensified. The IRA Volunteers inside the houses realised what was happening. Most of their shots were not having the impact they desired. The enemy was rapidly closing in on them.

Recognising the hopelessness of their situation, the last of the trapped Irishmen finally began streaming out of the village and up the hillside.

The British threw caution to the wind and hurriedly followed the rebels through the village. Once they were clear of the houses, the enemy too began scrambling up the incline after the retreating belligerents.

Turlough Molloy, Aran's and Gay's Irish-American comrade, had found a well-protected spot behind several large boulders and, taking up the challenge, had started firing at the advancing Crown forces. Two, three then four British soldiers fell to the ground writhing in pain one hundred yards below his position.

Seeing their mates fall, the English concentrated fire in Turlough's direction. He shot back but must have run out of ammunition for soon a white handkerchief tied to the end of his Lee-Enfield was visible. Three soldiers advanced and, no doubt, called out to him to surrender. Turlough slowly stood up, dropped his weapon and raised his hands in the air.

As Aran and Danny watched from above, the soldiers arrested him. Several of the other Sassenach troopers rushed over to their four wounded fellows. As the British infantry trio began leading Turlough back down the hillside, a Black and Tan officer came running up, drew his revolver and shot the Irish-American through the head without so much as a mind your leave. The executed man dropped to his knees and fell face forward down the hillside.

More IRA rifle shots rang out while the soldiers and the assassin ducked for cover. But before the Tan officer scrambled to safety, he looked back up the hill in Aran's direction. A disbelieving Aran recognised him through his powerful glasses. It was none other than

Tipperary's own, Captain Hawkins, now wearing the insignia of a RIC major but dressed in the uniform of a Black and Tan.

"Why that sodding bugger!" shouted Aran to Danny. "He's traded in the uniform of a British officer for one of the Black and Tans, and he's still dealing out his own version of vigilante justice. He's just shot Turlough in cold blood!"

Aran raised his rifle and fired two shots in Hawkins's direction, but he was too far away to be effective.

Defying reason, the Gort Rebel scrambled to his feet. He held up the two disfigured fingers of his right hand. He swore out loud and vowed that the two of them would have it out sooner rather than later.

Aran could see that the British soldiers had left Turlough lying face down among the heather that grew wild upon the mountainside. British covering fire allowed the three plus Hawkins to retreat down the hill dragging their wounded.

The enemy had now completely overrun the village and were fanning out over a three-hundred-yard area. Slowly, they began picking their way, a yard or two at a time, up through rocky terrain. They used the same tactics Caoimhin and Nick Robinson had used. Crawl forward under the protective fire of their rear guard, establish a new position higher up, then fire up the hill themselves while those below scrambled along behind them. Once new ground had been gained, they would repeat the process.

Just as the enemy was gradually coming within Aran's and Danny's firing range, Michael shouted, "Gay's fired twice and he's waving his left hand over his head! The Sassenach are coming around to our left...they'll be swinging around our left flank before long!"

Sure enough, several hundred yards above them, silhouetted against the summer-blue evening sky, Gay was signaling frantically to his three friends below.

Michael waved back at Gay to confirm they had received his warning signal.

Their path of retreat had been agreed upon in advance. With the enemy approaching from in front and the left, they were to take a path north by northeast back in the direction of Nad and O'Reilly's farm.

Looking back down the hillside, Aran counted nine IRA men still on their feet. Turlough was most likely dead and two others appeared wounded. They were on the ground trying to avoid the enemy's rifle fire.

Finding it very difficult to hike up the steep, uneven mountainside, let alone trying to carry a wounded comrade with them, the IRA soldiers were forced to leave their fallen mates behind. Gradually, the retreating men neared the outcropping behind which Aran and his two friends were tucked.

Michael began shouting to the men he knew to follow his lead. The Corkman moved off with his cohorts in tow. Carefully, they began working their way toward the western flank of Musheramore.

Danny took his cue from Michael. He called out the names of the Flying Gaels crawling uphill toward his position. Together, they began following the Cork lads.

By now, Nicholas and Caoimhin had reached Aran's well-protected spot. After catching their breaths, they began firing over the heads of their scrambling comrades and down into the advancing enemy line.

Try as he might, Aran could not pick out the familiar face of Major Hawkins. Suspecting that the man was really a coward in wolf's clothing, Aran imagined Hawkins was now safely out of harm's way, satisfied that he had done his dirty deed for the day.

Aran vaguely recalled Hawkins making some reference to Athy during his torturous interrogation in Tipperary last summer. Somewhere in the back of his mind he wondered if Hawkins had been involved in the cover-up surrounding Brigid's death? Gazing back down the rocky slope, Aran could see Turlough's motionless body lying face down on the hillside. He had become another victim of that spineless creature's cowardliness.

Aran, Caoimhin and Nick began firing at the enemy as the distance between the last retreating IRA soldier and the advancing enemy started to grow wider.

It seemed their bursts of gunfire were having their desired effect. With death staring the Stranger in the face, many of the British forces were growing tired of the chase. They were beginning to slowly retreat back down the mountainside. Several of the Tans, however, had decided to fight it out. They were enthusiastically trading shots with the three Irishmen.

Slowly and taking great care to aim, Aran managed to hit one of the Tans and two of the retreating soldiers. Their cries of pain were just audible over the sharp cracks of the rifle reports.

Disregarding common sense, Aran stood up again. He shouted down the hill, 'Tell your Major Hawkins that the Irish Rebel from Tipperary Town...the one with smashed fingers...sends his ficken regards!"

Then, ducking back down, Aran squeezed off two more rounds. Another enemy of Ireland took his last breath.

Caoimhin and Nick had a few successes of their own. Seven of the enemy now lay in pain or were dead on the rocky surface of Musheramore.

That did it. The British terminated their advance, strapped their rifles to their backs and, with white flags flying and their wounded mates in tow, turned back for the village of Ballynagree. It appeared they were unaware that reinforcements were on their way round the southern flank of the mountain.

Aran, Caoimhin and Nick decided not to wait around. They had no desire to face the reinforcements alone. Keeping low, just in case the Sassenach decided to pull one of their famous 'dirty tricks,' they dropped down to the spots where the two wounded IRA men lay. One of the Corkmen was dead but the other had only a shoulder wound. With the trio's help, the injured man, Jimmy McCooney from nearby Coachford, scrambled back up the hillside toward Nad and safety.

The local villagers would see to it that the two dead IRA men were given their last rites and that the bodies were returned to their families for proper tribute and burial. Aran and Gabriel would personally contact Turlough's uncle in Newcestown as soon as it was safe to do so. They would also write to his family back in Amerikay.

※

It was well after midnight when the three flying Gaels and the wounded McCooney lad reached the O'Reilly farm.

The others were anxiously waiting for them.

Safely back in the barn, Aran described the final stages of the battle and their retreat off the mountainside. With all the men on their knees, Aran offered up a prayer for their dead comrades. Besides the Corkman who had been killed, Turlough was the first Flying Gael to die in the line of duty. All the Volunteers were devastated by the two deaths.

With a heavy heart, Shadow conducted a summary briefing. Eleven of the enemy were down and no telling how many would never get up again. Unfortunately, no weapons were captured and much of the IRA's precious ammunition had been spent. But, all in all, it was a successful confrontation.

The coldhearted murder of Turlough Molloy by the Tans' Major Hawkins opened a few more eyes. Idle gossip had become painful reality as these Irish soldiers saw first hand the level of savagery this new branch of the RIC would resort to in their fight with the Irish Republication Army.

The Black and Tans' policy of 'give no quarter–take no quarter' intensified the growing sense of hatred and feelings of fear this group of English policemen struck in the hearts and minds of the Irish. But, it also further deepened the commitment of those same Irish people to resist to the bitter end the Tans' hostile and intrusive behaviour. The fight for Irish freedom was now out in the open. The bulk of the Eireann's people were coalescing under the banner of Sinn Fein, the Dail, the IRA and local guerrilla fighters like the Flying Gaels. The tide of freedom's violence was rising. At present, there appeared to be no way of stopping its terrible flood.

An hour later, after the new arrivals had eaten a cold supper and were settling down for some much needed sleep, Aran, Shadow, Danny, Gabriel and Michael O'Sullivan huddled together in one corner of the O'Reilly's barn.

They discussed the best decamping strategy for all those assembled. Quickly, a plan was finalised. Small groups of men would leave the Nad farm at various intervals throughout the next day and evening.

Before they all curled up in their blankets for the night, Michael turned to Aran. He thanked him for going back and saving the McCooney boy's life. He also complimented the Gaels for their bravery and fighting spirit.

"It's wonderful to see Irishmen come together, working for the common good. Two often in the past so, we've laboured in opposition to one another. Imagine that if ye will...like dogs scrapping over a bit of food we were. Wasn't I almost forgetting our own petty differences out there today. I can't tell you how good it felt to pull together and work as a team. 'Tis freedom we're after...not our own little self-interests."

Aran nodded and smiled. They talked on for several more minutes about the weals and woes of Irish history.

Sickened by Turlough's murder and thinking back on all that had happened during the past three days, Aran suddenly changed the subject. He was not tired in the least. Apologising to the Corkman for his own ignorance, Aran asked Michael about the origins and prosperity of the tiny bits of ground that served as farm and pastureland in this mountainous region of West Cork.

Michael smiled. Quietly, he launched into a fascinating history lesson that held Shadow, Danny, Gabby and Aran spellbound.

"A twenty-acre field even with a rock showing is indeed a rarity. And small level fields are rare enough. The vast majority are inclined at a more or less difficult angle to the horizontal. All have been reclaimed from the rock, the marsh, the bog, the heather, the brake, and worst of all, from the stony and eroded hillside. The quality of the soil is not good, even in the best pockets."[19-1]

Michael continued his story by rhetorically asking, "What of the people who made the little fields? The best on earth, I would say. Driven long ago from the fertile inland by successive plantations, they took root among the rocks. It is significant that all bear old Irish names. You will rarely find a Planter's name among them. If you do you will find that it is located on a spot worthy occupying."[19-2]

O'Sullivan talked on. "In time, and following a colossal expenditure of human tissue and with the worst of tools, the little fields and cabins showed signs of the owner's industry. They caught the Planter's eye.

"Now having made homes of a sort from hell's alternative, the tormented people expected that at least their right to the meagre fruits of their labour would not be disputed. But the greedy Sassenach eye saw a way further to persecute the mere Irish and at the same time to enrich himself."[19-3]

Without waiting for comment, Michael described how each stone-laden piece of ground was finally cleared of its rocky covering by hand and aching back. The offending boulders were removed and made into stone walls. Some of these constructions were actually five and six feet wide due to the excessive number of stones that had to be cleared from the land.

But then, the powers that be had the unmitigated gall to divide the rocky bits into estates. The overseers classified the Irish farmers' simple mud huts and little cleared fields as 'holdings' and grouped them together into estate 'belongings' for the newly arrived 'landlords' who now employed 'agents' to collect rents taken from the meagre returns the peasant farmers were able to scratch from their plots of land.[19-4]

Michael concluded his story by saying that was how generations of Irish before him came to know, mistrust and hate the greedy, heartless landlord system. It represented British imperialism at its worst.

Michael's Corkish accent suddenly sang out again, "No, life in these parts has never been easy. It has always been a struggle to feed all the mouths, to stay warm and dry in the best of times. But, it is virtually impossible to do so and survive in the worst of times. If it isn't the landlords and their agents, then it is famine, disease or some other act of God that tries to drive our people from the land. Many leave for better places...many died waiting for better times...some waste away in English prisons or at the end of British ropes...but many stay and try to make a go of it. It is a hard life...hard beyond description.

"Aran, I guess that's what we're after doing now, aren't we so? Just trying to make a go of it!" retorted the young Corkman.

"Yes, I think you're right. We're staying on and fighting so those next in line may be better off than the generations before us were...and, please God, better off than our lot today."

Michael's story stirred some deep emotions within Aran. The Gortman became lost in his own thoughts.

After a few moments of contemplation, however, Aran softly began singing a few verses of a song that his grandfather had often sung to him when he was little...a song about a special hero, an often forgotten giant...a man from his part of western Ireland...Michael Davitt.

> The Landlord's agents standing with their crowbars in their
>   hands,
> Four little children watch the fire and do not understand;
> Just another family evicted from their home,
> And the memory never faded for one brave man from Mayo.
>
> He grew up in an English town and ideas filled his head,
> He read about John Mitchel and what Finton Lawlor said;
> How the landed gentry with their property unearned,
> Took the food from millions gave them famine in return.
>
> Michael Davitt was nineteen when he joined the IRB,
> But the police they arrested him in 1870;
> And the lies of the informer sent Michael Davitt down,
> For fifteen years in Dartmoor as a traitor to the crown.
>
> The landlord and his agent wrote Davitt from his cell,
> For selfishness and cruelty they had no parallel;
> And the one thing they're entitled to these idle thoroughbreds,
> Is a one way ticket out of here third class to Holyhead.[19-5]

All thirty-one men in the barracks-barn were up on their elbows or gathered around Aran Roe, Michael and the others as the Irish Rebel finished the moving tribute to Davitt.

> O Forgotten Hero in poverty you came,
> But you never looked for riches and you never looked for fame;

The interest of the common man it was your life's aim,
Forgotten Hero never vanquished in the struggle.

On the ruins of the cottage where first he drew his breath,
Davitt said I hope that I may have the pleasure yet;
Of trampling on the ruins of this greedy useless band,
And driving Landlordism from shores of Ireland.

Davitt saw the Land War as the first step down the track,
And he hoped to see the end of the Queen and the end
of the Union Jack;
And I hope some tremor reached him where he lies in bleak
Mayo,
When they raise the Harp without the Crown above the GPO.

O Forgotten Hero in peace may you reset,
Your heart was always with the poor and the oppressed;
A prison cell could never quell the courage you possessed,
Forgotten Hero never vanquished in the struggle.[19-6]

❧

"GAY? ARAN? Is it ye I hear banging around down there in the
kitchen?"

A moment later, Sarah Anne came flying into the room that was
filled with all manner of good things to eat.

"Yes, by the grace of God, it is the two of you!" exclaimed the
overjoyed young woman.

The next thing Aran knew his sweetheart was in his arms. Her lips
were warmly wetting his as her eager mouth caressed his in return.

Growing jealous of his friend's reception, Gabriel interrupted their
passionate embrace with, "...dear sister and where might my Aine be
after keeping herself?"

Pulling back from Aran's arms, Sarah turned to her brother and
replied, "She's very well thank you. You just missed her. She's gone
over to the Murphys' and should be back within the hour."

Sarah's words were lost as the door banged shut behind her brother.
He was not about to wait an hour or more. He wanted to see his new
wife who two months ago began carrying their first child.

With the excitement of Aran and Gabriel's return filling the air,
Peter McCracken, his wife, Elizabeth, and two of the pub's employees
came down the hallway to greet the returning warriors.

The next minutes were filled with warm greetings and prayerful thanks for the two men's safe return. This was followed by the hurried preparation of a home-cooked meal and several rounds of good Irish stout. With Gay's and Aine's arrival, the two rebels gave detailed accounts of their adventures in West Cork.

As the McCrackens, Aran and Peter's employees sat around the crowded kitchen table, the flow of conversation and family devotion seemed to engulf each and everyone.

Looking around the room at the smiling faces of those present, Aran thought to himself that there was nothing more pleasurable than an Irish homecoming.

❧

As wanted men 'on-the-run,' Aran and Gabriel had to pick their overnight accommodations carefully. But with caution, they were able to spend the next two days with the McCrackens in Cahir.

Aran was still a novice when it came to expressing his love for Sarah. Besides his inexperience, he found it difficult to completely relax and give himself to her. His revolver or automatic were always within arm's reach. The Gortman's body tensed and his senses switched on to 'full alert' at every strange sound or unexpected voice.

Despite these frustrating circumstances, Sarah Anne was melting his heart. She understood Aran's edginess. In the last eight months, she had undertaken four courier missions for Michael Collins. Though each assignment had been successfully completed, Sarah knew the awful toll emotional strain placed on both the mind and body when one was continually exposed to danger and possible death. This, of course, was in addition to the severe physical demands that resulted from living life on-the-run. Thankfully, though, their time alone together became an important form of release. Besides having someone to talk to and to share pent-up thoughts and feelings with, the young couple began enjoying the pleasures of physical love. Just to be gently held and tenderly touched was a powerful balm that helped ease the strains of war. Annie's lips and fingers ignited a glow that Aran had never known. In turn, he was learning to give back to the one he loved.

They often talked about getting married, but the Gortman thought it best to wait until the conflict with England was resolved and Ireland was at peace. Scorning Gay's views on the matter, Aran thought wartime was not conducive to begin a marriage and all the other responsibilities that accompanied such an important commitment.

No, despite the deep-felt feelings Aran and Sarah Anne had for one another, they both agreed that postponing their wedding day until the fighting was over was the best thing to do.

Months ago Aran and Sarah Anne had put to rest his unsettled thoughts about Brigid and her sudden, tragic death. He had come to realise that his Athy feelings were both real and imagined. His youthful innocence had romanticised their forty-eight hours of togetherness in the spring of 1916. She had become a fantasy larger than life.

Yes, Brigid was a rare woman and the O'Mahony family was certainly wonderful, But, Aran in his abrupt desire to be understood, to find comfort and to know love had built a relationship based more on make-believe than on reality. That was not to say that the two of them might not have found true love together, but her tragic death ended that possibility.

Today, Aran took comfort in knowing that he had reserved a loving place in his heart for Brigid Eileen O'Mahony, a place filled with her spirit, her uniqueness and his warm memories of her.

After three years of knowing Sarah, however, Aran was sure of himself and of his love for her. She was his anchor. Annie held his life together amid all the uncertainty, violence and turmoil swirling around him. The Gortman knew that she was the woman for him. He was sure of her and she of him. Together, they hoped and prayed that this horror Ireland was living would soon end. They wanted to begin knitting their lives together...to begin sharing love as it was meant to be shared.

❧

Leaving his weapons and uniform in Gabriel and Sarah Anne's care, Aran rode one of the McCracken family bicycles back to Limerick and Shadow's safe-house west of town. He was careful to travel on little used roads and was fortunate to avoid any encounters with the military or police.

Aran spent several days with Shadow. The two of them renewed their friendship and discussed the results of the recent training exercise in the Boggeragh Mountains. They talked about the progress of the everexpanding war and what assignments would best befit the growing abilities and guerrilla confidence of the Flying Gaels.

They drew up a full report reviewing their military activities and sent it off to Michael Collins in Dublin via the postal train. For once it seemed Ireland had as many agents as did the British. It would be a week or more before they would receive a reply from GHQ, so Aran headed for Gort on his borrowed bicycle.

Again, keeping off the main roads, the Irish Rebel skirted Ennis Town. He slipped in the back door of his family home just in time for one of his mother's fine home-cooked meals.

※

As the summer stretched on, the level of hostilities on both sides continued to accelerate. Isolated detachments of British soldiers were often attacked and relieved of their weapons by small groups of IRA guerrilla fighters.

Late in June, at Jullundar, India, in the Punjab, over two hundred Irish soldiers, members of the famous Connaught Rangers, mutinied over the outrageous behaviour of British-backed forces, particularly the Tans, in Ireland. This legendary unit of fighting men from Ireland's rugged western province laid down their arms and refused any longer to soldier for England. The Rangers could not, in all good conscience, support and fight for an English government that was raining death and destruction on their families, friends and fellow countrymen.

Later, in early August, the British parliament passed and put into force the Restoration of Order in Ireland Act. This action gave the Crown's authorities in Ireland virtually unlimited power over the Irish. Eireann's people could be arrested and held without supporting evidence or benefit of a public trial. An Irishman apprehended carrying a revolver would most likely be shot on the spot...no questions asked...no considerations given.

In September, coroners' inquests became a thing of the past. No longer were official medical inquiries made into the death of IRA soldiers or innocent civilians. In their place, secret British military tribunals were held that effectively covered up any and all outrages committed in the name of preserving the peace and the Empire.

Finally, Irish towns, with their populations of inoffensive men, women and children, now were more frequently coming under attack. In most cases the violating party was England's new police replacements, the Black and Tans. Tuam, County Galway, was partly destroyed and its citizens terrorised while Balbriggan in County Dublin was virtually burned to the ground. Two of its village civilian population were murdered while the remaining inhabitants were forced to flee for their lives. Additionally, the towns of Ennistimon, Lehinch, Milltown Malbay, Fermoy, Lismore, Mallow and Thurles were all partially sacked, destroyed and/or ravaged by the uncontrolled fury of the Tans.

In all fairness, Aran knew that the IRA was not standing idly by while the Tans ran wild over the countryside. The military arm of the Dail was freely carrying out its own brand of death and terror.

Local IRA units continued to disrupt military and police movements by attacking the enemy when they travelled about the countryside. They stepped up their number of raids on barracks in their search for guns and ammunition. Specialised assassination teams sought out and shot spies, informers and government officials who had committed cruel and cowardly acts against the Irish civilian population.

Three individuals of note who tasted the vengeful hand of Michael Collins where District Inspectors Lea Wilson and Phil Kelleher, plus another man, a Mr. Swanzy.

Wilson's death was long overdue in Collins's eyes. Years before on a particular Saturday evening, 29 April 1916 to be exact, while Pearse's surrendered GPO troops spent the night huddled on the grounds of the Rotunda Hospital in Dublin, Captain Lea Wilson made his rounds humiliating and terrorising many of the helpless prisoners. In particular, he singled out fifty-nine-year-old Tom Clarke. Wilson forced Clarke to strip, parade naked in front of the hospital's windows and spend the night without proper clothing. Wilson's mistake was that he did his dirty deeds in front of a then unknown IRA captain by the name of Michael Collins. That night, Mick vowed to even the score. Finally, on the morning of 15 June 1920, Wilson was shot dead by several of the Big Fellow's personal aides. When Mick learned of Wilson's death, he replied, "Good, we got the bugger!"

The next person to taste Collins's personal brand of justice was a man identified simply as Mr. Swanzy. After many inquiries, it was determined that Swanzy was the man who had directed the assassination of Cork's Lord Mayor Thomas MacCurtain. On Collins's orders, he met his end on 22 August 1920. In addition to Swanzy, two other policemen were singled out and shot for assisting in the Mayor's murder. Since Dublin Castle would not act against those responsible for MacCurtain's death, Collins took it upon himself to do so in the name of justice and the Irish people.

Lastly and by some odd quirk of fate, Inspector Kelleher was gunned down in the small family hotel, the Granard Arms, run by Kitty Kiernan, Michael Collins's sweetheart. This County Longford assassination occurred on the evening of 31 October 1920 as retaliation for the British allowing MacCurtain's successor, Terence MacSwiney, to starve to death. Cork's Lord Mayor was protesting England's interference with Ireland's ability to have Eireann's publicly elected representatives and officials carry out their sworn civic duties.

MacSwiney died in late October, 1920 in England's Brixton Prison after surviving seventy-four days without food. During this entire time the British government turned a callous cheek and refused to negotiate a satisfactory solution to the stalemated conflict.

Word of these events were usually passed down to Aran from the frequent conversations he had with Shadow or Liam Mellowes.

As upsetting as these happenings were, Aran noticed one common thread that ran through both the British and IRA acts of violence.

The actions taken by the British government, via the Black and Tans, were often wild, irresponsible acts. They were nothing more than deeds of senseless, vengeful wrath frequently imposed on innocent civilians or their property. Aran speculated these atrocities were caused by the Sassenach's frustration at not being able to apprehend the elusive Irish Republican Army Volunteers. As a result, the enemy took out their vindictiveness on those most handy...the defenceless 'common folk.'

On the other hand, the IRA's violent actions were usually directed at British military units or RIC establishments whose stated purpose was to defeat the IRA and maintain Ireland as a peaceful colonial domain. In undeniable circumstances rebel forces did not hesitate to eliminate those individuals who had committed crimes against Eireann's people...be they military or civilian.

Though Aran detested these acts of violence that he and the IRA committed, the Gortman took comfort in knowing that in almost every case, they were carefully planned actions. They were not random acts of mindless violence. He also noted that the military conduct of the IRA were, whenever possible, directed in accordance with the agreed upon rules of international warfare.

It seemed that England, long known for her meticulous adherence to 'playing it by the book' had abandoned its code of honour, ethics and morality when pressed by an unseasoned band of poorly armed but highly motivated men...young men who would fight to the death to deliver a measure of freedom to Ireland's door.

❧

But of all the events that occurred during the middle months of 1920, the introduction of the Police Auxiliary Cadet Division into Ireland was probably the worst.

Aran learned of this new force, the Auxies as they were called, on a

Flying Gael training exercise in the Silvermines Mountains northeast of Limerick in early September, 1920.

Apparently, British Prime Minister Lloyd George was growing frustrated by the successes achieved by Ireland's upstart little republican army. So, to lessen some of the political pressure he was feeling, Lloyd George decided to give a more or less free rein to militant Cabinet Ministers Sir Hamar Greenwood, Ireland's Chief Secretary, and Winston Churchill, England's War Minister.

They were charged with reversing the direction of the 'situation' in Ireland by applying increased pressure on the Irish to conform to England's rules of law and authority.

Unlike the Black and Tans, who were former enlisted soldiers, the Auxies were chosen from a cadre of ex-British officers, the majority of whom were recruited in England, Scotland and Wales. But, fully one third of this new force were drawn from former British army officers living in the six northeastern counties of Ulster. It was this region of Ireland that had broken away and aligned itself with England. Now, once again, Ireland was to see Irishmen killing Irishmen for political, economic and religious gains.

Like the rest of the British army, this corps d'elite was a blend of fine and not so fine men. Being former officers, however, they appeared to be more intelligent than their counterparts, the Tans. In keeping with their lofty former status, they received one pound a day, twice the pay of their recently enlisted countrymen.

The Auxies, usually clad in smart dark-blue uniforms, wore distinctive black Glengarry caps as their personal signature. They also had the metallic letters 'AC' pinned to the epaulettes of their uniform jackets. Each man was personally armed with two revolvers and carried a rifle. They travelled in especially outfitted Crossley tenders and were supported by armoured cars equipped with Vickers Mark 1 machine guns. More importantly, however, they were not responsible to any other British army or RIC police unit. The Auxies had their own divisional military structure headed by Brigadier-General Frank Crozier. He was solely responsible for assigning individual Cadet units to various RIC barracks throughout Ireland. Their mission was to beef up the resident police force and put an end to all IRA activity in the area.

The Tans were free to commit terror while the Auxies were licensed to kill...and they did so, often without hesitation.

Rumour had it that this elite unit was ordered to carry their revolvers in their hands whenever they left the safety of their RIC barracks. They shot first and asked questions later. As a result, the Auxies's reputation for brutal and cruel behaviour grew rapidly and deservedly. They were a new and powerfully heinous force let loose upon the land.

By September, 1920 five hundred Auxies were stationed in southern Ireland while over twice that many Tans were assigned to supplement the RIC. The IRA was hard pressed to combat the might and strength of this new opponent.

❧

The autumn of 1920 witnessed two other tumultuous events, in addition to MacSwiney's death, that further shaped the future direction of the Irish War of Independence. Both proved to have a profound effect on the Irish struggle and Aran himself.

Beside their personal impact, the IRA was a direct beneficiary of the sudden upturn in violence. Almost overnight, more and more of the Irish population turned to actively support the Volunteers' fight for freedom and victory over England. Besides a jump in army enlistments, the Irish people increasingly provided the IRA with food, clothing, medical attention, safe-houses and messenger services. A general all-around feeling of national solidarity and community support blossomed.

The first dramatic event began on 20 September 1920. A young medical student, Kevin Barry, was arrested in Dublin for having taken part in a raid during which a British soldier was killed. The tragedy occurred in front of a bakery on Church Street just north of the River Liffey.

Most of Dublin came to the defence of the eighteen-year-old medical student. Public opinion used the persuasive argument that as a future doctor, Kevin Barry would soon be able to save the lives of countless other human beings. As a result, the authorities were urged to spare his life and only sentence him to prison. In support of this argument, Barry's lawyer offered evidence that the young man had not been the one who actually pulled the trigger. He had only been one of several individuals peripherally involved in the attack.

But, the British government would have none of it. They stood firm in their demand for Barry's execution. Led by the power of Winston Churchill's office, the authorities hung Kevin in Dublin's Mountjoy Jail on 1 November 1920.

The rationale behind Churchill's decision to execute Kevin centred around the strong worldwide criticism the English were receiving about the wild and uncontrolled, terrorist behaviour of the Black and Tans and the newly arrived Auxiliaries. Publicly, the Minister for War refused to condone the rash of illegal actions and killings going on in Ireland but privately he supported them. With the public clamour in the international press growing more embarrassing, Churchill decided official executions were more acceptable than the unjustified, freelance murders of Irish prisoners who were often 'shot while trying to escape.'

As the date for Barry's execution drew near, Collins became desperate. In early October, he organised a prison break to free the medical student, but it failed.

With time running out and nowhere else to turn, Michael Collins ordered Aran to Dublin. Mick had great faith in his young friend's ability to plan and execute escapes. The Big Fellow had seen the Irish Rebel in action before, both in England and in Dublin. This time, however, nothing seemed to go right. Aran's little group, assisted by two of Collins's associates, were unable to penetrate the added British security deployed in and around the prison.

Again, Ireland was thrown into a grieving posture as the memory of Kevin Barry, Eireann's newest dead hero, was honoured throughout Dublin Town. Then to make matters even worse, Dublin Castle refused to release his body for public burial. The young medical student was buried unceremoniously inside the confines of Mountjoy Jail.

❧

Mick was heartsick. No one could come near him for days. He kept to himself and refused to talk to even his closest associates.

Aran decided to stay on in Dublin, knowing that Collins might want his support after he had recovered from his sense of loss. Besides, the Gortman felt a special closeness toward his commander. He wanted to be with his friend during this sad and difficult time.

The Irish Rebel realised that Kevin Barry had been a sacrificial lamb. England needed to reverse the negative public image caused by the evil deeds committed by the Tans and Auxies. Thus, Britain's new policy of executing publicly convicted criminals, carried out with all the proper legal trappings, was an important step down the road toward rebuilding England's image as a fair and just nation. Her questionable policies regarding Ireland had to be sanitised so that no one at home or abroad could accuse her of criminal conduct unbecoming the Crown or its government.

It also dawned on Aran that Ireland's inner circles may have unofficially condoned Barry's execution as a crude way of drawing more Irish approval and support to its cause.

But none of these coldhearted possibilities made dealing with Barry's senseless death any easier for Aran Roe O'Neill.

Recently, the Irish War of Independence had taken many strange and confusing turns as political intrigue, miliary power grabbing and personal selfishness began assuming precedent over the real and stated reason for the fighting...Ireland's freedom from English rule.

Aran doubted if Patrick Pearse would have been a party to all the behind the scenes happenings that were now going on in Ireland. The purity of the 'wine-red blood' that now 'warmed' Eireann's battlefields in 1920 was not as pure and idealised as his headmaster had once imagined it to be. Aran remembered Pearse saying that slavery was more horrible than bloodshed but he wondered if some of the recent happenings in Dublin and London would also not rank right up there with slavery?

Again, Aran felt that growing feeling of dread returning to the pit of his stomach. It seemed to fester anew after he had learned of the political infighting and jealous backstabbing that had surfaced within the leadership of the Irish government and its military establishment. If Ireland was not careful, she would begin turning her own destructive actions inward. The consequences of such behaviour were too unimaginable for Aran to even think about.

❧

Two days after Kevin Barry's execution, Collins emerged from his cocoon of grief. Through some mysterious transformation, the Big Fellow was himself again. He acted as if nothing tragic had happened...that Kevin's hanging was just a bad dream. Once more, Mick was full of his old energy. With renewed vengeance, he again appeared ready to take on the full might of the British Empire.

The Irish Rebel marvelled at the Corkman's ability to put things behind him...to refocus on the tasks at hand.

Aran was glad he had stayed on in Dublin, for after Collins had conferred with Liam Tobin and Tom Cullen, two of Michael's best and closest friends, he asked to see Aran.

"First, I want to thank you again for all you did in trying to save poor Kevin, may God have mercy on his soul. He was a brave young man and certainly deserved a better fate. But now, Aran, it's our job to see that he didn't die in vain."

Captain O'Neill nodded his head in agreement at his Commander-in-Chief's remark.

Abruptly changing the subject, Collins continued, "As you no doubt are aware, Dublin's been besieged for the past few months with ficken little English spies. It seems there are almost as many of these bloody yokes as there are of us. In case you didn't know, most of these Secret Service agents have been recruited and sent over to us by one bastard of a man, Mr. Basil Thompson of Scotland Yard. Sure, our lot have nicknamed them the 'Cairo Gang' after that popular hangout they frequent in Grafton Street. But, in reality, some of those men did see active duty in the Middle East during the First War."

By now Collins was out of his chair. Like a caged animal, he paced back and forth in front of his cluttered desk.

"Aran, to put it simply, the bloody blighters are just getting too damn close to me and our men."

Again, Aran nodded.

"So, my young friend, we're going to have to take some decisive steps. We must put a halt to their little games once and for all."

Collins punctuated his utterances with several determined swipes at a persistent lock of curly hair that kept falling down onto his forehead.

"In a couple of weeks, the date's not yet fixed, small teams of men are going to pay the gang members a visit. We're going to put an end to their spying shyte. It'll be swift, well timed and very thorough.

"Sure, if we don't do something about them soon, they'll bloody-well do something about us...you can bet, sweet Jaysus, they will!"

By now Collins was pacing almost as fast as he was talking. His right fish pounded forcefully into his left palm. The sounding 'splats' of flesh against flesh seemed to punctuate his every word.

"I want the job pulled off without a hitch. It must be a lightning strike with shocking results, if the Castle is to get the idea we mean business...and it's after business we damn well mean!"

The Big Fellow stopped pacing. He leaned his hips against the edge of the desk. His steely eyes looked long and hard down at Aran seated before him.

"Aran, are you up to shooting a man in cold blood...possibly in his bed with his wife or girlfriend next to him?"

The question shot through Aran like a lightning bolt slamming into a tree trunk.

Narrowing his eyelids, Aran fixed his jaw. The Irish Rebel leaned forward and fired a determined look back at Michael Collins. "If that's what it takes to get those bastards out of Ireland, my answer is yes...YES! YES! YES!"

As Aran said that word over and over to Collins, he wondered to himself if he would live to regret his 'yes' replies.

"Ah indeed! As I'd hoped." Collins smiled. His mood seemed to soften.

He paused a moment, then continued, "I want you to move out of Vaughan's today. The Cairo boys are after watching it too closely. Here's a key to #5 Mespil Road. You remember the place. We all met there just after you returned from Amerikay. Liam, Shadow, Danny, Gabriel and his sister...we were all there...you remember?"

Without waiting for Aran's answer, he went on, "Ah sure, speaking of Gay's sister, I hear congratulations are in order...Shadow said you two were planning to marry. Sarah's a fine woman and a very able agent. She's one of the best I have!"

The fearful determination that had encased his last 'Yes' reply to Collins dissolved into a huge smile. "I knew Shadow could never keep that secret," retorted Aran. "But you're right. Sarah Anne is a wonderful woman and we do mean to marry...after this bloody business is behind us so. But Michael, do mind what you ask her to do, please God."

"You needn't worry your head on that score. Now, keep out of trouble for a few days and I'll let you know as soon as everything is arranged. It may take a while to organise...but certainly by the 25th. How does that suit?"

"Right well it does. You can count on me as always," answered Aran.

The Gortman stood up. He took the key from Collins's hand. Saluting his superior, he turned and walked to the door. Taking its handle in his hand, he hesitated and looked back at Collins.

All he could see was the wavy, dark-haired top of Collins's head. The Corkman was already pouring over the stacks of papers piled up on his desk.

❧

Two and a half weeks later, Aran received his final orders.

The Irish Rebel and a handpicked group of seventeen other men were to meet Michael Collins in the large backroom of the Printer

Union's headquarters at #35 Lower Gardiner Street. As this was going to be a joint operation, most of Collins's 'Twelve Apostles' or 'Squad' were present along with Dick McKee, Dublin Brigade OC, and some of his key officers. In addition to these men, Dick Mulcahy, IRA Chief-of-Staff, and Cathal Brugha, Minister for Defence, were standing against the back wall.

The mood in the room was hushed, serious but alive with energy. These men had come together to make a determined push for Ireland's freedom. Aran felt this could well be one of the most decisive moments in Ireland's long and storied history.

All had assembled except the Big Fellow. Time seemed to crawl as the waiting room grew restless. Had something possibly gone wrong?

Finally, Collins rushed into the room. His face appeared grim...his jaw firmly set.

Without any fanfare, Collins handed each man his assignment. They had been written out on little slips of paper. First, a location was carefully inscribed across the top. Below that, a man's name was neatly typed on the tiny document. Finally, a brief physical description of the intended target was noted.

Nine o'clock the following morning, Sunday, 21 November 1920, had been chosen as the moment when fifteen men, some of England's finest spies, would be shot to death in Dublin Town.

Collins asked if there were any questions.

There were none.

Snapping his briefcase closed, he warned the group to mind themselves. Then unexpectedly, Mick slammed the flat of his hand down on the table before him. "Gentlemen, some men have to die if Ireland is to live. Good luck...God bless ye all...and God Save Ireland!"

That was it. People left the meeting in twos and threes. All went directly to personally selected locations where they would pass on the details of their assigned 'job' to the other men they had chosen to assist them with the next morning's assassination assignment.

Aran, making sure he was not followed, proceeded to a public house just off Grafton Street called The Bailey at #2 Duke Street. He entered the front door, but instead of going into the ground floor saloon, he hurried up the steps to a first floor dining room. There he joined Gabriel McCracken and Liam McCullers who were seated at a table in the back of the room.

McCullers, from Galway Town, was the newest member of the Flying Gaels. He was on his first assignment with the column. Standing just under six feet tall with wavy blond hair, the man owned two of the deepest blue eyes Aran had ever seen. One of Liam's talents, that had first drawn Aran to him, was his unique ability to talk his way out of any imagined difficulty.

Liam's father had been killed by an Auxie one evening last August while he was walking home from work. The officer in charge of the street patrol had ordered him to stop and stand at attention. Apparently, Liam's father did not react fast enough to suit the peeler, so he cooly raised his revolver, shot Mr. McCullers in the head and left him for dead in the street.

Soon after that horrific event, Liam sought out Aran and applied for membership in the Gaels' flying column. Now, three months later, McCullers was sitting in a Dublin pub eagerly awaiting his first 'job.'

Their target, a man named Edward Smith, was a middle-aged Englishman. Aran's slip described him as tall, distinguished-looking, articulate and usually wearing fine gold-rimmed spectacles.

Mr. Smith, however, was no stranger to Aran. During the past year, the Gortman had made a habit of following the careers of English civil servants who were working to thwart Ireland's independence. Britain vainly advertised the careers and accomplishments of their leading politicians in *The Irish Times.*

Recalling what he had read, Aran filled his comrades in on their mark's past. "Our man Smith studied law at Trinity College in his early years. Later, he entered British government service and joined the King's army. He dabbled in military intelligence during the First War and worked for Churchill himself."

After the waiter had delivered three pints of porter to their table, Aran continued in hushed tones. "I know that under Churchill he had been instrumental in helping organise the Auxies.

"Tobin told me tonight that he was the number two man in the Cairo Gang. As a direct result of his bribery and intimidation, five members of Mick's intelligence division have been arrested over the past three months. Four of our best men were brutally beaten and tortured. The fifth, Tommy O'Brien, was 'shot while trying to escape.'"

Before he burned Collins's slip of death in the flame of the table's candle, the Irish Rebel softly read out the address and one other interesting bit,

> Edward Smith, Finbarr's Hotel, Lower
> Mount Street, Room #201 located at
> the head of the stairs with a window

view of the street below. It's rumoured he
has a strong liking for pretty young women.

With the paper evidence destroyed, Aran, Gay and Liam discussed their assignment. They decided that two of them would enter the hotel and do the 'job' while the third covered the main doorway leading out onto the street.

They agreed to draw lots with the odd man being the downstairs lookout.

As the hour was growing late, they ordered, ate a light supper and walked back to their Mespil Road lodgings, each taking a different route.

Just before retiring, the three men pulled slips of paper from Gay's hat. Aran drew the one with the 'x' on it. The responsibility of guarding the doorway was his. Gay and Liam would eliminate Smith.

Not another word was spoken between the three men. They all were lost in their own thoughts about tomorrow's assignment.

❦

A damp chill filled the cloudy morning air. Aran, Gay and Liam were up early, dressed and away from their temporary lodgings shortly after half eight.

The streets were empty. It was only a fifteen minute walk to Lower Mount Street and Smith's hotel.

Each man was well armed. If they were stopped by a patrol of Tans or Auxies, their lives would be forfeited on the spot. Of course, they would go down fighting but, then, their special assignment would be compromised. They knew Collins was expecting each team to successfully complete their assignment. If not, his carefully laid plans would not have their intended impact on the British authorities.

Aran carried his old friend, the Colt .45. Thomas Coogan, his benefactor, lived only a short distance away. He thought to himself, "if Thomas or Anna only knew what this gun has been through..."

In addition to the .45 tucked under his belt and concealed by his trench coat, Aran had his faithful Luger automatic strapped in its little holster beneath his jacket. The German pistol had seen its share of action as well. Aran recalled the shoot-out at the McCrackens farm back in Virginia. He remembered how Gabriel and he had taken on those deranged agents who had tried to kill them back in the autumn of 1916.

Walking nonchalantly, the trio turned down Percy Place and followed the Grand Canal toward Mount Street Bridge.

There on the corner overlooking the narrow canal and bridge was a spot that would go down in Irish history. Now all that remained of Clanwilliam House was a blackened hole. The building's destroyed shell had been pulled down. A yawning opening in the ground was all that was left of Willie Ronan's and his men's gallant fortress that had so bravely withstood Britain's advance into Dublin during Easter Week, 1916. Though the building was gone, the memory of their bravery would never fade in the hearts and minds of those who had fought in the Easter Rebellion.

It was ten minutes to nine. They were less than a block from Smith's hotel. The street was almost deserted. Two all-night celebrants were weaving their way along the footpath. Finally, they turned off into a narrow laneway and disappeared Several early-morning churchgoers were on their way to Mass. An old greying dog limped from door to door hoping to find a few forgotten scraps of something to eat.

Other than that, the street was deserted. All was quiet.

Aran and his two companions ducked into an alleyway. They carefully surveyed the hotel and its brick facade standing directly across the street from them.

An eerie stillness filled the gloomy morning light. A soft rain began falling. Aran pulled his coat collar up around his neck and tried to keep some of the annoying wetness out. With all his senses keenly sharpened, he noticed that the smell of coal smoke seemed unusually strong this morning...so strong he could taste its chalky bitterness on his cotton-dry tongue.

At two minutes to nine, the three men crossed the street and entered the hotel. Aran took up his position just inside the front door while his comrades slipped past him and walked into the building's little lobby. The Gortman had decided to leave the front door slightly ajar so as to have a partial view of the street outside.

Quietly but firmly, Gabriel ordered the sleepy hotel clerk out from behind his counter. He instructed him to lie face down on the floor in full view of Aran's roving eye.

Silently, the two men stole upstairs just as the bells of nearby St. Mary's Church began ringing the hour.

One...two...three...four...

His two comrades had just disappeared up the stairs when Aran noticed two people moving along the footpath several blocks away. There, walking toward him from the Merrion Square end of Lower Mount Street were two Auxiliary policemen. Each man held one of his two revolvers loosely in his hand. As they casually walked along the avenue, the duo appeared to be deeply engrossed in conversation.

Moments later, a woman's screaming voice shattered the stillness of the wet morning.

Most of what she shrieked was unintelligible, but twice the word "murderer" could be clearly discerned.

Seconds later three shots rang out.

The two cadets broke into a run toward Finbarr's hotel.

Aran turned and looked back at the stairs. No sign of Gay or Liam.

Refocusing his attention on the running policemen, Aran noticed they both had drawn their second revolvers. They quickly narrowed the distance between themselves and the hotel. The Auxies appeared eager for action.

Aran had only a moment to think. Gay's and Liam's lives were hanging in the balance...so was his.

He pulled his .45 out from under his belt with his left hand. Holding the weapon behind him, Aran rushed out of the hotel door, turned and ran slowly toward the policemen. As he went, he waved his right arm over his head crying, "Help, help...police...he's going to kill her...he's going to kill her!"

With the woman's screams still audible along the quiet street, Aran shouted down to the Auxies again, "Hurry, quick, a woman's just been shot...in my hotel no less!"

By now, the Auxies were only thirty yards away from Aran. With renewed energy, they ran even faster. As they sprinted towards him, their arms swung wildly back and forth. Their coat-tails billowed out from behind them like huge wings.

Their racing legs and flying arms greatly compromised their ability to accurately aim and fire their service revolvers.

With the distance between the three men rapidly closing, Aran slowed to a stop.

At fifteen yards, Aran swung his Colt .45 out from behind his back. He fired twice.

His bullets hit each man squarely in the chest.

As if dancing a ballet, the two men threw their arms up over their heads. For a long moment, they seemed to gracefully float through the air. But, gradually, their forward running momentum caused the policemen to lose their balance. Now, awkwardly, trying to maintain their footing, the two rozzers toppled earthward...their bullet-penetrated hearts were no longer able to sustain life. They crashed headlong onto the footpath, less than five feet from Aran.

Blood streamed out in two ever-growing pools of red from under their still forms, as life's final moments ebbed from their still twitching bodies.

Aran bent down. He twisted the four revolvers from their helpless fingers. He jammed the weapons in his trench coat pockets.

Turning, he rushed back to the hotel.

Thankfully, the woman had stopped screaming.

His two comrades, standing just inside the doorway, watched his hurried approach.

Gabriel's face was drawn. Tension etched tight lines of fear around the corners of his eyes and mouth. By contrast, Liam appeared surprisingly calm, even composed.

"Sure, are ye two all right?" Aran's words were clipped. They spilled out from between gasps of breath.

"Yes, we're in one piece," responded Gay.

"Did yis finish him off?" demanded Aran, looking toward the stairs.

"He's dead...and may God have mercy on us all," Gay's voice cracked.

"And the woman?"

"She fainted when I tried to gag her," answered Liam.

The three men stood for a brief second, wildly staring at one another.

"Well, then lads, let's get the hell out of here. Fast! Ye both know the plan. We'll meet again tonight."

Aran's words were lost as the three men bolted from the hotel. With accelerating steps, the troika dissolved...each heading off in a different direction.

❧

Moving swiftly through back laneways and side streets, Aran worked his way over to the quiet residential neighbourhood of Wilton Place. He ducked into Thomas's and Anna's carriage house that was tucked behind their nineteenth-century Victorian home.

He had hidden here once before...the Monday after Easter Week when he was first on the run from the British. This morning, the warmth of Thomas's revolver reminded him of its deadly presence as it pressed against his belly. Once again, the .45's loud, clear voice had called out in freedom's name, "Mo Roisin Dubh."

Aran carefully hid his two weapons and the four he had taken off the Auxies. He then settled down to spend the next five or six hours alone with his churning thoughts and emotions. The Irish Rebel wanted to stay out of harm's way for as long as necessary.

Little did Aran imagine the pain and death England would visit on Dublin Town later that day. The Sassenach did themselves proud revengefully repaying Michael Collins and his followers for their 'Bloody Sunday.'

20. Losing & Winning

There's an uneasy breeze a'rustlin the leaves
    in the bushes of Tyrone,
Mournful waves in Galway Bay are whimpering
    in restless tones,
An overcast sky still echoes the cry, a cry that
    never can cease,
Cause Ireland unfree will never be at peace...
Yes, only when she's free will Ireland ever be at
    peace.

Ireland Unfree/Unknown

*T*he level of unconscionable cruelty and unmitigated violence had swollen to unimaginable proportions. Death lurked around village street corners, behind flowery tangled hedgerows and over picturesque stone walls. The pressure to survive much less compete against the Crown's forces was taking a terrible toll on Ireland's soldiers and citizens alike. No one knew when or from where the next wave of hateful fury would descend. Most of life's normalities had ceased to exist. Behaviours too grotesque to imagine were becoming commonplace.

It was no longer wise or safe for Aran Roe O'Neill to visit his home. He and most other members of the Irish Republican Army were forced to seek the refuse of safe-houses in isolated parts of the Irish countryside. The danger of involving innocent family members and their property was too great. If a member of the IRA was discovered hiding in a home, it was often burned to the ground while its adult inhabitants were frequently executed.

The Irish Rebel lived in his clothes...day and night. He spent as much time glancing back over his shoulder as he did looking straight ahead. Every unidentifiable sound caused his heart to skip a beat. Each night he slept with his trusty Luger automatic on the table next to his bed.

❧

Aran did not return home after his 'Bloody Sunday' stint in Dublin. The number and viciousness of violent acts on both sides of the escalating war had multiplied a hundred fold. With the dramatic events of November, 1920, it had proven to be the bloodiest month of the almost two-year-old war.

In an effort to protect the lives and property of the ones they loved, Aran Roe O'Neill and Gabriel McCracken decided to return to the Galty Mountain cottage that had served as their haven of rest after Captain Hawkins so brutally beat them in the early days of July, 1919.

Amid wild and unsubstantiated rumours of a possible truce between the two warring belligerents, Aran and Gay left Dublin on December 13th. They rode bicycles procured for them by Michael Collins, who in addition to his other demanding duties, was now Acting President of Dail Eireann.

After their Sunday morning raid in Lower Mount Street, Aran, Gabriel and Liam McCullers eventually made it safely back to their hideaway in Mespil Road. They followed orders, stayed out of sight and waited for word from Collins.

To their great surprise, the Big Fellow himself arrived at their kitchen door early the next morning. He was in an unusual state of agitation and distress. Mick brought with him news of some truly unbelievable developments. As the three members of the Flying Gaels had been out of touch with the outside world, Collins's news came as a shock.

The word of the deaths of the twelve Cairo Gang members and two Auxiliary Cadets had spread quickly throughout Dublin...much as the bubonic plague had done in the Middle Ages. By noonday Sunday, the entire city was buzzing with the shocking details. Though disturbed at having to order the assassinations, Collins was pleased with the impact his scheme was having on Dublin Castle. English spies were coming out of the woodwork. They rushed, with half-filled suitcases, for the safety of the Castle with its plentiful guest apartments. Other secret agents were turning in their resignations and booking passage on the overnight mail boat to Holyhead and home. This flood of exiting touts, spies and undercover agents from Dublin was exactly what Collins had wanted. Additionally, members of the RIC's undercover Igoe Gang were reported to be leaving Dublin. They were returning to their home barracks in the Irish countryside.

Originally, the authorities had given Head Constable Igoe and his gang a free hand in arresting or, if necessary, executing Michael Collins. They were also assigned the task of putting an end to his associates' ruthless manoeuvres. But, the Big Fellow had turned the tables on them all. His swift and decisive actions had stemmed the Sassenach's espionage activities in Dublin. For all practical purposes, the Corkman seemed to have won 'the battle of the spies.' Needless to say, Collins and his IRB-IRA-Dail Eireann intimates were very pleased with the results of the morning's operation. But, this note of Irish optimist was doomed to be replaced by horror and sadness only hours later.

The Big Fellow knew that a large afternoon crowd was expected to gather at Croke Park for a Gaelic Athletic Association football match between Counties Dublin and Tipperary. Fearing a possible British reprisal, Collins decided, at the last minute, that it would be better to err on the side of caution. Collins tried to cancel the much anticipated sporting event. Unfortunately, word arrived too late to call it off. The contest went ahead as scheduled.

Michael's prophetic fears came to pass. Detachments of Black and Tans and squads of Cadets surrounded Croke Park. Under the guise of seeking out and arresting known Sinn Fein and IRA activists, they moved in. As the two teams battled it out on the pitch, matters suddenly turned violent. These English paramilitaries, enraged by the morning murders, opened fire on the crowd of unsuspecting civilians and athletes. When the final count was taken, thirteen spectators and one player, Michael Hogan from Tipperary, had been killed. Hundreds of other innocent spectators were either wounded or injured in the frightening scramble for safety after the first round of gunfire erupted.

As a crowning blow to the day's death and terror, two British agents, who luckily missed being shot to death by Collins's men that 'Bloody Sunday' morning, tortured and murdered Dick McKee, Peter Clancy and Conor Clune inside the walls of the Castle that night. This was a devastating blow to Collins's organisation as Peter and Dick were both key members of the IRA.

Late on Saturday night, McKee, Dublin's Brigade OC, and Clancy, its Vice Commandant, had been arrested in a British military sweep.

Clune, on the other hand, was an innocent university student. He was in Dublin to research an Irish language project he was working on and to watch the Sunday's football match at Croke Park. The young man had been mistaken for someone else when he was arrested at Vaughan's Hotel on Saturday evening.

With news of the Sunday morning assassinations, the two agents, a Captain King and a Lieutenant Hardy, flew into a rage. After trying to make their captives talk, they shot the three Sunday evening while 'they tried to escape.'

※

After 'Bloody Sunday,' things seemed to go from bad to worse. The war between England and Ireland reached new levels of death and destruction.

Five days later on November 26th, Arthur Griffith, President of the Dail, was arrested by British authorities during a general sweep of known Sinn Fein activists. This unwitting action by the British elevated Michael Collins to the position of Acting President of the Irish government. Now, the power of the country was truly concentrated in one man's hand...the hand of an extremist who would stop at nothing in his quest for Irish independence.

Once again England had shot itself in the foot. In arresting the Dail President, they had removed from circulation Griffith's moderating hand. In its place, the Crown had unwittingly allowed Collins to assume a more powerful and pervasive role in prosecuting the war.

Two days after that, Tom Barry and his newly formed County Cork flying column ambushed and killed seventeen Auxiliary Cadets at Kilmichael, south of Macroom. His attack matched, if not surmounted, the famous Galway-Athlone convoy raid that the Flying Gaels had taken part in during June, 1919.

Finally, in the last seventy-two hours, Lord French, the Lord Lieutenant and Britain's Governor General of Ireland, placed the counties of Cork, Kerry, Tipperary and Limerick under martial law while on December 11th, a mob of drunken, out-of-control Black and Tans burned and destroyed most of central Cork City.

※

Cycling south out of Dublin, Aran Roe and Gabriel McCracken had much to talk and worry about. Though they were travelling without their customary weapons concealed on their person, they still could be stopped for questioning or possible arrest.

Liam McCullers, the third man on their 'Bloody Sunday' team, was safely back in Galway. Only last week, Collins had arranged to have Aran and Gay's revolvers, some much needed rounds of .303 ammunition and two dozen British rifles shipped to the McCrackens' pub. They were expected to arrive on Friday in specially constructed porter barrels that bore the official Guinness Brewery stamp. They were to be part of the brewery's normal weekly delivery, so no one would be the wiser. This was another example of the wide and varied network of 'assistants' Collins had recruited to aid him in his war against the British authorities in Ireland.

Aran knew this journey to Cahir was going to be a sentimental one. Their planned route would take them along the western edge of the Wicklow Mountains, through Athy and on to Kilkenny, Clonmel and finally to the McCrackens' Tipperary pub.

Aran wanted to see how the O'Mahony family was getting on and he wished to introduce them to this friend Gay McCracken. Additionally, he had decided it was time to tell Gran, Hannah and the others about his pending marriage to Sarah Anne. The Irish Rebel hoped they would understand and offer him their blessings.

Surprisingly, the weather was fine for a December day. The two friends made the fifty-mile journey to the Athy farm in just under seven hours.

The spirit of Christmas was everywhere as they walked into the tidy cottage. Rory, now rising sixteen, was as tall as Aran. Mary had turned twelve a month ago and looked more like Brigid every day. Little Annie, two years younger than her sister, was not so little anymore. As Aran looked at the three children, he remembered that it was Annie who had always seemed to keep a special place in her heart for him...it was written all over the pretty freckled face.

Gran looked older. You could see that time and age were finally taking their toll, but her O'Mahony Clan's twinkling eyes still sparkled brightly. Hannah, who Aran had met briefly on his first visit to the farm after Brigid's death, had taken over most of the household responsibilities while Rory and the Ryans managed the farm.

Though they arrived unannounced, the O'Mahonys and the Ryans opened their doors and hearts to Aran and Gabriel. After visiting Brigid's grave, they all returned to the cottage for a lovely night of eating, storytelling and renewing of old friendships. Gran and the children celebrated Gabriel's news of his pending fatherhood and blessed Aran's announcement about his plans to marry Gay's sister, Sarah Anne. They all seemed to fathom the special place Brigid would always have in his heart while they also understood and approved of his desire to marry. Even in her old age, Gran still had a youthful heart. She reassured Aran that he had her blessing too. The elder O'Mahony even gave him a hug when they were alone for a moment in the kitchen after tea.

Relieved, delighted and refreshed by their visit, Aran and Gay headed toward Kilkenny the next day. They took the same route Aran and the great horse, Conor, had taken when he had sought Andrew O'Mahony's help in securing transportation to Limerick in his quest to locate Liam Mellowes after the Easter Rebellion.

Though the morning weather in Athy was fair and dry, it changed soon after they departed. Between lashing bouts of rain and a strong head wind, it took them most of the day to reach Andrew and Auntie O'Mahony's home. Again, they received a most cordial welcome.

Anxious to press on to Cahir and their long-awaited reunion with the McCracken Clan, the two lads declined Andrew's kind offer to stay an extra day to enjoy the pleasures of Auntie's cooking. They were too impatient to get home and did not want to even wait for the skies to clear.

Despite the foul weather and its wetness, the duo were glad for the protection it offered. Though they were travelling through known 'rebel territory,' the wind and rain would keep the Tans and Cadets in their barracks. The byroads were wide open to the two returning, homesick Irish soldiers.

❧

After a brief reunion with the McCrackens, Aran and Gabriel left Cahir and walked up onto the protective heights of the Galty Mountains. With their haversacks filled and their trusty revolvers hidden under their heavy winter coats, the two men again took up housekeeping in the little cabin.

Their lodgings were not quite as rustic as Aran's and Shadow's had been in the West Virginia mountains. In the Galtys they were closer to civilisation and their loved ones but far enough away from military patrols to reside in some degree of comfort and safety. Since Aine was eight months pregnant, she did not risk the difficult journey up into the mountains, but Sarah, Uncle Peter and individual members of the Gaels scheduled periodic visits to the cabin. The welcomed company always brought news of the war, additional supplies and friendly companionship.

❧

Under cover of night, the two rebels left their hidden retreat on Christmas eve. They celebrated that evening and most of the next day with the McCrackens in the pub's upstairs living quarters.

Aran and Sarah Anne hoped this would be the last Christmas they would have to spend apart and under such trying circumstances. The Gortman missed his own family very much but realised his presence at home would be too dangerous for all concerned.

Aran and Gay returned to the cabin on Christmas night. As they climbed the narrow boreen leading to the hideout, snow began falling. With full stomachs and mixed emotions, the rebels fell asleep dreaming of the day when this madness would come to a happy end.

❈

In reality, the difficult times were only just beginning. Two days before Christmas, the Better Government of Ireland Act had become law. In five months, the official division of Ireland was scheduled to take place. The Unionists had finally agreed on a six-county slice of the pie. This decision was a compromise. Originally, they had wanted all of Ulster's nine counties for their own while the nationalists had begrudgingly offered the Orangemen just four of Eirann's sacred thirty-two.

Now, the die was cast. The official division of Ireland into two separate entities was soon to become a reality. Aran could only imagine the troubles that would erupt because of it.

❈

The highlight of the next two months was the birth of Gabriel and Aine's daughter, Mary Margaret Brigid McCracken.

Two days before the child's birth, Aran and Gabriel left their mountain cabin and moved into the pub. On the morning of January 31st, Aran was awakened by the sounds of a newborn's cry. Mary Margaret had entered the world.

The two first names were in honour of Aine's and Gay's mothers' first names. The third name was for Ireland's famous saint or at least that is what Gabby told Aran when his friend queried him about their choice of names. But no matter what Gay said, the Gortman had his own ideas about their decision. Regardless of their motivations, Aran was pleased by the couple's choice of Brigid for their child's middle name.

❈

The next day was ancient Celtic Ireland's first day of spring, Imbolc. With mother and child doing well, the two men thought it best they return to their safe-house in the mountains.

Aran and Gabriel spent the next two weeks alone while the Cahir McCrackens attended to the new baby and its mother's needs. Once again, an Irishman was forced to make a monumental and heart-wrenching sacrifice. To be separated from Aine and Mary Margaret at such an important time was almost more than Gay could tolerate.

❧

In mid-February, Sarah rode up to the safe-house on horseback. Besides some much needed supplies and her own happy disposition, she brought a note to the two men from Shadow. Along with the usual reports of continuous rebel ambushing and RIC counter-attacks, Richard had some important news for them. They were to meet him at his family's mill beside the River Suir, north of Cahir, in two days' time. They were to bring their 'equipment' and should plan on spending the next several weeks 'travelling.'

❧

February was an unusually dirty month. The desperate weather seemed to continue day after day with no sign of letting up. But despite the cold and wetness, Aran and Gabriel were glad to get away from their hideout. The prospects of action appealed to them. They were hungry to get back into the thick of the fray again.

Aran had become aware of warfare's strange dichotomy. On the one hand, the dangers and horrors of fighting the enemy were frighteningly repulsive, but when he was away from the struggle for awhile, something inside him cried out for another round of tilting with the British.

Ever since the aftermath of 'Bloody Sunday' had subsided, Aran's troublesome stomach problems had disappeared. He did not know if he was becoming numb to the bloodshed or his mind somehow had learned to switch off from the revulsion of war. Maybe it had something to do with his resolving the shock and sense of loss over Brigid's death. The O'Mahony family had welcomed him back into their life and did not begrudge him his love for Sarah.

In the final analysis, however, Aran thought that Sarah Anne's presence and their love for each other was the real secret behind his renewed outlook on life. He felt at peace with himself, knowing that his love for Sarah was alive and blossoming. She was not some kind of ghostly substitute for his dead Brigid. She was her own person. She loved Aran for who and what he was. Aran eagerly welcomed her into his life.

Their devotion to a life together in a 'free' Ireland gave him a concrete reason for fighting. He now saw Eireann's continued struggle against the Sassenach as a very personal thing. No longer was he fighting for such vague concepts as national justice, political freedom or international recognition. As 1921 began, Aran was fighting a personal war...a war for Sarah Anne...for his family...for his brave comrades. He was risking his life so Ireland's people might live their lives in the manner they wished...in peaceful repose and rightful celebration of their own uniqueness. It sounded abstract when he talked about it with Gabriel but, in reality, it was a very real and personal matter to him.

❧

The Irish Rebel and the Irish-American slipped in through a side door of the deserted mill house just as night was darkening down. Shadow was alone in the small office next to the grinding room. The mill had been closed since Christmas and would not reopen until the first crop of grain had been harvested in the summer.

The three men had not seen one each other since August last. With brotherly affection, they embraced one another. Then the three men sat down to sandwiches and homemade biscuits that Shadow had thoughtfully brought with him. Gabriel produced a bottle of whiskey and they all toasted his newborn fatherhood. In turn, they saluted the small but continued successes the Irish Republican Army was having against the enemy in Munster.

Feeling sentimental, Aran fished down into his coat pocket and pulled out a tiny metal box. As he slid it open, two small objects fell out. Lying on the table, the Gortman's lily pin shone in the lamplight. It was identical to the one he head given his comrades in Dublin after their return from Amerikay in 1917. The other bit to tumble out was a gnarled piece of lead. Aran reminded his two friends that without their love and nurturing this bullet would have killed him.

The Irish Rebel's remembrances reminded Shadow of their narrow escape from Cratloe, the ship's doctor that saved the critically wounded rebel and the winter they had spent together in the mountains of West Virginia.

In turn, the bullet reminded Gabriel of his family back home in Virginia, the shoot-out with the foreign agents in their barnyard and the beating both he and Aran received at the hands of the deranged Captain Hawkins.

The thirty minutes was spent reliving old adventures and reviewing the events of the past six months.

Shadow still managed to keep the bakery in Limerick going strong despite spending more and more time away from the business, his wife Helen and their three growing daughters. The threat of arrest and IRA organisational duties pulled at him in every direction.

After they each had told a story or two and had finished their meal, Shadow put the kettle on for tea.

Sipping his hot, black concoction laced with good Irish whiskey, Shadow called the business portion of their meeting to order. Several new developments had occurred that concerned them all.

Clearing his throat and glancing at the Gortman in an understanding way, Shadow began, "Aran, the RIC policeman who pulled Brigid from her horse is dead."

He paused to give the Irish Rebel time to react, but Aran said nothing. He only stared down at the cup of tea in his hand.

After a moment, Shadow continued, "Somehow the man had miraculously recovered from his 'riding accident' but had suffered a permanent leg injury from the fall. As a result, he was discharged from the RIC some months later. But, instead of returning to his native Antrim home, he chose to settle in Kildare.

"During the past four years, the IRB has been after keeping an eye on your man. Gradually, they watched him succumb to the evils of drink. His stumbling drunkenness about the town were legend.

"Then, one evening just before Christmas last, he stumbled one time too many so. After coming out of a pub with is belly full of holiday cheer, the drunk collided with a Cadet who'd been drinking too. In the ensuing scramble, the Auxie, with gun in hand, shot your Brigid's tormentor to death. Sure, we'll never know if his death was intentional, accidental or what.

"According to my sources, there was no inquiry into the man's death. Nothing more was every heard about it. 'Twas all closed like the final chapter of some nightmarish book!"

Aran shifted his body in the chair and looked up at Shadow and Gay. "As ye may have guessed, I never really had the stomach to go after the man and blow his brains out so. I think that would have satisfied Collins but it would not have brought her back to me. For the longest time, that was all I ever wanted."

"Aye, 'tis better this way. One drunken eejit shot and killed by another crazy sod...may God have mercy on his rotting dead soul!"

Aran stood up and silently poured himself another tea and whiskey. In an effort to change the subject after a few awkward moments, the Irish Rebel quipped, "Thank God for Gay's whiskey, Shadow. If it wasn't for his spirits, I'd be getting a real strong taste of tea off this hot water of yours!"

The two others laughed. Aran's bit of humour seemed to break the spell of gloom that had befallen the mill's office.

After reloading his cup as well, the Limerick baker continued, "In addition to my Kildare sources, I've recently come across some interesting information about your dear friend, Major Hawkins. I think we can give it full credence. It came directly from an informer inside Dublin Castle. After the beating he gave ye both in Tipperary, I had my contact run a check on him."

Shadow pulled a slip of paper from his pocket and began reading aloud, "George Henry Hawkins, II; Born 1 April 1885...St. Albans, Hertfordshire; Parents: Mary Elizabeth and Colonel George Henry Hawkins; Siblings: one brother, Edward Allyn, two years younger...no sisters; Details: parents upper-middle class; father had a distinguished military career; retired after thirty years of service in His Majesty's army; presently serving as Professor of Military History...Cambridge University; mother: member of prominent London-society family with strong political connexions; Education: Hawkins...schooled at Eton and Oxford...received his commission as lieutenant in the British army in June, 1910; Career: served with various units in both Turkey and France during the First War."

Shadow looked up from his reading and smiled. His eyes glittered red in the lamplight. "Now, sure, this is the interesting bit. Apparently, he rose quickly to the rank of major. Then, in 1915, after some kind of heinous battlefield incident, Hawkins was demoted to sergeant.

"After being busted, he was assigned to the Royal Horse Artillery at Newbridge, the Curragh. But, as a result of some 'mysterious circumstances,' possibly Brigid's death, Hawkins and another soldier were suddenly posted back to London.

"At that point, unfortunately, my source was after losing track of him for several years. However, we do know that in the spring of 1919 your man reappears again so...this time as a British army captain stationed in County Tipperary."

Shadow stood up and stretched his legs. He tore the slip of paper from which he had been referring into bits. Carefully, he tossed them into the fiery belly of the little stove that heated the office.

Turning to face his two comrades, he continued, "About two months after his arrival back in Ireland, Aran saw the blackguard in front of the RIC barracks in Craughwell. Several weeks later, he was after hammering the living daylights out of yis two in Tipperary.

"From all I have been able to gather so, he has a vicious temper, is disliked by the men under him, hates Ireland in general and the IRA in particular. Luckily for him, the bloody shyte is after having his father to thank for bailing him out of numerous scrapes."

Shadow took his seat again. In concluding his remarks, the rebel leader firmly stated, "The IRB Executive has given permission for the three of us to eliminate the bastard when and if we can."

Aran and Gay quickly glanced at one another after hearing Shadow's announcement that Hawkins's name had been placed on the list for elimination. Both were reminded of Michael Collins and his 'Bloody Sunday' assassination scheme.

The two men had spent many hours discussing Mick's tactics in the quiet of their Galty Mountain retreat. They had decided that they were both of one mind...Major Hawkins deserved to die...but only in a fair fight.

Aran said nothing but Gay passed an astute observation. "Shadow, sure after listening to your Hawkins's litany so, one thing strikes me as funny...the three-year gap in his military service record. Why isn't there something about what he'd been up to from the middle of '16 to the spring of '19?"

Answering his own questions, Gay continued, "When something like that happens, especially in the British military, the first thing I think of is 'undercover!' I'm wondering if he wasn't plucked out of the pack for special training?"

Shadow wagged his head in agreement. "It's very possible. His obvious repugnance of Paddies, his interrogation techniques and the ease at which he kills others certainly points in that direction so. When you add it all up, plus factoring in that mysterious time gap, his rapid rise back up the ranks and his new position with the Tans, sure, it certainly makes you wonder doesn't it?"

Aran had been quiet while all this speculation was being batted back and forth. Breaking the silence, the Gortman commented, "Indeed, if any of this is true, I wonder if the British command is holding something over him...like Brigid's death or even worse? Maybe the Limeys are after forcing him into being their dupe...or maybe he just entered the political underworld of his own free will?"

Pausing briefly, Shadow thoughtfully replied, "From all I can gather about this blackguard and his behaviour, I'd guess he went willingly."

Aran agreeing said, "Ah, probably so, Shadow...yes, I'm inclined to agree with you..."

Continuing, he added, "...but in thinking about Brigid...her death and his immediate transfer back to England...that's a big coincidence, no? Though we'll probably never be certain, sure, I'm thinking he was one of the two soldiers involved in attacking her that day...those ficken shytes!"

"If that's true, Aran, does it change your opinion about eliminating him?"

"No, Gay...I don't think so. He's a bloody louser any way you cut it, but I'd rather see him get his in a right fair fight sure. At least my conscience would sleep better that way!"

Leaning forward in his chair, Shadow softly interjected, "I'm after having one other piece of information that may have a bearing on our mutual desire to repay Hawkins for all his dirty tricks. Do ye both remember Mellowes's pledge to solve the mystery of how the British found out we were leaving Ireland in '16?

"Well, after months and months of careful investigation, Liam and I have been able to narrow down the list of possibilities to just one man...Kenny McCoy of Kilrush. Everything seems to fit. He was one of my more hurried Volunteer recruits back in those days. Sure and if he wasn't on guard duty at the safe-house that night. Certainly, he knew of our escape plan. Curiously enough, in going back over the day's happenings, he didn't accompany us on our ride out to Cratloe that morning. For some unexplained reason, he stayed behind.

"Lads, as ye know, we've also had some other problems with the Sassenach knowing in advance about some of our ambushes and raids.

"After careful review, Kenny was the only one of the trusted Gaels who has been in on all of those schemes that went awry so. Never a leader...always a follower, Kenny has played his cards carefully. He only seems to tip off the authorities when something particularly damaging to the British is about to happen."

Aran and Gabriel looked at one another in utter amazement.

"How did ye ever find him out, Shadow?"

"By process of careful elimination, Gay. That, plus some damning information Liam was able to gather from one of his sources inside British military intelligence.

"Mellowes found out that though McCoy was born in County Limerick, his family had moved to London when he was a child. With the possibility of a world war looming on the horizon in late '13, Kenny, probably wishing to avoid possible conscription, moved back to Kilrush. He took up residence with his grandparents. Sure and all this time, if his father hadn't worked his way up the ladder until now he held an important position with a large bank in London's financial district.

"Now, this part is only supposition mind ye, but our best guess is that the British Secret Service found out about the family's Irish connexion and Kenny's sudden move. They must have applied some pressure on the younger McCoy to keep the RIC informed of Volunteer activities in his area. They may have even 'suggested' he enlist in the first place. As a threat if he didn't cooperate, they'd be after impugning his father's banking reputation. That would result in the shattering of his family's professional and social standing in London."

"Those bloody lousers will stop at nothing to get what they want!" exclaimed Gabriel.

"More of the Limeys' dirty tricks, Gay! They're a past master at that art," quipped the Irish Rebel.

"Yes, the world of British intrigue and deception seems to have no conscience and no end," replied Shadow. "But the mistake Kenny made was not tipping us off to the situation in the first place. Once he started passing secrets, he was in over his head. Sure, I'm guessing, he figured there was no way out...no way we'd ever understand. Indeed, he knew we'd kick his bollocks for being the bloody spy that he was. But it's a crying shame! Rather than turn counterspy, he tried to keep both sides happy with his lies and dirty deeds."

"Well, now that you think you have the traitor identified, Shadow, what are we going to do about him?" asked Gay.

"We're going to test the theory while we try and kill two birds with one stone," chuckled the baker.

"As ye well know, ever since our return from Amerikay, Liam and I have never rendezvoused at the same place twice. We keep our personal conferencing strictly to ourselves. That way there's never a danger of someone else finding out where and when we're after planning to meet.

"For the past three years that arrangement has worked out perfectly. But now, we're going to change that just a wee bit. Danny Kelly, Liam and the three of us are going to lay a little trap for Kenny and, if we're lucky, Major Hawkins might fall into it as well.

"I'm going to let it slip to McCoy that our little group plans to meet at my safe-house on the 27th. It'll be for the express purpose of planning the assassination of the 'good' major himself. Kenny knows of the beating ye two suffered at his hands and how Hawkins murdered Turlough in West Cork last summer. I'll also go on about having heard of other IRA atrocities that Hawkins has been involved in and how an IRA death warrant has been sworn out in his name.

"That piece of information should be meaty enough to interest him and draw Hawkins out at the same time. If the major thinks he can eliminate Mellowes and the rest of us in one fell swoop, I'm after betting he won't be able to resist the temptation."

Aran's only reply was, "Sounds pretty dangerous to me, Shadow. Sure, holding ourselves up as bait to that divil of a man could easily backfire if we're not careful."

"It is a bit chancy, I'll admit, but Mellowes wants to clear up the spy-in-our-midst business and nail Hawkins in the process."

⁂

Everything was set. Shadow had let slip the necessary information to McCoy. According to plan, Richard, Danny and Kenny would spend the night of the 26th at the safe-house in preparation for the scheduled meeting the following day.

Aran, Gabriel and a handpicked group of Flying Gaels would meet in Kilmurry, north of Limerick, that same day. These twenty-five men were not to be given any details of their mission or destination. Beside the five close friends, only McCoy knew of the proposed meeting on the 27th.

The scheme entailed Liam Mellowes, again disguised as a priest, arriving at the cottage shortly before dusk. Aran and Gabriel were scheduled to walk in soon afterwards.

Unknown to Kenny, Mellowes actually would be in Dublin on the 27th, meeting with Collins. Aran would don Liam's disguise and Gabriel would deploy the Flying Gaels around the perimeter of the cottage. The Volunteers would be issued an extra supply of ammunition and instructed to be prepared to engage a large contingent of enemy troops.

⁂

The appointed day dawned soft and dreary. Aran and Gay had their forces well hidden and in position by half eleven in the morning. They were dug in along the rise behind the cottage. Nine others took over four of the dwellings at the safe-house end of the little village. All of these home owners were in full accord with the IRA's presence except one. Unfortunately, that woman had to be restrained. She was confined to one of her upstairs bedrooms for safekeeping.

Finally, eight other men occupied key spots at the other end of the village. They were to guard against an enemy advance or retreat from that direction.

At quarter to four in the afternoon, Aran, in his priestly garb and driving a duplicate of Mellowes's famous 2.5 HP Sun motor bike, approached the safe-house from the west. Both his Luger automatic and his Colt .45 were strapped to his legs beneath his religious vestments.

Throughout the day lookouts had been posted, but there had been no signs of any enemy activity in the area. Shadow's cottage door had remained undisturbed as well. Aran and Gay began wondering if Kenny McCoy was really the guilty party that Shadow and Liam sought. Maybe the RIC smelled a trap and were choosing to ignore McCoy's information. British intelligence might have had an accurate fix on Mellowes's whereabouts and wisely had guessed that the scheduled cottage rendezvous was a setup. But with nightfall fast approaching, it was time to put their plan into action.

The late afternoon's first step required Aran driving up to the cottage and parking the motor bike around in back.

The Gortman's suspicions were immediately aroused when no answering knock greeted his coded rapping. Despite his feeling of confidence with Gay and the Gaels covering the cottage, Aran bent down and, from beneath his robes, unstrapped his Colt .45.

With the blackout curtains in place, the exterior of the cottage appeared dark and unoccupied, but whiffs of smoke were visible curling up from the chimney.

The Irish Rebel carefully pushed down on the door's handle. Responding to his pressure, the normally bolted barrier creaked open. Peering inside, Aran saw that the room was dark except for the fire's reddish glow.

With his eyes still unaccustomed to the room's blackness, Aran cautiously stepped inside. Questioningly, he called out, "Shadow...Danny...are yis here?"

His words were still ringing in his ears when Aran felt the cold, barrel-end of a shotgun pressed against the back of his neck.

From behind the door's protective barrier boomed the voice of Kenny McCoy. "Well, look at what we've here...a wolf dressed in sheep's clothing! Aran O'Neill is it! This is a surprise! I was expecting Liam Mellowes himself to be after showing up at this hour."

Kenny jammed his shotgun into the middle of Aran's back. "Drop that revolver of yours and give it a good kick across the room."

Aran hesitated for just a moment.

"I said now or I'll let me gun do the next talking!"

The Gortman dropped his revolver and kicked it into the corner.

"Now, it's down on the floor with you...hands behind your back."

Aran did as he was told.

From his prone position, Aran's eyes darted around the room. There, seated up against the far wall, were Shadow and Danny. Their hands were cuffed in front of them and their legs looked securely tied together with some heavy rope. Both were gagged.

Aran felt, then heard handcuffs being snapped around his wrists.

"Sit over against the wall next to your two friends." Kenny McCoy issued the order like a seasoned military veteran.

The Judas looped a stout rope around Aran's ankles and securely tied it off.

McCoy patted Aran down and discovered his Luger strapped to his right leg. With a dull thud, it joined the Colt across the room.

"What a fecken lot yis are! When it comes to dealing with a professional, ye are after totally outclassed."

All Aran could do was to exchange surprised and angry looks with his two comrades. He could not believe they had allowed this wretched blighter of a British agent get the drop on them.

"O'Neill, how many did ye bring with you?" ordered McCoy.

"More than necessary to do the job on you and your crowd," bragged an infuriated Aran.

McCoy tied a gag over Aran's mouth.

The three captives kept their eyes fixed on the impostor as he lighted the oil lamp and pulled a chair up to the table. He put his shotgun down on its wooden surface and glared at his prisoners.

The cabin's silence was interrupted by a knocking at the door.

Whispering, Kenny warned his captives, "Not a sound out of ye or you're all dead...is that clear?"

Aran glared at the turncoat.

Shadow, recognising the knock, nudged Aran with his elbow. A wild, frightened look spread over his face.

The Gortman recognised his friend's alarm but was helpless to reply.

Aran had also heard those four familiar insistent raps before. Where had it been? Then, suddenly, it hit him...it was Helen, Shadow's wife, knocking at the door. It was the same code she had used back in May, 1916...the night she had first brought him to the cottage to meet Mellowes and her husband.

"What in the world was she doing here?" questioned Aran to himself. Shadow had told him that she and the girls were going to her mother's for a week. With Helen out of harm's way, there was no need to worry her about their little scheme.

With great alarm, Aran realised something must have gone wrong for Helen to be here this evening.

Without waiting to give the coded reply, Kenny pulled open the door. He grabbed a dumbfounded Helen by the arm and quickly pulled her inside the cottage. Helen screamed upon seeing her husband and his two comrades tied up on the floor with their backs against the wall.

McCoy raised his fist and landed a hard blow directly onto her unguarded chin.

Helen slumped to the ground.

McCoy slammed the door shut, tied Helen's hands behind her back and left the woman lying on the flagstoned floor.

McCoy was becoming unnerved. He rushed over to Aran. With his shotgun pointed down at his former comrade, McCoy ordered, "Tell me who and how many are waiting outside?"

Gagged, Aran simply shook his head.

With anger and fear pasted on his face, the erstwhile Flying Gael delivered a hard slap to the side of Aran's face.

Realising he was getting nowhere fast, McCoy spun around, grabbing a groggy Helen by the arm. He roughly pulled the woman to her feet. With a crisp command, "Move!" he half-hauled, half-marched the still-dazed woman to the door.

With a fistful of Helen's hair in one hand, Kenny threw open the cabin's door. Using Shadow's wife as a shield, he yelled out at the night, "I've Doyle, Kelly and O'Neill tied up inside! Doyle's wife is right here with me. If anyone so much as fires a single shot, I'll kill all four of them!

"The Tans are on the way to collect me...so, if yis want to see your friends alive...hold your fire! Understood?"

With that, Kenny dragged Helen back inside the cottage, slammed the door shut and securely bolted it.

Shoving Helen over against the wall with the others, he checked his weapon. Aran could see Kenny's hands shaking as he sat down at the table before his four hostages.

Minutes later the sounds of several lorries filled the evening air. The walls of the little cabin shuddered with their pending arrival.

❧

Gabriel and the other men outside did not have a clue that anything was wrong until Kenny and Helen stepped out of the little house. Yes, they had seen Helen arrive at the cottage door. Gabby questioned her presence on the scene but had dismissed it, speculating she was simply window dressing. But he thought to himself, "My God, Shadow's really playing this one up. I'd never involve my wife in such a dangerous game."

With the unexpected turn of events, the Flying Gaels surrounding the safe-house felt trapped themselves. It seemed like a hopeless imbroglio. If they opened fire and rushed the cottage, McCoy said he would kill their friends and Helen. If they waited for the troops to arrive, their three comrades and possible Helen would be hauled away to face some unknown fate...probably a firing squad...'shot while trying to escape!'

Gabriel did not know what to do next. So, he decided to wait, hoping time would buy him a better alternative.

Minutes later three lorries raced up the narrow road and stopped just before Shadow's cottage.

In the following vehicle's headlamps, Gay could see that the first Tan to hit the ground was none other than Major Hawkins himself. A total of thirty-six men swiftly dismounted from the three vehicles and lined up waiting for further orders. The individual lorry drivers stayed put, manning their steering wheels.

Moments later, the safe-house's front door burst open. McCoy, pushing Helen in front of him, emerged and stood in the lorries' lights.

Partially blinded by their brightness, McCoy called out, "Major...Major Hawkins...is that you?"

"Who the hell do you think it..."

But before Hawkins could finish his admonishment, McCoy yelled out, "It's a trap...it's a bloody trap...we're all surrounded!"

For just a split second, Hawkins appeared paralysed.

McCoy screamed out again, "I've got Doyle, Kelly and O'Neill tied up inside the cabin. What do you want..."

Turning to face his men, the major ordered, "Spread out! Take cover! Fire at anything that moves!"

The commands were barely out of his mouth when Hawkins abruptly wheeled around. With both of his service revolvers blazing, Major Hawkins, the epitome of evil and deception, fired five or six shots into the couple standing in the open doorway.

That was enough for Gabriel. He opened fire with his Lee-Enfield. The low hill bordering the cottage and the street in front suddenly exploded into a cloud of smoke and fiery death. The bark of shotguns and the loud eruptions from several Howth rifles filled the air.

Gay's first three shots tore through Hawkins's body a moment after the force of Hawkins's gunfire had hammered Helen Doyle and Kenny McCoy backwards onto the cottage floor.

Helen was dead before she hit the ground. Shadow watched her die in helpless horror. The love of his life and mother of his children lay dead on the floor across from him. The twisted body of Major Hawkins, lying in the muddy laneway, was partially visible through the doorway. It offered Shadow nothing in the way of satisfaction.

The gunfight outside was short-lived. With their commanding officer down and no place to run, the Black and Tans dropped their weapons, shouting, "We surrender...don't shoot...we give up!"

Ordered to line up facing the lorries with their hands raised overhead, the captured Tans did as they were told. Being alert for possible hidden enemy snipers, the Flying Gaels slowly came out of hiding and surrounded the policemen.

During the next few minutes most of the IRA were busy collecting rifles, revolvers and tying up their captives. In all, twenty-three policemen were arrested. Eight were dead and nine had been wounded. In addition, three lorries plus a large quantity of weapons had been captured.

Gabriel and two others raced to the safe-house. Inside the cottage there was nothing to celebrate. After confirming the death of the man and woman on the floor, they released their three comrades with McCoy's keys found on the table.

Shadow was in shock. Aran and Danny tried to comfort him but it was no use. He heard nothing.

It was not until later that evening that Shadow learned the horrifying details. Helen had returned home unexpectedly because their youngest daughter was ill. Rather than stay with her mother in Sixmilebridge, Helen decided to come home. She wanted Shadow to mind the two older girls while she took their youngest to their neighbouring family doctor. Not knowing anything about her husband's secret plans to trap McCoy, she went looking for him at the safe-house.

It was a freakishly bizarre turn of events. Shadow felt he was to blame for all that went wrong. He cursed himself for not telling Helen of the trap or of not instructing her to stay away from the cottage. He condemned himself for misjudging McCoy and letting him get the drop on Danny and him. He damned himself for his soldier of fortune attitude...for thinking he was indestructible...that he could go out and do battle with a hateful, dishonourable and despicable foe like the Black and Tans and not pay the costs. This enemy was below the level of human contempt...they were subhuman...beyond salvation.

To compound his heartbreak, Shadow knew he would not be able to grieve or even bury his beloved. If he remained at home, he would surely be arrested and most likely shot for his role in this evening's affair.

Aran stayed by his friend's side. He instructed a few of the Gaels to locate a horse and cart with which to take Helen's body back home.

The captured Tans, now tied hand and foot, were loaded into two of the lorries. The dead and wounded were placed onboard the third. With Volunteers behind each wheel, the three vehicles were driven into the outskirts of Limerick. They were emptied of their human cargo and set afire.

Scrawled on a sheet of writing paper and placed in one of the Tan's pocket's was a warning:

> If anyone in or around the scene of this evening's attack is harmed or their property destroyed, every RIC policeman in Limerick will be hunted down and shot to death.

The letter was signed...the Irish Republican Army.

Thirty-nine of the forty Tans were returned and accounted for...that is, all except one. Gabriel directed a detail of four men to take Major Hawkins's body out into a nearby bog. They buried his body in an unmarked grave so the final resting place of this evil man would remain a secret forever.

Aran drove the procured horse and cart back to Shadow's house. His mourning friend sat in back holding Helen's dead body in his arms.

The neighbours were summoned...so was the doctor and a priest. Gabriel dispatched a Volunteer to Sixmilebridge with instructions to notify Helen's family of the tragedy. Shadow gathered his children around him and told them the terrible news. Outside, the Flying Gaels maintained a neighbourhood watch, just in case the Tans decided to retaliate.

Thirty minutes later, Aran, Gabriel and Shadow left the Doyles' home on bicycles. They headed south toward the Galty Mountains. It was a night's ride to their lofty cabin retreat.

Danny Kelly headed off on his own. He travelled all night by bike and then by foot through the Mauherslieve Mountains. He planned to catch the morning train for Dublin in Thurles. The Flying Gael captain would personally report the evening's events to Generals Collins and Mellowes.

❧

So utterly profound was Shadow's sadness and grief that there was little Aran or Gabriel could do or say that would console their friend.

Aran remembered the support Shadow had given him at the McCracken farm in Virginia after he had learned of Brigid's death. He remembered Father and the times they had spent together talking about life and death. The older man's wisdom helped him understand the raging current of emotions that surged through him during those first few weeks of his grief and pain.

Now, it was his turn to help his friend, but nothing seemed to make any difference. His heart went out to Shadow. He did the best he could, but in the end, he felt so inadequate and powerless.

All Shadow wanted was to be with his three girls, but he knew his presence would only jeopardise their safety. His fears were confirmed at the end of their second week in the mountains when they read about the murders of Limerick's Lord Mayor George Clancy and his predecessor Michael O'Callaghan. The Tans had murdered them both in cold blood, in their homes, in front of their defenceless wives.

Shadow was all for calling out the Flying Gaels and going on his own murdering campaign. Somehow, though, Aran and Gabriel were able to talk him out of it.

Less than a week later, however, they received a cryptic message from Tom Barry. Because of his success at Kilmichael on November last, he and his flying column had become folk heroes among the people of West Cork. In his communique, Barry asked for the Gaels' help at a 'meeting' he was organising in a week's time.

With the prospects of returning to action and taking on the enemy, Shadow's dreary mood lifted. He almost seemed his old self again, as plans were made, messages sent out and rendezvouses arranged.

On the night of March 15th, the Flying Gaels came together in a farmhouse just west of Mallow. Danny had contacted the Galway and Clare men. Aine's brother, Pat Grogan, had informed the Limerick and Tipperary contingent.

The first hour was difficult for Shadow. As the men drifted in, each took turns expressing his sorrow over Helen's death. But, once he was up in front of the men giving orders, answering questions and making assignments, Shadow was his old self.

The 'meeting' Barry referred to turned out to be a well organised ambush at Shippool, directly opposite the old castle of Dun-na-Long. After lying in wait for a day and a half without encountering the enemy, Barry's men, reinforced by thirty-seven members of the Flying Gaels, withdrew a few short miles to the northwest. On the evening of March 18th, they proceeded to take up positions along the narrow road leading west out of the village of Crossbarry.

This time luck was on their side. With the arrival of daybreak and a brilliant sunrise, came the unexpected appearance of a larger than usual contingent of British military. They were moving out from their barracks in Bandon.

The veteran Irish guerrillas successfully engaged this enemy convoy containing more than a score of lorries. It proved to be the most momentous battle of the war's West Cork campaign to date.

As the battle raged, the Sassenach's ranks mysteriously swelled. Aran wondered if the British had used the lorries as bait. Seemingly, from out of nowhere, hundreds of fresh British military personnel suddenly appeared and tried to encircle the republican forces.

After several hours of fierce battling, the rebels managed to slip between the enemy's fingers. The partisans disappeared into the surrounding hills and lush countryside.

During the fighting, Aran, Shadow and Gabriel fought side by side. Never before had the Irish Rebel seen the old guerrilla fighter take so many chances and subject himself so often to the Sassenach's fire. On several occasions, the thought flashed through Aran's head that Shadow was daring the enemy to kill him. This death-wish behaviour frightened Aran. He made a mental note to confront his friend with his concern when the fighting was over. The Gortman guessed it was all tied to Helen's murder and Shadow's uncertainty over his living his life without her.

After making good their getaway, the Gaels hightailed it out of West Cork. Shadow and Danny headed for Sixmilebridge and a reunion with Richard's three daughters.

Aran and Gay returned to the Galtys. They spent the next month slipping in and out of Cahir visiting Sarah Anne, Aine and Mary Margaret.

❧

Amid renewed rumours of a truce and cease fire, the War of Independence slowly ground on. Actual face-to-face fighting was now almost entirely restricted to the occasional ambush or weapons raid. Tom Barry's Crossbarry encounter had embarrassed and deflated the British. Press releases stated that Crown troops had lost two men with nine wounded. The truth was that a great many more than two had fallen victim to the IRA. As for the Irish Republican Army, three men had been killed with just two injured. On the IRA plus side, which was never reported, the enemy lost many of their military vehicles and a large quantity arms and ammunition.[20-1]

Lately, the enemy seemed to be keeping to their barracks and military compounds. They acted as if they were afraid of the rebels and appeared unwilling to engage them in combat.

Ah! If the British only knew just how thin the republican forces were stretched. Aran and Gabriel understood how bad things really were for Ireland's army, as they were privy to Mellowes's and Collins's communiques with Shadow. The art of the Irish bluff had been honed to a fine degree. Luckily, the Sassenach had decided not to call the rebel separatists out.

There was one 'official' policy, however, that the British aggressively did practice during the early months of 1921. In an attempt to frighten, intimidate and economically devastate Ireland's citizenry, the Tans, Cadets and British military began burning Irish homes, businesses and, particularly, local creameries and mills. With the milk and grain processing centres destroyed, coupled with the constant disruption of local fairs and markets, much of Ireland's rural economy ground to a halt.

As this new Royal policy of 'authorised reprisals' became apparent, the IRA issued its own warning...if the burnings did not stop immediately, the republicans would burn two Anglo-Irish homes for every Irish house or business that was torched.

It did not take long. After several prominent 'big houses' were burned to the ground, political pressure was brought to bear on the British authorities. Their 'scorched earth policy' was quickly put to a stop.

❧

Just prior to Christmas, 1920, Eamon de Valera had returned to Ireland. He had spent eighteen months in Amerikay raising money for the burgeoning Irish government and trying to gain political recognition for an independent Ireland. His diplomatic skills and inspiring personage gradually became a rallying point for some members of the Dail and much of the Irish populace during the early months of 1921.

One of his statements that garnered particular favour among republicans was de Valera's defence of IRA tactics. When Lloyd George and Churchill complained about Irish 'dirty tricks,' de Valera fired back, "If they (the British) use their tanks and steel-armoured cars, why should we (the IRA) hesitate to use the cover of stone walls and ditches?"[20-2]

Back home again, the Dail's officially elected Prime Minister continued his little charade of calling himself 'Ireland's President' just as he had done throughout his year-and-a-half fund-raising tour of Amerikay. Unfortunately, his presence back home only inflamed the differences that had erupted between key members of the Dail in his absence.

During the height of this intra-governmental squabbling in April, Collins was forced to make a 'flying visit' to his native West Cork. As part of Britain's ongoing reprisal policy in Ireland, Major Arthur Percival, Commander of the Essex Regiment stationed in Bandon, led a group of Cadets and British regulars on a burning campaign that included Michael's family home, Woodfield. On Mick's way back to Dublin, after he had inspected the damage to his family's property, the Big Fellow visited Aran, Gay and Shadow in their mountain retreat. During his brief stay, Collins poured out his frustrations to them about de Valera's constant attempts to interfere with the way he was conducting the war.

The 'Long Fellow,' as de Valera was affectionately called by his friends, had recently been renicknamed the 'Long Hoor' by Collins. This new moniker was earned largely because of Dev's constant interference with Mick's guerrilla warfare policies.

Dev wanted to stage large impressive monthly attacks on key British targets in Ireland. He thought that by pursuing such a strategy, the Irish would gain important international recognition. De Valera also speculated Eireann would receive increased sympathetic support from the United States. Collins disagreed. He maintained that the Irish did not have the manpower or firepower to engage in such a military strategy.

The onerous debate and behind-the-scenes bickering between the two men continued all spring. It caused a divisive split within the Irish cabinet. De Valera and his three political allies, Cathal Brugha, Austin Stack and Robert Barton, lined up against Collins and his backers, Arthur Griffith, William Cosgrave and IRA Chief-of-Staff Richard Mulcahy.

Things finally came to a head at the end of May when de Valera took charge. He ordered a massive attack on Dublin's Customs House on the evening of the 25th. Besides burning many public records, which effectively brought a halt to British governmental administration in Ireland, thousands of other important papers went up in flames. Many tax records and other irreplaceable historical documents were destroyed.

Though the Customs House assault, the largest Irish military manoeuvre since the Easter Rebellion of 1916, was a political and propaganda success, it was also a huge military disaster. On the one hand, it clearly pointed out to Britain and the rest of the world that England's current military campaign in Ireland was not succeeding. On the other hand, the Customs House attack resulted in massive losses for Dublin's beleaguered IRA forces. Six republican Volunteers were killed, a dozen more incurred serious injury and nearly one hundred others were taken captive by the enemy.[20-3, 20-4]

The losses to the Dublin Brigade were so devastating that Collins sent for the three Galty Mountain recluses and two dozen of their Flying Gael comrades.

Amid the renewal of anti-Catholic pogroms in Ulster, Aran, Shadow and Gabriel made their way to Dublin. Scheduled to join them were Pat Grogan, Caoimhin Donleavy, Liam McCullers, Nick Robinson and twenty others. Their job was to shore up the depleted ranks of the local IRA forces, strengthen the security web surrounding key government officials and help Collins refocus his flagging guerrilla campaign against the British.

The month of May, however, did bring some good news. Just prior to the Customs House debacle, Dublin's government received a tremendous vote of public confidence. In a national election, the Irish people voted to retain every standing republican officeholder. This second Dail election gave new life to Sinn Fein's struggling administration. In Ulster, however, the majority Unionist party, not unexpectedly, received the lion's share of its votes. This action ratified Lloyd George's and the Orangemen's successful partitioning of Ireland. There was nothing the southern nationalists could do except continue to arm their northern brothers in light of the increasingly vicious attacks of the Irish-Protestant, pro-unionists against their Irish-Catholic, pro-nationalist neighbours.

At the same time, in an attempt to financially cripple and economically embarrass their northern brethren, the Dail instituted an economic boycott. The importation of all Ulster goods into the south of Ireland was forbidden.

But, in spite of the growing bitterness between north and south, a note of optimism was struck in Belfast on June 22nd. King George V of England made a personal appearance. He formally opened the new Northern Irish parliament. In his speech, he expressed his sincerest hope that the Irish people would soon be at peace and that they could begin working together for the mutual benefit of all concerned.

This invitation by the Crown sparked a renewed round of peace talks between Dublin and London. Prime Ministers Eamon de Valera and Lloyd George began exchanging letters on a regular basis. The core of their paper discussions centred on two key issues. Who would the two governments choose to represent their respective sides at the bargaining table and what post-war political status would Ireland demand.

When Collins and his supporters tried to pin de Valera down as to what position the Irish government should take, Dev was his usual vague political self. Rather than offer his own personal opinion, he stated to his cabinet that the Irish people should have the freedom to choose between a free republic with some possible defensive treaty limitations and dominion status with few if any treaty restrictions.[20-5]

Back at their old haunt on Dublin's Mespil Road, Aran, Shadow and Gabriel spent many hours discussing the constantly changing political climate in Dublin. They felt that Collins's guerrilla war policies had been winning the war for Ireland. Thanks to the IRA's past efforts, the British government was finally being forced to the negotiating table. As their late-night debates dragged on, Aran was always the first to remind his friends of the important role Collins had played in their fight to free Ireland from Britain's rule.

☘

"Women to the left. Men to the right. Queue up smartly you bloody lot!"

Sarah Anne was trapped. The British captain meant business. It was written all over his pockmarked red face. From his puffed appearance, it looked like his shirt was one size too small. Its collar pinched the soft flesh of his neck.

"Jesus, Mary and Joseph I pray to you, what'll I do now?" thought the young Irish-American woman, fighting back the urge to panic and run.

A quick look around told Annie that option was out of the question. There, standing along the quay, was a squad of some fifteen or twenty British soldiers. All armed, all poised for action.

Sarah was returning from England after completing another courier assignment for Michael Collins. Before she had left, the Big Fellow had told her that he thought this one might be the last time he would need her services. His words still rang in her ears, "I think those bloody lousers have finally had enough of Paddy's big toe!"

"Well sure," thought Sarah Anne, "This crowd in front of me doesn't look like they've their tails tucked between their legs. They look right smart and ready for anything."

Collins had said this journey would be her easiest. "Nothing to it, Sarah. Just deliver this communique to my old London Post Office friend, Sam Maguire." The message was on a half page of paper, folded once.

"Here's ten pounds for expenses."

Clutching the document in her hand, Sarah Anne watched the Corkman smile and tilt back in his chair. "Ah, yes indeed," he began. "Ever since that Welsh wizzard Lloyd George declared he had 'murder by the throat,' little did he know it was himself not us he'd be throttling."

Sitting upright again, Collins swore, "That son-of-a-bitch has finally come to realise the IRA is no pushover. We gave him all he wanted and more!"

Sarah Anne nodded.

Flipping back the ever-present drooping lock of hair, Collins added, "Now, it's off with you. Good luck. God speed. Sam will be waiting for you in the fourth row back from the main altar of Brompton's Oratory on Wednesday between eleven and noon. It's in South Kensington. Do you know it?"

"I know it well so. I even went to Mass there on my last trip over."

"Good! Again, God bless..."

Michael Collins jumped up from his chair, pulled on his suit coat and disappeared out the door. Sarah could hear his boots pounding away down the hallway.

Modestly closing the office door, she pick up the folded piece of paper, lifted her skirt and was about to slip it into her hidden waist pouch when the letter fell to the floor.

In stooping to pick it up, Annie could not help but read its short message. "S, LG is begging for a sit down. But before I come over, nail up Henry's picture. M"

Sarah quickly picked up the paper, squirrelled it safely away under the folds of her clothing and left the Sinn Fein headquarter's building.

That was Tuesday morning. It was now two days later. The overnight mailboat from Holyhead had just pulled into Kingstown Harbour. Sarah Anne was only a few short steps from Irish soil.

But that is where it had suddenly stopped being easy. For some reason, the British authorities had decided to search each passenger and go through their cases before allowing anyone to debark.

Collins had told her there would be nothing for her to bring back, but Sam had insisted. He had just obtained six new 455 Webley & Scott Mark 1 automatic pistols and wanted Michael to have them. One by one, Annie's contact had slipped them from under his overcoat and into her small waiting case. "Besides," Sam whispered, "with your Red Cross identity, no one will give you a second look."

Usually that was the case. Twice Sarah had successfully smuggled weapons back into Ireland, not to mention the stacks of bank notes she had distributed to eager IRA commanders. But this time it looked like her luck had run out.

"Come along, Miss. Is that your bag there?"

Flashing her forged pass and American passport, Annie protested, "Corporal, I find this search highly irregular. As a Red Cross representative, I'm exempt from such barbarous tactics."

"Now, never you mind Miss...Miss McCracken, is it? This will only take a moment. Then you can be on your way."

"I insist most strongly. This is an affront to the America that fought by your side in France just three years ago. Have you forgotten already?"

"No, madam, I haven't. I'm just following orders."

By now, the captain in charge had stepped over to see what was causing the delay.

"Sir, me thinks the lady doth protest too much..."

"Corporal, search her suitcase!"

The corporal reached down and lifted Sarah's bag onto the small table setup at the head of the gangplank. Unbuckling its two straps, the soldier pulled it open and peered inside.

"There! Are you satisfied? Nothing but my nightdress and some personal things." Sarah was trying to put up a bold defence.

"What's down here?" the corporal asked. He gingerly began to probe under the top layer of clothing.

"Do you mind, sir! Those are women's things. There're not meant for you to be going through them like that!"

"Captain! Well, look at what we have here!" The solder was holding up one of the six Webleys by its trigger guard.

"Jesus! What in the hell?" The captain's red face turned a deeper shade of crimson as five more automatics were pulled from Sarah's bag. "Madam, I'm arresting you this instant in the name of the Crown. Sergeant, place this woman under close arrest. Transport her immediately to headquarters for questioning. Take that case and all its contents including the weapons with you for evidence."

"Yes, sir!"

The sergeant and three other soldiers surrounded Annie. With her bag in hand, they marched the young woman down the gangplank toward a waiting car.

"Jaysus, Gay! For God's sake, they've got Sarah!"

Aran Roe O'Neill and Gabriel McCracken could not believe their eyes. They had been waiting to surprise Sarah when she stepped off the mailboat. Michael Collins had even suggested it to his two comrades last night. "Yis three can go out to lunch and have a few drinks on me." Those were the Big Fellow's exact words. Grinning from ear to ear, the IRA chief had even slipped Aran a one-pound note.

Dumbfounded, the two veteran IRA men watched the fivesome move along the quay toward a parked Ford.

"Quick! Gay! Get to our motor. We've got to head them off before they take her to some barracks or station house." The two rebels pushed their way through the others who had gathered to meet the boat. Breaking free from the little knot of humanity, they raced toward their vehicle parked a short distance away.

"Gay, you drive. I'll dig out our weapons."

Gabriel started the motor car while Aran flipped up the back seat, exposing a small cache of weapons. With his Colt .45 in his left hand and the trusty Luger jammed under his belt, Aran slid Gay's revolver over onto his lap.

Aran took charge. "There they are...just coming off the quay. Drive right up behind them. We'll have to take them at our first opportunity. No telling if they'll stay here or head for Dublin."

Gabby's only response was, "Aye, aye." For the moment his hands were full dodging a delivery lorry and several strolling pedestrians. Skillfully, however, the Irish-American eased the car in behind their objective.

"Look, Gay. I can see Annie's head...she's there in the back between two Limeys. For God's sake, Gabby, don't let's be squeezing off any rounds from back here. We very well might hit her."

Gay nodded. "That's agreed. No shooting 'til we have a clear shot."

The two cars picked up speed. They headed toward the commercial centre of the little seaside town.

As they turned a corner, Gabriel pointed straight ahead. "Aran, the road narrows down just up ahead. I'm going to overtake them and force their motor off onto the footpath. You take the driver and the one next to him, no?"

The Gortman answered, "Jaysus, what a ficken mess we're in! All right. I'll get the two in front. You take the two with Annie."

The words were hardly out of Aran's mouth when Gay put his boot down. Their Ford jumped ahead. With one half of the rebel's car on the roadway and other half on the left-hand footpath, it pulled even with soldiers' vehicle. Still accelerating, Gay pulled ahead. When he was just over half a car length in front, he gave his steering wheel a hard yank to the right. The two cars made contact. The sound of screeching tyres and crunching metal could be heard for blocks.

The military vehicle was forced off the road. Crossing the footpath, it slammed into the side of a stone house bordering the roadway.

Gay abruptly swung his wheel back to the left, breaking free of the other car. Hitting the brakes hard, Gay almost sent Aran through the windscreen.

"Sweet Jesus in Heaven, Gay..." but the rest of Aran's words were indistinguishable. He flung open his car door and bound out of the vehicle. With his Colt in hand, Aran raced the short distance back to where the military motor was wedged up against the house.

Stopping, he quickly took aim then poured four shots into the driver and man seated next to him. "That'll even things up a wee bit," thought the Irish Rebel. Then in a loud voice, he added, "Your lot's taken one from me but you'll not take another, if I've any say in the matter."

Pulling out his Luger, Aran screamed, "Yis in the back seat...put 'em up, now!" Still stunned from the impact, the two did as they were told.

"You...there...by the door, out of it this instant or you'll be bleeding red all over those shiny brass buttons of yours."

Struggling to untangle himself, the British soldier swung his door open. Quickly he half climbed, half crawled out of the car. "Don't shoot, mister. We'll do what you like. Just leave us be, please."

"Flat on the ground you fecken louser and not another sound out of you!"

By now Gabriel had joined Aran. "I thought you said the two in the back were mine?"

"They are! You're welcome to have a go at them whenever you like."

Without waiting for an answer, the Irish Rebel shouted, "Sarah let's go. Michael's standing us to lunch."

Seconds later, Annie McCracken was beside the Irish Rebel with the troublesome case at her side. Reaching out, she put her hand on Aran's left forearm. Despite his jacket's covering, she could feel his taut, rock-hard muscles beneath the padded sleeve. Involuntarily, she uttered, "Aran, I love you so..."

Without taking his eyes off the man on the ground or the one still in the backseat of the motor car, Aran whispered in reply, "...and I you, my precious Annie."

Still somewhat dazed by the sudden turn of events, Saran Anne was scarcely aware of her brother's hand on her shoulder. "We've no time to waste so, Sarah. This way...now!"

Impatiently, Gabriel McCracken snatched the suitcase away from his sister. With his free hand, he grabbed her wrist. Before she had time to protest, Sarah found herself half-running, half-stumbling behind her brother toward the other motor car.

Aran waved his guns at the surrendered soldiers. "Yis can thank your lucky stars, I'm not a mindless killer like some of your crowd. Do as you're told and you'll only have to answer to your OC, not me. Now, not a sound or move out of ye, do yis hear me?"

He did not wait for their answer. By now Gay had reversed their car to within a few feet of where Aran was standing. "Come on will ye, you crazy Irishman...our tea's getting cold!"

❦

Aran arrived at Batt O'Connor's house at #1 Brendan Road just before nine in the evening. This had been one of Collins's safe-houses throughout the war. Willie Ronan's house was at the bottom of this very street. It had been the scene of Aran's gunfight with the British when he had fought to save Willie and the Walsh brothers from arrest during the aftermath of the Easter Rebellion.

Though the ceasefire was scheduled to take effect at noon the following day, there was no evidence of a pending celebration inside the house. All was quiet. The Irish Rebel wondered if anyone was at home. No one had answered his knock. Finding the door unlocked, he quietly let himself in. The soft light of late evening competed with the gas lamp in the hallway.

As Aran walked into the dimly lit parlour, Michael Collins rose from his chair, walked across the room and threw his arms around him. The Gortman tensed. He was prepared to defend his ears from one of the Big Fellow's infamous attacks, but none came. Instead, Aran received a warm hug and a firm handshake from his superior.

"Aran, we've done it...I'm not sure as yet what we've done but I do know one thing sure, the bloody lousers have had it...we've faced them fair and square and beat the pants off of them!"

Collins motioned the Irish Rebel to a settee. Without asking, the Big Fellow poured two large whiskeys.

With tumbler in hand, Aran stood up. He raised it to eye level. "Here's to you Michael Collins...the man who won the war..."

But, before Aran could finish his toast, Collins interrupted, "...and here's to you, Liam, Shadow, Gabriel, Danny, Sarah Anne and all the others who faced death...almost every day...for Ireland..."

"For Ireland!" repeated Aran.

They each took a swallow.

Once more Aran lifted his glass, "...and to the memory of Patrick Henry Pearse and the other brave men and women of '16...may God have mercy on their souls. They loved their country better than life itself."

Again, they drank a silent salute to their friends who had bravely died so Ireland might one day be free.

Thirty minutes passed quickly as the two friends talked about old business and future plans.

"Michael, the Sassenach were bloody lucky again. Though we made them pay a pretty penny, 'twas the Irish folk that had the worst of it. This fight was on our soil not theirs. It was our people and their belongings and property that paid the heavy price so. They're the innocent victims...the ones who simply wanted a taste of freedom. Sure, it's Ireland's folk who deserve our everlasting thanks for the terrible toll they were forced to pay."

"...and pay they did, Aran...but unless I'm mistaken, there's still a guinea or two to pay yet!"

"What do you mean, Michael?"

"I simply mean this, my friend. With the truce after taking effect tomorrow, what do you think will happen when our lads come out of hiding?"

Without giving Aran an opportunity to reply, Collins continued, "With our identities, strengths and weaknesses exposed, the IRA will be at a great disadvantage if the fighting is ever to resume. It will all be too late. The rabbit will be out of the hat...and sure, there'll be no way to get it back in!"

Shadow, Gabriel and he had already discussed the dangers such a situation posed. There were no easy answers to that eventuality.

Sitting back down, Collins told Aran that the Dail had recently sent money to Clan-na-Gael in New York in partial payment for the many things they had done in support of freedom's cause.

"Aran, my boy, part of that money was a reimbursement and 'a thank you' to Devoy for the Clan's minding Liam, Danny, Shadow and yourself while yis were in Amerikay. I'm planning on sending them more soon."

"I know its like preaching to the choir, Michael, but no amount of money will ever be after repaying all that crowd for what they did in Ireland's name."

Collins nodded his head and refilled their glasses.

Turning up the gas lamp a bit, Michael broke the surprising news to Aran that he wanted to be included in the initial ceasefire discussions over in London. "Can you imagine it Aran, that fecken Long Hoor is dragging his feet about having me on the team!

"You and I know the fighting's over, but there's going to be weeks and months of political wrangling before anything is finally decided."

"You're right, Michael. Sure, Ireland must have its strongest team in there opposite the British. They'll certainly have their best against us. I don't know of any other single person so able and so qualified to represent Ireland as yourself. Please God, Mick, don't let them leave you at home."

Michael Collins nodded again. His smile of appreciation was sincere and heartfelt.

"Aran, I know Shadow, Gay and you will be heading down the country soon...and right well ye should...but be on guard. I want yis to be ready. I may need your talents here in Dublin at a moment's notice."

"Michael, as my commander and friend, you know you only need ask..."

They talked on quietly for a few more minutes. Finally, Aran rose to go. He reached into his haversack and pulled out a scrolled-up piece of heavy paper. He handed it to Collins saying, "I thought you might like to have one of these so. I managed to save a couple. Sure, they're precious few of them around these days."

The Corkman untied the ribbon securing the document and carefully unrolled it. There in his hands was a perfectly preserved copy of the *Proclamation* that Pearse had read to the Irish people from the steps of the GPO on Easter Monday. It was the framework document announcing Ireland's intent to form a self-governing body to direct Eireann's newborn republic.

"I don't know where you got this, but it's something I've wanted from the very beginning. In all the confusion of that day and week that followed, I was never able to find one. Thank you, Aran. I'll be after treasuring this for as long as I live."

Holding the poster in one hand, Collins turned away from Aran. He reached behind the chair he had been sitting in and pulled out a parcel wrapped in brown paper.

"...and this, my Irish Rebel friend, is a little present from me to you."

Aran was surprised. Collins was not the sort of person to give gifts. Feeling a special sense of honour, Aran opened the package.

Carefully folded up inside the wrapping paper was a green flag. Sewn into the centre of it was a large golden harp.

"As you can see, sure, this harp doesn't have a damned crown sitting on top of it!"

Collins let out a laugh and continued, "I've heard you've made a few promises to some of your friends about hoisting one of these atop the GPO. I can't promise you how long it will stay up there, but hopefully, it'll fly from that lofty perch for a good long time."

❧

It was early afternoon. A bright warm sun shone from a cloudless sky on this eleventh day of July, 1921. It reminded Aran of that day five years ago when he proudly marched with Pearse and Connolly from Liberty Hall to the GPO. Looking back on that Easter Monday, he realised it was the day Ireland publicly graduated from constitutional nationalism and headed down the road of revolutionary conspiracy.

Today, in contrast to that historic occasion, Shadow, Gabriel and he were each dressed in their civilian clothes. They wished to hide their military identity from any observing touts. These rebels, however, had made one small concession to the cause they had fought so hard to win. Each wore a small white lily pin in the lapel of his jacket. These were the very badges Aran had given them on their return to Dublin in May, 1917. Each had kept his tucked away for just such an occasion.

As the three men made their way across town, they encountered groups of wildly celebrating Dubliners. The ceasefire had been in effect for the past two hours. As far as anyone could tell, it was holding.

Before they headed straightaway to Broadstone Station and their train bound for the west of Ireland, Aran asked if they could make one brief stop.

Turning right and crossing O'Connell Bridge, the troika headed up Sackville Street, the top and bottom of which were dominated by statues of Ireland's two constitutional heroes, Charles Stewart Parnell and Daniel O'Connell. Aran halted his comrades in front of the GPO. Reconstruction work had begun on the great structure, but it was progressing slowly.

Aran asked his two friends to wait for him on the street. There was something he needed to do. Carefully, concealing Collins's gift under his jacket, Aran hurried inside the skeletonlike interior of his former Easter Rebellion headquarters. Cautiously he made his way up the temporary stairs to his old duty post on the roof of the massive granite-blocked structure. Aran looked out over a Dublin crowned by a sun-filled, blue

Irish sky.

Walking over to the building's tall flagpole, Aran lowered the fluttering Union Jack of Great Britain. Letting it fall to this feet, the Irish Rebel pulled out the bright green flag emblazoned with the golden harp that Michael Collins had given him the evening before.

After carefully fastening the flag to the rope's brass clips, Aran paused. He lowered his head in prayer. The Irish Rebel thanked God for safely delivering him through these last years of war. He thanked him for his family, for his comrades, especially Turlough Molloy, for Father McCracken and old rebel of '67. He thanked God for the special angel he had sent to watch over him. Saying a blessing for all the men and women who had fought to see this flag flying above Dublin Town, Aran Roe O'Neill slowly raised the harp without the crown above the GPO.

Stepping back, he admired the beauty and the meaning of the moment. Aran reminded himself to thank Gabriel for keeping Sarah Anne safe and for fulfilling his promise to his parents back in Virginia. Sarah was his responsibility now. Together, hopefully, they would keep each other safe and out of harm's way.

A soft sea breeze from Dublin Bay and the Irish Sea beyond caught the flag. Its folds unfurled. The green banner proudly began waving over the Irish capital.

Aran imagined this fluttering symbol of unfetteredness was announcing to all the world that a new day had dawned...a day filled with hope, freedom and a bright new tomorrow. "Yes," he thought, "righteous men and women will make this a nation once again."

With his eyes fixed on the flag, Aran raised his hand in salute. Proudly he repeated to himself those celebrated words, "God Save Ireland!"

References

Introduction:
I-1:   C. Desmond Greaves. 1916 *As History: The Myth of the Blood Sacrifice.* Dublin, 1991, 30-33.
I-2:   Ruth Dudley Edwards. *Patrick Pearse: The Triumph of Failure.* London, 1990, 236.
I-3:   F.S.L. Lyons. *Ireland Since the Famine.* London, 1971, 336.
I-4:   Ibid., 337.
I-5:   Piaras Mac Lochlainn. *Last Words.* Dublin, 1990, 170-171.
I-6:   Ibid., 135.
I-7:   Ibid., 136.
I-8:   Ibid., 55-56.
I-9:   George Dangerfield. *The Damnable Question: A History of Anglo-Irish Relations.* New York, 1999, 207.
I-10: Ibid., 207.
I-11: Keith Jeffery, ed. *The Sinn Fein Rebellion As They Saw It.* Dublin, 1999, 64.
I-12: Alan J. Ward. *The Easter Rising: Revolution and Irish Nationalism.* Wheeling, IL, 1980, 143.
I-13: Richard English. *Ernie O'Malley: IRA Intellectual.* Oxford, England, 1998, 9.

Chapter 1:
1-1:   Mary Murry Delaney. *Of Irish Ways.* New York, 1973, 40.
1-2:   Patrick Pearse. *"O'Donovan Rossa's Funeral Address At Graveside."* Dublin, Undated.

Chapter 2:
2-1:   Padraic Pearse. *Selected Poems.* Dublin, 1993, 23-24.

Chapter 3:
3-1:   Unknown, *"These Are My Mountains."* Undated.

Chapter 6:
6-1:   Desmond Ryan. *Remembering Zion.* London, 1934, 119-120.
6-2:   Max Caufield. *The Easter Rebellion.* Dublin, 1995, 42.

Chapter 7:
7-1:   Ryan, op. cit., 117.
7-2:   Caufield, op. cit., 240.

Chapter 8:
8-1:   Mac Lochlainn, op. cit., 193.

Chapter 9:
9-1:   Ryan, op. cit., 34.

Chapter 10:
10-1: T. Ryle Dwyer. *De Valera: The Man & The Myths.* Dublin, 1991, 6-7.
10-2: Desmond Ryan. *The Rising.* Dublin, 1966, 260.
10-3: Thomas Moore. *"The Minstrel Boy,"* Walton's New Treasury of Irish Songs and Bal
       lads, Part 1. Dublin, 1968, 87.
10-4: Cathal Liam. *"Easter, 1916."* Unpublished poem.

Chapter 12:
12-1: Robert Kee. *The Green Flag, Volume II: The Bold Fenian Men.* London, 1972,
       148.
12-1: Donal P. McCracken. *"MacBride's Brigade in the Anglo-Boer War,"* History Ireland,
       Vol. 8, No. 1 (Spring 2000), 26-29.
12-3: Kee. op. cit., 148.
12-4: Ibid., 147.

Chapter 13:
13-1: Ibid., 49-51.
13-2: Ibid., 76-77.

Chapter 14:
14-1: Tim Pat Coogan. *The IRA: A History.* Niwott, CO, 1993, 10-11.
14-2: Walter Macken. *The Scorching Wind.* London, 1966, 126.

Chapter 15:
15-1: Robert Kee. *The Green Flag, Volume III: Ourselves Alone.* London, 1972, 20-21.
15-2: Ibid., 22.
15-3: Ibid., 22.
15-4: Patrick J. Twohig. *Green Tears for Hecuba.* Ballincollig, Ireland, 1994, 393.

Chapter 16:
16-1: T. Ryle Dwyer. *Michael Collins: The Man Who Won The War.* Dublin, 1990, 40.

Chapter 18:
18-1: Kee. *Ourselves Alone.* 79.
18-2: Ibid., 79.
18-3: Paul Johnson. *Ireland.* Chicago, 1980, 94.
18-4: Michael Kenny. *The Fenians.* Dublin, 1994, 13-14.
18-5: Liz Curtis. *The Cause of Ireland.* Dublin, 1994, 72.
18-6: Twohig, op. cit., 401.
18-7: Dan Breen. *My Fight for Irish Freedom.* Dublin, 1981, 81-95.

Chapter 19:
19-1: Michael O'Suilleabhain. *Where Mountainy Men Have Sown.* Dublin, 1965, 13.
19-2: Ibid., 13.

19-3: Ibid., 13-14.

19-4: Ibid., 14.

19-5: Andy Irvine. *"A Forgotten Hero."* (Song) Irish Times: Patrick Street (CD). Danbury, CT, 1990, cut 6.

19-6: Ibid.

Chapter 20:

20-1: Barry, op. cit., 138.

20-2: Twohig, op. cit., 417.

20-3: Coogan, op. cit., 207.

20-4: Dwyer, op. cit., 146.

20-5: T. Ryle Dwyer. *Michael Collins and The Treaty: His Differences with De Valera.* Dublin, 1988. 37.

Historical Notes

The following Historical Notes (HN) are included for the reader wishing additional insights into the persons and events described in the story.

HN-1:   This decision not to treat Collins as one of the 'dangerous ones' was one England would live to regret. It only illustrates that their famed intelligence network in Ireland was not so intelligent after all.

HN-2:   This morning departure was yet another example of the English not understanding the habits and customs of their oppressed neighbours. The Irish are notoriously late risers on weekends and holidays. This Easter Monday was no exception. The Rebellion was not scheduled to start at sunrise...it was meant to begin at twelve noon.

One other bit of British misinformation surrounding the Easter Rising centred upon whom the Stranger chose to point the finger of blame. The Sassenach constantly referred to the rebels as 'Shinners.' This label was slang for members of Ireland's new political party, Sinn Fein, which, loosely translated, meant 'we ourselves' rather than the oft translated 'ourselves alone.' The name expressed the party's desire for independence and self sufficiency instead of emphasing the notion of isolationism. Gradually, however, the party had become a front for Irish revolutionary separatists.

Sinn Fein, organised by Arthur Griffith in 1905, proposed a dual monarchy form of government possessing the freedom to determine its country's political and economic future. In his own mind, it was another nonviolent attempt to wrestle power away from the English. Because of his firmly held beliefs, Griffith wanted no part of any armed revolt. He refused to participate in the early stages of the Easter Week action. But as the fighting continued, he changed his mind and tried joining the rebels occupying the GPO. Connolly and others, however, gently but firmly rejected his offer and sent him back home. The rebellious leaders felt his leadership would be desperately needed after the fighting was over. They wished to keep him from harm's way.

Again, Britain totally misread their Irish opponent. It was not Sinn Fein who had planned the revolt, but rather the Irish Republican Brotherhood supported by Connolly's Citizen Army and selected leaders of the Irish Volunteers. The 'Shinners' were a small political force, not an armed group of rebels fighting for Irish freedom. The fact that some of the rebels belonged to Sinn Fein was incidental. But England, with all it's masterful and intrusive intelligence networks, failed to make that important distinction.

HN-3:   Five St. Enda's students were killed in the Rising while fifteen were arrested and imprisoned in England.

HN-4:   Arthur Griffith, opposed to IRB President Pearse's physical-force tactics, had not taken part in the Easter Rebellion, but that fact did not matter to the vengeful British.

HN-5:   Once before the initials 'IRA' had been used. In 1866, a group of impatient Irish-American soldiers executed a three-pronged attack on English positions in British North America (Canada) after the conclusion of the American Civil War. They hoped to occupy valuable land and a salt-sea port, then use their new possessions as bargaining chips for negotiating Ireland's independence. Though unsuccessful in their efforts, the idea of an Irish army of republicans had been born.

HN-6:   This tactical blunder, combined with Kitchener's inept war policies in Turkey, led to his removal from office. Unfortunately, however, his demotion came too late for many thousands of English, Irish and colonial soldiers and their grief-stricken families.

HN-7:   Though only second-in-command to Michael Mallin at St. Stephen's Green, the Countess Markievicz had dared the English authorities to treat her 'like a man' too. Constance's defiant gesture of kissing her 'Peter-the-Painter,' prior to handing it over to British Major de Courcy Wheeler beside the College of Surgeons, became one of the most celebrated gestures of Easter Week. Her femininity, much to her disappointment, won out in the end. Though sentenced to death for her role in the Rising, the Countess's conviction was commuted to penal servitude for life. On 18 June, 1917 Con Markievicz was released from the women's section of Aylesbury Jail, England. She and one-hundred-twenty-one other prisoners were the last of the Easter Rebellion rebels to be released. They returned to Ireland later that week to a tumultuous reception by the citizens of Dublin.

Glossary

Afrikaner: White South Africans of Dutch descent who settled in the Cape Town region during late seventeenth century as part of the Dutch East India Trading Company's efforts to colonise the area. As trading activity declined, many stayed on and became farmers in the South African, or Transvaal, Republic. Boer is Dutch for farmer.

Aine: Ann/Anne (Irish)

Amadan: Fool (Ir.)

Amerikay: America (Ir.)

Banshee: Wailing female spirit warning of death...'The white angel of death' (Ir.)

Bearna Baoghal: Gap of Danger (Ir.)

Bob: One shilling (1/20 of a pound–old money term used prior to Decimal Day, 15 February 1971)

Bog-trotter: Country hick/simpleton (Ir.)

Boot of a car: Automobile trunk (Ir.)

Boreen: Narrow country lane (Ir.)

Byre: Cowshed/barn

Caffler: A layabout (Ir.)

Cailin: Girl (Ir.)

Caoimhin: Kevin (Ir.)

Cathal: Charles (Ir.)

Ceile: Dance (Ir.)

Childer: Children (Ir.)

Chippings: Small stones

Clan-na-Gael: The IRB's sister organisation in Amerikay. Founded in New York (1867), it eclipsed the older Irish-American Fenian Brotherhood (1858) and continued the pursuit of a free Ireland.

Colleen: Girl (Ir.)

Connacht: One of Ireland's four provinces. The other three are Leinster, Munster and Ulster (Ir.)

Corn: Generic for any field-grown grain crop (Ir.)

Corncrake: Sandpiper-like shore bird with a distinctive, shrill call found in wetlands, especially along the River Shannon

Craic: Merriment/a good time (Ir.)

Cumann na mBan: 'The League of Women' established in 1914 as an auxiliary corps to the Irish Volunteers. Played a largely supportive role during the 1916 Rising but displayed a more active military presence in the War of Independence and Irish Civil War.

Demesne: Land adjacent to an estate, often walled

DMP: Dublin Metropolitan Police

Eejit: Idiot (Ir.)

Eireann/Eire: Ireland (Ir.)

Fecken: Ineffective, irresponsible

Fenian: Specifically, a member of the Fenian Brotherhood founded in United States (1858) whose stated purpose was liberating Ireland. Collectively, any Irish republican wishing to physically overthrow British rule in Ireland.

Furze: Gorse (Ir.)

Gaiters/Puttees: Cloth/leather lower leg coverings usually only worn by military personnel

Gaol: Jail (Ir.)

GHQ: General Headquarters

GOC: General Officer Commanding

GPO: General Post Office

HQ: Headquarters

Hob seat: Narrow shelf/seat built into wall of a fireplace

Hooker: Forty-four foot, wooden fishing/sailing boat (Ir.)

Hoor: Whore

Howth Rifle: 900 obsolete model 71 Mausers first issued to German Army in 1870-71 and later sold to the Russians. These rifles & ammunition were smuggled into Ireland at Howth Harbour, County Dublin on 26 July 1914. Additionally, another 600 rifles & ammunition were landed at Kilcoole, County Wicklow on 1 August 1914. Collectively, these Mausers were often called 'Howth rifles.' (More details available in John Pinkman's In The Legion of The Vanguard, 178-181.)

Humbug: Variety of hard mint sweet or candy

Innisfail: Ireland (Ir.)

IRA: Irish Republican Army

IRB: Originally, Irish Revolutionary Brotherhood (1858) but later changed to Irish Republican Brotherhood. Closely identified with the Fenian Brotherhood in Amerikay.

ICA: Irish Citizens Army

IVF: Irish Volunteer Force

Jumper: Sweater (Ir.)

Liam: William (Ir.)

Mauser rifle: Single loader, 11mm calibre German rifle usually firing a 385-grain bullet

Mheiricea: America (Ir.)

Miecal: Michael (Ir.)

Mo Roisin Dubh: Poetic name for Ireland/My Dark Rosaleen (Ir.)

Model Farm: Local/regional experimental agricultural farm

Navvy: A labourer

OC: Officer Commanding

Orangeman: Member of Orange Order (1795); usually of Protestant, pro-unionist and anti-Catholic, anti-nationalist leanings

Padraic/Padraig: Patrick (Ir.)

Peeler: Policeman (Slang)

Peter-the-Painter: German 7.63mm (sometimes modified to 9mm) Mauser automatic pistol (Parabellum) nicknamed for Peter Piaktow, a Russian anarchist, who participated in 1911 revolt in London, England.

Petrol: Gasoline

Pitch: Playing field

Planter: Usually, an English or Scottish colonist given land in Ireland as a reward or gift for the purpose of returning some economic, political or military advantage to the

Crown. Irish landholders were involuntarily displaced from their property by the authorities to make way for the newcomers.

Poitin: Home brew/moonshine (Ir.)

Press: Shelved cupboard; sometimes slang for a closet (Ir.)

Punt: Unit of currency = one pound (Ir.)

Quay: Dock/ship berth

RIC: Royal Irish Constabulary...Ireland's police force until 1922

Rozzer: Policeman (Slang)

Sassenach: The English who occupied Ireland (Ir.)

Scoil Eanna: St. Enda's School (Ir.)

Sean: John (Ir.)

Shinner: Member of Sinn Fein political party (Ir.)

Slagging: Having someone on...teasing

Saoirse: Freedom (Ir.)

Stone: Unit of weight...14 pounds

Sugan: Woven rope/reed-bottomed chair (Ir.)

Taig: Derogatory Protestant name for a Catholic (Ir.)

Tea time: Supper or evening meal

The Stranger: The English who occupied Ireland (Ir.)

Tory: Member of British Conservative political party

Truckle bed: Low bed on wheels

UVF: Ulster Volunteer Force

Whig: Member of British Liberal political party

Yeoman: An Anglo-Irish landowner loyal to the Crown. Often served as a member of a pro-British cavalry force in eighteenth century.

Selected Bibliography

Barry, Tom. *Guerilla Days in Ireland.* Dublin: Anvil Books, 1989.

Beaslai, Piaras. *Michael Collins and the Making of a New Ireland.* 2 vols. Dublin: Phoenix, 1926.

Bell, J. Bowyer. *The Gun in Politics: An Analysis of Irish Political Conflict, 1916-1986.* New Brunswick, NJ: Transaction Publishers, 1991.

Bennett, Richard. *The Black and Tans: The British Special Police in Ireland.* New York: Barnes & Noble, Inc., 1959.

Boylan, Henry. *A Dictionary of Irish Biography.* Niwot, CO: Roberts Rinehart Publishers, 1998.

Breen, Dan. *My Fight for Irish Freedom.* Dublin: Anvil Books, 1981.

Brennan-Whitmore, W.J. *Dublin Burning: The Easter Rising from Behind the Barricades.* Dublin: Gill & Macmillan, 1996.

Browne, Gretta Curran. *Tread Softly on My Dreams: Robert Emmet's Story.* Dublin: Wolfhound Press Ltd., 1998.

Caufield, Max. *The Easter Rebellion.* Dublin: Gill & Macmillan, 1995.

Coffey, Thomas M. *Agony at Easter: The 1916 Irish Uprising.* London: George G. Harrap & Co. Ltd., 1970.

Collins, Michael. *The Path to Freedom: Articles and speeches by Michael Collins.* Dublin: Mercier Press, 1995.

Connolly, Colm. *Michael Collins.* London: Weidenfeld & Nicolson, 1996.

Connolly, S.J., ed. *The Oxford Companion to Irish History.* Oxford, England: Oxford University Press, 1998.

Coogan, Tim Pat. *Michael Collins.* London: Arrow Books Limited, 1991.

Coogan, Tim Pat. *The IRA: A History.* Niwot, CO: Roberts Rinehard Publishers, 1993.

Coogan, Tim Pat. *The Man Who Made Ireland: The Life and Death of Michael Collins.* Niwot, CO: Roberts Rinehart Publishers, 1992.

Coogan, Timothy Patrick. *Ireland Since the Rising.* London: Pall Mall Press, 1966.

Coogan, Tim Pat and George Morrison. *The Irish Civil War.* Boulder, CO: Roberts Rinehart Publishers, 1998.

Corcoran, T. *John Mitchel: The Jail Journal (1848-1853).* Dublin: Browne and Nolan, Limited, Undated.

Costelle, Francis, ed. *Michael Collins: In His Own Words.* Dublin: Gill & Macmillan, 1997.

Crealey, Aidan H. *An Irish Almanac: Notable Events in Ireland from 1014 to the Present.* Dublin: Mercier Press, 1993.

Curtis, Liz. *The Cause of Ireland: From the United Irishmen to Partition.* Belfast: Beyond the Pale Publications, 1994.

Danaher, Kevin. *In Ireland Long Ago.* Dublin: The Mercier Press, 1962.

Dangerfield, George. *The Damnable Question: A History of Anglo-Irish Relations.* New York: Barnes & Noble Books, 1999.

David, Richard. *Arthur Griffith and Non-Violent Sinn Fein.* Dublin: Anvil Books, 1974.

De Paor, Liam, ed. *Milestones in Irish History.* Boulder, CO: Irish American Book Company, 1986.

De Paor, Liam. *The People of Ireland: From Prehistory to Modern Times.* London: Hutchinson & Co. Ltd, 1986.

De Rosa, Peter. *Rebels: The Irish Rising of 1916.* New York: Fawcett Columbine, 1990.

Deasy, Liam. *Towards Ireland Free: The West Cork Brigade in the War of Independence 1917- 1921.* Cork, Ireland: Royal Carbery Books Limited, 1992.

Delaney, Mary Murry. *Of Irish Ways.* New York: Harper & Row Publishers, 1973.

Doherty, Gabriel and Dermot Keogh, eds. *Michael Collins and the Making of the Irish State* Dublin: Mercier Press, 1998.

Doyle, Roddy. *A Star Called Henry.* New York: Viking, 1999.

Dwyer, T. Ryle. *Big Fellow, Long Fellow: A Joint Biography of Collins & de Valera.* New York: St. Martin's Press. 1998.

Dwyer, T. Ryle. *De Valera: The Man & the Myths.* Dublin: Poolbeg Press Ltd., 1991.

Dwyer, T. Ryle. *Eamon De Valera.* Dublin: Gill & Macmillan Ltd., 1998.

Dwyer, T. Ryle. *Michael Collins: The Man Who Won the War.* Dublin: Mercier Press, 1990.

Dwyer T. Ryle. *Michael Collins and the Treaty: His Differences with De Valera.* Dublin: The Mercier Press, 1981.

Edwards, Ruth Dudley. *Patrick Pearse: The Triumph of Failure.* London: Poolbeg Press Ltd., 1990.

English, Richard. *Ernie O'Malley: IRA Intellectual.* Oxford, England: Clarendon Press, 1998.

Flanagan, Thomas. *The End of the Hunt.* New York: Penguin Group, 1994.

Forester, Margery. *Michael Collins: The Lost Leader.* Dublin: Gill and Macmillan, 1971.

Foster, R.F., ed. *The Oxford Illustrated History of Ireland.* Oxford, England: Oxford University Press, 1989.

Foy, Michael and Brian Barton. *The Easter Rising.* Phoenix Mill Thrupp, Stroud, Gloucestershire, England: Sutton Publishing Limited, 1999.

Fry, Peter and Fiona Sommerset Fry. *A History of Ireland.* New York: Barnes & Noble Books, 1988.

Galvin Michael. *Kilmurry Volunteers: 1915-1921: Climax On Road to Independence 1775-1915.* County Cork, Ireland: Litho Press Co., Undated.

Garvin, Tom. *1922: The Birth of Irish Democracy,* Dublin: Gill & Macmillan, 1996.

Golway, Terry. *For the Cause of Liberty: A Thousand Years of Ireland's Heroes.* New York: Simon & Schuster, 2000.

Golway, Terry. *Irish Rebel: John Devoy and America's Fight for Ireland's Freedom.* New York: St. Martin's Press, 1998.

Good, Joe. *Enchanted by Dreams: The Journal of A Revolutionary.* Dingle, Ireland: Brandon, 1996.

Hachey, Thomas E. and Lawrence J. McCaffrey, eds. *Perspectives on Irish Nationalism.* Lexington, KY: The University Press of Kentucky, 1989.

Hart, Peter. *The I.R.A. & Its Enemies: Violence and Community in Cork 1916-1923.* Oxford, England: Oxford University Press, 1999.

Haverty, Anne. *Constance Markievicz: Irish Revolutionary.* London: Pandora, 1988.

Hogg, Ian V. and John S. Weeks. *Military Small Arms of the 20th Century,* 7th Ed. Iola, WI: Krause Publications, 2000.

Graves, C. Desmond. *1916 As History: The Myth of the Blood Sacrifice*. Dublin: The Fulcrum Press, 1991.

Griffith, Kenneth and Timothy O'Grady. *Ireland's Unfinished Revolution: An Oral History*. Boulder, CO: Roberts Rinehart Publishers, 1999.

Irvine, Andy. *"A Forgotten Hero," Irish Times: Patrick Street*. Danbury, CT: Green Linnet Records, Inc., 1990.

Jackson, Alvin. *Ireland 1978-1998*. Oxford, England: Blackwell, Publishers, 1999.

Jeffery, Keith, ed. *The Sinn Fein Rebellion As They Saw It*. Dublin: Irish Academic Press, 1999.

Johnson, Paul. *Ireland: A Concise History from the Twelfth Century to the Present Day*. Chicago: Academy Chicago Publishers, 1980.

Kee, Robert. *The Green Flag*. Vol. I, *The Most Distressful Country*. Dublin: Penguin Books, 1972.

Kee, Robert. *The Green Flag*, Vol. II, *The Bold Fenian Men*. Dublin: Penguin Books, 1972.

Kee, Robert. *The Green Flag*, Vol. III, *Ourselves Alone*. Dublin: Penguin Books, 1972.

Kenny, Michael. *The Fenians*. Dublin: Country House, 1994.

Kenny, Michael. *The Road to Freedom: Photographs and Memorabilia from the 1916 Rising and Afterwards*. Dublin: Country House, 1993.

Killeen, Richard. *A Short History of Ireland*. Dublin: Gill & Macmillan, 1994.

Killeen, Richard. *The Easter Rising*. Dublin: Gill & Macmillan, 1995.

Kostick, Conor. *Revolution in Ireland: Popular Militancy 1917 to 1923*. London: Pluto Press, 1996.

Laffan, Michael. *The Partition of Ireland 1911-1925*. Dundalk, Ireland: Dungalgan Press, 1983.

Lee, J.J. *Ireland 1912-1985: Politics and Society*. New York: Cambridge University Press, 1992.

Little, Niall. *"A Terrible Beauty Is Born": Ireland Begins Her Final Stand for Freedom*. Unpublished Historical Paper, Charlottesville, VA, 1996.

Litton, Helen. *Irish Rebellions 1798-1916: An Illustrated History*. Dublin: Wolfhound Press, 1998.

Llywelyn, Morgan. *1916: A Novel of the Irish Rebellion*. New York: Forge, 1998.

Lyons, F.S.L. *Charles Stewart Parnell*. London: Fontana Press, 1991.

Lyons, F.S.L. *Ireland Since the Famine*. London: Fontana Press, 1985.

Mac Lochlainn, Piaras F. *Last Words: Letters and Statements of the Leaders Executed After the Rising at Easter 1916*. Dublin: The Office of Public Works, 1990.

MacArdle, Dorothy. *The Irish Republic*. Dublin: Wolfhound Press, 1999.

MacDowell, Vincent. *Michael Collins and the Brotherhood*. Dublin: Ashfield Press, 1997.

MacKay, James. *Michael Collins: A Life*. Edinburgh: Mainstream Publishing, 1996.

Macken, Walter. *The Scorching Wind*. London: Pan Books, 1964.

MacManus, Seamus. *The Story of the Irish Race*. Avenel, New Jersey: Wings Books, 1966.

McCaffrey, Lawrence J. *The Irish Question: Two Centuries of Conflict*. Lexington, Kentucky: The University Press of Kentucky, 1995.

McRedmond, Louis, ed. *Ireland The Revolutionary Years: Photographs from the Cashman Collection Ireland 1910-30*. Dublin: Gill and Macmillan & Radio Telefís Eireann, 1992.

Moody, T.W. & F.X. martin, eds. *The Course of Irish History*. Dublin: The Mercier Press, 1995.

Murphy, Brian P. *Patrick Pearse and the Lost Republican Ideal.* Dublin: James Duffy, 1990.

Neligan, David. *The Spy in the Castle.* London: Prendeville Publishing Limited, 1999.

Ni Dhonnchadha, Mairin and Theo Dorgan, eds. *Revising the Rising.* Derry, Northern Ireland: Field Day, 1991.

O'Brien, Brendan. *A Pocket History of the IRA.* Dublin: The O'Brien Press, 1997.

O'Broin, Leon, ed. *In Great Haste: The Letters of Michael Collins and Kitty Kiernan.* Dublin: Gil & Macmillan, 1996.

O'Broin, Leon. *Michael Collins.* Dublin: Gill & Macmillan, 1980.

O'Connor, Batt. *With Michael Collins in the Fight for Irish Independence.* London: Peter Davies, Ltd., 1929.

O'Connor, Frank. *The Big Fellow.* Dublin: Poolbeg Press Ltd., 1979.

O'Connor, Seamus. *Tomorrow Was Another Day: Irreverent Memories of an Irish Rebel Schoolmaster.* Dublin: ROC Publications, 1987.

O'Connor, Ulick. *The Troubles.* London: Mandarin, 1975.

O'Donoghue, Florence. *No Other Law.* Dublin: Anvil Books Limited, 1986.

O'Farrell, Mick. *A Walk Through Rebel Dublin 1916.* Dublin: Mercier Press, 1999.

O'Farrell, Padraic. *Rebel Heart.* Dingle, Ireland: Brandon Book Publishers, Ltd., 1996.

O'Farrell, Padraic. *Sean Mac Eoin: The Blacksmith of Ballinalee.* Mullingar, Ireland: Uisneach Press, 1993.

O'Flaherty, Liam. *Insurrection.* Dublin: Wolfhound Press, 1993.

O'Hegarty, P.S. *The Victory of Sinn Fein.* Dublin: University College Dublin Press, 1998.

O'Laoi, Padraic. *Fr. Griffin 1892-1920.* Galway, Ireland: The Connacht Tribune Ltd., 1994.

O'Mahony, Sean. *Frongoch: University of Revolution.* Dublin: FDR Teoranta, 1987.

O'Malley, Ernie. *On Another Man's Wound.* Dublin: Anvil Books, 1979.

O'Malley, Ernie. *Raids and Rallies.* Dublin: Anvil Books Limited, 1982.

O'Rahilly, Aodogan. *Winding the Clock: O'Rahilly and the 1916 Rising.* Dublin: The Lilliput Press, 1991.

O'Siochain, P.A. *Ireland: Journey to Freedom.* Ireland: Kells Publishing Co. Ltd., Undated.

O'Suilleabhain, Michael. *Where Mountainy Men Have Sown: War and Peace in Rebel Cork in the Turbulent Years 1916-21.* Tralee, Ireland: Anvil Books, 1965.

Pearse, Padraic. *Selected Poems: Rogha Danta.* Dublin: New Island Books, 1993.

Pinkman, John A. *In The Legion of the Vanguard.* Boulder, CO: Mercier Press, 1998.

Ranelgah, John O'Beirne. *A Short History of Ireland.* Cambridge, England: Cambridge University Press, 1990.

Rosenthal, M.L., ed. *William Bulter Yeats: Selected Poems and Four Plays.* New York: Scribner Paperback Poetry, 1996.

Ryan, Desmond. *Michael Collins.* Dublin: Anvil Books, 1994.

Ryan, Desmond. *Remembering Zion.* Dublin: Arthur Barker, Limited, 1934.

Ryan, Desmond. *Sean Treacy and the 3rd. Tipperary Brigade.* Tralee, Ireland: The Kerryman Limited, 1945.

Ryan, Desmond. *The Rising: The Complete Story of Easter Week.* Dublin: Golden Eagle Books, Limited, 1966.

Ryan, Meda. *Michael Collins and the Women in His Life.* Dublin: Mercier Press, 1996.

Sexton, Sean. *Ireland: Photographs 1840-1930.* London: Laurence King Publishing, 1994.

Stephens, James. *The Insurrection in Dublin.* Gerrards Cross, England: Colin Smythe, 1992.

Taillon, Ruth. *The Women of 1916: When History Was Made.* Belfast: Beyond The Pale Publications, 1996.

Taylor, Rex. *Michael Collins.* London: Four Square, 1958.

The 1916 75th Anniversary Committee. *Souvenir Programme.* Dublin, 1991.

Townshend, Charles. *Ireland: The 20th Century.* New York: Oxford University Press Inc., 1999.

Twohig, Patrick J. *Blood on the Flag: Autobiography of a Freedom Fighter.* Ballincollig, Ireland: Tower Books, 1996.

Twohig, Patrick J. *Green Tears for Hecuba: Ireland's Fight for Freedom.* Ballincollig, Ireland: Tower Books, 1994.

Travers, Pauric. *Eamon De Valera.* Dublin: Dundalgan Press Ltd., 1994.

Uris, Leon. *Redemption.* New York: Harper Collins, 1995.

Uris, Leon. *Trinity.* New York: Bantam Books, 1976.

Walton's New Treasury of Irish Songs and Ballads, Part 1 & 2. Dublin, Walton's Musical Instrument Galleries Ltd., 1968.

Ward, Alan J. *The Easter Rising: Revolution and Irish Nationalism.* Wheeling, Illinois: Harlan Davidson, Inc., 1980.

Ward, Margaret. *In Their Own Voice: Women and Irish Nationalism.* Dublin: Attic Press, 1995.

Warwick-Haller, Adrian & Sally Warwick-Haller, eds. *Letters from Dublin, Easter 1916: Alfred Fannin's Diary of the Rising.* Dublin: Irish Academic Press, 1995.